Domains of Fear and Desire

Urdu Stories

edited by

Muhammad Umar Memon

TSAR

Toronto

1992

The publishers acknowledge generous assistance
from the Ontario Arts Council and the Canada Council.
© 1992 TSAR Publications on behalf of the authors and translators.

ISBN 0-920661-21-1

TSAR Publications
P.O. Box 6996, Station A
Toronto, M5W 1X7 Canada

Cover design: Natasha Ksonzek

in memory of

Zamiruddin Ahmad

(1925 – 1990)

Contents

Preface

Urdu is an Indo-European language which developed soon after Sultan Mahmud of Ghazna's incursion into northern India early in the eleventh century. It is written in the Perso-Arabic script and owes a significant percentage of its vocabulary to Arabic, Persian, and Turkish loanwords. A language of high literary refinement, Urdu today is spoken chiefly in India, where it is one of the official languages; Pakistan, where it is the national language; and in such Western countries with sizeable South Asian expatriate or emigré populations as the U.K. and Canada.

Urdu boasts of a radiant literary tradition, poetry being closest to its creative heart. Prose literature–particularly fiction, if the term could be applied at all–was predominantly oral before the nineteenth century and consisted of the *dastans*–enormous and anonymous story cycles recited in public by professional storytellers. But fiction as it is understood in the West didn't begin in Urdu until well into the nineteenth century. The novel came first, in the middle and later part of the century, but only in the sense of formalistic rudiments. This early–or proto–novel is most clearly represented by the works of Nazir Ahmad (1831-1912) and Pundit Ratan Nath Sarshar (1845-1903). The first recognizably modern novel, however, wasn't written until 1899, and this was Mirza Muhammad Hadi Ruswa's *Umrao Jan Ada* (named after a fictitious Lucknow courtesan). The short story, on the other hand, arrived roughly a quarter of a century later, and curiously, it has been used more deftly and with greater force by Urdu writers than has the novel. Critically speaking, there are better and artistically more refined short stories in Urdu than there are novels.

The short story emerged as a discrete narrative form with Munshi

Premchand (1880-1936) around the turn of the century. Except for a few works towards the end of his life, Premchand wrote more out of the need for social reform than any concern for the individual as an autonomous entity across history and culture. Still less did he worry about safeguarding the autonomy of literature. The same spirit characterized the bulk of fictional work produced under the aegis of the Progressive Writers' Movement, founded in 1936. In their need to break free from colonial rule and establish a just society along Marxist lines, the Progressives bypassed for the most part the form's great potential for probing into what lay beyond the immediate socio-economic reality. The fictional output of this period is rigidly circumscribed by the authorial notion of the short story then common in the literary canon. The emphasis is increasingly on social reality, to the growing exclusion of the individual himself or herself–the individual poised precariously between history and desire.

While ardent Progressives such as Sajjad Zaheer (d. 1973), Krishan Chandar (d. 1977), and Ismat Chughtai (d. 1991)–to name only a few–churned out story after story according to a formula forged in the crucible of Marxist ideology, independents such as Ahmed Ali (b. 1910), Saadat Hasan Manto (d. 1955), Urdu's greatest and most accomplished short story writer, and Muhammad Hasan Askari (d. 1978)–again, to mention but a few–elected to chronicle the events of the elusive and shimmering realms of the individual consciousness.

The two decades between the birth of the Progressives in 1936 and their demise in the 1950s may be considered the most propitious period for the development of the Urdu short story. In that period the short story both broadened its thematic horizon and showed greater willingness for technical innovation. Alongside of didacticism and purposiveness, which still characterized much of the Progressive writing of the period, one is able to see, primarily among the nonaligned writers, the use of the short story as a form fully aware of its inherent potential for the discovery and articulation of realities beyond the external and the social.

The meandering propensity for technical innovation enters a more daring, if sometimes precarious, phase in the sixth decade of this century. This modern product may be best described by the term "post-realist," indicating the collapse of the familiar space between the writer's persona and the reader. In other words, all the spatial and temporal coordinates are rigidly withheld in the hope of communicating experience in its pristine essence, without any kind of mediation. This results often in quite dizzying consequences for the reader.

In the present volume–which makes no claim to being definitive or comprehensive or even fully representative–I have tried to spare the reader some such very "private" stories. Instead, I have selected those that might yet be readable. However, like any selection, this one also cannot escape the biases of its editor. I have a very definite bias in favour of writers who have emerged since the partition of India in 1947. The reason is not a sinister one at all: Some of the earlier masters, such as Premchand, Krishan Chandar, Manto, Rajinder Singh Bedi, and others, have already been translated into English and Russian. It is time that someone looked at the generation that came after them, if only to see what it did with its heritage.

A few technical explanations are in order: Rather than transliterate, I have spelled the names of authors as they themselves spell them. Thus, Enver Sajjad, not Anwar Sajjad. To keep the text as clean and smooth as possible, original Urdu words are italicized only at first occurrence in a story. Italicization reflects only approximate spelling; it should not be taken for full or even partial transliteration, which is rigorously eschewed. I have also refrained from using italics for such Urdu words as have passed into English usage and are available in dictionaries. The meanings of the Urdu words retained are given when they cannot be guessed contextually and can be found in the "Notes and Glossary" section at the end of the book.

I would like to thank the editors of the following magazines for permission to reprint some of the pieces collected in this volume: *Annual of Urdu Studies* for "The Beggar Boy," *Journal of South Asian Literature* for "The Back Room," and *Temenos* for "Voices." Thanks are also due to Nurjehan Aziz for permission to reprint "The Refugees" from Abdullah Hussein's *Downfall by Degrees and Other Stories* (Toronto: TSAR Publications, 1987). Griffith Chaussée read some of the translations and offered invaluable editorial assistance. I would like to thank him too. I am also indebted to the kindness of the last named as well as Faruq Hassan, C.M. Naim, Javaid Qazi, and John Roosa who all undertook to translate especially for this volume.

Muhammad Umar Memon

Madison, 18 December 1991

ZAMIRUDDIN AHMAD

First Death

He was slightly out of breath because he had been walking fast. He looked around. It was all quiet in the alley. He climbed up the steps and put his ear flat against the big wooden door. It was totally silent on the other side; clearly, there was no one in the courtyard or in the veranda beyond. But there was someone in the latrine next to the courtyard: water was trickling out the hole into the gutter running right in the middle of the alley.

He opened the door gently and entered the house. A bird fluttered in the *neem* tree opposite the door. He heard the latrine door open and quickly hid behind the tree. He saw his older brother walking back towards the veranda, holding the ablution pot in one hand and tucking in his trouser string with the other. His brother suddenly stopped for no obvious reason, turned around, and greeted someone passing by the open door, *"Salam alaikum!"* and that someone else greeted back, *"Walaikum assalam!"*

Must be the Fat Uncle, he thought. *How pleased he'll be when they tell him what I've done! He never gets tired of telling me . . .*

"Why are you hiding behind the tree?" His brother's voice interrupted his thought: *How did he know I was hiding here?* He looked around; his cover was complete. *Must have been my crepe-sole shoes.*

"We are playing hide-and-seek," he said, coming out from behind the tree.

"Playing hide-and-seek, are you?" the brother said, looking rather suspiciously at him.

"Yes."

"Go look at yourself in the mirror. You're as white as a sheet. You look scared to death."

"Who, me?"

"No, *me!*"

"Nah! Why should I be scared," he said boldly. "I haven't done anything wrong; I'm only playing."

And indeed as he spoke a look of self-confidence replaced his earlier nervousness. All the same, the brother said, "You must have done something bad. Come on, let's go to mother." And with his free hand he grabbed the boy's shirt sleeve.

"No, I won't go," he said, wrenching his sleeve free.

"Alright! I'll go tell her."

"Go ahead. Tell her." He felt bolder.

The older boy crossed the veranda and entered the corridor that lead into the heart of the house, tracing as he walked patterns on the dirt floor with the water left in the ablution pot.

"Amma!"

Amma–huh! Sounds like a donkey! I'm not afraid of anyone. Not even abba.

Just then, he heard a din of jumbled voices rising from the cemetery and the alley. He closed the door and sat down on a charpoy under the neem. He was all ears now. Gradually, the voices grew louder, and he felt as if the ghoul he had left behind in the cemetery was about to assail him like a storm. *Let him come! I'm not scared. Why should I be? I haven't done anything wrong. Yes, why should I be?*

The ghoul stopped at the door. Silence. Then a voice pierced the silence: "Babu Ji."

Like a lamentation.

"Babu Ji!"

A faint, sinking voice.

"Babu Ji is not home."

"Babu Ji!"

"Told you, he is not at home."

"Please open the door."

It is Badsha. Wonder why they call him Badsha–the king. A gravedigger and a beggar. His real name, I think, is Ameera. Another travesty, for Ameera means "rich."

"Go away!"

"Knock with the chain," somebody suggested, and the chain started beating against the door.

This is Badsha's voice. But he wasn't there at the time!

He rushed to the door. "Go away, or . . ."

"We want to talk to Babu Ji."

The knocking grew louder and more insistent. Several voices were mixed in with it. Someone was laughing; another talking loudly. It seemed to him that the street kids he had been playing with a little while ago had all poured in here so as not to miss out on any fun.

Suddenly the voices died down. *"Bandigi Lala Ji!"*

"Hare Ram, Hare Ram!" He heard Lala Ji exclaim, "What happened?"

Before he could hear the answer, he heard his mother's voice. "What's the matter?"

"Nothing," he murmured and moved away from the door.

"I asked what is the matter," the mother repeated, crossing the veranda. "What is all this noise about? Have you gone deaf?"

In reply, he began crushing neem berries under his shoes.

"I knew he'd been up to something," the brother said, as he came trailing behind the mother.

"Why don't you answer me?" the mother demanded. She was now standing in front of him.

He still didn't answer. The crowd outside had obviously heard the mother's voice, so several of them shouted in unison, "Bibi Ji, Bibi Ji!"

"What's the matter?" she asked the crowd outside as she moved closer to the door.

"Mian broke open his head."

"No!" She could not believe her ears. "Whose head?"

"Enatwa's."

She looked at him with unbelieving eyes before peeping through a crack in the door. She turned pale. "He isn't lying," she whispered to the brother. "He's covered with blood."

The brother unlatched the door.

"Ask how it happened," the mother said to the brother.

The brother half opened the door and stepped out onto the threshold.

Enatwa was standing on one of the front steps; blood was trickling from the right side of his skull, staining his dirty, black *kurta*-shirt and red sarong. Two men were supporting him. Behind them were the street kids, some attentive, some sniggering, and some whispering to one another, but none showing any sign of sympathy for Enatwa.

"Ask him to sit down," the mother instructed the brother from behind the unopened panel of the door.

Enatwa sat down on the step he was standing on.

"What actually happened?"asked the brother.

"I'll tell you,"one of the boys volunteered.

"Shut up!" said one of the two men who had been supporting Enatwa by the shoulders.

That lousy Badsha again, the boy thought and crushed another neem berry.

"Mian was playing in the cemetery; he hit Enatwa with this big piece of brick and split open his head; that's what happened."

Liar! He won't tell what happened just before that.

"No," interrupted one of the kids, "Enatwa hit him first."

The mother and brother were both outraged. "He beat my son, this miserable beggar!"she said in some heat.

"He's lying, Bibi Ji, this bastard," Enatwa said glaring at the boy. "I didn't even so much as touch Mian."

"But he did beat up Maddan," insisted another boy.

"Yes, he did!" And he crushed several berries at once as he moved towards his mother. "He was beating Maddan with a shoe. The poor man was crying, but he went on hitting him. And he was dragging him too. Maddan's clothes were torn, but he didn't stop beating him–beating a grown-up man like that, in front of so many people, in the street!"

"But he didn't hit you, did he?" the mother asked.

"No. But he was beating Maddan with a shoe. Maddan was crying, and this man was dragging him by the feet over stones; Maddan's clothes were torn and he was bleeding."

"Mian is telling the truth," several boys said in unison.

"But Bibi Ji, that *sala* . . ."

"Tell him not to use foul language," the mother instructed the brother, who promptly asked the man to mind his language.

"Sorry, Bibi Ji," Enatwa said. "Maddan owes me ten rupees, but the bastard refuses to pay back. I bumped into him today. He again started making excuses . . ."

"But he promised to pay back in the month of Baqreid," said the boy. "I heard it with my own ears."

"Why did you get involved in their quarrel in the first place? What is Maddan to you anyway?" the mother scolded the boy.

4

Why doesn't she understand? This wretch Enatwa was beating the man. And why? For a lousy ten rupees! What's ten rupees! She had distributed luddoo-sweets worth as much on Munna's circumcision ceremony. If I were grown up, I wouldn't have hit him with a piece of brick, why, I would have given him a proper thrashing and saved Maddan. Nobody, not one of those people, came to his rescue.

"Yes, Bibi Ji, that's right. What is he to him, that bastard!" Enatwa said. "I lost ten rupees, and got my head broken in the bargain."

"He must have lost gallons of blood," Badsha remarked.

"Without any doubt!" Baldua agreed.

Liar!

"He wouldn't be alive if he had lost gallons of blood," observed the brother.

"Gallons or an ounce or two–the fact is that he has lost blood," the mother said. "However, what is done cannot be undone. What can we do now except," she looked angrily at him, "punish him."

He cringed, taking two steps backwards.

"But what about him, Bibi Ji?" Badsha said, looking at Enatwa, who made it look like he was about to faint. "He can't go back to work for Allah knows how many days. He won't be able to lift a spade, let alone dig a grave."

"And the medical expenses, who will pay them?" Baldua chimed in.

The mother felt inside the seam of her pajama and produced from it a silver rupee. "Give it to him," she said, handing the coin to the brother, who promptly gave it to Enatwa.

"Just one rupee!" Enatwa protested.

"That won't even buy him ointment or bandages," Baldua said.

"I'm sure the doctor will advise him to drink lots of milk in order to regain his strength," Badsha speculated.

The mother was beginning to feel anxious. She couldn't very well hand over to the wounded boy the five rupees her husband had given her earlier for the ghee–could she? No ghee, no seasoning for the lentils; and no seasoning could only mean the letting out of the secret.

The brother read the anxiety in his mother's face. "One rupee is enough," he said to Badsha. "You won't get a penny more."

This time Badsha and Baldua spoke with one voice: "This is really unfair, very unfair. Mian broke the poor man's head, and all you're offering is a mere rupee."

The mother signalled to the brother to say no more and said from behind the closed half of the door where she stood, "That's all I have now. You can come back for more later."

"But he needs it right now, Bibi Ji," Badsha said. "It wouldn't do him much good later."

After some hard thinking the mother concluded that these people were not going to be content with one rupee. Besides, there wasn't much time. Her husband would be home any minute. She must get rid of these louts, and get rid of them pretty quick. She asked the brother to go and get the five-rupee note she kept under the cup of catechu paste in the *pandan.*

When the boy handed over the five-rupee note to Enatwa, the three beggars protested again: five rupees were not enough; they couldn't accept anything less than ten rupees, though, considering the seriousness of the injury and the long time it would take for the wound to heal, even ten rupees weren't enough. But this time their protest sounded pretty feeble, and the mother and brother, pretty adamant. So they left, in something like a procession: the three beggars at the head, the street boys behind.

"Where do you think you're going?" asked his mother as he was crossing the courtyard.

When his brother had closed and latched the door, he saw his *nani,* his maternal grandmother, sitting on a settee on the veranda. He liked snuggling up to her, especially when he was threatened with punishment, though he knew quite well that she couldn't be of much help on such occasions as both his parents, particularly his father, had made it clear that she was not to spoil the boy with unnecessary affection. *Poor nani! She's all alone. That's why she's so afraid of abba.*

His feet had turned towards her of their own accord, it wasn't as if he was trying to run away. He stopped and looked through the corner of his eye at his mother's legs, clad in a tight markeen pajama, and her slippered feet coming flip-flopping towards him.

"Now tell me this," she said, twisting his ear, "why did you hit him?"

"I've already told you," he said, without making any attempt to free his smarting ear.

"What have you told her?" the brother, who was now standing beside the mother, asked.

And the mother repeated: "What have you told me?"

What's the use! She will not, she cannot understand. Still, the boy said, "Because he was beating Maddan with a shoe, and . . ."

"Again the same nonsense!" The mother let go of his ear and raised her right hand to slap him. "Is he any relation of yours, that Maddan, huh?"

"He's picked up bad habits hanging around with the street brats." The brother seemed bent on making things worse for him.

Why is he blabbering? Can't he keep his mouth shut? Huh!?

"I've told him over and over again not to play with boys of that sort, but he won't listen!" And she slapped him hard.

Blood rushed to his face. He felt the burning sting spread under the skin of his cheek. His eyes started to water. But he didn't cry.

The mother slapped him again. But this time there was no buzzing in his head. He felt the blood surge back from his face, feeding every muscle in his body and making it incredibly taut. And when he raised his left hand to fend off another slap, though his mother's raised hand was before his eyes, he saw the picture of a man, dressed in rags, being dragged along a limestone street, repeatedly raising first one, then the other hand to shield his head and face from a shoe hitting him again and again and again.

His mother caught him by the arm as he took a step backwards and said, "Promise you will never do it again."

He jerked his arm free and a "No" shot out of his mouth. He couldn't believe his own ears.

"How dare you!"

His mother chased after him as he ran towards the veranda; realizing that he was now out of her reach, she took off a slipper and hurled it at him. The slipper struck him on the head just as he was entering the veranda. He rose; the slipper had managed to do what two nasty slaps had failed to accomplish. He began to cry.

"That's enough, daughter!" nani said, putting down her rosary. "Never hit anybody with a shoe; it's written in the books."

"Didn't you hear what he said? Broke the man's head and says 'no.' God alone knows what he might do tomorrow! Why should he meddle in other people's affairs?"

I will, I will, I will!

Tears were trickling down his face, but he suppressed his sobs.

"So young but already hitting grown-ups!"

I will, I will, I will!

"Six rupees went down the drain because of him. Let his father come; he will teach him such a lesson that he'll never dare set foot out of the house again."

I will, I will, I will!

But the mention of his father slowed down the flow of tears, and he sat down on the settee close to his grandmother.

"No dinner for him tonight," the mother announced, looking for the slipper. The brother meanwhile went out.

The father, wearing a fez and twirling a walking stick, arrived a little while later. As usual, he went straight into the inner part of the house. The boy looked at the man from the corners of his eyes and when the man had moved out of sight, he concentrated on the sounds inside the house: slippers being dusted, betel-leaf juice being spat out, a throat being cleared, face being washed, and the father and the mother chatting. Other sounds followed: mother ladling pumpkin mash out of a cooking pot onto a metal plate; removing from the stove the plate of *mash*-lentils, ground in ghee, and putting it on a salver, taking *chapatis* out of the bread basket, carrying the salver to the charpoy, where abba, sitting cross-legged, regularly took his meals.

A few minutes later he heard someone rinsing his mouth, and the rattle of pots and pans. He walked softly towards the corridor. Grandmother, who never spoke when telling her beads, nevertheless made a "hummm!" sound. He stopped, but failing to understand what she might have meant by this, he entered the corridor anyway.

At the far end of the corridor a door opened onto another veranda, next to which was the kitchen, which he could see clearly from where he now stood. Facing the veranda was a rectangular courtyard, smaller than the first one, on the other side of which was a large room in which his parents and his little brother slept. The door was often closed. His father was pacing up and down the courtyard, his mother was busy in the kitchen.

He crossed the veranda slowly, went into the kitchen, and stood statue-like in front of his mother.

"Yes, what do you want?" she asked, angrily but softly.

"I'm hungry."

"I already told you, no dinner tonight."

"I'm very hungry," he pleaded abjectly.

"You will go to sleep hungry tonight, that's your punishment."

The father belched loudly. "What's the matter?" he asked, continuing to pace up and down the courtyard.

His voice had the usual deep throatiness that frightened him, but no hint of anger. *He isn't that bad! Don't know why mother makes me scared of him! He's loving, too; bought lemon drops for me yesterday.*

The boy got carried away. "Amma says she won't give me any dinner tonight."

"Why not?" the father asked the mother.

"Ask him." She stood up. "Ask him what he did today."

"What did he do?"

"Abba!" he came out of the kitchen into the courtyard. "That man, Enatwa . . ."

"Yes. What about him?"

"Well, he was beating Maddan with a shoe . . ."

"What for?"

"He said Maddan owed him ten rupees."

"These wretched beggars! Always quarrelling and fighting!"

"Yes abba! And he was dragging that poor man over stones and–"

"Enough of this," the mother cut in. "Now tell him what you did."

"What did he do?"

"Split open Enatwa's head, that's what he did."

The father stood still and wordless for a moment and then he asked, "Really?"

"Absolutely."

"How?"

"Hit him on the head with a brick."

"What on earth for?"

"Because he was beating Maddan," he answered his father's query, though it was not addressed to him.

"What is Maddan to you?" the mother asked.

"It must have been an accident," the father said.

"No. Enatwa came to our house to complain. He was bleeding; I saw it with my own eyes. And do you know what your son said when I told him off? He said he would do it again."

Amma should be ashamed of herself; she's telling a lie. I never said that; I only said "no!"

"There were so many people there, but not one would save Maddan."

"So you admit you broke Enatwa's head?"

He did not answer; he could sense the anger in his father's voice. "Speak up!"

He did not know what to say; he was frightened; he kept quiet.

"Such stubbornness! If he had slapped you or hit you, then it would have been a question of our honour. But if he *was* beating Maddan, was it any of your business? Just look at him, hardly three feet tall and already picking up the ways of hoodlums and criminals!"

"He must be dealt with severely, otherwise he'll only get worse. That's why I've decided not to give him dinner tonight."

"That isn't enough. He should be made *murgha.*" The father turned to him. "Did you hear me?"

But he remained still.

"Do as I told you, or . . ." the father roared and raised his hand.

He went into the veranda, assumed the posture of a rooster, and became a murgha.

The lanterns had been lit. All except he had their meals. The father and mother retired to their room. But his punishment continued. His arms were aching, his back was sore, his ears hurt, his face was flushed and his bent legs were trembling but he didn't cry. The punishment had hardened that something hidden within him which used to melt and flow out of his eyes whenever he was humiliated. The thought of quietly slipping into the kitchen and eating something on the sly, even a mere chapati, and then slipping back into his murgha position did cross his mind, but he didn't allow it to take hold of him. Inside him something had arched like a taut bow and would not permit him to countenance such a cowardly act; something that was telling him that this was outrage, that injustice was being done to him; something that was urging him to face this outrage and injustice no matter what it took, but never to stoop to stealing, not even a chapati. What would his brother say, reading his book, comfortably tucked in his bed? And nani who, for some unknown reason, was sitting up in her bed staring into the dark sky?

But inside him there was something else, too–something that slowly gnawed at his stomach and filled it with pain–a stabbing pain. Gradually, it overpowered all resistance. Tears began to roll from his eyes.

Nani got down from her bed, walked over to him, stroked his head with affection, and restored the murgha to upright, human form; and when the tired and trembling legs of this transformed murgha faltered, she drew him to her legs.

"I'm very hungry, nani!" he said, trying to stifle a sob.

"I know, my darling," she said. "Go and ask for abba's forgiveness; I'm sure he will forgive you."

Forgiveness! There was a lump in his throat; he choked. *You, too, nani!?*

She heard and understood his silent protest. "Otherwise you won't get any dinner at all tonight and will have to remain a murgha for who knows how long."

He crossed the courtyard in a thousand long moments and came to the door of the room on the other side. The gurgle of a hookah came from behind the closed door. He kept his hearing tuned to this sound for many more long moments, and then finally spoke to the closed door: "Please forgive me, abba. I will never do it again!"

The sound of his last word was still ringing in his ears when the arched, taut bow inside him suddenly snapped, and a flood of tears and sobs swept him away like a reed.

Translated by the author and Muhammad Umar Memon

QUDRATULLAH SHAHAB

The Plague in Jammu

It was summer in Jammu and the plague was rapidly spreading. In Akbar Islamia High School I had the job of cleaning the fourth graders' classroom. One day after school when I was alone cleaning the classroom, I found a dead rat under a desk. I picked it up by the tail, took it outside, and after twirling it around in the air, let it fly into the bushes by the side of the road. On seeing this, Lal Din shrieked. He hurried towards me, dragging his limp leg, but halted some distance away. Lal Din was our school's only peon. He used to ring the school bell, serve water to the boys, and even sell cookies and stale *pakoras.*

"Hey stupid!" Lal Din was yelling. "That was a plague rat. Why did you touch it? Now you'll die and kill us in the bargain."

Resting on his cane, Lal Din delivered a detailed lecture on the symptoms of the plague. First, a strong fever hits. Then the swelling appears which gradually gets as big as an ear of corn. Then the whole body puffs up like a balloon. Then your nose, ears, and mouth all drip blood; pus flows from your sores and, within four or five days–good lord!–it will be all over for you.

Several days later, as I was walking down Residency Road, a rat suddenly bolted onto the road. It stopped, then swayed like a drunk and staggered. Two or three times it somersaulted then hit the ground with a thud and lay with its mouth open. I came close to it and poked at it with my foot. It was already dead. Without thinking I lifted it up by the tail and tossed it over to the side of the road. Some pedestrians who had stopped to watch this whole affair from a distance now began screaming, "Plague rat! Plague rat! Run home and wash yourself before the swelling comes!" These people also gave an impressive discourse on the plague's symptoms from which I learned a good deal more.

In those days ten to fifteen people were dying every day in Jammu from the plague. All around, in every street and alleyway, the pall of fear was nearly palpable. Customers in shops looked around suspiciously in case there were rats running around among boxes, canisters, or bags. The shopkeepers would stare at the customers and wonder if indeed there was a case of the plague in their house. People had stopped going out to visit and socialize. Passersby would give each other plenty of room on the sidewalk. Every house in the city was cut off from the others as though it were a fort in which the besieged people, with wide eyes and panic-stricken faces, quietly awaited their own infection. The Municipal Committee people sniffed about doorways on the trail of the diseased. Where one of their raids met with success, they would, like Marjina in the story "Ali Baba and the Forty Thieves," mark the door with whitewash. For a small bribe the mark could be erased from one's door and even put on an enemy's door. The symptoms of the plague came like a death sentence, one which enjoined surviving members of the household to walk around hiding their faces like fugitive criminals. Even the custom of shaking hands almost entirely ended; people would fulfill the obligations of customary politeness by greeting each other only from a distance.

Even though I had touched two plague-infected rats, the predicted swelling did not appear. I began to feel as bold as a lion. I would start to laugh when I saw the fearful, terrorized faces around me. A hundred different pranks sprang up in my head as I became emboldened by others' helplessness.

Hakim Gorandetamal's store was located in Raghunath Bazaar. One day Hakim Sahib was alone, sitting on his chair, shooing away the flies that kept landing on his nose. I came and stood next to him, my body touching his, and said in an agitated voice: "Hakim Sahib, I need some medicine for the plague, quick."

Hearing the word *plague*, Hakim Sahib started and then scolded me: "Why are you breathing down my throat? Move away from me and talk. Who's got the plague?"

I had soaked a ball of cotton in iodine and tied it to my underarm with a rather dirty bandage. I slid even closer towards Hakim Sahib and, bringing my arm out of my shirtsleeve, began to move it closer to his face for inspection. His eyes filled with fear and bulged out of their sockets.

Hakim Sahib sprang up so quickly that his chair fell back with a crash. Standing far back inside the store, he began yelling, "This is a store—a store—not a hospital for contagious diseases! Get out and get to a hospital or I'll call the police!"

On Hakim Sahib's table there was a jar of sugared rose petals. I quickly lifted the lid, plunged my hand in the syrup, and grabbed a handful of the moist candies. I rushed out of the store.

Hakim Gorandetamal had one special virtue: he never let anything in the store go to waste. One time he spotted a dead lizard in an open bottle of almond oil. He lifted it out with a pair of tongs and then hung it for some time at the bottle's mouth so that every last drop would fall from the lizard back into the bottle.

The success of my trick on Hakim Sahib doubled my courage and heightened my spirit. Listening to people's conversations and reading the notices of the sanitation department posted on the walls, and then freely exercising my own imagination, I formulated an especially long-winded and terrifying speech on the plague's symptoms, states, and consequences. I first tried it out informally on a few people and was pleased with the results. Even good, healthy, and well-mannered types would, at some point or another, be affected by the mention of the plague, and suddenly a darkness would spread across their stolid and sober faces. On occasion my success would overwhelm me with that drunkenness one feels at a *qawwali* party when, on some word or another, one impulsively gets up and whirls about in a trance.

At the high school, the young and recently married Maulvi Abdul Hannan was our Urdu and Islam teacher. He was exuberant, jocular, and very kind. His light-skinned face was defined by a sharp nose and an auburn goatee. His clothes were always elegant and well cut. In the middle of teaching class he would often suddenly become quiet, close his eyes and start swaying, and say in his soft, soft voice: "Allah be praised! What a blessing life is."

One day Maulvi Abdul Hannan came to class worn out and depressed. He put his feet up on the table and leaned back in his chair. Shutting his eyes, he said sadly, "Today I'm not feeling well. There won't be any class."

The rest of the boys were soon laughing and playing around. I came and sat on the floor next to the Maulvi with a serious and worried look on my face. His nostrils were inflamed and his eyes were bleary. His ears were bright red and his face was contorted with torment. In other words, he was an excellent candidate for my lecture. I tried two or three times to tell him the town's most recent news about the plague, but each time he sharply interrupted and shut me up. Seeing that my strategy was failing, I began to complain that Lal Din, the peon, didn't clean the school with much care.

"So what? Why are you backbiting Lal Din anyway?" Maulvi Sahib said sternly. "What's the poor fellow done?"

"But Maulvi Sahib," I protested, "even in this classroom there was a plague rat lying dead."

The arrow hit the bull's eye. Maulvi Sahib jerked up from his chair as though the infected rat was still lying around. He asked for God's protection several times under his breath and then angrily left the room, probably to look for Lal Din.

After this he didn't show up at school for two days. The third day I went to his house to inquire about him. When I arrived, he was lying half-conscious on the charpoi under a sheet. His slender and beautiful new wife was sitting by his side and fanning him. Her henna-stained hands had coloured the fan's handle with the same redness. When she moved her hand it seemed as if a fountain of blood would begin to fall on Maulvi Sahib's auburn beard.

Maulvi Sahib was very happy to see me. Sadiqa Begum gave me a homemade fruit drink in which she had stirred some *sattu*. Then she took out some money from a small basket and handed it to me saying that I should bring back some potatoes, peas, cilantro, and meat from the bazaar. I didn't have any experience with the ways of the bazaar but with some effort I did the shopping and came back. For each item I gave a price that was considerably lower than the price I had paid. I made up the difference with my own pocket money. Sadiqa Begum was delighted and said, as she stroked my head, "My, my, you've shown yourself to be pretty smart. You shop very well. You must come to see Maulvi Sahib more often and then you can do the shopping for me."

I was greatly pleased by Sadiqa Begum's suggestion. Instead of going to school I went straight to Maulvi Sahib's house every day. On some excuse or another I managed to get a little extra money from my parents in addition to my pocket money and spend it all on shopping for Sadiqa Begum. After greeting Maulvi Sahib, I would go and sit by

Sadiqa Begum in the kitchen. Sometimes I would shell the peas, sometimes I would chop the onions, sometimes grind the spices. Whatever work she began I would come running over and try to take away from her.

I arrived one day to find Sadiqa Begum sitting in spotlessly clean clothes. She had bathed and appeared ready to go somewhere. A black silk *burqa* was lying next to her. Maulvi Sahib was lying down quietly covered from head to foot. I asked about his health and he moaned from under the covers, "Allah, Allah, it's not good."

"Has the swelling started yet?" My voice was full of hope.

"Don't be silly," Sadiqa Begum angrily hissed. "This isn't a swelling sickness, this is just a plain old fever."

Tears swelled up in her dark blue velvety eyes like shattered crystals. She wiped her tears away with the edge of her *dupatta* and then raised her henna-stained hands in prayer. Her slender lips were like rose petals, stained with the deep red of walnut bark. Her face reflected the colour of both gold and silver as though she had just bathed in milk and honey. After praying she lightly blew her breath over Maulvi Sahib. She donned her black silk burqa and appeared just like a doll dressed in a gown. She turned to me and asked, "Kaka, you'll come with me?"

I stood up eagerly and happily, as if to go to Magic Mountain.

"We have to go make an offering to Roshan Shah Wali's shrine," Sadiqa Begum said. "Come on."

I'd heard about this Roshan Shah Wali. I had even seen his shrine once from a distance. His large grave rested on a high marble platform. Green sheets were continually laid atop his grave and at night a whole array of lamps burned near the head of it. On coming inside, Muslims read the *fatiha* and *darud* or made their offerings. But some Hindu Dogras also came to pay their respects and would reverently walk around the grave keeping their hand on the shiny, glass-like walls. Quickly, I assured Sadiqa Begum that I knew the way to Roshan Shah Wali's shrine very well and that I'd take her there without a hitch.

The offering of sweet rice was in a china bowl. After covering it with a lace handkerchief, Sadiqa Begum handed the bowl over to me. In a show of great respect, I drew up my cheeks and loudly said *bismillah arrahman arrahim* while carefully holding the dish with both hands. Sadiqa Begum folded a brand new coarse-woven sheet for placing on the grave and carried it with her. Upon leaving Maulvi Sahib's neighbourhood, we hired a tonga. I wanted nothing more than to sit right next to Sadiqa Begum in the back seat but, to maintain the tonga's balance, the coachman had me sit up front. At first I felt dejected but when the tonga hit the paved road I started feeling happier. From the warmth of the sun the blacktop had become as soft as a quilt. The clopping of the galloping horse, the whizzing of the turning rubber tires, and the flapping of the black silk burqa in the wind sounded to me like a sitar and *tabla* concert. My heart began to sing. I imagined I had leapt from the tonga right onto the fabled genie-borne throne of King Solomon. Outside, the whole world moving about on the street appeared to me very sad, poor, extremely insignificant, and infinitely bereft. Drunk with my good fortune, I drew back the lace handkerchief without thinking, grabbed a huge mouthful of the sweet rice, and began to eat with relish. On seeing this, the tonga driver began grunting and roaring at Sadiqa Begum, "Oh, Bibi Ji, look at this, your kid is polluting your offering. Now your wish will never come true."

Sadiqa Begum lifted her veil and looked at me helplessly. In her eyes again the crystals formed and began breaking. I hung my head down like a stray dog and sat quietly.

When we reached Roshan Shah Wali's shrine, Sadiqa Begum dejectedly sat down on the steps of the shrine.

"Kaka, why did you do that?" she asked. "You ruined the offering. Now what are we going to give to the shrine?"

Large teardrops began to fall from her eyes like a steady stream of hot wax dripping from a candle. I put my head on her knees and I also began to wail and cry. One of the dervishes of the shrine, on seeing us crying, got up and walked over to us. In a thundering voice he said, "May your descendents prosper. May the *pir* fulfill all your desires. Here, Bibi, give me your offering and I'll present it to His Highness."

Seizing the opportunity, I immediately handed over the plate of sweet rice to him and Sadiqa Begum gave him the coarse woven sheet. As the dervish unfolded the sheet and measured it with his arms, he shook his head and said in a disappointed tone: "It's a very small sheet. This won't cover but half. Don't you see Bibi how the shrine of a big saint is also big?"

Sadiqa Begum began to sob uncontrollably and convulsively. Perhaps the dervish felt pity. He said, "Alright Bibi, offer a rupee and a quarter along with it and the King will accept it."

Sadiqa Begum counted out her change. I chipped in a couple of annas and with great difficulty we managed to come up with a rupee and a quarter to hand over to the dervish.

On the way back we didn't have enough money for the tonga ride. There was only one and a half annas left in my pocket. When we came to the *pan* shop on the corner of Raghunath Bazaar, I ran to get two sweet pans, which cost two paisas each. I brought them back wrapped in paper. In the vegetable market baskets of jujube fruits were laid out everywhere. I had two paisa's worth of the best ones weighed out and then thrown into my cap. Then we ate our fill of jujube fruits, talking and laughing all the while. I was intentionally taking the long way home so that our trip would stretch out forever. In one alley a vendor of flavoured ices was walking around with his wooden chest wrapped under one arm while barking out his sales pitch. I sprang up and had two paisa's worth of ice placed on a *peepul* leaf. Then I ran back to Sadiqa Begum and gave it to her. Underneath her veil she quickly gobbled up the ice and I licked the leaf clean. By the time we reached the market near the old palaces of the Maharaja my pocket was empty. Otherwise, I certainly would have hit upon the idea of buying one of the palaces for Sadiqa Begum.

We came to Maulvi Sahib's neighbourhood and spontaneously the prayer burst from my heart: please Lord, may Maulvi Sahib be dead from the plague before we arrive home and may I continue wandering the streets and alleys with Sadiqa Begum, chewing pan, eating jujube fruits, and savouring ice. But, unfortunately, Maulvi Sahib was alive and well. He was lying as usual on a charpoi, covered from head to foot, waiting for the swelling to come.

That night I didn't sleep at all. I'd doze off a bit, then the flying ships of my vivid dreams would lift me up from one place and hurl me down onto another. I waited in torture for the night to pass. When the dawn finally broke I quickly made my bed and sprinted off to Maulvi Sahib's house. He himself wasn't in the front room but Sadiqa Begum was lying there in a deep sleep on her charpoi covered by a muslin dupatta. I went to the kitchen and he wasn't there either. I looked into another room and it too was empty. With happiness the hope stirred in my heart like a small snake uncoiling that perhaps Maulvi Sahib had died and had even been buried in the middle of the night. But then suddenly from the back room his voice came as though he were speaking from inside a grave: "Son. Listen here."

I immediately darted towards the back room and asked with great brio: "Maulvi Sahib, has the swelling come yet?"

"Don't talk nonsense," Maulvi Sahib scolded. He had placed his bed in the most distant part of this narrow and dark room. He was sitting on it eating breakfast. While dipping shortbread in his tea, he instructed me to stay outside of the room and told me in a heavy voice that Sadiqa Begum had developed a strong fever. During the night the swelling of the plague appeared under her right arm. He had sent the news to her parents, who would probably be arriving any moment.

"Son, until they come, go sit with her and look after her." Maulvi Sahib threw some coins in my direction and said, "Bring some ice from the bazaar and put it on her head. Make some fruit drinks for her and wash the glass outside in the street tap. Also, keep it near her bed and don't mix it up with the other dishes in the kitchen."

Having brought the ice, I broke off a bit and began to rub it on Sadiqa Begum's forehead like a bar of soap. The ice melted like butter on a hot griddle. Its drops of water began to flow in tiny canals over her eyes, ears and cheeks. A few moments later, Sadiqa Begum opened her eyes and stared at me in surprise. Then she pushed me away from her charpoi.

"Oh don't Kaka! Don't sit near me. I've got the plague. May God keep you safe."

I quickly got up and made a fruit drink with lots of crushed ice. Sadiqa Begum gulped down the whole glass in one breath. I was about to make another one when she stopped me, "Enough, Kaka, not now. May God keep you well."

For a long time she lay on her bed staring at the ceiling. Then she said, "My mouth is getting a very bitter taste, Kaka. Can you bring me a sweet pan?" She began to take some money out from her pocket but I had already taken off in a flash. Raghunath Bazaar was about two miles away. I ran all the way to the stall where we had eaten sweet pan the day before. I bought four pans and ran back breathless and exhausted. In the meantime, Sadiqa Begum's relatives had already invaded the house. A couple of women had commandeered the kitchen and three or four people sat around her bed as though laying siege to her. As I began to give Sadiqa Begum a packet of pan her father rebuked me and snatched the packet out of my hand.

For a while I wandered around the house useless as a piece of junk. Then I headed for the back room to talk with Maulvi Sahib. He was lying motionless, covered from head to foot with a sheet. On hearing my voice he brought his hand out from under the sheet and waved it at me like a red flag. He told me to stay outside the room and get lost. Since no one paid any attention to me I felt compelled to return home.

At night I told my mother that the wife of my Islam teacher had come down with the plague and that Maulvi Sahib himself was just about to be hit with the plague's swelling. I said I had made an offering on their behalf and I asked her to cook an offering for me to take to Roshan Shah Wali's shrine.

"Allah have mercy on us all!" mother said. "I'll cook an offering the first thing in the morning and on the way to school you can go present it at the shrine. You can also say some prayers there. But son, look out, don't go near their house. It's a contagious disease. Allah, have mercy on us all!"

Early in the morning, mother cooked sweet rice and mixed raisins, apricot kernels, and coconut into it. She put this in a big clay bowl for the offering. Then she brought out a new muslin dupatta to lay on the shrine which she folded and placed on top of the bowl. With my school bag in one hand and the offerings in the other, I left the house in a joyous mood. But on the way to Roshan Shah Wali's shrine, all my happiness dissipated. As I was walking down the road I recalled the shrine's dervish who exacted a fine of a rupee and a quarter from Sadiqa Begum for laying a small coarse sheet on a big shrine. The muslin dupatta I had was even shorter than that sheet. I didn't have any money to compensate for its shortness but, even if I did, I definitely didn't want to waste it on that fat dervish. Just then I saw the ugly vulture-like dervish hovering around the shrine of Roshan Shah Wali. At that moment a huge burden was lifted from my chest. I paid my respects to the shrine from afar and sat down on the side of the road and ate half of the sweet rice myself. I gave the rest to an old hunchbacked woman who was sitting nearby patting out cakes of cowdung.

I folded the white muslin dupatta and put it in my school bag between my books. While I was walking along I cooked up a lot of schemes in my head. One plan was to go straight to Ataullah's shop and have the dupatta dyed. Deep red, pink, turquoise, lilac, purple, yellow–one by one, hundreds of colours flashed across my mind's eye. There wasn't a single colour that would not have blossomed like a flower on Sadiqa Begum. I racked my brain trying to think which colour Sadiqa Begum herself would have preferred. But nothing came to mind. She had never even mentioned which colours she liked or didn't like. But today, one way or another, I would get her to tell me which colour was her favourite. If she told me straight out then fine; but if not, I had devised another plan. I would have the dupatta dyed by Din Muhammad Butt who was famous throughout the city for his colourful striped scarves and turbans. When women school teachers and college boys appeared wearing on their heads the adornment of his handiwork, it looked as though a veritable spring had burst forth in the street.

I was weaving this rainbow of colours and pleasant scents around in my imagination when I arrived at the Maulvi Sahib's. There, all my best-laid plans fell to the ground with a crash. Sadiqa Begum's bier was laying in the doorway. Eight to ten men were hovering around in the alleyway like vultures, waiting to walk to the graveyard.

I ran to Maulvi Sahib in a great commotion. He was sitting in the back room wrapped in a shawl. With sobs and sniffles, he was reading the Qur'an. On seeing me coming towards him, he waved me away with his left hand and screamed with anger, "Why are you coming headlong at me? Go take part in her funeral."

He wiped away his tears with the edge of his shirt and then thundered, "Do you remember the funeral prayer or have you forgotten it? I've already taught it several times in class."

"Yes, yes, I remember it," I replied in a high and forceful voice, and then I muttered some filthy curses at the funeral prayer and at the Maulvi's mother and sister too.

"What's this 'yes, yes'," Maulvi Sahib hissed like a snake, "you mean 'no', you pig."

In my mind I swore at him several more times. Then I stuck out my tongue and made a face at him. Fortunately, I was able to dodge the shoe which Maulvi Sahib had quickly grabbed and wildly hurled at me.

When we started, about a dozen men were in the funeral procession, but by the time we reached the graveyard only about half that number were left. There was a great bustle in the graveyard and the gravediggers were busy at work. They were digging three to four graves side by side and they very nimbly lowered Sadiqa Begum into one of them. Then, quickly moving their shovels, they built up a heap of dark brown earth over her body. One man sprinkled half a barrel of water over the grave. After reciting the fatiha, everyone returned home.

I thought that the least I could do was to lay the muslin dupatta on Sadiqa Begum's grave. For me, her grave had become a shrine. But there were some people standing nearby attending other funerals. I felt embarrassed and so tucked my schoolbag under my arm and quietly went away.

Translated by John Roosa

INTIZAR HUSAIN

The Back Room

The threshold of the back room appeared to her to be a boundary to a dark land. As she stepped across the dust-coated sill, her heart began pounding. She moved slowly and deliberately into the dark room, always apprehensive and on the verge of turning back. Her perception of this room had changed many times. Out there, on the other side of the sill, was another world: dark but comforting and familiar. Often after playing in the scorching sun in the lane or courtyard, she entered the back room to hide behind its doors or slip behind the dirty tarnished cauldron in one of the corners. The cooling darkness quenched her flushed, warm body. Her feet luxuriated in the chill of the soft soil. Mother was living then. Whenever she saw her going in or out of the back room she chided her, "Hey, you little pack rat! What are you doing rummaging around in all that junk? It's dark in there . . . what if a bug bites you?"

But the childhood had departed, so had mother and with them, even that comforting darkness. The existence of the back room had become dulled in her memory—so dulled she rarely thought that besides many rooms, porticos and courtyards, the house also had a back room.

The back room had remained closed for many years except when necessity required its opening at the changing of a season. Sometimes particular seasonal supplies were needed. Occasionally it was also opened to store a broken charpoy or to take out a broken water pot or a bucket splitting at the seams for repair.

This year with the arrival of summer the back room was opened again. The advent of this summer signaled another change in her perception of the room. She entered and arranged the winter quilts and mattresses on the upper shelf. As she descended she noticed a braided hair piece hanging on a peg in front of her. She began thinking how oily and soiled her own had become. This one had a much nicer sheen, she was convinced. "Why not take it?"

Suddenly her glance fell to the dusty floor below. God knows how many years had passed since it had been swept last. A broad, undulating line extended in the dirt from one corner, where an old dusty chest containing pots was stored, and disappeared behind the tarnished cauldron in the corner near the door. She stared at it intently. Her feelings balanced on surprise and trepidation. She suspected something and contemplated calling apaji. Then she noticed the ropes of the charpoy were lying loose and felt she had concluded hastily–"It was probably only the imprint of the open charpoy lacings."

Whenever she passed by the back room while sweeping in the main rooms and courtyard, she thought of its dirt floor; a place where the dust was so deep that if she were to step inside, her bare feet would surely be enveloped by the soft powdery earth. No matter how many times it was swept there would always be more dirt. And that wavy line was there too, undulating across from the big chest to the copper cauldron. Its image billowed up in her mind and she tried to suppress it. But after a while her determination weakened and the coiling tracklike line in the dark soil emerged in her imagination and swayed on into the darkness of the past . . .

"No, daughter, no! Don't ever call it out loud by its name!" mother admonished apaji. "It has extra-sensitive ears and hears its name the moment it is spoken. I'll tell you about the experience I had once. I got up after my nap one afternoon and put on my slippers, and right in front of me in the courtyard was the cursed thing lying there looking half-dead. I called for your husband. But curses! As soon as I uttered its name it went slithering off."

Apaji was speechless, huddled up with her chin on her knee, her eyes fixed on mother's face. Mother started again:

"It is a very ancient one. We've heard tales about it ever since we first settled in this house. Our dear old mother-in-law–God rest her soul–used to go into the back room to get things without ever bothering to take a lamp with her. The poor old woman was nearsighted and tottered haphazardly into the room. There were a few times when it heard her footsteps and quickly slithered under the chest. But once she escaped by just a hair's breadth. She entered the room and began mumbling, 'Hey, who threw this hair piece on the ground?' She reached down to pick it up and, lordy, it was that snake!"

Apaji sat motionless. A shiver ran through her. "Personally," she said, "I'd have never thought of such a thing. But now I remember a similar thing happened to your son. One day at high noon I went into the room to get the cot with the canvas strappings which I knew were grimy and needed washing. I didn't realize it at the time but he had followed in behind me. I was busy tugging at the cot when I heard him begin to mutter, 'Who threw this cane on the ground? It was ordered special from Naini Tal and they're hard to come by. Once it's broken that'll be the end of it.' He was about to put his hand on it when, mother, it suddenly recoiled and slithered instantly out of sight."

Mother confirmed, "It's true. One moment he shows himself and the next he's disappeared . . . I pray to Allah that we be spared from all evil spirits."

Apaji drifted off into her thoughts. Shuddering, she returned to her senses. "Yes, may Allah protect us from every evil, and especially from that dreadful thing whose very name gives me gooseflesh."

"But, daughter," mother responded, "each man has his own fate. Those destined with good fortune will receive it even from their enemies. God bless our mother-in-law, she used to tell us this story: Once a prince was tricked by the family of his betrothed. They put a common old hag in the marriage palanquin instead of the princess. She was toothless and grey-headed. Her body was listless and her skin was as wrinkled as a prune. On the wedding night she sat waiting on the nuptial bed covered by a beautiful red mantle. She trembled, fearing the prince's arrival and the disastrous moment when he would lift her veil. Then suddenly a very strange thing happened. A black snake hung by his tail from the rafters just over her head. His mouth was gaping. He glided down some, and then a little more until his mouth touched her hair. The poor thing froze stiff with fear. Then the most bizarre thing happened. He drew a strand of her hair into his mouth and then dropped it. The strand turned completely black and was so long that it extended all the way down to her waist. He took another and another until her whole head of hair had turned completely black and was so long that it extended all the way down to her waist. When the prince entered he was overwhelmed. He thought he had entered the boudoir of a fairy princess rather than an ordinary bridal suite.

The fairy princess was his bride; her face shone like the moon, her body was supple and fair as flour, her tresses were sinuous and serpentine. His heart and soul were captured by her beauty."

Apaji fixed her gaze on mother's face. She was astounded by the story.

"Mother," she asked, "how could she turn into a princess?"

"My dear, when fate is set in motion, even the physical body can change."

"But mother, a change like that?" apaji exclaimed incredulously.

Wrinkles formed on mother's brow. "Do you think I would tell you a lie and wager my chances for heaven?" she said. "If it's a lie, then the punishment goes to the one who first told the story. I told you just what I heard. But, daughter, the important point is that every person lives according to the decrees of his fate. Normally that creature wouldn't hesitate to harm anyone. Snakes are poisonous enemies of mankind. They are such stubborn things that neither disease nor death can subdue them."

"Oh, mother! What are you saying?" apaji couldn't contain her words of wonder and disbelief.

"Girl, you doubt everything. You may not believe this either, but it's said that a snake only begins to age after a thousand years. He sheds his skin a hundred times and just like that he's rejuvenated. He never dies a natural death. If someone were to bash his head in, well, that's a different matter."

Apaji thought for a while, then asked, "Mother, why doesn't he die?"

"Because he's eaten a charmed herb, that's why," mother replied and went on. "Long, long ago–and you may doubt this too, if you like– there lived a king in Babylonia. He had a minister–a very chivalrous minister it is said. Together the king and his minister conquered one territory after another. Then one day the minister died unexpectedly. That shook the king's spirit but he bore the loss courageously and solemnly pledged to conquer death itself. A wise old dervish told him about one of the Seven Seas which contained a special herb. The king followed his directions and journeyed heedlessly, without thought of food or water, until at last he reached his destination. As soon as he arrived at the spot he plunged into the water and brought the charmed herb up from the bottom. Had he but eaten it, he would have rid himself of death once and for all. But as luck would have it, on his return journey, the king came upon a river. He was exhausted and decided to bathe and cool his body in the river. Leaving his clothes on the bank he splashed into the river. Meanwhile, back on the bank a snake snatched the herb into his mouth and slithered quickly away. The king dashed out of the water and ran after the snake. He trampled the whole jungle, turning it upside down, searching every tree, examining every cave. But, girl, the creature had completely vanished."

Again and again things appeared and vanished; lighting would flash before her eyes, then darkness. This illusiveness of things was a constant source of bewilderment. She recalled her childhood and her playmate Battu. They played together untroubled by the time of day or concerns outside of their own amusement. And Battu–so unique in his ability to disappear at any instant from her sight! Those days were merely a dream to her now. How he could hide in the back room when they played cops-and-robbers! The corner where the big cauldron was stored, the big chest of cooking pots, the charpoy standing up on end–all those things slowly, slowly began to emerge in the darkness . . . everything but Battu. "Oh God, where's he disappeared to? Which cave is he hiding in? Has he been swallowed up by the earth or eaten by the sky?" And just then, as she would be thinking all that, a dark, black head would begin inching its way up from behind the chest of pots. She would spring forward and grab him. "Ah hah! The thief is caught!"

Sometimes when they played hide-and-seek the back room offered the ideal hiding place. They would both enter it and hide themselves in a corner. A long time would pass while they stood without a sound. Slowly, very slowly the darkness would begin its work. It seeped into their bodies and then departed, establishing a new relationship between the inner and the outer worlds. The world of sound and sight seemed to have remained far in the distance and the world of darkness had begun. A journey of infinite leagues. No signs, no stopping points. With the sound of footsteps in the courtyard the world of darkness contracted . . .

Or when they played blindman's bluff. Battu, the blindman, entered the back room with such confidence as if everything was visible to him. He neared the cauldron and suddenly clamped his hands on her, catching her braid so forcefully that she had to let out a scream.

Only recently she had started using a hair piece. There was a time when her hair was so long that it was actually a nuisance to care for. It was long, lustrous hair that braided into a thick black whip. It waved over her back far below her waist. Before taking a bath she used to sit on the small bath stool and loosen her hair to wash it with soap-nut powder she had prepared. The tresses bobbed against the wet floor. But a sudden, violent attack of cerebral meningitis had left her hair dull and spotty. During the severe days of the illness she was in a coma for three days. She lost all sense of who or where she was. Now she thought about those three days as a long journey into darkness. She passed from one black boundary to another, each opening into a new, dark land. And finally, into the ultimate black kingdom. Again and again she approached the limits and turned back, returning to the world of sound and light. The effects of that long, fearful journey were apparent on her body that had declined and on her hair that had become thin and short, its luster dulled. Now, only with the addition of the hair piece could her braid assume its former length.

While passing through the courtyard her feet often led her in the direction of the back room. She remembered the oily, matted hair piece. God knows how many years it has hung there on the peg. "Would it be worth bothering to weave it into my own braid?"

Repeatedly she abandoned the impulse to go in and take it down from the peg. But unconsciously her glance returned to the back room, spurring thoughts of the hair piece and the impulse to go there. She approached the door, halted and retraced her steps. The thread of her imagination began to lengthen and wind into the nooks and corners of days past . . .

"Mother, there was plenty of oil! I shook the lantern at bedtime and checked it myself. I think the wick must have fallen inside."

"Well then, why did you turn it down so low?" mother demanded. "These are uncertain times; God knows what may come up. The lantern must never be extinguished! Poor me, I didn't know what to do. It was so dark in here I couldn't tell one hand from the other. I heard a rustling sound but couldn't make out what it was. I thought maybe it was a snake but wasn't sure if I was just imagining things. All of a sudden the chickens in the pen began cackling. As soon as I looked towards the pen I saw it . . . you can't imagine how long it was!

I almost dropped dead. I couldn't utter a sound. Finally I managed enough courage to call you."

"Mother, I don't remember you calling me."

"My dear girl, you sleep like a log. Even if this house were filled with the tumult of Judgment Day or kettle drums played right on your ear–they still wouldn't wake you up. A sleeping man's like a dead man; woe to such a sleep! Anyway, I then called Naseeban. I kept calling her for a long time but she seemed to have dropped dead too. What could I do? I sat stone-still the whole night and kept reciting verses from the Qur'an. I was afraid lest I should fall asleep and someone might get up to go to the toilet and . . . especially Safia–she has this terrible habit of getting up out of bed and sleepwalking barefooted to the outhouse. I was in this predicament when the sun finally rose and it gradually became lighter . . ."

"Safia! what are you doing?" apaji's voice shot up from the kitchen. Safia mumbled something and instantly her thoughts vanished. Then she became so immersed in her household chores that she lost consciousness of her mind and body. She spread the brassware and kitchen utensils out in front of her and taking fistfuls of ash from the plate she dropped some into each vessel. She scrubbed each one so vigorously with the jute pad that when she rinsed them in the tapwater and lined them up on the brick platform they reflected the sunlight like mirrors. They appeared gilded rather than scoured. When her ash-covered hands brushed against the running water the light blue glass bangles on her wrists made delicate tinkling sounds. Her fair fingers and wrists glistened with the water and a ray of light danced across her forearm.

Soon afterwards her glimmering fingers became covered with dough and the breadboard began ringing unceasingly from the steady motion of her fists. The moist dough stuck to her wrists and even one or two of her bracelets. Safia kneaded it to the perfect consistency. She rolled out paper-thin *rotis* and put them on the griddle to bake. Then she placed each one on the open coals to puff them up and stacked them in the bread basket.

In the dusky light of evening when she removed the griddle from the hearth and turned it upside down, the countless flying red sparks looked like so many stars floating in the black soot.

"Apaji, the griddle's laughing!"

"The laughing of a griddle is not a good omen," apaji answered in a concerned tone. "Put some ash on it."

Even while performing these household tasks her thoughts would stray elsewhere. Sweeping the courtyard or tightening the straps on the canvas-laced cot, or undoing the skeins of silken thread, the cellar of her imagination would open into its own world, independently of the motion of her hands. The wavy line began to reach into the darkness of forgotten days. The thought of mother brought with it the memory of her gossip sessions and stories. She remembered how calmly she could pass over the most astounding things and yet be so shocked at banal matters. Once when she was cleaning a cauldron stored in a corner of the back room, she uncovered a snake skin with her hand. She picked it up nonchalantly and tucked it carefully away, saying, "Basheeran could use it to prepare a syrup for her daughter who's ill with whooping cough." There was another time too when the stiff carcass of a white pigeon found in the pigeon hole one morning made mother suddenly remember the hissing sound she had heard coming from the vicinity of the dovecote in the middle of the night.

She envied mother, a person to whom invisible things revealed themselves. As for herself, ever since childhood her path had been covered by markings and clues of the phenomenal world, but the substance always eluded her. Shadows crossed her path at every turn, but never the figure that cast the shadow. Sometimes the traces appeared so fresh she thought a step or two more and she would catch up. Such a thought invariably set her heart pounding and made her body tremble and her feet too heavy to move.

It rained that day when she and Battu arose at early dawn and left the house in search of rain bugs. At the edge of the black mango orchard a drenched *neem* tree lay fallen on the soggy earth. It was long, serpentlike, and its trunk was jet black. It looked like someone had just flayed it with an axe and the white fat lay scattered everywhere around. They were stunned by this scene.

"Lightning struck last night."

"Lightning?"

"Don't you know," Battu began, "it rained all night and the lightning struck real hard. It seemed like it landed right on our roof..." He babbled on, "A black snake used to live in the hollow of this tree. He was a very ancient one. He must have come out in the night. Lightning strikes dark, black things–you know."

"Where did he go then?" she asked fearfully.

"Where did he go!" He laughed at her ignorance. "The lightning ripped him to pieces."

Contemplating these things brought an overwhelming longing for those days to return; that someone might seize the spotted snake of the past by its head and reverse the direction of the meandering procession of names and relics. To again hear mother tell stories and pontificate, but to ignore all that and dart out early at dawn, barefooted, in pelting rain, towards the jungle to search out rain bugs. If there were no rain bugs, there were always cuckoos; and if there were no cuckoos, then at least there were always toadstools.

The awning overhanging the front part of the balcony was so old its wood had rotted and turned dark; when it rained it looked darker still. After a few showers a white pulplike substance pushed through its cracks and joints. Gradually black and white umbrella-cap mushrooms began to unfold. Some mushrooms were chalky white, some were black speckled and others were striped. Picking them was often an inviting challenge. The toadstools growing on the awning were within the reach of both of them, but the big fat ones growing directly below it on the wall even Battu could not reach, let alone she. Once, however, supporting himself with the lattice and bracing his foot on the ledge, Battu did manage to raise himself high enough just to touch the awning–but the fattest ones still remained beyond his reach. That did not bother him, for no matter how far a thing was from his grasp, Battu was sure to make a daring attempt, at least once.

On the path to the mango orchard lay an old abandoned well. It was so shaded over by the dense foliage of a sprawling banyan tree that unless she bent over and peered hard she didn't see any water at all. Battu would crawl out on one of the branches directly above the well and announce audaciously, "I'm going to jump . . ."

The ground seemed to slip from underneath her feet and she would find herself entreating, "No, Battu, no!" From Battu's expression it was evident that her ardent pleadings made no impression on him at all and that he would jump into the well any moment. But he would not; instead, he would slide down the trunk of the tree to the ground. One day he jumped, though–jumped or fell or what, she could never know. He had gone there alone that day. She only heard the commotion afterwards. Shabrati, the water carrier, came running and began pounding on the door of Battu's house. Battu's father ran out, shaken and anxious, and made straight for the well, followed by many other people from the neighbourhood. Those who stayed behind stood about in small groups, dumbfounded.

"Who? Battu?"

"He fell into the old well–how?"

"My God, that child's really wild!"

Apaji was saying, "That boy's a real daredevil. Whenever he came here, all he did was hang from the awning or the fence of the roof. He'd make my heart flip. I scolded him a thousand times for performing his acrobatics here. I even spanked Safia once for being crazy right along with him. But, I'm sure the ghouls ride that boy's back. He never listened to a word I said, nor anyone else's for that matter."

"He's the only son of his poor parents," interjected mother. "May Allah have mercy on them."

Apaji's tone of voice changed, "Yes, may Allah have mercy on them. I pray that he be spared, but I want to make it perfectly clear that whatever happens our girl will never become his. How can one trust such a youngster? Who knows what he might do!"

"Well, this is a problem for another time." Mother heaved a sigh. "Right now, God have mercy on the poor fellow. There's evil in that dark well. Every year someone's sacrificed to it."

Evening came and some people brought him home stretched out on a cot. His clothes were drenched from the water, his hair was matted, face pale and sallow, and body limp, lying unconscious. For some time deathly silence settled over the lane–the same silence which was to return once again many years later and, again, on account of Battu: the day the telegram came. God knows what got into Battu's head that, without telling a word to anybody at home, he enlisted in the army and volunteered for frontline duty. For a year or two there was no news of him. When finally it did arrive, it came in the form of the announcement of his death while serving in a foreign country.

"Good Lord, a telegram about Battu!"

"A telegram about Battu? Allah, be merciful!"

Apaji, who was baking rotis, suddenly turned the griddle over and snuffed out the fire. For a short time the lane was filled with a silence.

People stood about in small groups, shocked, communicating only through their eyes. As Battu's father read the telegram his hands began to shake and without raising his head he went inside.

She shuddered back into the present. She had put soap nuts in a bowl to soak and placed the bowl itself outside in the sun on the brick ledge; the soap nuts had ballooned up by now. Hastily she loosened her hair. The grey suds in her hair made it look even more off-colour. She finished bathing and went out into the midafternoon sun and stood a moment near the brick ledge. She tossed her hair from side to side a couple of times and then walked into the room and stood before the mirror. Some of the body and softness had been doubtless revived, but the qualities it once had when it waved over her shoulders or when she made a bun which swung freely like a shining platter were gone. For hours mother combed it, arranged it and braided it. Performing a ritual, she would pull it back into coiled strands and blow on them while reciting auspicious Qur'anic verses. Then taking a small hank of hair she would tuck it away in a chink of the brick wall. Now–now her hair is lifeless and thin. Mother's comb and skillful fingers are gone too. She turned her focus from her hair to her face–a face which used to radiate the essence of beauty. The previous glow of her body had begun ebbing also. She remembered hearing the whispers exchanged between an elderly woman and apaji in a gossip session just a few days ago.

"Apaji, how long do you people intend to keep this girl at your hearth? She is already past the age. She'll get impatient if you aren't careful."

"Do you think I want to keep her around at home any longer? It's hardly the time for her to be sitting around here . . . but what can I do?"

"As soon as someone comes along, marry her off, I'd say."

She shook herself again and began combing her hair somewhat energetically. Arranging her hair with her fingers she noticed that it was dry and brittle despite all the oil she applied. Dullness had over-shadowed its lustrous shine. While braiding it she picked up the hair-piece. It appeared thinner than her real hair, more greasy and matted than thinner. She put it down and went out into the courtyard towards the back room. She walked hypnotically, as if in a dream, as if some-one had snared her into a magic spell. She put her foot on the door sill and opened the latch. She gave the door panels a slight jerk and shoved them open. As she entered the back room she suddenly became aware she was stepping into *that* realm of darkness. She recalled the wavy line coiling from the large chest to the cauldron. Her heartbeat quickened. She moved further into the darkness, as if descending below where the earth beckoned. Another wave of delirium rushed her senses. A state of intoxication, a vague fear that some great trial might confront her–the mystery unknown. Moving on into the darkness she felt the soft earth beneath her feet–the same powdery earth which she had walked on many times before, where the details of her footprints would appear as etchings in the dust. She looked at the floor coated with fine dust beneath her feet–where was that wavy line? Had it been rubbed out or was it never really here? She reached towards the peg and took the hairpiece down. It was oily, matted, coated with dust. She put it back. As she came out of the back room, the intoxication which had flooded her mind had already vanished. And a dullness like that of her dry pallid hair began settling over her body like a fine mist.

Translated by Caroline J. Beeson and Muhammad Umar Memon

QURRATULAIN HYDER

Hyena's Laughter

The valleys between the Himalayas and the Shivalik hills are known as "doons"–Dehra Doon being one of them. The Corbett National Park, spread over a hundred square miles, is located in one of the doons of the Naini Tal district. The Ram Ganga descends the mountains here and enters the Park. On one bank is the mountain range; on the other, the dense forest of *sal* trees. The forest is inhabited by tigers, leopards and the deer; the Ram Ganga by alligators who, unconcerned with our time, exist in the geological age of the dinosaurs, much like hippopotami and the elephants. Hearing the sound of a jeep on the forest road, the tigers, the leopards, and the antelopes suddenly disappear into the dense forest. One hears only the rustle of leaves or sees just a fleeting glimpse or a shadow–as if the disappearing animal were an idea hidden within the jungle of the human mind. Or sometimes, at night, one sees within the range of the headlights of a car or a jeep a hyena or an otter or a black bear–as if an unsuspected fear within one's own mind had suddenly materialized.

The forest is filled with the music of the deer, the colourful birds, the snakes, and the pitch-dark night; the silent symphony of the flowing river, the sleeping alligators, the birds and beasts, the snowy winters, the crawling mists and the darkness.

This year in December, all kinds of people were staying in the compound of the rest house at one end of the forest: a retired British army officer and his memsahib, travelling in their caravan car; a few students from the University of Cambridge come to study the flora and fauna in the Himalayas; and some European young men, all staying and sleeping in their camping tents. A little distance from them, in open tents, were a few workers and building contractors, busy putting up new buildings in the compound. The number of visitors to the Corbett National Park has increased steadily every year.

After dinner, the chief elephant man brought down all the elephants, who had been taught to bend down on their knees to greet the foreigners. The memsahibs fed every elephant a piece of bread. Then all living creatures went into their resting places—rooms, tents, huts, burrows, caves, nests, anthills—and to sleep until the next morning when the sun looked in on the Ram Ganga, and the forest and the compound woke up. Then each creature had his breakfast of goat meat, or live deer meat, or dead buffalo meat, or occasional human flesh, or raw meat, or worms and ants, or fried eggs, porridge and cornflakes, or toast and jam, jellies, marmalades and tea, or *puri bhaji* or dry bread or *parathas*, before starting his day.

And then quietly, on tiptoe, Buddhu, the pig, entered the compound. He would stand in front of the new building. The Rampuri waiter would shout: "Buddhu is here." Taking her walk on the road old Mrs. Freemantle would say, "Hello Boodoo, good morning!" and Brigadier Freemantle growl, "Hello, Boodoo, old rascal." The American tourists would smile and say, "Hi, Boodoo." And some American girl would exclaim, "Isn't he cute?"

Buddhu comes to the compound twice a day. He gets his breakfast and leaves; then he comes back for his supper and goes away again.

Evening. A green jeep wagon arrived during that misty evening and stopped in front of the new building. Two men and a young woman stepped out. The servants from the new rest house ran to haul their luggage in, for the visitors seemed affluent tourists, carrying a colourful, matching American-made suitcase, hold-all, bag and an expensive picnic basket. The three of them entered the reception room which had a shiny bar in front. The girl raised her eyebrows and looked around in annoyance, as though the only hotels she ever went to were five-star hotels.

Brigadier Freemantle was sitting alone at the bar. One of the newcomers walked in, clad in Jodhpurs and a turban on his head, with one ear pierced, and sporting a sharp, pointed moustache. One still encounters such characters in the landscape of Rohil Khand. He raised his finger to order "a brandy and soda" from the bartender—a young man from the northern hill country—and sat down on a crimson leather barstool. A few minutes later he noticed the Brigadier and tried to attract his attention. But the latter took no notice of him. Some Indians, in the presence of a white foreigner, often become very self-conscious. Immediately they slip into speaking English with an affected accent and seem proud to be talking to a white man. A curious meekness and humility takes possession of their entire demeanor. The Westerners on such occasions silently laugh at them. More often than not, these very Indians speak rudely to their own countrymen.

The other newcomer was a thin, balding runt of a man, with hooded, listless eyes–like those of a sloth–which he moved about lackadaisically. He was talking in low tones to the manager of the rest house. The girl stood nearby looking bored. She could have been a starlet or an expensive model–beautiful, fair-skinned, tall and healthy, with hazel eyes. She wore diamonds. The runt looked twice her age. A few minutes later they both went upstairs. The man with the pierced ear kept sitting at the bar drinking brandy. The roar of the tigers could be heard outside.

"What a shame that this wonderful tiger country is going to be drowned in the Kalagarh Dam," the man with the pierced ear commented.

"Yes, it is, isn't it?" The Brigadier responded briefly.

"I used to arrange hunts for the princes. Gone are those days. What about you?"

"I come here from England every year to do some fishing," the Brigadier answered.

"Can I be of any service?" the man with the pierced ear inquired.

"No, thank you," the Brigadier said curtly.

Outside, the sounds of the night were becoming louder. A quarter of an hour passed. The man with the pierced ear stared at the Brigadier. One of his eyes was bloodshot. "The valley around is really very romantic," he said. "If you sometimes . . ."

This fellow is not one of those who just like to make small talk with the foreigners, the Brigadier thought and got up from the stool. He lit his cigar, said "goodbye," and walked out rather quickly.

The man with the pierced ear began to drum with his fingers on the bar top. He finished his drink and asked the bartender for the number of his companion's room and then said, "Send the bill upstairs, to the sahib who was with the young lady. Which way is the staircase?"

The bartender told him.

Upstairs, he knocked at a door. From inside someone asked him to come in. The door was open. He walked in. The girl, reclining on the bed, was turning through the pages of Jim Corbett's *Man-Eaters of Kumaon,* a copy of which had been placed in every room for the benefit of the tourists. The runt lay on the other bed staring at the ceiling. He ordered, "Go now," in a voice that did not seem quite compatible with his meager body.

"Alright. I'll be out of Dhakala during the night. At Najibabad, you can . . ."

"Go," the runt interrupted him.

"Good night," he said to the girl, "I'll be back on Sunday morning. Be ready."

"Go," the runt repeated.

The man with the pierced ear bowed a farewell and went out.

The runt got up and opened one of the suitcases. He took out a whip and a leather belt and tossed the two towards the girl. Then he locked the door.

Early in the morning Mrs. Freemantle was hanging up her laundry in front of her caravan car. Her husband sat in a chair nearby reading the newspaper. Suddenly she said, "Poor girl. The poor thing!"

The Brigadier kept quiet.

"The poor Indian child bride! Can we not do something for her, Henry?"

"What is it, Doris?" the Brigadier asked, a little peeved.

"That girl who came here last night, she was taking a walk this morning wrapped in a shawl. There were whipping marks on her back under the sari. I think her husband flogs her. Can we not . . .?"

"Doris, don't poke your nose in other people's affairs."

"But , Henry . . .!"

At eleven in the morning, the girl stood in front of the mirror getting ready. She had put on a safari suit. The runt was a man of taste: while applying the Swiss pentane to the remnants of his salt-and-pepper hair, he broke into joyful song: "In forest alone does the heart cheer / Love hungers after beauty there."

The girl listened to the song with attention.

"This is an old film song. Goes back before your time," he said, picking up his camera and binoculars.

Both came out and locked the door. Then they came down the stairs and went towards the platform for elephant rides. They climbed up the few stairs to the top of the platform and sat down in the howdah on the elephant's back. The elephant was waiting alongside the platform like an automobile.

In the howdah the girl burst out laughing. She was happy like a child. Her diamonds glittered in the sun. The mahout, a lanky man wearing a soiled khaki jacket, held the poker in his hand carefully and gently nudged the elephant: "Come on, daughter Ramkali, get going. In the name of God . . ."

Ramkali started towards the gate at an amble. Coming out of the compound, they passed through the farmland along the river and moved towards the forest. Excitedly and happily the girl looked all around through her binoculars, and time and again drew her companion's attention by saying, "Look, look, a peacock . . . a stag. Look there, an alligator. My God, how incredibly huge! Mahout, what animal is that one, over there?"

"An antelope, memsahib. But don't talk. The animals vanish as soon as they hear human voices."

Ramkali went into the thick forest. The nests of the weaverbird hung like chandeliers from the trees. From afar they saw two other elephants carrying the English students from Cambridge.

Having gone through one part of the forest, the trained Ramkali turned around. Reaching the rest house the girl tipped the mahout twenty rupees. Among the servants of the rest house, the girl had already acquired something of a reputation for her wealth and large-heartedness. One waiter, to please her, moved forward and pointed out, "Memsahib, look. Buddhu is here."

"Buddhu? Don't let him go. I'll feed him myself today," she said and went in.

The dining hall was depressing. The girl, who had felt exhilarated in the forest, now sat down disheartened to have her meal.

At that time there was only one other family in the hall. Bored, she watched them. The wife's hair was oily, drawn back tightly into a bun; she was wearing a faded chintz nylon sari; she had gold bangles, vermilion in the parting in her hair and a blue plastic *bindi* on her forehead; all the children were dressed in ready-made *baba* clothes; the husband sat with the latest issue of *Dharmyug* in his hands. Everyone seemed thoroughly sick of the others.

The waiter served her meal. He was a thin man from Rampur and resembled the well-known *tabla* player, Ahmad Jan Thirakwa. Life seemed such a colourless, shallow, embarrassing, absurd thing.

After the meal she brought out a plate of food for Buddhu, and later she went out for a walk along the river. On the way she met the woman with the plastic bindi, who looked her over critically. The girl smiled; the woman was obliged to smile back. The two began talking.

The woman asked, "What's your caste?"

"Brahmin," the girl replied.

"And what's your name?"

"Bandevi–the forest goddess," she said.

"Is that man your husband?"

"Who did you think he was?" the girl asked, cheerily.

The woman moved on, frowning.

Coming out of the compound the girl came to the area where the construction workers had pitched their tents. They were putting up a new building. At that moment they were congregated at one edge of the forest, busy saying their prayer. Rich foods were cooking on open pits. One man, having finished the prayer, asked, "Yes, memsahib, what can we do for you?"

"Nothing, nothing. I was just passing by. What are you cooking here?"

"Why don't you give it a try? Hey, Dilawar, get some dessert for the memsahib." He offered her the chair and continued talking, "We're from Bijnor. Have been here for a year, waiting for the project to finish. Only then can we return."

"Don't give her the dessert from the tray for the offering," one man said in low tones to Dilawar. The man had a white beard and looked very pious. The girl had overheard his comment.

Dilawar brought some yellow rice pudding in a flowered, enamelled dish. The girl smiled and asked, "Who was the offering for?"

"The Saint of Baghdad," Dilawar answered, a little embarrassed.

The girl tried a spoonful of the dessert and gave a twenty-rupee bill to Dilawar.

"Very kind of you, ma'am," the contractor said politely.

She said goodbye to them and went back to the compound. The Bijnoris looked at each other in astonishment.

40

Eleven a.m. the third day. The Brigadier sat in the sun reading the newspaper. The runt came towards him in a rush and said, "I have to go to town on an urgent errand. I'll be back by nightfall or tomorrow morning. Would you and Mrs. Freemantle be kind enough to look after my wife?" Having said this he hopped into his jeep and drove out through the gate.

Mrs. Freemantle said, "The brute! Beats up on a sweet and gentle girl like her. I'm sure her poor parents sold the pitiable thing to him for money. It's so common in the East."

Buddhu came and stood next to her chair. Mrs. Freemantle lovingly stroked his snout. Buddhu was a wild boar who used to emerge from the forest only for some entertainment and then go back. The people in the compound called him Buddhu (The Fool).

The girl came out of the rest house, said "Good morning," and sat in a chair.

"Boodoo," said the Brigadier, "is the best public relations officer of the forest, the animals' representative who maintains a liaison with the world of the human forest."

"Who knows what his forest is like," the girl said.

"You've been in there, haven't you?"

"Yes, but not deep enough."

"It must seem the same to the animals as our world does to us. When we and the Japs were fighting in the forests of Burma, we both looked like beasts."

During the last two days, this sociable girl had become quite friendly with the English couple.

Mrs. Freemantle went towards the caravan car.

"Can I stay with you until lunch?" the girl asked the Brigadier.

"Of course. Even your husband asked us to . . ."

She giggled. "He's not my husband. I met him at the racecourse in Calcutta. He is a jockey and loaded with money. Has a wife and children. He is a pervert. I've been with him for the past six months and am tired of him now and want to leave but he wouldn't let me. I've squeezed more money out of him than I could have earned in a whole year. Look at these diamonds. Blue Belgium."

"Oh, I see," the Brigadier said. He was a man of the world. "But take care not to repeat any of this in front of my wife. She's an old-fashioned lady. She'll never speak to you again."

"Very well, Brigadier."

"But you look like a respectable girl from a decent family. . . ."

"Are you going to say what everybody else does: how come a nice girl like you is doing something like this? The answer to that, sir, is that there's big money in it. Actually, now our business is becoming international. Some of my colleagues have even been to the Middle East and the West already. My parents and brother know about it. They live in New Delhi."

"Who was that frightful chap who arrived with you?" the Brigadier inquired.

"My public relations man."

The Brigadier said gently, "But, my dear, don't you sometimes feel afraid? You might run into someone who is half insane or a sadist, or– there's really a very fine line between sanity and insanity."

"This man is a sadist too, but I know how to handle him. And in any case, there are always occupational hazards. One of my schoolmates became a nurse and went to Germany. There she gave up nursing and joined the Eros Palace in Hamburg. Within days she became a millionaire. Has a magnificent house, swimming pool, a beautiful car. If I get a chance, that's what I'm going to do."

"What are you going to do?" Mrs. Freemantle asked, returning from her caravan car.

"Social work, community service, Mrs. Freemantle," the girl answered with firmness.

"Really!" the Brigadier said under his breath.

A little later she left for lunch. In the afternoon she came out on the porch. A wounded bird, flapping his wings, hit a doorpost and fell down. The girl picked it up and began stroking it out of real sorrow and compassion. Suddenly she had an idea. She hid the bird under the edge of her sari and went off towards the camp of the Cambridge students.

The five of them were sitting in front of a small, open tent. Three boys and two girls. The young men were healthy, tall, golden haired, golden bearded, the gods of the northern forests of Europe, progeny of the sun god; the girls milk-white, blonde and fresh-looking, the goddesses of the forest. How magnificent these Europeans looked, she thought. On the other hand, we Indians are so grubby, dark, emaciated, deformed and ugly; such miserable runts; mere insects– crickets and grasshoppers. She kept watching the five of them fondly.

Then hesitating, she moved a little closer to them. They were busy discussing some issue. The books on their subjects lay near them.

"Good afternoon," she said. "Excuse me!"

"Hello. Good afternoon," one golden-haired god approached her.

She offered him the wounded sparrow. "You people are studying the life in the forest. I thought you might be interested," she said.

"Oh! How very nice of you. Thanks." The boy cupped the bird carefully in his hands and hurried towards his companions. They immediately began tending to the bird's injuries.

For a few minutes she stood there waiting, hoping that they would strike up a conversation with her. Then, disappointed, she went back to the compound.

In the evening, as she stood weary and bored in the patio, she spotted the same English boy going towards the bar. She rushed inside and seated herself in a sofa. The boy bought some bottled beer and walked towards the door. She waved at him and said hello. He smiled with a slight bow and came towards her.

"Good evening, ma'am . . . Mrs . . . ?"

"Mrs. Ale."

"How are you, Mrs. Ale?"

"My name is Rum."

"Ale and Rum–you're pulling my leg?"

"No, I'm not. I call my husband Ale. He has become known by that name. My real name is Rumbha who in Hindu mythology is a celestial dancer."

"How interesting!" the boy said. "My name is simply Bernard Craig."

"Sit down, Bernard. Have a coffee with me." She called the waiter. Suddenly she looked happy and hopeful. "How's your bird now?" she asked.

"He became well after we bandaged him up. Flew back to his woodland." The boy sat down and began making small talk with her.

"I think we too should go back to our jungle, that is, the civilized world. It's not easy to spend time here. Time is so stationary here. But the captain wants to stay on for a few more days and go on the big hunt, at the foot of the mountains where the Ram Ganga begins."

"We too came here to visit the places where the rivers begin," the sun god said. A halo of golden hair. Golden beard, luminous like the sun itself in the dim light of the bar.

She didn't take her eyes off him. He was saying: "I like India so much that I'm almost tempted to marry some Indian girl. My friends in England who have Indian wives are very happy. They say you people prove to be very loyal and obliging wives, quite unlike the English girls."

She blushed, feeling restless.

The waiter brought the coffee and she got busy pouring it into the cups. Then she asked him, "Have you seen any tiger yet?"

"No. The trap was set the day before yesterday. We waited on the scaffold for quite some time, but the tiger didn't show up. In two or three days we'll be in New Delhi, and then it's back to England."

The girl began to talk in a low, sad voice. "My father, His Highness of Karanpur, was a well-known hunter of his time. I've been on many big-game hunts with him. My brother is also an expert hunter."

The young Englishman was listening to her with fond attention. She continued: "When the princedoms here were abolished, I was very small. It changed our entire way of life. When I grew up I had to become an air hostess." She lifted her hand to show him the ring. "This blue Belgium is the last relic of our family treasure."

"Fascinating! So you were a flying princess!"

"It was during one of my flights that I struck up a friendship with the captain. We got married. He started drinking heavily, so he was grounded. He has become intolerable. Now, I'm in the process of getting a divorce from him. I wish . . ."

The young man kept quiet.

"This place is part of nature. Here one is obliged to speak the truth. That's why I'm telling you all this."

"I am honoured, Mrs. Ale," he said gently.

A man clad in a heavy black overcoat walked into the room. Bernard observed him and said, "Mrs. Ale, have you ever wondered how some people resemble animals? For example, doesn't this man look like a Himalayan bear? And yesterday we saw a tiny fellow. He looked exactly like a sloth."

"And what animal do I look like?" the girl asked smiling.

The boy looked at her probingly and said, "A leopard . . . or a lynx maybe . . ."

"Thanks. Because of my eyes? Yes, there is a lot common between human and animal eyes. The badger has unlucky eyes; fish have cold eyes and the ox has stupid eyes."

"Look there, an ibex just jumped on to the barstool," the boy said jovially.

She too laughed. "Some people look like frogs, others like elephants or rhinos or grasshoppers or cattle or herons. Some women look like geckos, or silly sparrows."

"We're all in the same family," Bernard said. "A Hindu friend of mine tells me that all living creatures are a family and according to the theory of the transmigration of souls each has to go through eighty thousand incarnations."

"Really?" the girl asked surprised.

"You're not a Hindu?"

"My mum, Her Highness of Kiranpur, was a Christian."

"Oh!" Bernard gave her a long and deep look. He finished his coffee and stood up. "Thanks for the coffee. Good night, Princess. See you tomorrow!"

He walked out a little quickly and disappeared in the mist.

The fourth morning the Cambridge students were busy studying in the shade of a tree. She walked by them, but they did not see her. ("I'm almost tempted to marry some Indian girl. I'm almost tempted. . . .") Walking quickly she reached the tents of the Bijnoris. The old man with the radiant face sat on a prayer rug.

"Assalamo alaikum!" she uttered the Muslim form of greeting.

"Walaikumus salam!" the old man responded but observed her a little suspiciously.

In a pleading tone, she spoke slowly, "Sir, pray for me. Pray to your saint for me. Beg him to show me some favour so that my life gets on the right course. Please, please. Do something quickly. Here, take it," she took out two hundred-rupee bills from her purse, placed them in front of him and returned. The old man sat there, bewildered, watching her.

The runt was back by evening; he was standing on the porch supervising the loading of the fishing gear into the jeep. He ordered a porter: "Go tell the memsahib to hurry up!"

The porter went upstairs and knocked on the door. She was dressed in a grey trousersuit and stood before the mirror putting on her make-up. She opened the door and asked the porter to reassure the sahib that she'd be down soon. Then clambering down the back stairs she ran towards the Cambridge students' camp.

Bernard was sitting on a stone under a banyan tree, smoking his pipe. Surprised he said, "Good evening, Mrs. Ale."

"Rum," the girl corrected him, smiling.

He kept quiet. He didn't want to complicate his life by getting involved with a married woman.

"I'm not Mrs. Ale." She seemed deeply troubled. "Please give me your address in New Delhi. I want to get out of this mess. I'd like to go to Britain. Will you help me?"

"This is absurd. Every Indian I meet wants me to help him get to Britain," he answered sourly.

"I'll tell you the whole story. Everything. Just give me your address in New Delhi."

"We haven't decided yet where we're going to stay in New Delhi."

The jeep came and stopped near her and the runt asked her coldly to get in. Flustered she looked at Bernard and then got into the jeep. Near the gate the jeep got stuck in the sand. Brigadier Freemantle was strolling nearby. He called a few men. Together they gave the vehicle a push, and it went out of the gate. The girl looked back. The Brigadier wiped his face and balding pate with his handkerchief and waved her goodbye. Lights were lit in the students' camp in the distance.

It was pitch dark on the way to the woods. Frightened, she slid closer to him. "It's very scary here. Go back to the rest house . . ." she said.

"Tomorrow, that hunt-guide brother of yours is coming back. Is that why you've asked him to come? I'll see how you leave!"

She thought: I'm not going with him either. Right now the bearded old man will be saying a prayer for me. Mrs. Bernard Craig. I'm determined to prove a dutiful, loyal wife. If that doesn't work, then the Eros Palace in Germany. "Stupid ass," she heard the voice of the man with the pierced ear. She imagined him sitting on the scaffold with a gun in hand, and she was tied up on the ground like a trapped goat, waiting to lure a tiger. She thought again of the Bijnori old man's radiant face and felt light-hearted, safe and happy. She said to the runt, "Sing us that song again."

He acted as if someone had just placed a needle on a record, immediately starting to sing:

"In the forest alone does the heart cheer
Love hungers after beauty there
Here people drink from the cup of love
The strangers don't know what love is about
We can't make a song
That opens the blossom of a heart
My heart never blossomed before . . ."

He parked the jeep on the sand. She jumped down and began helping him bring out the fishing gear.

The Ram Ganga glittered like molten silver. The man took out his hip flask and took a swig.

"It's even colder here," the girl said shivering.

"What did you expect on a December night on the river bank? A heat wave?" the man answered. "Take a jog. It'll drive the cold away."

She started jogging on the sand. He too followed her at a terrier's trot. But he soon sat down panting. Suddenly startled by the scene before her, the girl exclaimed, "Oh, what a beautiful place!" She took off the strap of the coffee flask from her shoulder and plopped down on the sand.

Across from her, on the other side of the river, a hill belonging to the Shivalik range stood like a stone wall. The light reflecting from the water shimmered on the walls of a cave cut by the current of the river. It looked like the palace of the water nymphs. The man plunked down next to her. He put the hip flask to his lips and, a little tipsily, began purring and waxing poetic: "On the bank of the river, in a moonlit night, a drink in your hand, your lover close by; a loaf of bread, a jug of wine; come on, have a sip, love."

"No, I'll have coffee." Then she said to herself: Maulvi sahib, the bearded cleric, would be saying a prayer for me at this very moment. How can I be sitting here drinking?

He rambled on: "My lover close by, my stupid lover, my blackguard, rascally lover, . . ." and downed the whole flask. He sat there looking like a mouse whose insides were full of molten lead. He shut his eyes: his head was falling forward.

The girl grumbled, "Is this the time or the season for fishing? Come on, take me back, or I'm going to die of pneumonia."

He was lost to her.

"I'm going to go sit in the jeep," she said.

He did not stir.

"Orangutan!"

No movement.

"Badger!"

Still no movement.

"Insect! Midget!"

He kept quiet.

"Doddering old grasshopper."

Suddenly he stood up and gave her a hard kick. She slipped and fell into the water.

"Help! Help! Save me!" she screamed. The receding current carried her deeper into the water. Across, the image of the cave trembled on the water. An alligator, awakened from its prehistoric, timeless sleep, slowly slid down the rock. Entering the water it moved towards the drowning girl.

Scrambling furiously, the girl raised her head above the surface. She saw that the water, glistening in the cool light of the moon, was all around her, and a black alligator, its jaws wide open, was advancing towards her.

The alligator grabbed the girl's legs in its jaws. She uttered a deafening scream. Then there was silence. The girl had died of the dread even before going into the alligator's mouth.

Holding her in its jaws, the alligator swam towards the cave. It rested for a second under the stone wall. At that moment it was alive in a bygone age of the earth, as were the Himalayan rivers issuing from the snow, the mountains, the forests, the rocks. The alligator started dismembering the girl's body and devouring her. A few tiny eddies of blood appeared on the surface of the water, and clumps of hair and pieces of flesh and torn clothes began floating above. Calmly and unhurriedly the alligator was having his dinner.

The runt saw all this from the bank. The hair on his body and head stood on end. With fear, his sloth's listless eyes popped wide open and stayed open. Panic-stricken he ran towards the jeep that stood near an old tree, far from the bank. The trunk of the thick tree, eaten up by the white ants, had snake pits in it. The leaves rustled with the commotion. A boa constrictor peeped out of the pit, and a doe woke up. Shaking, the man turned to look behind him: the Ram Ganga was peaceful, flowing like molten silver. He started the engine. The rumble of the engine was horrifying in that silence. Blindly racing the jeep, he came back on the forest road. Suddenly, a hyena came smack in front of the headlights and laughed loudly.

The night passed. The moon had set. The sun appeared on the Ram Ganga. The forest awoke. At breakfast time, Buddhu came out of the trees into the compound. He came under the porch of the rest house and stood there, his head bowed, waiting for the girl who used to feed him every morning.

Translated by Faruq Hassan and Muhammad Umar Memon

ABDULLAH HUSSEIN

The Refugees

An event occurred thirty years ago and brutally took hold of Aftab's life. This is the story of that event. Events don't occur in a void, but are related to the great unknowns that flank them on either side. Human life, too, is a continuum. For although we can measure an individual life within a definite time span, we cannot separate it from the flow of time. And just as man's greatest asset is the duration that is his life, so the essence of a story is the event on which it is based. This story, too, derives its meaning from just two days in Aftab's life. That some thirty years separate those two days is quite another matter.

20 June 1940

It was well past the noon hour but the heat hadn't let up at all. The sky, a crisp bright blue in another season, was a blazing sheet of silver now. One couldn't even look up.

Shaikh Umar Daraz and his son had just performed the midday prayer in the mosque and got up from the prayer mat. On one side along the wall his boots lay on their sides, soles nestled against each other, with his khaki sun hat thrown over them. Shaikh Umar Daraz bent down, picked up his possessions, and started out. His son walked to the outer courtyard, where he had left his sandals, sat down at the edge and began slipping them on.

Before leaving the mosque, Shaikh Umar Daraz wet his large square handkerchief under the tap, wrung it out thoroughly and threw it over his head. Over the handkerchief he fixed his sun hat rather carefully. The white kerchief was about the size of a small towel and conveniently come down over the nape of his neck and ears, though on the forehead it sort of flapped an inch or so above the eyes. If you looked at it casually, you might even have thought the hat had a fringe stuck to it.

Shaikh Umar Daraz's skin was a healthy pink. His face reminded one of those sepia photographs in which British colonial officers sporting knickerbockers or breeches, their heads covered with handkerchiefs and hats in a similar fashion, were photographed against a background of tropical jungles or sun-scorched deserts. Even the expression on his face was the same–as if he didn't belong to his immediate world and lived comfortably away from it, like those colonial officers.

Of the travels of his youth just these two mementos remained with Shaikh Umar Daraz: the fringed sun hat, and that faraway look in his eyes. Below his face he was just an ordinary man: clad in a white *shalwar-qamis* suit and a pair of boots. Occasionally during winters, though, he would slip on a pair of khaki breeches and full boots. But then, instead of mounting a horse, he would hop on his bicycle and ride to work, or, if it were evening, stroll down to his grainfields, ostensibly to inspect them, all the way twirling his walking stick with a flourish.

As father and son stepped out of the mosque compound, a gust of hot wind slapped their faces. "Aftab," Shaikh Umar Daraz said, "you go on home. I'm going out to the fields. I'll be along soon."

"Now?" The boy was surprised.

"Yes. I have something to take care of."

"I'll come along."

"No. You go on home. The wind is awfully hot."

"I'll fetch a towel," the boy insisted. "Please let me come along."

Shaikh Umar Daraz looked around uncertainly for a moment, then decided it was all right for the boy to come along. "But make sure you wet the towel well," he shouted at the boy who in the meanwhile had sprinted off to the house.

Minutes later the boy returned, his head and face covered with a wet towel. The two started off. The dry, white walls in the alleys shimmered in the sun. The hot wind would gust in, hit the walls and bounce back like a ball of fire. The pair quickened their pace and soon came out of the complex of alleyways. A single thought occupied their minds: To get out of the city as fast as they could and hit the blacktop highway where you at least had some large shady trees. Within about ten minutes they had walked to the city's edge.

A hot, shimmering desolation enveloped the city. Although it was a district headquarters, the city was marked by a simple peasant ambience. Only the presence of a bazaar, a hospital, the Friday congregational mosque and *'idgah,* a district court, a cinema, a horse-show ground, an assembly place, an intermediate college, and two high schools set it apart from a *qasba*-town. A twenty-minute walk in any direction from the centre of the town and one would be out of the city limits and in a countryside of open spaces and farmland.

Coming to the Grand Trunk Road, the father and son felt a bit relieved. *Tahli* and *sharin* trees bordering the highway provided a welcome refuge from the heat and glare. Their dense shade somehow filtered out the heat from the scorching summer wind. They had barely walked a few paces down the highway when a tonga came up from behind and stopped beside them. "Come Shaikhji, hop in," the coachman said slapping the front seat to wipe it clean of dust. "You're headed to your fields, I guess?"

"Yes, Qurban," Shaikh Umar Daraz said. "But you go on. It isn't much of a walk . . . really."

"All the same, hop in. The carriage is all yours." Qurban climbed down from the tonga and respectfully stood beside it.

There were two other passengers in the tonga already: a peasant, settled in the front seat, and his wife, all bundled up in a white flowing sheet, behind him. Shaikh Umar Daraz climbed up and occupied part of the front seat, and a happy Aftab jumped into the rear next to the woman. The woman flinched, squirmed to the corner of the seat, leaving some empty space between the boy and herself. Qurban, balancing himself with one foot on the footrest and the other planted firmly on the floor of the cab, urged the animal to move again.

"Shaikhji is our provider," Qurban said, seemingly to the peasant. "We live by his kindness."

Here and there the sun had burned holes into the highway and a thick, molten tar oozed from them. Every now and then the wheels of the tonga would land in one of these potholes, come out laced with the tar, and leave a long, tacky black trail behind them.

"Shaikhji works as Head Clerk to the Deputy Sahib," Qurban proudly enlightened the peasant.

Duly impressed, the peasant looked at the strange man sitting next to him, gathered his sarong respectfully and shrank to the corner of the seat.

"It's a scorcher, Shaikhji," Qurban continued. "The poor animal, it can't speak, but it feels the heat all right. He's dearer to me than my own children. But what can I do, I have to fill my stomach somehow."

Shaikh Umar Daraz nodded and said, "That's true, Qurban."

About a quarter of a mile down the highway, Qurban stopped the carriage. Shaikh Umar Daraz and his boy got down. From this point, the way to their cropland was mostly narrow dirt trails snaking through the fields.

The older man patted the horse's back and said, "You've got a fine animal, Qurban." He kept looking at the gorgeous animal, while caressing its body.

"If I'd my way, Shaikhji, I would never let him off my front steps," Qurban proudly said, "but I have to fill my stomach somehow."

Qurban raised his hand to his forehead to say goodbye and made a clucking sound to urge the animal on.

"Father, do you own this tonga?" Aftab asked.

Shaikh Umar Daraz laughed. "Qurban was just being nice. You see, I had him released from police custody the other day."

"Had he beaten someone up?"

"No. He was talking to his horse . . . the idiot!"

"Talking to his horse?"

"Yes. He was telling the horse to go on undaunted just as Hitler did," Shaikh Umar Daraz laughed again.

"And the cops got him for that? . . . Just that?"

"Yes. You see, the war is on. And Hitler is our enemy."

"Father, do you think we will win the war?"

"Who knows? Things don't look good."

They would stop briefly under an acacia or an ancient *peepul* along the trail to shield themselves against the relentless sun and then they would start on again. The last wheat had almost all been gathered and the parched fields, scarred and crusted by the sun, rolled out to infinity. The gusts of scorching wind would blow away the few remaining dried wheat stalks lying randomly in the stark fields. The monotony of the sun-drenched white landscape was broken only by the solitary green of an occasional hayfield, which also served as a reminder that the area was not a wasteland after all. The farmers had now begun to gaze at the sky in hopes of rain clouds.

On summer afternoons, Aftab found two sounds very comforting: the screeching of a kite flying high in the sky and the soft, sonorous cooing of a mourning dove. The latter invariably made him want to withdraw to a quiet corner and listen to it uninterruptedly. For the dove's music was permeated with the dead stillness of the lazy summer afternoons and soothed him in the gentlest of ways. On the other hand, the screech of the high-soaring kite always filled his youthful imagination with distant thoughts.

"Father," the boy said, "why do you finish the *du'a* so quickly?"

"Do I? Whatever do you mean?"

"You barely raise and join your hands and run them quickly over your face."

"That's already long enough."

"What do you ask God for in so short a time?"

"Forgiveness."

"For what?"

"Sins."

"You commit sins?"

"Oh, come on now. I don't on purpose, but sometimes maybe I do without wanting to. Just happens . . ."

"And you don't know about it?"

"Sometimes I don't, but sometimes I do."

"How can that be?"

"Oh, well, man is a fallible being."

"Does mother also commit sins?"

"Maybe. But surely less frequently than I do."

"When she prays, she prays for a long time."

"That's her habit."

"Is it a good habit to pray?"

After a prolonged silence Shaikh Umar Daraz said in a feeble voice, "Perhaps."

The boy continued, "You only pray for forgiveness?"

"Yes."

"And mother, what does she ask God for?"

54

"That, you must ask her." Shaikh Umar Daraz looked at his son and smiled. "Young man, you do like to badger me with questions. You'll make a good lawyer when you grow up."

That made the boy's thoughts take off on a different tangent: What would he want to be when he grew up?

"Father, you had run off to Bombay–is that right?"

"When?" Shaikh Umar Daraz flinched and looked at his son.

"When you were young," the boy looked up at his father triumphantly. "Mother told me all about it."

A smile quivered on the older man's lips. "Yes," he said, "I did."

"You were very young then?" Aftab asked.

"I was a young adult then."

"How old is a young adult?"

"About twenty, twenty-two years."

"And just a plain young man?"

"I'd say about eighteen, maybe twenty."

"So is a twenty year old a young adult or just a young man?"

"Damn it, you'll surely become a lawyer," Shaikh Umar Daraz said as he smiled again.

"You had run off to become a movie actor?"

Suddenly, for the first time, the older man's colour changed. It was as if his son had pierced the thin, invisible membrane on the other side of which he lived in his world of terrible solitude. But this was not a colour of worry; if anything, it betrayed a distant emotion that had surprised him with its sudden, inexorable closeness.

The boy, finding no answer, lifted his face to his father, but the shimmering sun flooded his eyes.

"Mother told me," the boy said, "that you'd gone off to become a movie star."

"That's true."

"So did you?"

"Well, yes. I did work in a movie."

"Did it show in our hometown?"

"Oh well, in those days only a couple of big cities had movie theaters."

"What did you play?"

"A soldier."

"Like a police constable?"

"No. An army soldier."

"So did you fight in a war?"

"A big one. Between the British and the Muslims."

"Where?"

"Up in the hills . . . in the deserts . . ."

"Are there hills in a desert?"

"In some, yes. This sort of terrain is ideal for battles. I had a white stallion."

Suddenly the boy had the feeling that his father was now not just answering his questions, but also taking a lively interest in the conversation which he had deftly veered towards things closer to his heart. And that made the boy very happy. This strange, wordless communication dispensed with even the need to know on whose side the father had fought. The boy knew, as certainly as his own being, that his father had opted for the role of a British cavalry man.

Finally the boy asked "Who won?"

"We did, of course. But the Muslims, too, put up a good fight. It was a fascinating script. The movie cost hundreds of thousands of rupees. That's like millions today. Our costumes came straight from England. A hundred and twenty horses were bought. They were later sold back, though. But those were gorgeous animals. Each had its separate groom. The white charger I was given was a real thoroughbred. I never saw a nobler animal. The first time I ever rode him, he bore me with such spontaneity and ease, as though we had known each other for a lifetime. I had him for a whole month. For the whole of that month nobody else ever dared touch him. For a full thirty days . . ." Shaikh Umar Daraz suddenly stopped, as if savouring a fond memory. "For a full thirty days I alone owned that animal."

Aftab's mind had stopped straying. He had been imagining the whole scene.

"Did they use rifles in the battle?" Aftab asked with visible impatience.

"Yes. We started out with guns. Then when the armies began to fight hand-to-hand we threw away our rifles and drew our swords."

The boy didn't realize that sometime during the conversation both he and his father had stopped walking. With the montage of desert scenes, of hilly tracks, of the fierce battle between the British cavalry and the brave Muslims running, inexorably, through his mind, Aftab involuntarily raised the branch in his hands and wielded it a couple of times in the air like an accomplished swordsman. Shaikh Umar Daraz stretched his hand and took the *shisham* branch from Aftab's hand. The boy lifted his head and looked straight into his father's eyes, even though the shimmering sky still dazzled him. Before him was the same bright face with its sharp, sculptured features, but flushed with the heat of some uncontrollable inner excitement. It was as if the thin shisham branch had changed, the moment it came into the older man's hand, into a sharp-edged sword, its point having pierced the membrane separating the two.

Shaikh Umar Daraz was standing next to a dead, stunted, leafless acacia. A few round, dried-out limbs poked randomly into the air.

"Imagine it to be a horse–" Shaikh Umar Daraz suddenly leapt into the air and landed precisely on one of the limbs, mounting it as if it were some charger. He raised his left hand in the air to take hold of the imaginary reins, and with the other started whirling the "sword" all around him with dazzling agility, his eyes shining with awesome brilliance. He seemed to be in the thick of battle, cutting down enemy soldiers by the dozen. "And now my horse is wounded . . . it falls," he shouted as he quickly dismounted, but the frenzied movement of his arms continued unabated.

That was a most bizarre scene. In the dead stillness of a sunswept afternoon, in the middle of a parched field, a man wearing a fringed sun hat, his arms and legs outstretched, was brandishing a thin shisham branch with painful concentration, kicking up storms of blinding dust. A couple of fields away a few village brats, driving their buffalo home, momentarily stopped to watch this comic sight. But for the little boy, who stood close to the sword-swishing man, the scene was all too sublime; it certainly wasn't ridiculous. Oblivious to himself, and with total absorption and wonderment, the boy watched his father who, standing beside his dying horse, attacked the enemy soldiers to the right and left of him, in back and in front of him, making short work of them with his shining sword. His eyes glowed with animal fierceness and his body moved with uncommon alacrity, as the sword swished and struck the air.

The towel had rolled down Aftab's head and was dangling from one shoulder. In that instant the boy was impervious to everything: to the incandescent, blinding glare, to the scorching heat. Pure human emotion and animal passion had come together in that instant–an instant in which every boy comes to recognize, unmistakably, his father in the man before him, regardless whether the two are joined by blood. What is important, what counts, is the man's ability to capture fully the boy's attention.

But those moments flew away as fast as they had come.

Shaikh Umar Daraz abruptly stopped thrashing his sword about, thrust the slim shisham switch back into his son's hands, and laughed gently. He had broken into a fine sweat, and beads of perspiration rolled down his face. He picked up the sun hat which had fallen on the ground with one hand and with the other dried his face on the handkerchief. Then he carefully spread the kerchief back on his head, over which he fixed his hat, and started to walk on again. The shisham branch had turned back into a mere switch in Aftab's hands. Its thinner, flayed end had broken off. Within those few short moments the boy had stolen a fleeting view of a wondrous, expansive world where the days didn't burn, nor did the nights strangle. His heart was suddenly like a bird–soaring uninhibited into unchartered space.

In a corner of ten acres of irrigated land stood a well shaded by tall, dense trees. Aftab had already counted all of those trees many times over. He knew trees didn't grow so fast as to increase their number in a matter of days, but he still would count them each time he came to their cropland. There were eighteen *dharaik* trees, four big sharins, a single one of *jaman,* and two tahlis. So dense was their shade that the sun never managed to penetrate all the way down to the ground underneath.

Father and son sat down on a cot lying in the shade and each drank a cup of refreshing salted buttermilk. Then Aftab got up to go through his ritual. He would come to a tree, touch the trunk, count it, and then move on to the next one and repeat the routine. Generally he would thread his way through the grove, passing by the left of one tree and the right of the next one. This made his trail a winding, snakelike one, which pleased him very much. Sometimes he would turn around after he had come to the last tree and loop his way back to the first, but without breaking the count. Then when he had returned to the first tree, he would divide fifty by two. This made him feel that he had completed a round, that the count was what it should be, but, more importantly, that the invisible circle he had drawn around the trees would somehow protect and keep them green.

In the meantime the sharecropper had come out of the hut, holding a hookah in his hand, and sat down near the cot on the bare ground. He began to tell them about the crops.

Shaikh Umar Daraz's face once again looked normal. He was lying on the cot, his head propped up on the pillow of his folded hands, gazing into the trees above. From his manner of responding, it was obvious that he was only half listening to the man. The sharecropper had become used to it. Unbothered, he went on talking to the older man. That peaceful look of mild self-absorption on his father's face generated a feeling of strength and fondness in the boy's heart. It was as if a gentle secret had come to be lodged there. Kneeling on the ground and resting his elbows on the thick, low wall, he leaned over the well and peered deep into the cavity–way down to the mercury platter of water–to catch a reflection of his head. A few yellowed dharaik leaves floated on the surface. Soon the peculiar smell of the water–musty, cool, aged, but above all, permeated by a sense of a certain past time (his grandfather had built this well)–began to rise up to his nostrils. Nothing, absolutely nothing, ever smelled like that. The boy, as if to retrieve that certain, long lost time from the bowels of the earth, emitted a medley of sounds, some shrill, some heavy and hoarse, and listened to the well return them only as a volley of deep and muffled echoes.

It was not an electric well: a pair of oxen pulled the rope that raised the water bucket to the ground level where it was emptied into the irrigation ditch. If he came at irrigation time, Aftab would himself drive the oxen, until his head began to reel. This afternoon, all was quiet at the well and the oxen quietly grazed on the fodder in one corner in the shade. Aftab got up from the well and walked over to the oxen. The cool, comforting smell of the well, which recalled his grandfather's image for him, still lingered in him. He also carried another presence within him, that of his old father, which now began to grow like a tiny drop of ink spreading out on a blotter. For the first time, the boy, barely ten years old, felt the passage of ancestral time through his being. And it filled his heart with a certain uncanny satisfaction.

The boy's eyes fell on a puppy dog which had sneaked up on him from behind and was now standing at his feet. It was a pup the colour of gold, and so tiny that it wobbled all over even as it stood. When the boy bent over to pick it up, it shrank back, yapping shrilly, and tumbled off to the wall and disappeared behind it. The boy followed the pup. Behind the wall he noticed the dog belonging to their sharecropper lying with her young in a hollow. The dog knew the boy.

She cocked her ears once, and finding that her pup was safe, went on leisurely suckling her litter with her full teats sagging to one side. Only last week the boy had seen the dog with her ballooned stomach swaying from side to side, but it never occurred to him that she was about to give birth. He came to the hollow, squatted down at the edge and stared enraptured at the pups. He could see only four pups: Three were black and white, busy attacking the dog's full teats with their eyes closed shut, and the fourth, this gold-coloured one, that had just returned from its adventures outside the hollow and looked more outgoing than the rest. It had abandoned the teats and was struggling to climb up the dog's stomach. The sharecropper's son, seeing the boy's utter fascination, grabbed the gold-coloured pup and stuffed it in the boy's hands. The pup began to yelp. The dog raised her head and growled a bit, then quieted down. The boy, holding the pup against his chest, came to his father and asked, "May I take it home?"

With half-opened eyes Shaikh Umar Daraz looked at the pup that was still making faint noises and said, "He's so tiny. He needs his mother's milk. Wait till he's grown a bit."

The boy, still holding the puppy, returned to the hollow. Shaikh Umar Daraz dozed off for a while. His hands were still folded under his head. The sharecropper went on rambling between puffs of his hookah. The boy again sat back on his heels at the edge of the hollow and, supporting his chin on his hands with his elbows on his knees, returned to staring at the gold-coloured pup in quiet ecstasy.

On the way back many thoughts occurred to Aftab, among them to remind his father that the latter had skipped his afternoon prayer. But that was nothing new. Shaikh Umar Daraz offered his prayers only when the fancy struck him; other times he'd be content with just being by himself, happily self-absorbed. The strange thing though, was that whenever he put off his ritual prayers, he never felt the slightest remorse. On the other hand, if Aftab's mother ever forgot to pray at the prescribed time, she'd be so upset that just about everybody would know about the incident. Only much later, after he had grown up, did the boy come to know that the state of being at prayer was the state of being happily self-preoccupied.

The sun had begun its descent and the temperature had dropped some. As they passed by the green hayfields, a gust of fresh cool air would sweep over them. Many times during the walk home the thought occurred to Aftab to ask if that movie also had some pretty

English memsahibs. He couldn't bring himself to, though. He was strangely aware that that incident, which only he knew about, had entered his heart surreptitiously, like a secret, and that he was never to let anyone in on it. If ever he broached it with anyone, the sense of a certain wholeness would be shattered forever. Many times he looked at his father to find his face still permeated by the same softness and serenity.

On their return trek through open spaces along shaded paths, it didn't feel so uncomfortably hot, but the moment they entered the city, broiling heat and eddies of hot grit and stinging dust struck them with oppressive force. After the paralyzing midday heat, the city was returning to normal activity. People–freshly bathed, neatly combed and clad in gauzy *malmal kurtas*–had sauntered out of their houses and were now milling around in alleyways or crowding up storefronts. Circular Road was again busy with tonga traffic. An old, beat-up rickety bus zoomed past them, kicking up clouds of dust and sending a few bicyclists in front scrambling off to the sides. Dust particles, fired by the day's heat, cut into Aftab's body. A water carrier was squirting water along the edge of the street.

Shaikh Umar Daraz bought Aftab an ice from a vendor and said gently, "Your mother doesn't like dogs. She thinks dogs are unclean. Don't tell her anything about the pup. I'll talk to her about it myself." Then, after a pause, he added, "Let's go visit Chaudhri Nazeer."

They turned into an alley, abandoning the path leading home.

Chaudhri Nazeer, Shaikh Umar Daraz's childhood friend, emerged from the house wearing only an undershirt and a white sheet wrapped around his lower body. Aftab always found the man a bit too intimidating: not only was he the vice-principal of one of the two local high schools, but he also had this habit of talking to children with an air of unnerving seriousness. With Shaikh Umar Daraz, though, he appeared altogether relaxed, even informal, and addressed him as Shaikhji, sometimes as just Umar. With him he wouldn't mind even laughing heartily, slapping him on the hand every now and then with great informal joy.

Chaudhri Sahib led them into the small outer sitting room and later served them a sweet iced drink. A while later he started to pull energetically at the cord of the hand-operated ceiling fan and talk somewhat secretively but in a loud voice, his bespectacled face thrust slightly forward. This feeling of closeness and informality was reserved only for Shaikh Umar Daraz. Only with Chaudhri Sahib did the boy find his otherwise reticent father talk a lot, be perfectly at ease, and sometimes even break into gales of laughter.

By now Aftab was quite beside himself with the heat. The cool drink brought rivers of sweat gushing out of his body. Suddenly he wanted to leave this horribly stuffy room, dash off home, peel the clothes off his scalding body and throw himself under the streaming tap.

"Jot down the file number," Shaikh Umar Daraz said to Chaudhri Sahib. "Who knows, I might forget it."

The Chaudhri looked unbelievingly at Shaikh Umar Daraz. "Umar," he said, "you have never forgotten anything in your whole life; how will you forget my file number?"

"All the same, write it down," Shaikh Umar Daraz laughed gently. "It might just come in handy."

The Chaudhri suddenly became silent and gave the other man's face a deep, probing look. Shaikh Umar Daraz quickly turned his face around to look out through the open door. The Chaudhri extended his arm, put his hand over his friend's and said in a concerned voice, "You're all right, Umar, aren't you?"

"I'm fine," Shaikh Umar Daraz laughed. "I'm just fine."

The heat was now stinging Aftab and he was beginning to lose patience with Chaudhri Sahib, who was needlessly prolonging the conversation, asking after his father's health over and over again. Finally, when the two got up and started for home, Aftab's heart began to pound fitfully as if Chaudhri Nazeer's silent fear had somehow crawled into the boy's heart where it was generating numerous other fears, large and small. Suddenly the boy felt he no longer wanted to go back home. Mother would be sitting on the wooden prayer platform, he imagined, and Bedi would be filling the earthen water jars under the tap. But these thoughts failed to ease his heart. His mother's voice kept hammering away at him. "Your father would have been a magistrate today," she often said. "If only he hadn't wasted his time in his youth." Adding a little later, "He has a brilliant mind. He just doesn't pay attention. We don't even make a penny from the land; the sharecroppers eat up everything."

His mother was a wonderful woman–forbearing and affable–and he loved her very much. Right now, though, the heat emitted by the closed alleyways was so oppressive that the boy was overwhelmed by the desire to get out of the steaming city once again with his father, walk down the shaded highway, then along the cool, comforting hayfields, till they returned to the well. Abruptly an irrepressible desire arose in the boy's heart to shout and ask, "Father, why did you come back from Bombay?" But when he lifted his face, the stern look of his father completely unnerved him.

At home it was exactly as he had imagined: in the small, brick courtyard, his mother was sitting on the low, wooden prayer platform, telling her beads in quiet absorption as her body swayed gently from side to side; and Bedi, done with sprinkling water over the bricks from which arose a soothing, moist, warm aroma, was now filling the water pots at the tap. Aftab went straight to his mother and sat down beside her on the platform. She patted him affectionately on the head and pressed him to her side. Shaikh Umar Daraz entered and greeted, *"Assalamu alaikum!"* It was an old habit. Every time he entered the house he would say those words, even if no one were around. His wife threw a casual glance at him and greeted him with a slight nod of the head, still preoccupied with her beads. Shaikh Umar Daraz stood awhile in the middle of the courtyard, looking around blankly, and then quietly repaired to the sitting room.

The moment he was gone, Aftab hurriedly peeled off all his clothes and made a dash for the tap. The cold crisp water streamed over his body and tickled it. The boy began to shiver and scream with delight. The girl laughed at his ecstatic squeals and worked the hand pump harder. A couple of minutes later Aftab's body stopped shivering. He wet his head under the spout, sucked into the streaming water to catch a few cold gulps and choked over them, then stuck his head under the stream and with his eyes closed began to enjoy the cool sensation of the refreshing water flowing over his body. The dark, uneasy feeling that had earlier gripped him at Chaudhri Sahib's had now completely disappeared, and he was feeling nicely hungry. He knew that after he had dried and changed, his mother would get up from the platform and bake fresh *chapatis* and they would all eat a hearty meal right here in the courtyard. He was happy.

Daylight was fast ebbing away in the sitting room. Shaikh Umar Daraz, a creature of habit, would always leave the sitting room door and windows open in the evening. Today, he didn't though. In the stuffy, closed room he sat sunk in his rattan chair. Today, in fact, he hadn't done anything according to his routine: he had neither taken off his sun hat and set it on the table, nor removed his boots, nor even turned on the table fan in the corner. Fat drops of sweat oozed out from under the hat's fringe and flowed down over his forehead to the web of his thick, bushy eyebrows where they hung poised. For some time he sat motionless and quiet, as if exhausted from his long daytime trek through the summer heat, then, as one suddenly remembers something, he removed the hat with both his hands and set it carefully down on the table. He dried the sweat off his skull and forehead with the handkerchief and then let it hang from the chair arm. Then, instead of bowing down to remove his boots, he got up from the chair, walked over to the door opening into the house, closed the door and latched it noiselessly. He opened the wardrobe, took his double-barrelled shotgun and stuffed a pair of cartridges in the chambers. He put the rifle butt on the ground and lowered his ear directly over the round, dark barrels, as if straining to catch some elusive sound. Then he extended his arm, stuck his fingers into the trigger guard and pulled both triggers down forcefully.

20 June 1970

A little before noon a tallish man got down from the train at the railroad station, accompanied by a boy of about nine or ten. In facial features and gait, the boy bore a striking resemblance to the older man. They were father and son. The former, Aftab Umar, was a lawyer who practiced in Lahore. He had come to this city with a single purpose in mind.

The sun was spewing fire overhead and the gusting wind rose in blazing fire balls as it bounced off the scorched brick platform. To escape the sun, Aftab Umar snapped open his umbrella and quickened his pace along the platform, carefully keeping both himself and the boy in the shade of the umbrella. Coming to the long roofed porch of the platform he stopped, threw his attaché case on the bench, yanked out a handkerchief from his pants pocket and began drying his face and neck with it. Then he extended his arm to do the same for his son, who flinched, jerked his face away, quickly pulled out his own handkerchief and used it instead to dry himself. Both unfolded their handkerchiefs, examined the lines left on them by sweat and dirt, and stuffed them back into their pockets. Aftab squinted in the glare at the platform.

"When I left here," he said, "the station didn't have this platform."

"Didn't the train stop here?"

"It did. But the platform wasn't here."

"Where did the train stop then?"

"On the bare ground."

The boy, a bit confused, looked at the platform and asked, "So when was the platform built?"

"A few years ago."

"You never saw it before?"

"No."

Twenty years ago a single peepul tree stood outside the station building–everything else was the sun above and the raw earth below. Now the space directly opposite the terminal was paved and lined by tall shishams. Standing under their shade on the ground covered with pollen-packed tiny white flowers were many tongas, too many to count. A half dozen private cars were parked in the small parking area reserved for automobiles. The cars, all except one, were being loaded and people, those who had just disembarked from the train as well as those who had come to receive them, stood near them talking animatedly, laughing, fanning themselves with a magazine or newspaper. Next to the area for car parking was a stand for scooters and bicycles. All these developments had fundamentally altered the look of the railway station Aftab once knew.

All at once a number of coachmen swarmed up to Aftab and the boy, each trying to offer his tonga for hire. Aftab looked intently at their faces, but failed to recognize a single one. Finally he got into a tonga and said to the coachman, "Take us to a good hotel."

"Rivaz Hotel is the best. Very clean and quite close to the court-house. Gulnaz isn't bad, either, but it's got a bad name. Respectable people stay away from it. Sir, you look as though you don't live here–right?"

The street was still the same–broken and riddled with potholes–but many new shops had sprung up on either side. It was almost noon and, despite the hot wind which had started blowing, all you saw around you was a surging sea of heads. Automobiles, scooters, tongas and bicycles crowded the street. Aftab took out his sunglasses, put them on and stared at every passing face from behind the cool lenses. He strained to recognize a single familiar face, but in the twenty-minute ride found none and began to doubt if he had spent the first twenty years of his life here. Twenty years ago, when he had left here, he had just finished his B.A. in the newly opened college. He knew hundreds of people. Where had they all run off to? he wondered. It seemed as though the entire population of the city of his time had been physically lifted and relocated elsewhere, making room for a population of strangers.

Aftab was familiar with the Rivaz Hotel. But it was not the old, smallish, bungalow-style building he expected to see; a box-shaped, off-white, four-storey tall monster with cement floral vines crawling along the windows greeted him instead.

A gust of mouldy smell, characteristic of entombed places, struck Aftab's nose as he opened the door to his third-floor room. He quickly flung the window open. The rooms had all been built disregarding the prevailing air currents. In this season of hellish heat, Aftab marvelled at this architectural travesty. The hotel attendant, trailing behind them, had in the meantime checked out the light switch by flipping it on and off a few times and was now dutifully trying to get the ceiling fan to work. A couple of wires had perhaps come off loose in the fan's regulator, which was covered with fly specks.

"Would you like me to bring up the meal, sir?" the attendant asked.

"We'll eat downstairs in the hall . . . after a while," Aftab said. "Could you bring us some ice water for now?"

"Right away, sir."

"I think I'll take a bath." Aftab said to his son as he took off his shirt.

"Daddy, let me take a bath first."

"Tell you what. Let's slip on our shorts and take a bath together."

"Aftab opened the attaché case and took out a towel, bar of soap, comb, talcum powder, two clean boxer shorts, a big and a small one, and piled them all up on the bed. The room was furnished along modern lines. Two single beds with a side table wedged in between, all lay flush against the wall. The sheets were clean and a crisp white. The bathroom boasted of a shower, but the pressure was too weak to pump the water high enough for the shower to work properly. Water flowed down in a faint stream from the shower-head and was collected below in a bucket with an enameled mug set close beside it. Aftab gazed wide-eyed at everything, hoping to find at least one familiar object. He stepped back into the room and sat down on the bed. His son stood in the middle of the room with only his boxer shorts on, cooling himself under the ceiling fan.

"Daddy, where was your house?"

"There–" Aftab pointed in a direction.

"Who lives in it now?"

"God knows. I sold it before I left."

The attendant returned with a jug of iced water. It was an iron jug and its handle was riddled with reddish gold welding marks. They had a glass each and stepped into the bathroom.

The marble-chip floor of the dining room was messy with dried up gravy spots. Even though curtains had been lowered over the doors and windows, it didn't much help against the attacks of pesky flies. They swarmed on tables, chairs, plates, on people's arms and incessantly working jaws–just about everywhere. Gingerly, like an actor on his first appearance on an unfamiliar stage, Aftab entered the half-lit dining room. He had briefly hesitated at the door and looked cautiously around, as if startled–becoming aware, suddenly, of an awesome loneliness crawling into the dead centre of his heart.

"Daddy, aren't you going to tell me the story? Remember, you promised?" the boy reminded Aftab over the food.

"Not now."

"When?"

"When we go out for a stroll."

"At four o'clock?"

"Yes, about that time. After the sun's gone down a bit."

After they had returned from the dining room the boy lay down on the bed and read his comic book for a while, then turned over and fell asleep. Aftab also tried to sleep, but couldn't. He got up and walked over to the window. Opening out before him was a view of the city's busiest square at the busiest time of the day. People were returning from work; young men and women from schools and colleges. There was a messy traffic jam. Seemingly, the passage of twenty years had left the square's appearance intact. The same businesses were still around: three shoe shops, including Bata, a tailor's shop, a dentist's clinic, a stationery store, and the cigarette-and-*pan* stall. The atmosphere in these stores hadn't changed either, nor had the ambience of the streets where girls, crammed into tongas, most of them without their veils, were on their way home from school. Aftab had heard that an all girls' college had been opened here. This was his hometown. He had passed through this square countless times on his way to and from school, and then later as a college student. Hundreds of times in these very streets, he and his friend Mustafa had chased after the perky Government School girls who were always bundled up in their black *burqas*. A quarter of a mile down the street into the inner city was the house where he was born. Even today, if he climbed down the three flights of stairs of the hotel and took himself to the square, he could walk blindfolded to his house or, for that matter, in any direction, as though he had never left here. Between him and his city there were just these forty-five stairs.

All at once he was overwhelmed by just such a desire: to climb down the flight of stairs to the square, remove his sunglasses, look up old acquaintances among the milling crowd, shake hands with them, talk to them, and then push on to his house, or to Mustafa's. Mustafa's father might still be alive, he thought.

Aftab took off his sunglasses for a second. The glare stung his eyes. The traffic was thinning out in the square and the shops were closing one by one for the noon break. Within an hour the square will be deserted, he thought.

Nothing, absolutely nothing in the city, now belonged to him. He was nineteen years old when he had got his B.A. and landed a job in the Government Secretariat at Lahore. A year later, during his mother's sudden and fatal illness, he had briefly returned to his hometown to dispose of everything, house and all, and permanently settled down in Lahore in a new house outside the city in the Model Town suburb. He was still living in that house. After getting a law degree he had given up his old job and set up his own practice. Every year he would promise himself a visit to his hometown and childhood friends, some of whom dropped by now and then to visit him or to ask a favour. They had all been married and raised children. Mustafa had died in action in the 1965 Indo-Pakistani war and Aftab hadn't been able even to go visit his survivors and console them; managing, instead, a letter of condolence. When Iqbal, another friend, fell seriously ill, he had him brought to Lahore and admitted to Mayo Hospital. But in the past twenty years he hadn't once been able to travel these seventy miles to his hometown. How on earth could he now go and stand in the square? Standing in his hotel suite, the thought that he was now gone from this city for good hit Aftab with a chilling finality.

"Daddy–" his son's groggy voice called at him.

Aftab turned around. "You're up?"

"Imran's daddy has bought a brand new chair."

"Oh. What kind of chair?"

"A swivel chair."

"Is that so?"

The thought of visiting his hometown had emerged so suddenly, so unexpectedly. Not even a whole day had passed. Faruq, his son, was playing with his friend Imran in their backyard. Aftab, too, had come out in the yard after his shower and was now seated comfortably in a chair studying a brief. Nasreen, his wife, was sitting in the chair opposite him browsing through a magazine. Aftab removed his feet from his slippers and slowly put them on the ground, letting the cool grass tickle his soles. Once during his work he casually lifted his head and his eyes fell directly on his son. And the whole matter gelled in that single instant.

All his thoughts became ineluctably focused on that frozen instant of time. In that instant much went swirling through his mind: It was 19 June today; tomorrow it would be the 20th. Faruq, his son, was ten years old, while he himself was reaching his fortieth year. Exactly 30 years ago he was ten and his own father, forty. These uncanny resemblances, these striking harmonies became concentrated, inexorably, in that whirling instant which swept over him like a magic spell. Aftab became oblivious to the brief of the case due to start the next day lying open in his lap, his wife sitting opposite him, everything. He felt as if that instant was whirling round a pivot which drew him irresistibly towards it. Slowly it dawned on him that the pivot was none other than his hometown.

Then and there, sitting immobile in the grip of that spell, Aftab decided that it was time he visited his hometown. He told his wife about his decision. She could understand his desire, but not why he should insist on dragging Faruq along in the miserable heat. But she didn't fuss over it, thinking that, after all, his parents were buried there and that he had never once gone back.

Aftab sent for his assistant and gave him instructions about the court hearings scheduled for the next day, June 20th. He talked Faruq into accompanying him with a promise of showing him around his hometown and telling him a fascinating story once they got there.

That night he couldn't sleep a wink. His thoughts remained fixed on that instant, where time seemed to have hit a dead end and halted. As the night progressed the thought that that instant was steeped in a mystery became a conviction. That mystery had, in fact, kept a part of his mind paralyzed for thirty years. Perhaps the time had come to solve it!

"I tried it out myself," Faruq said.

"Hmmm."

"I mean the chair."

"You did?" Aftab said absentmindedly. "You said it's a swivel chair?"

"Yes. It goes round and round," Faruq explained, tracing circles in the air with his hand. "Yes, daddy, it does–round and round!"

"Hmmm."

"What time is it?"

"Four o'clock."

"Let's go." Faruq was impatient for the "fascinating" story his father had promised to tell.

"All right," Aftab said, "Let's go."

It was getting on towards late afternoon but the city still hadn't fully snapped back into action; here and there, though, some tentative signs of life had begun to show: water was being sprinkled in places and shops were again opening, but it would be a while before the customers showed up. The only people who were there now were shopkeepers' acquaintances and friends who regularly dropped in for an idle evening chat.

Carefully huddled under the shade of the umbrella both Aftab and Faruq walked into the bazaar. Aftab stared at some faces and for the first time recognized a few, vaguely though, just as one does trees and dwellings. What he thought he recognized were the timeless, anonymous faces of shopkeepers whom he had seen all his life glued to their storefronts. Some had visibly aged, with a pronounced grey showing in their beards, while others looked strangely unaffected by time. None of them, however, paid any attention to Aftab. He walked through the bazaar unnoticed, hidden behind the anonymity of dark sunglasses and an umbrella. At the spot in the road where they had to take a turn towards Circular Road, Tunda–who sold spicy grilled shish kababs–was just setting up. On the front of his box-shaped stall lay the flat, rectangular open barbecue grill which he had filled with charcoal, but hadn't got it going yet. Instead, he was scrubbing the dozen or so skewers with a piece of dirty rag. An old, beat-up small fan was set beside the grill which he used to blow on the coals. Perhaps it was the same fan, Aftab imagined, which Tunda had used twenty years ago. Shortly smoke will bellow out of the grill, he thought, carrying the appetizing aroma of roasting spiced meat, and bring otherwise perfectly satiated people scrambling out to Tunda's stall. Already before the time for the sunset prayer a crowd could be seen milling around his stall and wouldn't begin to thin out until it was time for the night prayer. Then, as the cry of the muezzin arose from the neighbourhood mosque, Tunda would wash the skewers in the large empty bowl in which he kept the spiced ground meat for the kababs and carefully put them away. Then he would empty the grill in the gutter, where a few coals, still red-hot under a layer of ashes, would expire hissing loudly and sending up clouds of smoke; he would put the grill back into the stall, lock up the stall and make for home. Although Tunda's left hand was intact, his right had been amputated just below the elbow. In spite of the handicap, he did all his work alone. From the time Aftab was a mere child, he had always found Tunda perched on the platform of his stall, no bigger than a chicken coop, working away using the one hand with a deftness and speed that defied description. Tunda was famous throughout the city for his delicious kababs.

Suppose he were to take off his sunglasses, Aftab toyed with the idea, and install himself in front of Tunda and accost him, would he, Tunda, recognize him? Surely he would. Had he not, after all, from childhood right up to his late teens found himself twice a week standing in the crowd at Tunda's stall waiting for his turn to buy a few sizzling-hot, crackling kababs smeared with peppery-hot onion sauce, which Tunda would wrap for him in a piece of newspaper, before dashing home with his mouth watering?

Passing by the stall Aftab turned his head to look behind. Tunda was still busy scouring the skewers.

By now the two had crossed the bazaar and reached Circular Road. The traffic was sparse, mostly tongas and bicycles; the irritating dust had not yet begun to rise. They walked on Circular Road for a while and then, instead of following the curve, walked straight up and got on the path connecting the city's centre with the Grand Trunk Road. This barely half a mile long stretch stood in Aftab's memory as a dusty, unpaved path which looked deserted even in daytime. Not so now. It had been paved and an assortment of big and small factories had sprung up along both sides, with large and small bungalows wedged in between them. A completely new neighbourhood! Pools of stinking water, covered with mosquitoes, had formed next to the factories and residential houses. Aftab hurriedly strode out of the area.

The moment they got on the Grand Trunk Road, Aftab felt as though time had suddenly reversed itself and then stopped, preserving unchanged in its core a pristine vision of the world as he once knew it. And, today, still very much the child he once was, he had returned to play in that world.

The open fields, the land, were still the same: ancient and familiar. The same shisham trees lined the road and swayed in the wind and provided, with their shade, a refuge from the scalding winds.

Aftab snapped shut the umbrella, removed his sunglasses and put them back into his pocket. The glare no longer hurt his eyes. Off the road the landscape was dotted with the same old fields. Wheat had already been harvested and the parched fields looked mournfully sad in their stark nakedness, their surface riddled with dark rodent holes where freshly dug-up dirt was piled in tiny hills. Dry wheat chaff lay strewn all around the fields. These mouse holes, Aftab remembered, used to scare the daylights out of him because as a boy he had always thought they harboured vipers. Today he knew they were just mouse holes. He still couldn't look at them without fear. He told his son to give them good clearance. Walking by a hayfield he bent down a little, broke a long green leaf and began to chew on it.

That dead, ancient tree was still there in the field. Aftab stood a few feet from it and gawked at it; he couldn't believe his eyes. All along he had been thinking that when he got there chances were the tree wouldn't be there; and even if it were, he would have to look around quite a bit to find it (he was obsessed by the desire to return to it once again and narrate the whole story to Faruq right beside it) but as soon as he had crossed over the tall hedge of bushes, what do you know, the tree stood right in front of him, immobile as a statue. Aftab took a few slow steps to the tree, and then extended his hands gingerly to touch a twisted, black branch, as if afraid that the merest touch would send the whole tree crashing down. But the tree stood firm. And although every single fiber in that tree had been dead and dry for a long time, its stiffness, its mournful spread and the tremendous force with which its roots gripped the earth had not changed at all. Even the line left behind by the stripped bark was in its place. It was as if the tree had become frozen in the moment of its death and become a permanent mark on the earth's topography. The single thing that didn't fit in

Aftab's memory of the tree was this new, awesome-looking shisham that had sprung up a few yards from it. After the incident thirty years ago, Aftab had stopped coming to their land. Later his mother had rented it out. And though he did come here once or twice as a young man, it was by chance; and then again he didn't walk but bicycled down to it on the paved highway recently built by the District Board, the highway which passed by their well and went to Ahmad Pur Sharif.

Aftab lifted his head and looked into the dense shisham foliage above.

"Daddy, I'm tired," Faruq said.

Aftab wiped his son's sweaty face with his handkerchief and said, "We're almost there." He ran his fingers through Faruq's hair. "There, you can almost see it."

"Where?"

"That grove of trees . . . you see it?" Aftab pointed in a direction.

"Yes."

"There's a well under those trees," he said. "Around the well are many fields. Well, that used to be our land."

"But Daddy, I'm really tired," Faruq said, whimpering a little.

"It's cool and shady down there," Aftab said. "Come on, it isn't all that far–really."

"Unh-nh-nh!" the boy whined. "The sun's killing me. I don't want to go there." He flopped down under the shisham.

Aftab looked ardently and let his eyes linger awhile on the familiar dark, dense foliage of the grove a quarter of a mile down the trail and felt its comforting cool touch on his sunburnt cheeks. The touch seemed so familiar, so recent he thought he was in the grove only a fortnight ago, catching his breath awhile in its shade. His throat was badly parched and a desperate longing arose in his heart to gulp down a bowlful of that refreshing salted buttermilk. Who might be living here now?–he wondered, with a trace of confusion and anguish.

"Daddy, let's go back home."

That sensation of comforting shade suddenly vanished. Aftab walked over to his son and sat down beside him leaning against the shisham trunk. Then he said, "Son, let's rest awhile here and then we'll go."

"Daddy, when will you tell me the story?" they boy said in an exasperated voice, tired of waiting.

Aftab lifted his eyes and looked far into the bright sun. Way down, the dead tree stood still in its stark nakedness, mutilated, terribly mangled–like a frightening nightmare. Aftab put his sunglasses back on and started to tell his son the story . . . that story.

In a soft and collected voice he recounted the event that had occurred thirty years ago and had paralyzed his life since. The entire incident was fresh in his memory, and yet he couldn't begin relating it without a certain diffidence. He was having difficulty talking about it; he felt as if something was buried deep inside the earth and he had to actually dig and pry it out of there. For a while he talked haltingly, as if trying to press disjointed events into a rational order but finding them too stubborn to connect; later his voice grew more confident and coherent as randomness coalesced into order, and each insipid detail became vibrant with life. His words formed into slithering links which closed in on him like a chain. He was now speaking with flow and smoothness, the words flying out of his mouth like birds following the track of sound which terminated in a frozen moment of time.

In that sun-soaked, broiling afternoon, sitting under that intruding shisham, Aftab saw the dark, long tunnel of his life recede to reveal a tiny point of light at the other end. The speck of light gradually moved towards him and stopped in front of his eyes, causing everything and every moment to ripple over Aftab's skin with remarkable tactile sensation. It felt as though the past thirty years had been suddenly divested of all meaning–that not only time and life but even man's own body had no significance at all before his inexorable memory–a memory that integrated one generation into the other and gave the world its sole meaning.

Aftab raised his head to look at his enraptured son and ran his fingers into his hair, as if transmitting through touch the end of the chain. He had hit the end of his story.

In relating that incident, Aftab had made one change: he never did reveal that the man with whom he had gone out on a stroll through the fields exactly thirty years ago, the man who had on returning from the stroll shot himself without uttering a word, was in fact his own father. He didn't have the courage to let his son in on the secret; instead, he told him that the man was a neighbour of theirs.

The story told, both got up and started back. In spite of the blazing sun, Aftab neither popped open the umbrella nor put the sunglasses back over his eyes, but kept walking into the sun, impervious to its searing heat and blinding glare. A crushing load was suddenly off his heart and his body felt strangely unstrung and weightless–weightless, but strong. And although his mind was empty of thought, his body vibrated with the feeling that this city of his childhood was still very much his own. These fields, these trees, these streets now alive with traffic, tongas and automobiles that zoomed past kicking up clouds of dust, the bazaars full of popsicle vendors and sellers of fragrant *motiya* garlands, the alleyways where women sat on their house fronts or doorways fanning themselves as they chatted with their neighbours, mouths thrown open from the deep heat, the children who tumbled and rolled and capered about in the dust as they played unbothered by the heat, the houses from which rose the sound of metal bowls striking against earthen water jars, or the pungent aroma of frying or sauteed onion or garlic spreading everywhere around–all these places and sights and smells Aftab felt, through an unbroken continuous sensation, to be his own. He had left his hometown for good twenty years ago, but throughout that time and at no place–Lahore where he had settled down, the cities where he was obliged to spend some time on business, and those other places which he had merely passed through–nowhere, absolutely nowhere had he experienced the state he was in now, the state in which one becomes oblivious even to one's body. Although for thirty years his heart had remained numb, his body had shivered every instant with a nameless fear, as if somebody would sneak up on him from behind and grab him. Only now his body had stopped trembling and become light, every muscle in it perfectly unstrung, relaxed and calm, he not even aware that he had a body. Only the heart was the seat of every sensation and knowledge. For the first time in his life, Aftab found out what exactly the two words "My hometown" meant, which he had so often heard people say.

Sitting across a table from each other in the small front garden of the hotel Aftab and Faruq were sipping Coke from chilled bottles. Condensation formed into droplets in the smudge marks left by their fingerprints and trickled down, cutting crooked pathways into the frosted surface. It was getting on towards evening. Beyond the three-foot-high garden wall, a second wave of traffic had started to funnel down the street. The time for the last evening trains was approaching and the anxious coachmen were crying "Station! Anyone for the station!" People, freshly bathed, neatly combed and wearing fine malmal shirts, had come out of their houses for the evening stroll. Faruq got up, walked over to the chair near the wall, sat down in it, leaned back and resting his feet on the wall began reading his comic book. A little later, Aftab too got up, grabbed his Coke, walked over to his son and slumped down in the chair next to him.

"So, did you like the story?" he asked.

Faruq inattentively mumbled something and went on reading the comic in the fading daylight. A naked lightbulb burned in the hotel veranda, its light too far and too feeble to do him any good. After a while, Faruq got tired, stopped reading, looked up and suddenly asked, "Daddy, are you going to write this story?"

Aftab thought for a while and then said, "I might."

"Daddy, you could become the world's greatest lawyer if you didn't write stories."

"Oh!" Aftab broke into laughter. "Whoever told you that?"

"Mummy."

"Really? What does she say?"

"Just that if daddy didn't waste his time writing stories he could become the biggest lawyer."

Aftab laughed again and became silent. After a while he said, "Faruq," he put his elbows down on the table, "shall I write this story? What do you say?"

Again the boy emitted a faint, uninterested sound and began looking at the street.

Aftab continued, "Tell me one thing."

"What?"

"Why did the man kill himself?"

"I don't know why."

"Come on. Think about it." Aftab insisted. "Only when you tell me that will I write the story."

"Why?"

"Because I myself don't understand why the man shot himself."

The boy stared unbelievingly at his father, then turned around to look at the street, as if thinking. Both remained silent for a while. Aftab's heart pounded violently. He shifted his weight on his elbows and lowered himself over the table. The same old fear his body knew so well began to return.

Suddenly Faruq turned around to look at Aftab. There was a strange glint in the boy's eyes.

"Perhaps he loved horses," the boy said.

The fog began to lift from in front of Aftab's eyes and narrowed into a tiny bright dot of uncommon intensity. The dot slowly expanded into a large pool of light in the middle of which Aftab saw a shimmering white stallion galloping away. The sun poured over its body with such brilliance that the eye skidded off and could not behold it. Every muscle in the horse's taut body was so firm, so prominent as though it had been carved out of granite. A rider was firmly mounted on the horse's back, confidently holding the reins. The rider was outfitted in the white uniform of a British soldier, with a sun hat stuck on his head. He held a bared sword pointing to the sky. With each gallop, the horse and the rider soared into space in such unison that it seemed they were a single body which would jump across the length of the earth in one gigantic bound. In the ebbing light, still leaning on his elbows, Aftab stared at this scintillating picture of perfect beauty and harmony, until the fog rose again and obscured his eyes. The scene disappeared as fast as it had appeared, but it left in its narrow wake the knowledge that that was the finest moment of his father's life.

It was getting dark. The momentary brightness was gone. In the crowding darkness something quite new had emerged. It was as though that swift-footed bright moment had left its dark shadow behind. Something was found, but something was lost too; something was revealed, but something had also become forever hidden: "This city," Aftab found himself thinking, "this city where my father had lived his whole life had finally lost its appeal to him. And here I am; I left it for good, only to return and be fully alive again. Anyway, what does it all mean?"

The confusion that had been gnawing at his heart had certainly been removed. Or perhaps it hadn't been. If there was anything he knew with certainty, it was this: he belonged here . . .

It was night now. Street lights had come up. Faruq, his legs still resting on the low wall, was again browsing through his comic in the dim light of the electric pole in front.

"Daddy," Faruq said suddenly, "I'll go to America when I grow up."

Startled, Aftab looked at his son. The boy's eyes were sparkling. Aftab stared at him for the longest time, then, somewhat casually, said, "Is that so?"

"When I grow up I'll become a doctor. And then I'll go to America."

In the comic book that lay open in the boy's lap, a gigantic black man was crossing the street with his giant-size strides, while a string of cars funnelled through his wide-apart legs. Faruq turned his face to look at the street again, his eyes still gleaming with an illicit, faraway look.

A little later Aftab got up from the chair and looked at his son, as if contemplating whether to say something, but then said nothing. He left the boy in the garden and went into the hotel. In the hall he stopped and looked around for a few moments and then slowly began to climb up the stairs.

A few minutes later, Faruq too decided to return. When he opened the door, it was dark inside. He jumped up and turned on the light. His father, still in his day clothes, his feet in socks and shoes, was lying stretched out on the bed. His arms were gently folded over his chest and his face was drenched in sweat. It was terribly hot and stuffy inside the room.

"Daddy, shall I turn on the fan?" Faruq asked.

Aftab remained immobile. Faruq walked over to him and called out gently, "Daddy!"

Aftab opened his eyes and stared at the ceiling, as if trying to recognize it. "You may, if you like," he said in a faint voice.

"Daddy, I'm hungry."

Aftab got up. He went into the bathroom, washed his face with cold water and dried it on a towel. Then, taking the boy along, he walked out of the room.

"Daddy, when will we go back home?"

"Early in the morning."

The two began climbing down the stairs to the dining hall.

Translated by Muhammad Umar Memon

NAIYER MASUD

Obscure Domains of Fear and Desire

Thou holdest mine eyes waking;
I am so troubled that I cannot speak.
I have considered the days of old,
the years of ancient times.

Psalm 77

"We kept on looking at each other in silence for the longest time. Our faces didn't betray any kind of curiosity. His eyes had an intensity and brightness. Never for a moment throughout this time did they seem to me devoid of feelings. All the same, I couldn't at all understand whether his eyes were expressing something or just observing. I did feel as though we were coming to some silent understanding between us. All of a sudden a terrible feeling of despair came over me. This was the first time I'd felt like this since I'd come to this house. At this point his nurse placed her hand on my arm and led me out of the room.

"Outside, as I spoke with his nurse, time after time I realized that my speech was a shortcoming and that the patient was travelling far ahead of me on a road which I knew nothing about."

I have given up talking, not looking. It isn't easy to stop looking if one happens to possess a pair of eyes. Keeping quiet, even though one has a tongue, is relatively easy. And yet at times I do get an urge to close my eyes. But so far they are still open. This may be due to the presence of the person who is looking after me. She is my last link with that old house where I opened my eyes for the first time and learned to talk. When I lived in that house, she was just a cute little doll, only a year-

79

and-a-half old. And so affectionate towards me. I would call for her as soon as I entered the house and then, as long as I remained there, she would cling to me.

Now she has no memory of those days. All she's been told is that I am the last representative of her family. She does not know much else about me. In spite of this, she is very fond of me. She thinks that this is the very first time she has seen me. She does not remember that I used to call her my "Little Bride." Actually, I started calling her that because she began to refer to me as her bridegroom whenever someone in the family asked her who I was. This amused everyone. They would all laugh and then just to tease her, someone would claim me as a "bridegroom." When she heard this she would have herself a regular little tantrum. Among those who teased her, there were several older relatives, both male and female. In those days, her small world was crowded with rivals. But, even then, the ranks of her rivals did not include the woman for whom she had the warmest feelings, not counting her mother or myself. And in return, this woman cared more deeply for this little girl than anyone else.

1.

She was at least two years older than me. Twelve years prior to the time I'm talking about, I had seen her at my older brother's wedding. She was the younger sister of my brother's wife. But due to a complicated pattern of kinship, she also happened to be my aunt.

At the time of my brother's marriage, she was a mature young woman and I was a mere boy–a shy, awkward stripling. She affected towards me an attitude of someone much older than myself. Of course, we often chatted, shared jokes and teased each other. But in spite of all this informality, she maintained the air of an elder. I never detected any fakery in that attitude, which perhaps would have irritated me. She treated me not as though she were much older than me, but as though I were quite a bit younger than her. And I liked that.

There were times, however, when I got the distinct impression that I was, after all, just her young nephew. This happened when she compared her hometown with mine and insisted that hers was a much better place. I would immediately leap to the defence of my town and argue with her endlessly in a rather childish manner. During those years, she visited us once in a while and stayed with us for long periods of time. And during this particular visit which I am speaking of, she had been with us for three or four days.

I came into the house and, as usual, I called out to my "Little Bride" as soon as I'd stepped into the courtyard. But the house was silent. No one seemed to be home. However, Aunt was there. She had just emerged from the bathroom and had sat down in a sunlit spot to dry her hair. I asked her where all the others were and she said that they had all gone to attend a wedding somewhere. Not knowing what else to say, I asked her about my "Little Bride" even though I had a hunch that she might have gone to the wedding with the others. I went and sat next to Aunt and we started talking about this and that. Most of the time we talked about my "Little Bride" and chuckled over her antics. After a while her hair was dry and she stood up to tie it in a bun. In an effort to arrange her hair, she raised both arms with her hands at the back of her head. Her bare waist arched just slightly and her bust rose a little and then slightly moved backwards, causing her locks to fall away from her. I saw this in a fraction of a second and remained unaffected. She continued to put up her hair in a chignon and we went on talking. Suddenly one of her earrings came off and landed near her foot. I quickly bent down to retrieve it for her. As I knelt at her feet, my eyes fell upon the pale curve of her instep and I was reminded once again that she had just taken a bath. I picked up the earring and tried to put it back in her ear while I kept up a rapid patter of conversation. I could smell the musky odour which arose from her moist body. She continued to fiddle with her hair and I kept on trying to put her earring back on. But for some reason, I couldn't get it to stay and her earlobe started to turn red. I must have jabbed her with the post of the earring. A little cry broke from her throat and she chided me mildly. She then took the earring from me with a smile and by herself quickly put it on. And soon afterwards, she went up to her room and I went into mine.

A little later, I went upstairs looking for a book. On the way back, I glanced over towards Aunt's room. She stood in front of the bamboo screen. Her hair hung loosely about her shoulders and her eyes looked as though she had just woken up. I went into her room and again we started talking about odds and ends. She started to tie up her hair all over again and once again I saw what I had seen earlier. Seeing her waist bend backwards once again, I felt a bit uneasy. We talked about the wedding that my entire family had gone to attend and I told her that there was a great difference in height between the bride and bridegroom. Exaggerating rather wildly, I insisted that the bride barely came up to the waist of the bridegroom.

Aunt laughed at this and said, "Anyway, at least she's a little taller than your bride."

We started talking about my "Little Bride" once again, whose absence made the house seem quite empty. I was about to introduce some other topic, when Aunt got off the bed and came towards me.

"Let's see if you are taller than me," she said with a smile.

Grinning we came and stood facing each other. She moved closer to me. Once again I became aware of the fragrance which arose from her body, a warm, moist odour which reminded me that she had just taken bath. We drew still closer and her forehead almost touched my lips.

"You're much shorter than me," I told her.

"Of course not," she retorted and stood up on her toes. Then she giggled: "How about this?"

I grabbed her waist with both hands and tried to push her downwards.

"You're cheating," I told her. And bending down, I grabbed both her ankles and tried to plant them back on the floor. When I got up again, she wasn't laughing anymore. I clasped her waist firmly with both hands once again.

"You're being unfair," I said to her as the grip of my hands tightened on her waist.

Her arms rose, moved towards my neck, but then they stopped. I felt like I was standing in a vast pool of silence which stretched all around us. My hold on her waist tightened still more.

"The door," she said in a faint whisper.

I brought her close to the door without letting go of her waist. Then I released her slowly, bolted the door and turned towards her again. I remembered how she had always behaved like an older relative towards me and I felt angry at her for the first time, but then just as suddenly this anger turned into an awareness of her tremendous physical appeal. I bent over and held her legs. I was still bent over with my grip around her legs progressively tightening when I felt her fingers twist my hair. I held both her feet and helped her to the bed. She pulled me up with a violent intensity and my head bumped against her chest. Then, with her fingers still locked in my hair, she moved back towards the bed. When we got to the edge of the bed, I put my arms around her waist and began to push her backwards. But she suddenly broke free and stood up. I looked at her.

She murmured: "The door that leads up the stairs . . . it's open."

"But there's no one in the house."

"Someone will come."

Silently we went down the stairs and bolted the door that led up them. Then we came back up together, went into her room and bolted the door from the inside. Apart from the tremors running through our bodies, we seemed to be fairly calm, exactly the way we were when we talked to each other under normal circumstances. She paused near the bed, adjusted her hair once again and taking off the earrings she put them next to the pillow. In a flash of recollection, I remembered all those stories I'd heard about love affairs that started after the lovers stood together and compared their heights. But I decided right away that these stories were all imaginary, wishful tales and the only true reality was this experience which this woman, who was a distant aunt–but an aunt who also happened to be the younger sister of my brother's wife–and I were going through together. I picked her up gently and made her lie down on the bed, thinking how just a few minutes earlier I had entered the house calling for my "Little Bride." It is possible that the same thought may have crossed her mind. A light tremor went through our bodies. I had just begun to lean towards her when she suddenly sat up straight. Fear flickered in her eyes.

"Someone is watching," she said softly and pointed at the door. I turned my head to look and also got the impression that someone was peeking through the crack between the door panels. The person appeared to move away and then return to look again. This went on for a few minutes. Both of us continued to stare in silence. Finally, I got up and opened the door. The bamboo screen which hung in front was swaying back and forth gently. I pushed at it with my hands and then closed the door once again. The sunlight streaming in through the cracks created a pattern of shifting light and shade even as the bamboo screen moved in the breeze. I turned back towards Aunt. A weak smile flickered around her lips but I could hear her heart throbbing loudly in her chest, and her hands and feet were cold as ice. I sat down in a chair next to her bed and began telling her tall tales of strange optical illusions. She told me a few similar stories and pretty soon we were chatting away the way we always did. Not one word was exchanged about anything which had transpired only a few minutes earlier. At length she said to me: "The others should be coming home soon."

That moment it occurred to me that the door leading up the stairs had been bolted from the inside. Just then we began to hear the voices of family members. I got up, opened wide the door of the room and came out. Aunt was right behind me. I unbolted the door that led up the stairs and then we came back to her room and continued to talk about sundry matters. After a while, I heard a noise and saw that my "Little Bride" stood at the door. She really did look like a bride. Aunt uttered a joyful shout, grabbed the little girl, pulled her into her lap and started to kiss her over and over again with a passionate intensity. The little girl shrieked with laughter and struggled to escape from her embrace. Apparently, in the house where the wedding had taken place, some overly-enthusiastic girls had painted her up like a bride and decked her out with garlands. A few minutes later, her mother came up to the room along with some of the other children. At this time the little girl was sitting in my lap and I was asking her about the fancy food she'd eaten at the house where the wedding had taken place. She could only pronounce the names of a few dishes and kept repeating them over and over. Her mother tried to pick her up but she refused to budge from my lap.

"Oh, she is such a shameless bride," Aunt said and everyone burst out laughing.

At some point we all came down into the veranda where the other members of the family had gathered. Aunt continued to teach my "Little Bride" how to act shy and every now and then bursts of laughter rose up from the assembled throng.

2.

By the time the sun had gone down, I'd made many attempts to catch her alone. But she sat imprisoned in a circle of women, listening to anecdotes about the wedding. During the night, I tried three times to open the door that lead up the stairs but it appeared to be bolted from the other side. I knew that a couple of women–themselves never married and perpetual hangers-on in the household–also slept in her room but in spite of this I wanted to go upstairs. Next day, from morning till noon, I saw her sitting with the other ladies of the family. I never did like spending much time with women, so I uttered some casual remarks to her and did my best to stay away. By the late afternoon all my family members had retired to their rooms and most of the doors which opened onto the courtyard were now bolted from within. I went up the stairs and lifted the bamboo screen from Aunt's door. She lay on the bed fast asleep. I looked at her for the longest time. I had a hunch that she was merely pretending to be asleep. She lay with her head tilted backwards on the pillow and her hands were clenched tightly into fists. She had removed her earrings and placed them next to her pillow. The scenes which had taken place in this very room just the day before flashed through my mind, but I drew a complete blank when I tried to remember what had happened during the moments that followed. It seemed to me that I had just picked her up in my arms and placed her on the bed. I stepped in the room and turned to close the door but noticed one of those superfluous women sitting with her back against the balcony, winding some woollen yarn into a ball. She gave me an enthusiastic greeting and the utterly useless bit of information that Aunt was sleeping. I pretended to be looking for a book and then, complaining about not being able to find it, I left the room. But while I was searching, I looked over at Aunt several times. She really did seem to be fast asleep after all.

Late in the afternoon, I saw the superfluous woman come downstairs and once again I went up and peered into Aunt's room. She stood in front of a mirror combing her hair with her back towards me, while another superfluous woman recited a tale of woe about the first time she was beaten by her husband. I'd heard this story many times before. In fact, it had been a source of entertainment in our house for quite some time. Aunt laughed and then noticing me in the mirror, she asked me to sit down. But I questioned her about the imaginary book which I had been searching for and came down once again.

I was away from the house through most of the evening. I was sent to take care of some family matter, but I botched the whole business and returned home late at night. The doors of all the rooms were closed from within, including the one that lead up the stairs. I went into my room and closed the door. For a while I tried to summon the image of Aunt but I failed. I did manage though to evoke her scent very briefly. As I slipped into sleep, I felt sure I would see her in my dreams. But the first phase of my sleep remained blank. Then towards midnight I dreamt that the superfluous women were dressed up as brides and were making obscene gestures at each other. Soon after that I woke up and only managed to fall back to sleep towards dawn. At daybreak I woke up again from a dreamless sleep. My head felt foggy and confused. I decided to go and take a shower. In the bathroom, I got the feeling that Aunt had just been there, and I shook my head again and again to clear my senses. When I emerged from the bathroom I saw Aunt sitting in the sun drying her hair. One of my elders went up to her and began a lengthy discourse on the various ancient branches of our family. On the veranda, the same two superfluous women I had seen yesterday were quarreling over something, but the presence of the old gentleman forced them to keep their voices low. Three other superfluous women soon joined the fray and contributed their half-witted views, to reconcile the two, or adding fuel to the fire perhaps. Aunt listened to the elderly relative very attentively and covered her head as a sign of respect. I left her talking to this gentleman and went upstairs. But I came to a dead stop outside Aunt's room. Another superfluous woman was standing outside the bamboo screen. She asked me if Aunt had taken her bath. I told the old hag that I wasn't responsible for bathing Aunt and came downstairs again. Before all this, I had no idea we had so many superfluous women crawling about our house. Their only practical use seemed to be to help out with all domestic chores, whether exacting or easy. Downstairs, the elderly gentleman still paced in front of Aunt. He had dealt with the past history of the family and was starting on the present.

Late in the afternoon, I was sent out once again. But the situation that I'd been trying to deal with since yesterday deteriorated even more and I returned without accomplishing anything. That night I woke up many times. It occurred to me that the customary visit of Aunt as our houseguest was almost at an end and the hour of her return was drawing close. In the morning, I felt as though my head were full of fog once again and in spite of a cold shower I couldn't get rid of this heavy-headedness. I felt sure that if I found Aunt alone somewhere, I would surely kill her. I didn't much care how I'd do this either. I decided that I'd better stay away from her that day.

Much later, I saw her just as I emerged from my room. She sat talking with some other women of the family and motioned with her hand

for me to come over. The veranda was unusually quiet. The little girl
slept in her mother's lap. Clearly she was ill. I took her up in my lap
and questioned her mother about her condition. Then the old
gentleman, one of my elders, came into the veranda and the atmosphere became even more sombre. He made an effort to suppress his
loud voice and asked about the child. But the little girl woke up. She
looked as though she had almost recovered. The old gentleman began
to tease her about her bridegroom. From the way the child responded,
it became clear to us that she had not realized she was in my lap. The
old gentleman then queried her regarding my whereabouts. Her
response made everyone laugh. Finally, I tickled her lightly. She realized who I was and she began to giggle in embarrassment. The elderly relative picked her up and took her away. She was also quite fond
of him and had woken up several times during the night calling for
him.

As soon as the old gentleman left, the atmosphere of the room
changed and peals of laughter rang out again and again. While they
were all talking, Aunt and I began to argue about what the date was
that day. As we debated back and forth, the others looked on with
keen interest. Aunt simply couldn't be convinced. From where we sat,
I could see the corner of a calendar that hung in a room next to the
veranda. Long ago a relative had drawn it up for us. With it you could
tell the date of any day in any year. But this took a long time and you
had to do several lengthy calculations. Eager to prove our cases, we
both got up to examine this calendar. Both of us entered the room
together. But as soon as we were behind the door we hugged each
other convulsively and almost sank to the floor. Then just as abruptly
we got up and came out. The little girl's mother asked us if we had
decided who was right, but just then there was some laughter, and
then some more. Aunt was looking pale. Anyone coming in upon us
just then would undoubtedly have assumed that we had just emerged
from the room after spending quite a long time together.

That day I successfully finished the task I had mishandled twice
before, and returned home even later than the previous night.
Everybody was in bed, so I also went in and lay down. From the moment that Aunt had risen from the bed and come towards me, to the
time we had entered the room with the millennium calendar, I had not
given much thought to how she might be feeling. I had not even con-

sidered that she might be totally unaffected by it all. All the same, I thought about killing her. All night long, I was assaulted in turn by remorse, her physical charms, and the longing to meet her alone again.

In the morning, when I came out of my room after a sleepless night, I was in the throes of remorse. So when a superfluous woman, the first one to rise, told me that Aunt's brother had arrived late at night with some bad news and that they had both gone away together, the only thought that came to my fogged brain was that I wished I'd been able to apologize to her.

All the elders in my family couldn't believe it when I told them that I had grown tired of my sheltered life and that I wanted to be on my own. And when they expressed reluctance, I was never quite able to assuage their doubts and concerns. Nevertheless, I did succeed in making them give in to my demands, mainly because they cared for me a great deal. Upon seeing all the elaborate arrangements that they made for my journey, I realized how comfortable and secure I had been in that house and felt rather fed up with myself. A few days before my departure they gave me a small stone amulet inscribed with sacred names to wear around my neck. It was an heirloom which had been in our family for many generations. This increased my annoyance. Quietly I took the amulet off and put it back in the chest full of old clothes where it had always been kept.

My elders said goodbye to me in a subdued manner, and as I walked away from my home the voices which I kept hearing the longest were the voices of all the superfluous women. They were praying for my safe return.

3.

I faced great hardships as I struggled to make myself independent. And finally, it was the good name of the family elders which helped me along. Thus, without moving a finger, indeed without even being aware of it, they helped me to stand on my own two feet. The work that I had undertaken involved inspecting houses. Initially, I had the feeling that I would fail in this profession because back then, apart from my own house, all other houses looked to me like piles of inorganic nature or vegetation only half alive. Sometimes I felt a vague hostility towards them, sometimes they looked like cheerless toys to me, and sometimes I stared at them for a long time as though they were just like foolish children, trying to hide something from me. Perhaps, this is why, though I cannot seem to recall exactly when, houses began to assume a life of their own right before my eyes.

In the beginning, I had no interest in the humanity that existed in these houses, though by merely looking at one I could make an estimate of how old it was, how and when certain improvements had been made over the years as well as the speed with which Time passed inside these structures. I was sure that the speed of Time within these houses was not the same as it was on the outside. I also believed that the speed of Time could vary from one part of a house to the next. Therefore, when I calculated the rate of a home's deterioration and the years still left in the structure, the estimate usually bore no relationship with the outward appearance of the place. Still, none of my calculations ever proved to be right or wrong, because even the smallest estimate of the years left in the life of a house was always larger than the years remaining in mine.

One day, as I was standing in front of a house, something about its closed front door made me think that it had covered its face either out of fear or to shield itself from something or, perhaps, out of a sense of shame. I was unable to assess this house. Therefore, when I went in I examined every nook and cranny, every ceiling, wall and floor very carefully. I wasted the entire day there without coming to any conclusion and at length came home only to spend most of the night thinking about this place. I reconsidered my assessment strategy and tried to remember all the details. At some point, it finally occurred to me that there was one part of this house which aroused fear and there was another part where one felt that some unknown desire was about to be fulfilled.

The next day I found myself standing in front of another house. The front door was closed, but it seemed to me that the house was staring at me with fearless, wide-open eyes. A short while later I was wandering inside it. When I entered a certain part of this house, I became very apprehensive. Now I awaited the second sensation, and sure enough, in another part of the house, I got the feeling that some significant but unexpressed wish of mine was about to come true.

I was surprised at myself for having overlooked this fact until now.

I returned to the houses I had seen many times and located these domains of fear and desire. No house, whether old or new, or one among many of the same basic design, was without these domains. Looking for these domains of fear and desire became a vocation with me and, ultimately, this vocation proved harmful to my business. Because I was becoming convinced, without even needing the least bit of proof, that it was impossible to assess the life span of these homes when they contained these domains of fear and desire. After suffering tremendous losses, I felt as though I had turned into an idiot or was losing my mind altogether and I decided to give up this vocation. But inspecting houses was my work and even if I did not look for these domains of fear and desire consciously, I would instinctively come to know where they were. All the same, I did make an effort to cut down my interest in them.

Then one day I discovered a house where fear and desire existed in the same domain.

I stood there for a while, trying to decide whether I was experiencing fear or desire but I could not separate the two feelings. In this house fear was desire and desire, fear. I stood there for the longest time. The lady who owned the house wondered if I was having some kind of fit. She was a young woman and at the time there was no one else in the house except the two of us. She came close to me to examine me carefully and I realized that this domain of fear and desire was affecting her as well. She grabbed both my hands and then with a strange, cautious boldness she advised me to rest for a short while in the front room. I told her that I was quite well and after a few minutes of conversation with her about business matters, I left the house. Perhaps, it was after this day that I started taking interest in the humanity that lived in these houses.

Eventually I could not imagine one without the other. In fact, at times I felt as though both were one and the same, because both intrigued me equally.

This interest increased my involvement with houses. Now I could look at a house in the most cursory manner and yet discover passageways that were secret or wide-open, in use or abandoned. I could tell whether voices rising from one part of the house could reach other parts of the house. I'd examine each room very carefully to ascertain which parts of the room were visible from the crack between the door panels, or from the windows, or the skylights, and which parts could not be seen. In every room, I found a part which was not visible from the crack between the door panels nor from any window, nor from any skylight. In order to isolate this part, I would stand in the middle of the room and paint the whole place black in my imagination. Then, using only my eyes, I would spread white paint on all those parts which could be seen from the cracks or windows. In this manner, the parts which still looked black were found to be the truly invisible parts of the room. Apart from certain rooms which were meant for children, I never did find a room in which the invisible part could not provide a hiding place for at least one man and one woman. Around this time, I began to concentrate on the shapes of these invisible parts. These shapes made up the outlines of different images and at times they had a truly amazing resemblance to certain objects. But I never did find a complete picture of anything. Everything appeared to be incomplete or broken, even though I examined countless such "invisible" parts. Some of these images had familiar shapes–of a lion, for instance, or a crab, or a pair of scales, and so on–but they all seemed like fragments. Other images resembled unknown objects and they looked incomplete in spite of the fact that they were unfamiliar. They left a strange effect on the mind, which it was impossible to articulate.

One day I was in the outer room of a new house, looking at the image of the invisible part of the room. The image had an unfamiliar shape. As I examined this shape it occurred to me that long, long ago I had seen a decrepit old house in which the domain of desire had exactly the same shape.

Until now I had only ascertained the boundaries of the domains of fear and desire in these houses. I had not thought about the shapes which could be formed from these outlines. But now I began to recall many–or, perhaps, all–shapes, and it occurred to me once again that either I was turning into an idiot or I was losing my mind altogether. Anyway, I became convinced that no one else could look at houses the way I did. I was also quite overwhelmed by the thought that no one else had the kind of rights that I had over the humanity that lived in these houses.

4.

I didn't stay in any one place. I wandered through many cities and moved in and out of many homes. To me, at least, it began to look as though the cities were crowded with houses and the houses were filled with women. And every woman seemed to be within easy reach. Many women made advances towards me and I made advances towards many. In this I also committed many blunders. For instance, some women whom I thought to be empty of, or unfamiliar with, or even full of hate for desires, turned out to be saturated with them and very willing to do the utmost in order to fulfill them. In fact, at times they made advances so boldly that they frightened me. Other women, who seemed to me to be oozing with desire and just waiting for the slightest sign from me, turned out to be so naive that when I made a pass at them they were unable to understand my intentions altogether. Some were overcome by depression, others were terrified. In fact, one got so worked up that she abandoned her calm and tranquil domestic life and actually left her home. She had a habit of arranging and rearranging her lustrous black tresses. I thought she wanted to draw my attention to her hair. She went away. That was totally unexpected. So I set out looking for her. I just wanted to tell her that her black hair had misled me, but she kept running away from me. Perhaps she thought that I was pursuing her like some sex-crazed animal. I never did find her and I suspect that the fear I induced in her may have been the cause of her death. But I often console myself with the thought that she might have accidentally fallen into the river and resurfaced somewhere and been rescued.

5.

After this, I gave up making passes at women. Instead, I took to waiting, wanting them to come after me. At times, these waiting periods became rather protracted. During one such lengthy interval, I went to a new city where no one knew me. One morning, as I was wandering around the main bazaar of this city, a woman standing in front of some shops smiled at me and made a sign with her hand. She wanted me to come near. At first, I thought she might be a "professional" and I kept on walking. But then she called out my name. I stopped and turned towards her and she hurried up to me.

"Don't you know who I am?" she said with a smile.

I finally did recognize her. Many years before she and I had been very close. She hadn't changed much except for the fact that she looked a little older. I was rather surprised that I had not been able to recognize her. But I was also pleased to run into someone in a strange town who actually knew me.

"What are you doing here?" I asked her.

"I live here," she said.

In a few minutes we were chatting away with the greatest informality. Again and again, I got the feeling that she had become a prostitute. I had no experience with such professionals. I couldn't even tell them apart from ordinary women. Then why did I suspect she was a professional? As I stood there staring at her, I became more and more suspicious. She noticed that I was examining her and a smug sort of look came over her face, revealing the source of my suspicions. For quite some time, she had been making a play for me, with words, eyes and even body language. In the past, I used to be the one who made advances. Several years earlier, during the period when I'd known her, she was already a woman of some maturity. And now she stood there acting all coquettish and coy like a teenage girl. This saddened me. I examined her closely once again. Even now she was quite attractive. But she had also changed a great deal. As I stood there talking to this woman, I felt as though Time were speeding up, there, in that bazaar.

"Where do you live?" I asked her.

She pointed towards a neighbourhood behind the shops.

"Come, I'll show you my house," she said. "If you have the time."

I had time. In the past, our relationship had begun pretty much in the same manner. She had showed me her house where she lived by herself in those days. Now we started walking side by side through the busy street. At a shop she stopped and bought a big padlock. She placed the lock and one key that went with it in her bag, and dangled the other key casually between her thumb and forefinger as she discussed the merits of a certain type of lock with the locksmith. Then, in a rather absent-minded way she handed me the key she had in her hand and we walked on.

She wants everything the way it once used to be, I thought to myself, and once again it seemed to me that Time was speeding up in that bazaar.

"How much farther?" I asked her.

"We're almost there," she said, and turned into a broad side street. Presently we found ourselves standing in front of an ancient wooden door that had just been given a fresh coat of paint. She removed the padlock that hung on this door, put it in her bag and went inside. I stayed where I was. Then a smaller side door adjacent to the main door opened and she stepped out. She now had the new lock in her hand.

"You haven't forgotten, have you?" she asked me and flashed a bold smile at me.

"I remember," I said.

I took the lock from her and she went back into the house through the small side door. I bolted the main door and locked it with my key and went into the house through the small side door, bolting it behind me. Now I found myself in a large room which contained many niches and alcoves but nothing in the way of furniture. I came out of the room and stepped into a spacious courtyard which had been enclosed by a wall. I noticed that a tall window made of weathered wood had been built into this wall. I started walking towards it when I heard a voice to my right:

"No, not there. Over here."

I turned and saw that adjacent to one corner of the wall and behind several small trees there was a veranda. The woman stood there under an arch. I went and sat down on a divan which had been placed there. Behind me there was a door. She opened the door and we went into a room. The room contained a bed and other domestic odds and ends which had been arranged neatly. She fell on the bed heavily as though she were very tired and I took a chair.

"So do you live here alone?" I asked her.

"Alone . . . well, you could think of it as living alone. Actually, I live here with an old acquaintance–an elderly woman."

"Where is she now?"

"I really don't know. A few days ago she burst into tears abruptly and cried quietly all night long. In the morning she said, with the greatest reluctance, that she missed a certain home. Then, all of a sudden, she longed to be in the house where she'd spent her childhood. Soon afterwards she packed up all her things and went away. I'll introduce you to her when she returns."

"Why should I want to meet a melancholy old crone?"

"No, no. You don't understand. She can be very amusing. One minute she'll be telling you what a marvelous man her husband was. And the very next, she launches into a story about how he used to beat her up. She can be murderously funny."

"I have no desire to be murdered by the anecdotes of some old hag," I said and left the room.

She came after me.

"What's the matter?" she asked.

"I'd like to see the house," I responded and went down into the courtyard.

"There isn't much to see," she said. "There is this veranda and the room, and that outer chamber. The rest of the structure has collapsed."

We were standing some distance away from the window which had been built into the courtyard wall. I examined the wall carefully. It was apparent that the house had been one large structure and the wall had been put up to divide it into two halves.

"Who lives on the other side?" I asked her.

"I don't know," she said. "Perhaps no one."

Now we were standing near the window. The window had been poorly constructed out of rough planks. A board had been nailed diagonally across the two panels in order to seal it permanently. I was drumming softly on this board when I felt the ground under my feet shift. I placed my hands around the woman's waist and pulled her close to me. She looked a little surprised. I was also amazed at myself. I took a few steps back and then let her go. So the domain of desire is right here, I said to myself and then going close to the window I turned towards the woman again. She looked up at me and smiled.

"You've become rather aggressive," she said.

Once more the ground shifted under my feet and I shuddered.

And the domain of fear also, I thought with a causeless melancholy.

The woman stood in front of me, smiling. Somehow, she had succeeded in simulating a look of arousal. I lingered near the window for quite a while. There was a strip of ground barely two feet wide adjoining the window. The rest of the domain lay on the other side of that window.

"Who lives on the other side?" I asked.

"I told you, Mr. Aggressive, no one."

"Come, let's go," I said, moving close to her. We proceeded towards the veranda. Now she had begun really to feel aroused and she put her arms around my shoulders.

"It's too closed-in and oppressive in there," she said in a whisper and we stopped where we were. I recollected our old encounters when passion used to sweep her off her feet like a wind storm, and now, here in this house, she was either supposing or leading me to believe that she was being overwhelmed by a storm of desire once again. In this house, or, at the very least, in this particular part of the house, Time moved at a higher rate of speed than it did in the bazaar. A kind of affection began to stir in me for this woman who happened to be the only person I knew in this strange city.

"You haven't changed at all," she said softly.

"Well, along with Time . . ." I began and then suddenly, glancing upwards at the window, I saw something shiny in the crack between the frame and the upper edge of the panels. At exactly this time, the woman started to slip away from my grasp. She had closed her eyes, the way she used to in the past. I took her in my arms and looked at the window once again. A pair of dark eyes were looking at us through the crack at the top. As I bent over the woman in my arms, I caught a fleeting glimpse of a red dress through the chinks between the boards. Slyly I looked up once again. The bright black eyes were locked on us. They were not looking into my eyes. They were focusing on our bodies. The idea that we were being watched by an unknown woman who was under the impression that I was unaware of her presence, produced something of an excitement in me and I averted my face.

At this point we were standing very near the window. Slowly, very slowly I lowered my head down on the ground and placed it on the sill. I had a vague sensation that there was a woman with me and that I was holding onto her with both my hands. I fixed my eyes on the lowest chink in the window. Just beyond the chink, I saw a bare foot. Had the toe of this bare foot not twitched again and again, I would have thought that it had been molded in pure white wax. Behind the foot, at a distance which I could not determine, I saw an ancient arch of dark wood and the lower portion of a column. The foot became suffused with the glow of the red dress, and I sensed the fragrance of a body in which another, more ancient odour was also implicated.

The toe rose from the ground and I saw that a long black string had been tied around it. I couldn't tell where the string led. If I'd wanted to, I could have reached over and grabbed this string, and, perhaps, I had even decided to do exactly that. But the woman with me gripped my hands. Then she opened her eyes briefly and closed them tight again. She may have suspected that I wasn't focusing on her. So I became attentive to her. After a while, she rearranged her hair and said, "You haven't changed at all."

I looked at the window once again. There was no one on the other side. It was then that a question bobbed up inside me. Had this woman wanted to stage a show for a girlfriend? I kept on staring at the window for the longest time and then suddenly I turned towards the woman again and examined her face intently.

But a vacant look of satiation had settled over her expressionless face.

"You haven't changed either," I said to her and went onto the veranda.

6.

I went to see this woman nearly every day.

"Until the elderly lady returns," she told me the very first day, "this house is yours."

And, frankly, I did begin to think of it as my own house and went there whenever I felt the urge. If the main door happened to be closed from the inside, I would knock and she would come and open it. I would sit and talk with her for a little while and then I'd go away. If the main door had a lock on it, I would produce my key, open the lock and enter the house. Then I'd come back out through the side door, put the lock on the main door, re-enter the house through the side door and bolt it behind me. She would meet me either on the veranda or in the room and I would end up returning late that day. But lately it seemed that almost every time I went to see her, I found the main door locked from the inside. I'd have to knock to be let in. She'd open the door and we would spend some time laughing and joking and then I would leave her.

One day I knocked on the door for a long time before realizing that it was locked from outside. It dawned on me that I had become used to knocking. I unlocked the door and went in. Then I came back out from the side door, put the lock on the main door, re-entered the house through the side door, bolted it behind me and walked towards the veranda. The woman was not on the veranda and the door to her room was closed from outside. A couple of times in the past, she'd come home some time after my arrival. I opened the door to her room and lay down on her bed. I must have stayed there for a long time, in a state of partial sleep. Eventually, I left the room and came out onto the veranda. The afternoon was fading into evening. I was somewhat surprised at myself for having waited so long for her. Anyway, I waited a little longer and then came out through the side door, unlocked the main door and went into the house again. I bolted the side door from the inside and was about to go out the main door when I stopped suddenly and turned back towards the veranda. I walked across the veranda into her room and changed the position of the bed.

She should know, I thought, and came back out onto the courtyard. I was going towards the main door when something made me stop in my tracks. I turned around slowly and looked at the window in the wall. A pair of dark eyes was looking straight into mine through a chink below the window frame. I turned back towards the main door.

I should have known, I thought with causeless melancholy and slowly turned and walked back towards the veranda. I went into the woman's room once again and pushed the bed back to its original position. Then I came out into the courtyard and crept along the wall that ran at an angle to the veranda. Staying close to the wall, I slowly inched forward in the direction of the window. When I got close to it, I bent down so far that my head almost touched the ground. Through the gap at the bottom I could see the waxen foot with the black string still attached to the big toe. At first it remained perfectly still, but then it looked as though it had started to pull back. I reached under the crack suddenly, grabbed the black string and gave it several quick turns around two of my fingers. The foot struggled to retreat, but I pulled it back with equal force. Now, between my eyes and this foot, there was my intervening hand with the black string wrapped around the fingers. The string, apparently of silk, was very strong and it became obvious that my fingers would be sliced off any minute. I gave it several more turns around my fingers and then suddenly my hand came into contact with the toe.

The pull of the string was making it impossible for me to think clearly. When I had moved from the veranda towards the window, I had made up my mind to make a play for her but now I couldn't figure out what to do and my fingers were just about ready to drop off. The evening gloom fell over my eyes like a heavy blanket of darkness. I felt a cutting pain, but, along with the pain, it became possible for me to think. The very first thing that occurred to me was that I was not the only one in pain. In contrast to my tough and masculine hand, the delicate feminine foot was infinitely soft and the thread that was cutting into my fingers was also tied to that foot. I pressed the toe gently and caressed the foot with two fingers that were free. It felt even softer than I had imagined it to be, but it was also cold as ice. Even so, I could feel the warm current of blood surging under the delicate skin.

By now the blackness of night had spread everywhere and I could barely see the silhouettes of the small trees. I am inflicting pain on her, I thought. Suddenly it occurred to me that up till now I had only pulled the string towards me once. I loosened the string around my fingers by a few turns and groped about the window with the other hand. I grasped the board which had been nailed obliquely across the window and tried to get up. But the board came loose and, precisely at that moment, the string got disentangled from my fingers. I placed both hands on the window to keep my balance, but the window fell open since there was nothing to keep it closed now. Suddenly, I found myself on the other side of the window. In the darkness, I could barely see the dim outline of the dark wooden arch and a shadow moving slowly towards it.

I followed the shadow into a region of dense gloom beneath the arch and soon lost sight of myself.

This was my first experience with total darkness. I passed through the arch and went forward for a short distance. But then I found myself stopping. I tried to move north, east, south, west–in all four directions–but the darkness made it impossible for me to advance. I lost all sense of my whereabouts. Nor could I determine the position of the arch anymore. All I knew was that I was with an unknown woman in an unknown house and that–I was sure of this–we were alone. My long association with women and houses had given me the keen instincts of an animal. And now as I stood in the darkness, I peered about keenly like an animal. I took a deep breath. I was certain that the characteristic perfume emitted by ancient houses, which I'd begun to smell outside the door, would soon assail my nostrils. But this did not happen. And even though I knew it to be futile, I squinted into the darkness with such intensity that my features must have surely looked frightening. In spite of this, I could not cut through the darkness. And, as far as the sounds of voices were concerned, I had ceased to be conscious of them the moment I gave the very first turn to the black string around my finger. Still, I made an unsuccessful effort to listen. It felt as though I had been standing there, straining my senses for a very long time. Then it seemed as though I had just passed under the arch. Soon afterwards I felt two soft hands brush up against mine. I grasped them firmly and pulled them towards myself.

After a long interval, I relaxed my grip, and my hands, exploring the elbows, arms, and shoulders, began to move towards the face. I tried to estimate individual features. But apart from a suspicion of long, thick eyelashes, I could not get an idea of anything else. My hands wandered across her body, went along the legs and down to the feet until my head touched the ground. I tugged at the string gently and then stood up. Now, once again I felt soft hands clutching my own. Her palms pressed against my palms. And then in the darkness, my hands became aware of colour for the first time. Two white palms, upon which a pattern had been traced with red henna, moved from my palms to my wrists, then to the elbows, and from there to my shoulders and then further up until they cupped my face. Her fingers, which had red rings around them, passed over my cheeks and came to a stop at my neck. She tapped my neck three times and then her palms came to rest over my shoulders and stayed there for the longest time. Then groping slowly across my clothes, they reached down to my feet and then, after vanishing from that darkened scene for a few seconds, came to rest on my shoulders again. I remembered that ancient scent which had wafted towards me once and was mingled with the odour of femininity. This odour belonged among those smells that are as old as the earth and were around long before flowers came into existence. It was an odour which brought to mind half-forgotten memories. However, at this moment it did not remind me of anything. In fact, I was fast forgetting what little I did remember.

The pressure of hands on my shoulders increased and then relaxed. And now, all at once I became aware of the fulsome, tactile presence of a female body. It occurred to me that I was with a woman who had seen me with another woman–at least once–in broad daylight. I also realized that it was useless to try and see in the dark. I closed my eyes. I knew that closing them would not make any difference. And, honestly, there was no difference, not for a while at least. But just when I'd forgotten the physical limitations of my eyes, I saw that I was slowly sinking into a lake of clear water. At the bottom of this lake I could see the ruins of ancient temples. I opened my eyes and was relieved to see only darkness all around. I recalled that there was a woman with me in this gloom. My breath felt the heat that was rising from her body. She is being swept along by a storm, I thought. Once more my eyes began to close and I could not keep them open no matter how hard I tried. Once again I saw the same clear water lake. The ruins of ancient temples drifted up towards me until they bumped against my feet. But I couldn't feel them. Then, even as I was watching, the clear water of the lake became very dark and the ruins disappeared.

I don't know how long it was before I woke up. It was still pitch dark all around me. But on one side I saw the outline of the arch and beyond it the beginnings of dawn. I turned to the body lying motionless in the dark and let my hands wander all over, touching each and every part. I placed my palms on hers, waiting, for a long while, for them to become moist with warmth. But they remained cold and dry. However, my hands did feel once again the bright red pattern on one of the palms. The shape of this pattern represented something unfamiliar. I stared hard at this shape and it became clear to me that the same shape resembled the domain of fear in a certain house, the same shape resembled the domain of desire in a certain house, and the same shape resembled the invisible part of a certain room. I tried to remember all the places where I had seen this shape and then it occurred to me that even though the shape was unfamiliar, it was, nevertheless, quite complete. For this reason, I had to struggle to convince myself that I had never seen this shape anywhere before. I made a futile attempt to pick up this shape from the palm of her hand. Then I touched it with my forehead and walked through the wooden arch and went outside. The window resembled a dark stain. I went through it and emerged on the other side.

When I crossed the courtyard and made my way towards the main door, the morning birds were chirping in the small trees directly across from the veranda and some old woman there was coughing away.

7.

I did not suddenly stop speaking. First of all, it never even dawned on me that I had given up speech. This because I never have been very talkative in the first place. The fact is, I just started devoting more time to thinking. After I came away from that house, I slept for two days straight. I caught myself thinking even in my dreams and I continued to think after I woke up. The first thing that occurred to me was that I had gotten through that night with only the sense of touch to guide me. I had experienced everything by touch alone; rather, all that I had experienced was merely transformed reflection of my sense of touch. But even so, I missed nothing and except for the first few minutes I imagined that all five senses of mine were being fully satisfied.

I never did feel any curiosity about that woman. This reaction rather surprised me and I tried to force myself to think about her. But my mind rejected every image of her that I conjured up. I struggled with myself for many days but I was eventually forced to accept defeat. In the entire fierce encounter with my mind, I did come to one conclusion: I would not be able to recognize her even if I saw her from very close. But she would recognize me instantly, whenever and wherever she saw me. This thought did not disturb me that much, but then neither did it make me feel very easy. I accepted it like some worn out and exhausted truth and gave up thinking about it. At about this time, I realized that I had, more or less, also given up talking.

I have not sworn an oath of silence. It's just that I do not need to speak. This has been made possible for me by the kind people who live in this house. They spotted me somewhere, recognized me, and told me that for many generations our families had been very close. They brought me to this spacious house and, graciously, urged me to pick out whatever place I liked for my living quarters. I looked over the whole house and chose for myself–who knows, this might have pleased them–a section which had been unoccupied for a long time.

My bed is positioned exactly on top of the domain of fear. I have not been able to discover the domain of desire in this house. But that cannot be. So I have now become convinced that fear and desire converge here in exactly the same spot and that I have dominion over it.

Once I was walking about my room in the middle of the night, when I happened to see this spot. It had assumed a black shape. This shape had an unfamiliar but complete silhouette. I kept on staring at this image for a long time. Then I examined the entire room carefully, peeking into each and every crevice, every window, every skylight. I stained the room white with my eyes, but the black shape remained untouched by this whiteness.

The shape of the invisible part–I thought . . . At exactly this moment, I began to hear the chirping of the morning birds outside. I felt very strongly that if I tried even a little, I would remember where I had seen this shape before. But I made something of a pact with myself never to make this effort. From that moment on, I gave up talking.

Then, the same day that I was introduced to my nurse, I moved a part of my bed a little distance away from the domain of fear and desire. She sits on this part of my bed and I just keep looking at her. I believe that in this way I'm protecting her and also protecting myself.

Translated by Javaid Qazi and Muhammad Umar Memon

HASAN MANZAR

The Beggar Boy

It was that time of afternoon when beggars came to the door asking for a little flour.

The usual call of the beggar echoed in the alley. The sun was oppressively hot, the air moist and heavy, and the acid of his sweat had begun to sting the beggar boy's nape and underarms. The boy, about twelve or thirteen years old, lifted the heavy sack curtain, peeked inside the door . . . and was startled.

The girl who was kneading dough in front of him didn't move away. It pleased him to look at her, light pink and sitting on the low wooden stool. The boy was dark-skinned; his knees had nearly turned white from being down on the ground so much; and a lock of hair–a *chirki*–longer than the rest of his hair, sprouted awkwardly from the oval of his head like a sudden mushroom rising from an unsuspecting patch of grass.

The beggar boy had been calling at this door regularly for the past few days. At first, they would scold him and chase him away; later, they would throw him a paisa or two; but today–today nobody had so much as looked at him even though he had been standing at the door for quite a while.

Once again he repeated his begging call . . . to the walls.

"Who is it?" a woman asked from inside the house.

"It's the same beggar boy," the fair-coloured girl replied.

"Ask him if he is ready to embrace Islam."

"Hey, you, will you become a Muslim?"

The dark-skinned boy gawked at her briefly and moved on without caring to reply. The city was quite far. The prospect of dragging himself all the way to the city to collect his daily crumbs disheartened the boy. If only he had managed to collect some alms at this house, which fell midway between his village and the market in the city, he would have been spared the toils of a long, exhausting walk. But one does not fight over alms!

Coming on to the path, the boy thought, "What kind of people are they? What has begging got to do with religion?"

Apparently the thought of abandoning his religion was as painful to the boy as the sting of a scorpion.

While the beggar boy was trudging along his path to the city, the children of the family, their play over, came dashing back into the house one by one. They had just come back from watching the wondrous sight of elephants picking up piles of sugarcane and loading them on the empty cars of the freight train. The elephants belonged to the Raja, just as the platform belonged to him. The name of the Raja was also inscribed on two stone slabs on either end of the red-gravel platform. This station was that Raja's *Pur,* as in Hastinapur–another city.

But Hastinapur has nothing to do with our story. For one thing, our story isn't all that old; for another, in the days of Hastinapur's eminence, people didn't go about persuading others to change their religion.

The pack of children attacked the food. Back at the station, the wondrous spectacle of the elephants was still in progress, and Ragghu had promised to give them a ride as soon as Bare Babu, the station master, had left for home.

In a small shed not far from the house, the oldest boy of the family, who had arrived from school a week ago to spend his vacation at home, was busy playing a different game with a village girl–a game which we had better not mention in this story lest these sheets fall into the hands of impressionable children. At any rate, the girl was furious and was threatening the boy. He quickly stuffed a shiny, silver four-anna coin in the girl's hand, and the two quietly walked out of the shed, one behind the other.

The girl's skin was taut, smooth and shiny black. She had wrapped her *laihnga* tightly around her legs. Out of the shed, she headed for the railroad tracks, climbed the steep front slope, crossed the tracks, and slowly climbed down the back slope. The boy–his sense of smell still flooded with the girl's strong body odour mixed with the smell of sweat rising from her clothes–was lost in the gentle, tingling music that had risen from her rustic jewelry. Then, after a while, he too started off for home. He was feeling pleasantly hungry.

After everyone had sat down to eat, in walked Bare Babu, the station master. He was a rather rotund man; whenever he laughed, his shirt flapped over his belly as if it harboured an entire colony of leaping frogs.

In a family whose members are all alive and well, whose daughters have not yet been married off and whose boys have returned for vacation–in that family who doesn't have a gargantuan appetite! In Bare Babu's house, just about everyone was a glutton.

As soon as Bare Babu had sat down to eat he called Sanjhli, the third daughter.

In one of the back rooms overlooking the railroad tracks, Sanjhli was standing at the window, her hands holding the bars, her eyes straying beyond the farther slope, her mind searching out a few elegant but meaningless sentences for a piece she was doing for some women's magazine. On the third or fourth of each month, this magazine would arrive by mail in that "Pur". Everyone, even the children, would rush to have a look at it. The manila wrapper which bore the station master's name and title would be carefully unwrapped and stored in the desk drawer. Sometimes, one of these wrappers would find its way–either tucked away inside a book or inadvertently wrapped over something or other–into the house of one of Bare Babu's acquaintances in the village. Mostly, however, it was used as a book cover.

Sanjhli had somewhat sharp features and a pale white complexion like *champa* flowers. She had been contributing regularly to this magazine. What exactly she wrote nobody knew. Her pieces, rather harmless and oversweet and addressed always to an imaginary girlfriend, read rather well. Presently as well, standing by the window, she was trying to fix up some phrases–as usual full of sweet nothings, but mysterious and charming all the same–in her mind. It seemed the stillness of the desolate railroad station had completely absorbed her youthful heart.

She saw the village girl climb up the front slope and disappear behind the tracks, heard her father call her, and left the room to join everybody in the courtyard.

The children hurried through their meal and dashed out, where at the station Ragghu–or rather, the elephants–were waiting for them.

The oldest boy was called Manjhla–the middle one. Nobody knew why. The most one could say was that perhaps he had an older brother who had died or disappeared. Anyway, he sat at some distance from his father, lest the colour of his face or the odour of the village girl still clinging to his clothes give him away. Next to him sat his soft-brained brother who was called the Idiot. The oldest, the middle and the third daughters sat near the father. The mistress of the house, who had been supervising the meal in the kitchen, was the last to join the lunch. Behind her came Choti–the little one–trailing her loose, baggy pajama pants. Always sloppy, she managed to keep herself dirty and remained unbathed even when she knew a bath was overdue.

Why the girls were called Bari (the oldest), Manjhli (the middle one), Sanjhli (the third one), and Choti (the little one) was something of a mystery, all the more so since the "little one" had been followed by two other girls. Perhaps because the birth of the last two had not been planned.

Everyone sat down to eat. The subject of the beggar boy with the chirki was broached. In the meantime, the beggar boy was dragging his swarthy, emaciated legs along the path to the city market, in the dwindling hope of receiving some grain, a fruit, or a few coins in charity.

The mistress of the house was again expecting. Her skin was the same fresh pink colour as the girls'; the boys, though, had acquired a dark tan as a result of too much running about in the sun.

The mistress of the house asked, "Did you give the brat something?"

"No."

"Why?"

"The moment I mentioned about him becoming a Muslim he just bolted."

Bare Babu felt he had bit on a red, hot chilly. Everyone tensed. In the past three days the family had scarcely discussed anything except the beggar's possible conversion. Will he . . . or won't he? The question was so crucial it had preoccupied everyone, big or small, even the Idiot, although it was Choti's considered opinion that the Idiot's feelings ought not to count: he was always too distracted to perform his ritual prayers properly–worse still, he even performed them in the same clothes he had on when he had cuddled the puppy dog.

Although everyone offered the ritual prayers, most did but half-heartedly. The younger boys went to the *'idgah* with Bare Babu only twice a year on the occasions of Eid and Baqar Eid; the older ones had literally to be dragged to the mosque for the congregational prayer every Friday. It would seem each one had the uncanny ability to know what was brewing inside the mind of another member of the family. For instance, Manjhla knew very well what kind of man Bare Babu–his father–had been.

Years ago he had once visited Allahabad with Bare Babu. Father and son stayed in the Railway Rest House. In the morning the father went out to take care of some business, and the boy spent the whole morning picking fallen *neem* berries. The father returned past the noon hour and took the boy out to show him around town. The city was quite big. Throughout, Manjhla could not fail to notice a strange change in his father's attitude–the kind of change which the sons of bad-tempered fathers notice only once or twice in their lives when their fathers unexpectedly become very kind and the sons diffidently try to laugh with them. Anyway, Bare Babu and Manjhla tramped around the city for quite a while.

Bare Babu bought quite a few things: gramophone discs, a thermos, some clothes, magazines for Sanjhli and toys for the other children.

Those toys–they brought back a strange memory. The festival of Divali was only a few days away, and the only kinds of toys you could buy were made of either sweetmeats or clay: men with elephant trunks, six-handed women, weird-looking men mounted on equally bizarre-looking animals with bodies of dogs and heads of tigers, blue-bodied men, monkeys holding maces, and oxen made of coarse brown sugar.

At some point in the shopping Bare Babu suddenly told the boy to stay put and himself took off in another direction. The boy was absorbed in the toys. With one eye glued to a row of toy peacocks, he looked with the other at his father who had meanwhile crossed the street and was now climbing up the stairs of the corner house.

Soon bored with looking at the toys, the boy yawned a few times and then crossed the street and came to the eaves of that house. In one of the shops at the street level of the house, a *panwari* was deftly applying different watery pastes to *pan* leaves with a pair of wooden sticks.

The boy asked him, "Who lives upstairs?"

The panwari looked at the boy briefly, then, lowering his eyes back to the pan, said, "Kali Jan."

To a child of any other Muslim family the name "Kali Jan" might have sounded unusual, but not to Manjhla. Long time ago, a Pathan girl called Marjan had worked in Bare Babu's household. The boy right away concluded that this "Kali Jan" must be a woman. And the realization made his heart beat hard.

With his small legs, which suddenly seemed too heavy for walking, the boy crossed the street at a run. A horse-drawn carriage went past him perilously close, and the whip of the coachman cracked inches above his head. His heart began to pound even more fitfully. He hurried back to the toy shop.

He could scarcely remember when Bare Babu returned and towed him along to the station. But he could remember all too well that his mother tolerated those toys for a day or two and then her patience ran out. She had them thrown out in the alley. Janki's kids gathered the trove and walked away with it. Somebody had asked the soft-brained brother, "Brand new toys–why throw them out?"

"My mother says they are Hindu gods," the Idiot replied.

Whenever the girls saw some Hindu worshipper bow reverently before a smooth, shiny stone lying at the foot of a *peepul* tree, they would start to ridicule the poor fellow by mumbling something that sounded like a Sanskrit prayer.

There was not much to do at home but quite a crowd available to do whatever needed to be done. A half dozen daughters, two or three servants, a few relatives who regularly hung around–this left the mother and Manjhli with plenty of time to do their needlework, and Sanjhli to pursue her writing unhindered.

Then suddenly one day the beggar boy appeared on the scene. The first day they scolded and shooed him away–all because he had a chirki on his head. Had he been Muslim or at least not had this damnable token of Hindu religion, certainly some charity would have been in order. That a Hindu child had the audacity to come begging at a Muslim house meant that he was woefully ignorant about the religion of its occupants. Or else he was a nitwit who scarcely knew the difference between Hindus and Muslims.

The second day he showed up, it was raining so hard that the alley had become a veritable pool. Dripping wet, he came, lifted the heavy sack curtain, and installed himself in the doorway. Right above the door hung a branch of the banyan tree on which perched a row of crows huddled against the rain. One of the girls asked the boy to come in, but he remained rooted to his place. The girl asked him a second time.

Just then the rumble of a freight train arose at the back of the house. Through the grill of a window, the boy watched the locomotive chug slowly along, its image distorted and trembling in the misty air. Two of the boys began to count the cars in the train.

After the train had passed–and it always took an eternity to pass– the boy begged for a paisa or two; he was even prepared to accept a pinch of flour.

A woman came out of the room, swinging her ballooned stomach sideways like a pregnant goat, and asked, "Who is it?"

"The beggar boy," replied the girl.

"Why did you let him come in?" the woman asked with some irritation.

The boy started and quickly withdrew to the doorway, where he remained waiting for charity.

A little later a boy came out of the room and handed him a small coin. "May Ram bless you!" the beggar boy exclaimed and caught on his way out the pregnant woman's angry "Away, get the hell out of here!"

The next day he was back again, standing in the same spot.

"What is your name?" asked the woman.

"Ramsarna."

"Ramsarna! Ramsarna!" the children aped, making fun of his name, and laughed.

The "little one" said, "Ramsarna! Why, only elephants have such a name."

"No, they don't," the other girl observed, rather emphatically.

The male elephants under Ragghu's care had such names as Jhabbu, Masta, Tumbul; the female elephants, names like Champa and Kishori. Even so, the children named the beggar, "Ramsarna the elephant." The "little one" would often ask, "Ramsarna the elephant, give us some sugarcane." And when he would be given flour, the same girl would say, "Now Ramsarna the elephant is going to bake himself some bread."

Ramsarna developed a liking for the children. He would come around noon time, stand at the doorway, and ask for a pinch of flour. *"Dhut! Dhut!"* the children would make the sound used to urge elephants to kneel. Ramsarna would bring his feeble posterior down, put his begging bowl behind him on the ground, and sit supporting himself on his palms, in the manner of elephants, or so it seemed to him. Often sitting in that posture, he would watch the train go by at the back of the house.

Hearing his begging call for a pinch of flour, the Idiot would throw his hand in the drum, grab literally a pinch of flour between his thumb and the index finger, and thrust it out to the beggar boy: "Everybody watch! Ramsarna the elephant will eat flour and give milk."

One day the beggar boy again came when it was pouring down hard. The mistress of the house herself asked him to come in the veranda. The children were jumping around inside the room on cots; the older girls were scattered everywhere in the house; and Bare Babu was away on his job at the railway station. The mistress had a knife in her hand. Her thumb was swathed with a bandage.

"Bahu Ji, you have cut your thumb?" Ramsarna asked.

"Yes."

"Ram! Ram!" the beggar boy exclaimed in a concerned voice.

A thought flitted across the mistress's mind. "Why didn't Ramsarna exclaim 'Oh, Allah!'? Or some other expression, such as, 'Oh, Ali!', as some people do?"

After a while she asked, "What village do you come from?"

"Bhojpur."

"Is it far?"

"Quite far."

"You have a mother?"

"No."

"Father?"

"No."

"Any relatives?"

"No, Bahu Ji, no one," Ramsarna said, with touching but feigned ruefulness. He had been wielding this weapon to his advantage for years now and had become quite adept at it. A ray of hope glimmered in his heart. If Bahu Ji could take pity on him, she would make his day.

When the mistress asked him about his kith and kin and his home, Ramsarna realized that beyond a few begging calls he had learnt to parrot, he knew absolutely nothing, or–perhaps–more than that, his life really didn't amount to much.

His mother had died some five or six years ago. Died–as it often happened with low-caste women–of incessant vomiting and diarrhoea after gorging herself on a rotten melon. But who was his father? Where had he come from? And where did he disappear to? Nobody in all of Bhojpur had an answer to these questions. Perhaps he was one of those people who quietly melt away in the crowd of this world without leaving a trace.

Stranger still was the chirki which sat on his head like a black bee. Ramsarna perhaps could not even tell how long he had had it and why exactly he wore it.

After the beggar boy had collected the alms–a bit of cornflour–and gone, the pregnant lady of the house sat for a long time thinking about him. She remembered the band of people who had set out for some villages in the east, to spread Islam among people. Missionaries–she knew–who proselytized. Yes, that's it. Why not convert Ramsarna?

That night the whole family openly talked about Ramsarna. Bare Babu spoke at length about Aurangzeb's religious policies, with which Manjhla found himself in agreement. The oldest, the middle, the third and the fourth daughters also talked with fervour and excitement. In that desolate, out-of-the-way station–through which most trains sped by so fast they shook the house to its roots–it seemed that finally a mail train had ground to a halt, causing the entire atmosphere to take on the gaiety and exuberance of a country fair.

Slowly the discussion veered to other religious matters. Who used to spread out the prayer rug on the surface of the river and offer ritual prayers? And who on a bedsheet hanging in midair? As is normal in such discussions, the thought of eventual death crept into everybody. The same wrenching fear gripped them which had gripped the family of Nusuh following the outbreak of the cholera epidemic in that novel by Nazeer Ahmad.

The mother offered her dawn prayer, and the younger girls, who had gone to bed trembling from fear of the torment meted out in the grave, right away sat down to recite from the Holy Qur'an. Dawn broke.

A couple of times during his work, Bare Babu gave a start. His older brother, the civil surgeon, had developed his own spiritual powers to the point where he could communicate with spirits. For the first time ever, Bare Babu felt the distance which the maddening pursuits of his life had created between them. What was he–Bare Babu? At most a man who unabashedly desired material things. But life's sole purpose was not just to eat, drink and be merry, was it?

The whole of that day Manjhla looked as though he had a lot on his mind. He remembered the time when he was about twelve or thirteen years old and had been caught fooling around with Sukhdaiya, a good eight or ten years his senior. His sister Manjhli had surprised them. She wanted to report the matter to her parents but didn't know quite how to. Finally, she scribbled a few cryptic sentences on a scrap of paper and gave it to her mother, who couldn't make out what the words meant. From that day on, God knows how many Sukhdaiyas had come into his life and, after gratifying his desire for a while, gone away. During this time, the boy did not feel as though he missed them, nor, chances are, did those women themselves feel the need to remember the joys of their brief encounters with their adolescent lover.

Anyway, Manjhla, like his sisters, remained quite distracted that day. And the day after.

About noon, Ramsarna, clad as usual in rags, reappeared. The children saw him all right but remained silent. One of the girls came out to give him a small coin and went back in. The mistress also came out of a room, hesitated for a few moments in the veranda, as though thinking deep and hard about something, then she too went back in. The house was gripped by an eerie silence. Even the back of the house seemed strangely still. The older girl breezed in, and then withdrew. The beggar boy hesitated at the doorway for a while and then went away.

He was thinking: "Strange people! Today they gave me handsome alms but no attention. Why didn't the children feel overjoyed to see me, as they usually did before?"

No sooner had he left than the otherwise dead house became vibrant and alive. The mistress asked, "Gone–already? I was just coming out to talk to him."

"No, mother, you weren't," the eldest girl snapped. "You went back in as soon as you saw him."

"But so did you," Choti, the ill-mannered girl, retorted.

When Bare Babu returned home for lunch, his very first question was, "Did Ramsarna show up?"

"Yes," somebody replied.

"So?"

"So–nothing." Everyone looked around silently, as if wishing to slip away somewhere.

"Well?" he said, a bit shocked.

"He isn't running away, is he? . . . maybe tomorrow."

But the next day, when they suggested he embrace Islam, Ramsarna took off like a bullet. True, he was poor; but that didn't mean he would readily give up his faith. So, that's it, then: their charity had a motive! They hoped to convert him!

Many times along the way Ramsarna's feet slowed down to the point where they were barely moving. A spiraling anger seemed to have drained them of all energy. Then he would think with horror of arriving late at the market, and his feet would automatically begin to move faster.

He stopped briefly on the way to wash his face and feet in the river. Then, crossing over to the other bank, he came to a peepul tree and prostrated himself in reverential worship before the stone that lay at its foot. For the first time ever, love for his religion had suddenly blossomed in his heart.

When he reached the market, the fair was winding down. People were leaving; those that still remained seemed irritated by the heat.

That night Ramsarna went to bed without a morsel to eat, just as he often used to before he started begging at Bare Babu's.

The next day he found himself standing before Bare Babu's doorway at his usual time. The children, as soon as they heard his begging call, shouted, "Ramsarna the elephant is back!" Choti urged him with *"Dhut! Dhut!"* The beggar boy blushed, hesitated a bit and then sat down, supporting himself on his emaciated legs.

"Keep quiet!" the mistress said to the noisy kids. "Let me talk. . . . Hey, Ramsarna, why did you run away yesterday?"

"Oh, nothing, Bahu Ji."

"Can't be. You left without receiving anything, didn't you?"

Ramsarna remained silent. Two of the children planted themselves on the cot in the yard and began staring at Ramsarna as though he were about to perform some trick.

"Did you get anything to eat yesterday?" the mistress asked.

"Don't you see his face, Mother, he's famished," the oldest girl observed.

"Who is it?" Manjhli shouted from inside.

"It's Ramsarna the elephant, Baji," the children replied in unison.

"No, children, no!" the mother chided. "We don't call human

beings elephants and horses! He's human like you are."

The children cowered.

Ramsarna was overcome with emotion and began to cry. Nobody in the entire village had ever stood up for him. The other children were forbidden to play with him. Everywhere he went, he was greeted with abuse and driven away. He had never seen people's dwellings from inside. He could not even imagine what their kitchens looked like. And here was this kind woman scolding her own children for his sake! Warm tears flowed down his cheeks to the corners of his mouth, where he licked them off with the tip of his tongue.

"Want to eat something?" the lady asked.

Ramsarna nodded.

One of the girls quickly brought him some bread and the beggar boy hurriedly began to eat it as if he would have died of hunger.

He was still busy eating when, suddenly, the woman urged him in a solicitous voice, "Listen, become a Muslim and I will give you nice clothes to wear. Begging is no good. It won't fill all your needs. No home, no place to go, not even a soul to care for you. Stay with us. You can play with the kids. . ."

"And I will even teach you to read and write," Manjhli butted in. "Once you have education, you will become a real *babu*, a real clerk."

Ramsarna thought: the girls were really nice to him; Bahu Ji treated him like a mother; all those days of starvation; the chilly nights of Magh; people treating him like an untouchable, or as if he had some incurable disease–not even a whiff of all that in this household! He sat silently listening to the lady's persuasive words.

"So, what do you think? Will you become a Muslim?" the lady repeated. "Two meals a day–the same food we eat, not some rotten bread thrown at beggars. . ."

This fresh assault of temptation's tidal wave washed away the last shreds of his hesitation as if it were a dirt embankment.

"Yes," Ramsarna consented in a dead voice.

One of the boys made a dash for the station. Within minutes Bare Babu arrived, huffing and puffing.

One of the girls began energetically to work the handle of the water pump. Ramsarna was now being scrubbed and bathed. Under the cleansing soap his body began to sparkle wherever water touched it. Surprisingly, he wasn't as dark as the dust had made him look.

Inside, the mistress was searching for her younger boys' old clothes. Soon a pile collected on the cot in the veranda.

Ramsarna was tremendously enjoying his bath and didn't at all feel like coming out from under the streaming water. Even his own mother had never bathed and scrubbed him so lovingly.

"Come on, that's enough," Bare Babu shouted, "or else he will catch cold."

One of the girls ran to fetch a towel. Ramsarna was at a loss: he didn't know what to do with this piece of thick, pelted cloth. Just then someone asked, "Ramsarna the elephant, aren't you going to dry yourself?" And the mistress ordered, "Hey, dry yourself."

Ramsarna just stood there, dumbly looking at the towel, when Bare Babu, too, urged him, "Your body! Come on, dry your body with it."

Ramsarna began to do as he was told. He looked like the monkey who, acting on the signals of its trainer, occasionally misses a cue and then stands dumbly, not knowing what to do.

The mistress was preoccupied with a thought of her own: the happy occasion called for a *milad*. Why not? And Bare Babu was absorbed in the merry thought that the news of his tremendous feat would even surprise his elder brother.

Although Manjhla had taken no active part in persuading the beggar boy to become a Muslim, his satisfaction was no less: lately he had been somehow avoiding his earlier rakish activities.

Nobody was unhappy in that house that day. Sadness of any kind was out of place in a family whose members were all alive and well, whose daughters had not yet been married off, whose boys had returned home to spend the vacation, and which had been graced with the good fortune of sound faith.

Ramsarna was given a pair of pajama pants and told to go in a secluded corner and change. While he was slipping into his new pants, Manjhla brought him a shirt, and later one of the younger girls, overwhelmed by the spirit of charity, gave him her old pair of black shoes. When he emerged from the corner, the mistress exclaimed, "Now you look like a prince!"

The beggar boy found himself standing in the veranda–dumb, lost, uncomprehending. He could not think of anything to say. He was overwhelmed, like everyone else, by so much excitement. But the reason behind the excitement–everyone seemed to have already forgotten it.

The mistress grabbed the boy's hand and brought him to a low, wooden stool. As he was being seated, somebody pulled him up again; he was seated only after Choti had brought a prayer rug and spread it on the stool first.

"Now, there–make a Muslim out of him!" the mistress said to Bare Babu.

"Hunh?" Bare Babu took a few steps forward, then backed off, not knowing exactly what to do.

"What are you waiting for?" the mistress demanded.

"You are doing the right thing. I'll do my part tomorrow." Bare Babu looked at his wife as though he had thrown a riddle at her to solve.

The mistress asked the boy, "You are becoming a Muslim out of your own free will–aren't you?"

Ramsarna remained silent.

"Come on, say that you are. Aren't you?" The mistress shook his shoulder.

"What, Bahu Ji?" Ramsarna asked.

"I'm asking you to say that you aren't accepting Islam under duress–right? Look, nobody is threatening you, nobody is strangling you either . . . you are converting happily, right?"

"Out of your own free will," Bare Babu chimed in.

Ramsarna indicated with a nod that it was so. But everyone asked again, "Say it!"

"Enough!" Bare Babu said, "you have asked him three times already. That'll do."

"From today your name is Khuda Bakhsh."

Ramsarna shook his head in affirmation. To having a new name he had no objection at all.

"Now we must have Bakhshu recite the *kalima*," one of the girls said, "Come on, Bakhshu, say *La ilaha. . .*"

"*La ilaha. . .*"

"*. . . il-lal-lah.*"

"*. . . il-lal-lah.*"

"No, that won't do," Bare Babu butted in. "First put a cap on his head."

"And the chirki?" the Idiot had a brainstorm. "How can he become a Muslim with his chirki intact?"

Yes, the chirki? How can he? The words were charged with magic. The soft-brained brother had hit upon the most important thing!

One of the girls dashed off, returning seconds later with a pair of scissors; and the oldest boy moved forward to clip off the chirki. Suddenly the beggar boy threw both his hands over his head and closed them tightly over that small tuft of extra-long hair, as though he was guarding with his life his sole asset. If he lost it, he would truly become a pauper.

"Hey, let go of it," Manjhla chided. "Let me get rid of it for you."

"No, no. I won't let you do it," the boy broke into tears.

"Er-r-r . . . what's the matter with him?" the mistress said in disbelief.

A real tug-of-war broke out over the beggar boy's head. Meanwhile the boy had started to sob violently.

"How are you going to become a Muslim if you won't get rid of the chirki? Damn it, you will remain a beggar for the rest of your life."

"I won't let you cut it," said the boy firmly.

"I'll see how you won't. I will. . ." Bare Babu fumed.

"I won't let you."

Hell broke loose over the boy's head. A lot of tugging and pulling went on for quite a while, then someone pushed him off the stool, and another shouted, "Get the hell out of here."

The beggar boy picked himself up and moved away with feet drained of all energy. He passed by the hand pump where his torn shirt lay crumpled. At the door he picked up his begging bowl. Just then someone shouted from inside, "Grab him!"

Ramsarna leaped out of the door into the alley.

Back in the house everyone was thrown into a wistful mood as though they had just returned from a funeral. Bare Babu went back to the station; the younger kids went out to put stones on the train tracks; the Idiot took out his collection of empty cigarette packets and began to count them; and Manjhli noticed that Manjhla was again climbing up the slope way down by the tracks.

Manjhli was suddenly overwhelmed by an urgent desire to write a letter addressed to her imaginary girlfriend, describing the loneliness, the silence that pervaded her surroundings, broken only by the occasional rumble of a bullock cart as it passed along the path, and returning, like a surface of water disturbed and then calmed.

Somewhere along a narrow path the beggar boy was immersed in a thought of his own: What had happened with him? If it was all a joke, why did he panic and take off? But if it was not a joke and meant really abandoning his religion, then it had been a narrow escape indeed, and he must thank his stars for that.

He didn't feel like returning to his village. His new clothes seemed to please him, and after the refreshing bath he was also feeling nicely hungry. He fished around for something to eat in the vegetation on either side of the narrow path. Finding nothing, he set out in the direction of the city.

The sun had all but set by the time Ramsarna made it to the city. He had scarcely called at two or three doors when it got quite dark. He settled on a jutting raised porch outside a shop and began to munch from the small leaf basket which a sweetmeat seller had given him. The contents were mostly sweetmeat crumbs, stuck with ant legs, and had somehow become mixed with a bit of salted yogurt.

The sky, turning a flaming red for a few moments, became completely dark. The worshippers who had come for the evening service in the temple across from where he was sitting returned home. The priest came out and sat down on the elevated, flat unroofed porch outside.

The air was stuffy. The priest looked like a dark statue. A bird flapped its wings and flew above Ramsarna's head. Feeling bored and lonely, the boy got up and walked over to the priest. Since afternoon he had been feeling rather restless, needing to unburden himself about what had happened.

"Who is it?" the priest asked in a stern voice.

"*Maharaj,* it is me, Ramsarna."

"So?"

"Nothing. I just came to pay my respects."

"Where do you live?"

"In Bhojpur."

"A beggar?"

"Yes."

"Have parents?"

"No."

"Sit down."

Ramsarna sat down.

"Your caste?"

Ramsarna remained silent. So did the priest.

After a while, twirling the chirki around his finger, Ramsarna said, "Maharaj, there is a house on my way. Muslims live in it. A man there wanted to cut off my chirki today."

"Who's that scoundrel?" the priest asked.

"He's called Bare Babu."

"So did you let him do it?"

"No, Maharaj."

"What else did they want?"

"They said, 'Become a Muslim. Stay with us. We will give you clothes, and you will have plenty of food to eat.' "

Ramsarna took a long time relating his tale of misfortune, which the priest every now and then punctuated with cries of "Scoundrels! Rascals!" When Ramsarna had finished, the priest gestured for him to come close and began examining his chirki. Then, holding the boy's hand, the priest praised him for a long time. In his opinion, Ramsarna had performed a meritorious deed which only members of the highest caste were capable of. "Tomorrow, I'll relate this story to everyone," he said. "I'll tell them how such-and-such a child valiantly defended his religion. I'm sure some noble soul or the other will take you in."

His belly full, Ramsarna fell fast asleep in the temple courtyard. Suddenly he felt someone's warm breath over his face. Fear gripped him. In his confusion, he tried to jump up, but felt as though his slight, emaciated body had been pinned down by a heavy stone. He tried to scream, but the priest pressed his hand down hard on Ramsarna's mouth. The two tangled. Ramsarna had no doubts about the priest's intentions. Like every orphaned, indigent boy who tramped the streets begging, he had come to know, despite his rather young age, life's many unpleasant secrets.

Finally, the boy succeeded in wrenching himself free of the priest, just as a snake shakes its head free of the grip of a mongoose, and dashed out of the temple. He kept running madly for quite some distance, though he didn't have to, for the priest thought it pointless to pursue him.

Roaming around for a while Ramsarna found himself in front of a cattle lock-up. This was the last brick building at the city's outermost edge. A river flowed by it and the bridge spanning it led towards the path to the village. Ramsarna, however, didn't find enough courage in himself to return to his village so late at night. Instead, he climbed the wall of the cattle lock-up and jumped down into the compound where he spotted a donkey. In the darkness the donkey looked as though it were sleeping. A little distance from the animal, Ramsarna laid his tired body down on a heap of hay and dozed off.

The next morning as he was walking back to the village, Ramsarna thought: why did those people want to make him a Muslim? What would they have gained by that? They didn't love him; and they certainly wouldn't have fed him forever.

Then the thought occurred to him: the priest was no well-wisher of his, either. Why, then, did he want him to remain a Hindu? What good would it have done him? Those other high-caste Hindus–they wouldn't have taken him in.

After thinking long and hard, Ramsarna concluded: let's just say there are people who do many things without a reason. Bare Babu and his family were like that. So was the priest. And so had been his own father earlier.

Translated by Muhammad Umar Memon

KHALIDA HUSAIN

Recognition

I once had a dream but soon forgot it. When Nusrat invited me to the fair, I remembered it–well, sort of. At the time, I was embroidering flowers on Munna's bush shirt and he–my husband–was sitting near-by in an armchair reading the newspaper.

"Listen, Kaneez and Bilquees are also coming along. You really should get out of the house sometime." Nusrat took a gibe at me once again for remaining glued to the house. Her remark distressed me, as it always did, and then an all-too-familiar dread began to rise inside me–something like a scorching fireball turning deep inside my guts.

"Yes, why don't you?" he urged, turning over the page.

"But Munna?"

"Take him along too. The other children can stay home." He put his eyeglasses down on the table and rubbed his eyes with his palms. Meanwhile, Tai Ji walked in with the hookah she had just freshened up.

"This will give mother a chance to get out of the house too." He looked at the clock and got up.

It was time for his tennis practice. I took out a pair of clean white shorts and a half-sleeve t-shirt and laid them on the bed, and then I started for the kitchen to fix tea. That very instant, Nusrat, wrapping herself in the *burqa,* said, "Well, then, see you tomorrow, at five-thir-ty. Kaneez and Bilquees will be with me." And then she climbed down the stairs.

Tai Ji stuck the spout of the hookah in her mouth and, spreading a quantity of rice on a large flat metal tray, started to look through it for stones. As I brewed the tea, I felt the same penetrating dread assault me again and again, and with it the urge to dash after Nusrat and tell her that I wasn't going to go. But he had changed and was ready to go out; he had already reached the staircase. I brought him his tea; he drank it standing up. He was about to go down when I noticed his loose shoelaces. Immediately I bent down and secured them tightly. He said goodbye in his usual manner and went downstairs with the tennis racket in one hand. His large shoulders, stout neck, and thick, bushy hair always looked the same to me. But today, watching him go down the stairs, I suddenly remembered my forgotten dream:

I'm hurrying along in the alley, which is completely deserted; there isn't a soul anywhere in sight. I'm mortally frightened of being alone. Suddenly I see him come along, up ahead, there, racket in hand, clad in his tennis whites, sticky with sweat. I take heart. But even as he is looking at me, he doesn't appear to see me. I cannot understand. I'm fazed. I lift my veil to let him see that it is I, but he doesn't; he just walks away, passing close beside me. I try to call after him but feel as though my throat is locked. So I run after him. The sound of my footsteps makes him turn around, but his face has completely changed. It's someone else. God knows who. I'm terrified. A doubt descends upon me: perhaps *my* face has changed too. I look for my house but find that all the houses in the alley seem curiously anonymous.

Remembering the dream I felt an emptiness inside my chest and stomach, and my ears began to buzz. I closed the staircase door and came over to Tai Ji. I sat down beside her and returned to work on Munna's bush shirt. I've known all along that he is someone else past this staircase, past this alley. People see him differently, perceive him differently. I cannot see him in that light at all. That's why even when he is with me, it is as if he is outside the alley, a place where I do not know him at all. He knows it too; what's more, he wants to keep it that way. That's why often his body is just that to me–a body. This frightens me. But he knows that already . . . and wants to keep it that way.

And so I worked away on the sewing machine, faster and faster. But now, all of a sudden, the dark emptiness inside my stomach began to stab at me–that same hot, fiery dread, burning through my insides. Ever since Munna, the dark emptiness inside my stomach often leaps up before me, without warning, without any effort on my part. It reminds me of the warm heaviness I felt before his birth, a time when I seemed to walk with a firmer gait, and had not yet had a dream quite like this one. But I bore Guttu, Naseem and Ruhi before Munna, didn't I? So why is it that I can't remember anything about their birth? Is it because Munna is the last one to be born, so that everything is fresh in my mind? But with the other three I could manage to sleep through the night, and if they bawled it was mostly Tai Ji who rushed up to quiet them. But if Munna, even so much as snores, I hear him crying, in my sleep. I wake up and look around. I see a Munna, there, fast asleep, and another Munna crying away somewhere. I start to wonder whether this other Munna might not be mine as well. Try as hard as I might, I cannot remember. If Munna isn't crying somewhere else, then where does this cry I hear come from? And if Munna is in fact lying beside me, fast asleep and snoring, then who is this other Munna that is crying? Wide awake, I try to put my mind to rest: this is me and this is Munna; he is lying beside me, fast asleep; there isn't another Munna in the whole house: not inside me, not outside me. And so I manage to go back to sleep.

I also remember that while I was still carrying Munna, I had never thought much of the alley, nor had the alley itself ever appeared to me in the way it did now. He would go in and out of the alley umpteen times during the course of a day, and although I knew he was a different man outside the alley, where people saw and perceived him differently than I ever would, I still didn't think much of the alley and the world beyond it. Perhaps because I was so heavy in those days that the courtyard, the rooms, indeed the whole house seemed to be filled with me, and I always felt thick with sleep. But as the days pass since Munna, I feel I'm becoming increasingly lighter, but not in actual appearance though, for I still have the same old rotund body. I can see as much in the mirror every day. No, not in appearance. Yet there is no getting around the fact that I am becoming lighter, how and in what parts of my body, I don't know. Sometimes I feel as though my feet are lifting off the ground. Which makes me laugh. For just the other day Ruhi remarked, "Mother, you're getting a little wider at the waist." This, and the casual suggestion he made not long ago: "When spring comes, we'll go out for walks in the morning. It keeps the body in shape."

"Mummy! Mummy!" Munna sneaked up behind me and draped his little arms around my neck so I couldn't turn the sewing machine handle.

"Where did you go?"

The moist warmth from his tiny hands began to work its way into the skin of my neck.

"Cheesy! cheesy!" He let go of my neck and darted over to Tai Ji to hug her.

"Come over here, Munna. Put this on and show me how you look." I tried the bush shirt on him. Watching him in front of me I marveled how only a few years ago he used to be inside me. Part of my own weight. I looked at him closely: his face did seem different–a little, perhaps. Immediately I looked away from him.

Late in the evening after he had returned and I had laid out dinner for him, I said, "I shouldn't have said yes to Nusrat. I don't feel like going."

He stopped breaking the bread midway and gave out a laugh–his usual indifferent laugh which always makes me feel that he has nothing to do with me. Which isn't wrong either, perhaps. He could be sitting right next to me and at the same time couldn't be farther away. I was expecting him to say something about my going to the fair with Nusrat, or not going there, but he just laughed himself into silence. So I spoke instead, "God knows what is it with me: the very thought of stepping out of the house terrifies me."

"What can one say to such craziness," he said, drying his hands on a towel.

He turned on the radio and picked up a book from the table. Naseem and Guttu were fighting in the courtyard over something. "What's the matter with them? Naseem!" he called in a heavy, resounding voice. Immediately silence swept across the courtyard, broken only by the steady gurgle rising from Tai Ji's hookah. He lit a cigarette and puffed along as he read his book. Frightened, I looked away from his face. Seen from up close, even *his* face seemed somewhat unfamiliar.

The next day Nusrat came with Bilquees and Kaneez, and I went down into the alley with Tai Ji and Munna. Without wanting to I looked back at my house and felt that the windows, doors, grey awning and red walls all looked unfamiliar to me. I grabbed Munna's hand securely, and we all walked until we came to the end of the alley.

The street outside the alley had just been sprinkled with water and its grey surface was divided into two neat zones of wet and dry running parallel down the street's length. Up ahead, the open drain descended into the dirt track and ran along past the last of the houses. The tea stall next to Ditte's barber shop was open. The coloured poster of an actress, all decked out in her finery, hung on one wall inside the tea stall. I vaguely felt that I had seen her in some movie, but couldn't remember which one. Next to the poster in a glass frame appeared the noble *kalima*–the Muslim profession of faith–done in colourful calligraphy. And a mirror in a golden frame hung on another wall. The radio was blaring away.

I could see all this in such detail because Nusrat had asked us to wait there for the tonga. I was holding Munna's hand so tightly that our perspiration started to run together. I looked to my right in search of a tonga–a funeral procession was coming along. Jasmine and roses were heaped upon the black funeral sheet, and one could almost see the crisp rustling white of the bleached shroud spill out through the wooden latticework on the sides of the bier. Immediately, Tai Ji recited the kalima in a loud voice. Two individuals moved forward and exchanged places with the other two who had been carrying the bier on their shoulders. Munna clutched my hand even more tightly.

"Who died, mother?" he asked, searching for my eyes behind the screen of my veil.

"No one," I said and quickly recited the kalima myself. The funeral black, the pristine white of the jasmine and the blush of roses flashed across the tea stall mirror for an instant, leaving behind only a scent, so different from the smell of the flower strings he used to bring me now and then.

"So will you take us?" Nusrat had finally succeeded in stopping an empty tonga.

"Yes, sister. But five adult riders. That's a lot. Well, all right–"

Nusrat and Bilquees took the front seat, Tai Ji, Kaneez, Munna and I the back one. The movement of the tonga caused Munna to keep sliding down off the slippery leather seat, so I pulled him into my lap and folded my arms around him securely.

We turned onto the street which led to the fairground. It was crammed with numerous cars and tongas just like ours, and with crowds of men, women, and children who jostled about on the sidewalks. A flood of humans spread out as far as you could see.

"Good gracious, what a crowd! Just look at them–they keep swarming in like insects!"

"Why not? This isn't an everyday occasion," Kaneez said, full of exhilaration, and shifted to one side.

Can't she sit still for even a little while? Must she keep shifting back and forth all the time? Her elbows had already jabbed me in the side several times.

"Exactly like a column of ants. Have a look, Rasheeda." Tai Ji nudged me and I looked out.

Indeed, people were walking antlike in unbroken lines–anonymous, stripped of personal identity. How did one distinguish between two ants? Perhaps the ants themselves didn't know quite how. And neither did we humans. The thought made me laugh. I looked closely at the black burqa canopies: one couldn't tell them apart. Suddenly I felt an entire colony of ants crawling on my back. Once again the dark emptiness of my stomach surged up before me. And once again I felt I was becoming lighter, that my feet had no mass or density. I hugged Munna even more tightly to myself.

The fairground was just up ahead. A city of all sorts of lights was flashing before us. Some lights swayed like seven-layered necklaces, others went round and round like spinning umbrellas, and still others just cascaded down like a waterfall. The tonga went down a gentle slope and pulled into an open space. We got down. Nusrat sprinted off to the ticket booth. Minutes later we were entering the fairground through the main gate. A sea of humanity was surging inside.

"See," Bilquees said, beaming with joy, "how festive and lively the place looks!"

"Gracious, what a crowd!" Tai Ji exclaimed, her voice tinged with both joy and fear.

"All right, let's start from the right end," Nusrat, who had been here once before, said.

We had barely walked up to the shop that sold mirrorwork apparel when the announcement went up:

THE WELL-OF-DEATH! THE WELL-OF-DEATH! LADIES AND GENTLEMEN, THE TRULY STUNNING PER-FORMANCE IS ABOUT TO BEGIN. IN JUST TEN MINUTES.

"Mummy, mummy," Munna tugged at my burqa, "let's go watch the Well-of-Death!"

"All right, we will. But for now keep holding my hand," I said as I clutched his hand in mine. The place was crawling with fair goers. They jostled past me on either side brushing my shoulders.

"The Well, the Well," Munna whined.

"Come on, let's first make Munna happy," Nusrat said, walking towards the round wooden shell with a staircase leading up to the top.

People were slowly gathering around the shell's mouth. Close by, on the wooden platform, a woman in tight black pants and a red blouse sat on a stool. She wore garish red lipstick and her eyes were smeared with collyrium. She had a white scarf tied round her neck and her blonde hair was puffed up like a beehive. She would look at the people, throw a smile at them, then take a long, deep drag on her cigarette, and send up a series of smoke rings. Next to her a midget in a yellow shirt and wide-skirted *shalwar*-trousers danced away to the tune of some film songs, tapping the string of miniature bells tied round his wrists.

The midget's stern, long face seemed to go all the way down to his waist, and every time he spun, the hump on his back jutted out into the space like an outcropping of rock. His hands were wide and unusually short, as if somebody had lopped off the ends of his fingers. Collyrium, running from his eyes, had smudged his cheeks, and his nostrils quivered fitfully above his long, dark, bushy moustache. As he danced, he threw a glance backwards at the blonde every now and then and smiled, exposing his buck teeth. I realized that the dwarf certainly stood apart from everybody else: he could never have been lost, no matter how thick the crowd.

We were still on our way to the Well when Bilquees, seeing a large crowd by the pond, suddenly broke her stride.

"What is this?" she raised herself on her toes to look. The people at the water's edge were peering up at the sky. We also looked up and saw a man clad in layer upon layer of thick, heavy clothes standing on the end of an iron ladder extending upward to the sky itself. He was very high on the ladder, so high that the lights at that elevation looked feeble. In order to see him, we had to bend our heads so far back that my neck began to hurt from the stab of an over-stretched vertebra.

"What is it?" Munna tugged at my veil. I picked him up. "Look," I said, "this man is going to set fire to himself and then jump."

The man took a bottle and doused himself with gasoline. He bowed and greeted everybody. The bespectacled woman standing next to me adjusted her thick glasses and the boy who stood by her asked, "What will happen now? What is he going to do?"

The woman relaxed her tired head and said, "Can't see a thing." After a while, she raised it up again and started to watch. Behind the glasses, her eyes looked cloudy. The man on the aerial ladder struck a match and touched it to his clothes and instantly turned into a ball of fire. The ball of fire then took a leap and fell into the pond with a resounding slap. Several oil slicks quickly materialized on the muddy surface and began to dance. Some of the spectators rushed forward to help the showman out. Then everyone went on their way.

"That's all?" Munna asked, and then tugging at my veil renewed his request, "The Well, the Well." But by then I had pretty much lost track of myself. I was inundated by a deluge of humanity none of whom—except the midget, the showman on his aerial ladder, and the woman who sat on the wooden platform, her art concealed within her—had any identity at all. That same torrid fear was starting up again deep inside me. Perhaps I was feeling hungry.

We walked over to the Well-of-Death. A show had just ended and spectators for the next one were just beginning to gather. The midget was back dancing. But the blonde was nowhere to be seen. Nearby, on a white canvas flap hanging over the entrance to a show tent, big red letters proclaimed: A CIRCUS WITH REAL GIRL GYMNASTS, accompanied by pictures of girls in shorts. Kaneez halted in front of the tent.

"Shall we?" asked Nusrat. Before Kaneez could reply, the barker—a bald man in khaki pants and a white bush shirt—came up to us. "Come in, please, come in," he invited us solicitously, as his unusually bright eyes probed our faces behind the meshwork of our veils, moving from one veil to the second, and then on to the third.

"You're just in time. The show's about to begin! Only eight annas! Only eight annas!"

Some people were going in through the canvas flap. The flap lifted a little and revealed a cluster of small girls in their minuscule red shorts and tiny blue blouses standing in the middle of the floor past the rows of seats. Their skin was a rich dark brown and their eyes looked slightly dilated. Between their emaciated arms and spindly legs heaved their ribcages. One girl arched backwards, supporting herself on her palms and feet in the shape of a bow, while another jumped up and down over the other's arched ribs. All of a sudden, I felt a pounding in my side, and a similar one in Munna's. I groped for Munna's ribs, and quickly withdrew from the flap.

"Mummy, the Well! the Well!" Munna tugged at my burqa again, growing insistent.

"All right."

But there was still some time before the show and seats were filling up fast on the Ferris wheel nearby.

"Let's ride," Nusrat dragged me towards the wheel.

"No, it will scare the hell out of Munna," I said.

"You can leave him with me," Tai Ji offered, sitting down on a wooden bench.

I was still uncertain. I was thinking of the last time, years ago as an unmarried woman, when I had a ride on the Ferris wheel: how each downward turn of the contraption brought a sinking feeling to the heart. Meanwhile, Nusrat had already bought the tickets. So the four of us poured ourselves into a gondola. Up at the top, two gondolas were still empty. When they came down to be filled, ours catapulted up, above the rest. All the lights were now below us, and a dark city stretched beyond the last lights. The fair looked like a toy, the people mere wriggling worms. Up on top, I was frightened of losing my weight. I peered into the crowd below, trying to spot Munna. But I felt disoriented, my sense of direction impaired. Where did I leave them, Munna and Tai Ji?–I wondered. I tried to locate the Well-of-Death. That helped restore my sense of direction a little. Finally, I spotted Tai Ji's white burqa canopy and, next to her, Munna, in blue shorts and bush shirt. I was certain that Munna would look up at me, but he didn't; he was busy looking elsewhere, at the balloons perhaps. "Munna! Munna!" I called out to him, but my voice failed to reach him. Just then I felt as though I heard a boy crying. Some Munna was crying away, without letting up. I felt as if it was my own Munna who was crying somewhere in the crowd. But I quickly figured out: I had no other Munna, within me or without, besides the one who stood down there. Yes, my Munna was standing down there, playing with the balloons. Good! But then who was this other Munna who was crying?

Meanwhile, the Ferris wheel started up: up and down, up and down. The whole world was spinning. Every time our gondola plunged downward, a hot, fiery dread wrenched my insides, causing me to see the emptiness inside my belly again and yet again. On every downward swing, the riders, all of them, first shrieked out of fear and the sheer torture, and then broke into peals of laughter. Nusrat, Bilquees, and Kaneez were laughing wildly, while I looked down from the turning wheel for Munna, wondering whether he would look up at me at all. He didn't. Not even once.

The wheel stopped and we got down from the car. Tai Ji, to my surprise, was sitting in a different place from the one where I thought I had seen her, and Munna was actually sitting in her lap, eating a candy. I looked foolishly around, wondering who I might have been looking at from the Ferris wheel. Later too, my eyes searched for them but I never did see that woman and that child anywhere at the fair again.

The Well-of-Death was ready to start. The blond woman in the red top had returned to her stool on the platform. She would puff at her cigarette and smile. Nearby, the midget with his droopy face, jutting hump, and truncated fingers danced away.

"Let's go," Bilquees started towards the steps. I climbed up behind her, holding Munna's hand. Upstairs, we stood flush against the mouth of the wooden shell. Way down in the pit stood two motorcycles, one red, the other green.

"Is this the Well?" Munna asked.

"Yes."

Presently the small door at the bottom of the shell opened and in walked two men wearing tight pants and white half-sleeve t-shirts, followed by the blonde in her red blouse, black pants, and garish makeup. She began talking jovially with her male partners who meanwhile kick-started the motorcycles, drowning out every other sound inside the shell, indeed throughout the fair. The men mounted the motorcycles and started circling around the bottom of the Well slowly. The woman hopped on the green motorcycle behind the male rider. Suddenly, the motorcycles picked up speed and climbed on the wooden walls, rattling and shaking them perilously. At times it felt as though the motorcycles would fall out the shell's mouth, and each time when they came very close to the shell's edge, people stepped back quickly. Then, suddenly, the blonde untwined her hands from the waist of her companion, flung them into the air, and smiled throwing back her head. The veins in her neck swelled and her light brown teeth shown in the light. Thus she kept going round and round the inside of the Well.

Cries of "Oh, no! Oh, my God!" went up continuously all around. Black burqas were packed on either side of me, so close that I could not tell which one, in fact, covered me. Already, I was feeling light in the head from the deafening roar of the motorcycles. The throng pressed down on me so closely that someone else's breathing felt like my own.

The motorcycles finally stopped. The riders bowed and exited from the small door. The spectators began to file down the narrow staircase. We let the people just ahead of us get down first. Later, after the crowd had thinned some, first Nusrat and then the rest of us began to descend. Stepping down the first stair, I tried to grab Munna's hand to help him down.

But where was he? I looked frantically around everywhere. There was no Munna.

"Munna–where is Munna?" I asked myself . . . and everyone else.

"Munna!" Tai Ji called out, feeling anxious, and scanned the area around. Then all of us went around the Well-of-Death at least a couple of dozen times, looking in utter desperation for Munna. But he was nowhere.

"Where is Munna?" I asked again. But Munna was nowhere.

Later, we searched for him in shop after shop.

"He was wearing a blue outfit and red shoes, wasn't he?" Bilquees asked.

"Yes," I replied.

"God will look after him! God will protect him!" Tai Ji kept comforting me.

I saw blue outfits and red shoes in every shop, though not Munna's. And as I went looking for him in the crowd, I began to doubt whether there ever was a Munna in the first place. Was he really there? Was he there and then got lost? Or was he never there and got lost? Suddenly, in the middle of my stride, I began to feel terribly heavy, as though the entire fairground had filled up with me. The dark emptiness inside my stomach had been filled. Was Munna there? Apart from me? I wondered. Or did he exist while I did not? Or if we both in fact did exist separately, then how could we possible become *lost?*

Nusrat suggested: "Rasheeda, maybe we should go to the fair office and have them make an announcement. Besides, lost children are usually turned in there."

We made our way to a small room near the exit. Inside, four men were sitting round a table covered with a red tablecloth. We came up to them.

"Yes?" the man with the eyeglasses asked.

"We have lost our child," Nusrat said.

"Oh no! Do sit down, please." He promptly took out a notepad and pencil from the drawer. "Can you tell me about him? Age? What is he wearing? What does he look like? Any distinguishing marks? Can he talk?"

I tried hard to remember but drew a complete blank. Tai Ji, however, was able to give those men a lot of information. The man with the glasses then made an announcement on the loudspeaker. He repeated it for a long time; the entire fairground resonated with his voice. He asked us to wait awhile. We sat down. Tai Ji kept repeating pious prayers, and Kaneez, Bilquees, and Nusrat continued to give me hope. The men in the office offered me tea. But the very first sip stuck in my throat like a tacky bitterness. I began to look outside the window at the crowds. Only the midget could never be lost. The man who set fire to himself and then jumped into the pond, only he and the riders in the Well-of-Death and those little girls in A CIRCUS WITH REAL GIRL GYMNASTS possessed any identity at all. Nobody else did. I remembered the dream in which I turned around and looked, only to find that all the houses in the alley bore that same curious anonymity. Suddenly I saw that Munna was standing straight ahead of me in the doorway. I tried to speak but could not. I could not even stir from my place at all.

"Thank you God." Tai Ji darted from her chair.

"Where did you wander off to, Munna? Who brought you back?" Kaneez asked as she grabbed Munna's hand.

"Oh she–" Munna pointed at the empty door as he took out a bunch of candies from his pocket and began to count them.

I took hold of Munna's hand and we walked out of the fairground.

"Where did you go, huh?" Tai Ji wanted to know.

"Nowhere." Munna was now ensconced in my lap. "I was walking holding mummy's hand. Later, when I looked at her, it was somebody else. It wasn't mummy."

"Who was she?" I asked him.

"At first, she was mummy; but some distance down the path, she wasn't."

"Poor little thing!" Bilquees exclaimed. "These veils, they must have confused him."

But walking down the dimly-lit street I kept hearing Munna's cries coming after me from the fairground, even as Munna was tucked comfortably in my lap, eating candies.

"Who was she?" I asked as I stepped into our alley. The scent of jasmine and roses strewn over the black sheet still lingered in the alley and the heavily decked-out actress still stood laughing inside the tea stall, and anonymous houses in anonymous alleys were filled with anonymous light. I asked again, going up the stairs of my house, and yet again in the darkness of the night when Munna and I were alone: "Who was she?"

"First she was mummy, then she was not!"

Munna will give the same answer throughout the centuries.

Translated by Muhammad Umar Memon

MUHAMMAD SALIM-UR-RAHMAN

Voices

"I want to keep dogs."

"What for?" the woman's voice flickered in the darkness.

"I want to keep dogs."

"What for? Because we are lonely? Come to think of it, Suraiya hasn't written in a long time. Good, she must be happy with her husband. And Nasim–well, he's practically forgotten us. He never writes. What's that place in America? Sannata? Sansanata? That picture postcard . . . it was so lovely, no? God knows where I put it away. He hasn't sent us anything since–has he? Tell me! You haven't been keeping his letters from me? God knows what time it is."

It was pitch dark inside the room. There had been a power failure. A chilly October night, with jumbled sounds drifting in from afar, like faint lines appearing and dissolving on a thick, darkened screen. The man felt he was lying on an ocean floor, splayed out among a profusion of oysters, shells, corals, seaweed, smooth round pebbles, fish eggs–splayed out like a fish, with his fish-wife, his *fishette*–could there be such a word, he wondered–right beside him. He caressed her thigh. "My fish."

The woman laughed softly. "My dog."

The man smiled. The woman couldn't see him smiling.

"Dogs!" he said.

"Wouldn't one dog be enough?" she asked.

"This too is a dream. Many dogs, all kinds of dogs: black, brown, white, chocolate, black-and-white, brindled, pied–even perhaps green, yellow, colourless–as colourless as water. I'm out hunting with them. Evening. A green expanse rolling out as far as the eye can see, in which we are speeding along like splashes of so many colours, speeding along. I want to hunt down the moon."

135

"You are mad," the woman said.

There was a silence. "Oh, still quite a while before daybreak," the woman thought. "The night is like a mountain. We are climbing down ... or up. Must be down. There isn't strength any more to go up. Down and down and down. Perhaps that might help in falling asleep." Thousands of stairs–black-and-white, black-white. A hurricane lantern's moving right along, as if by itself.

"I'd go mad if you weren't with me," she said.

"You are with me, all the same I'm mad," the man said.

She plunged her fingers in the man's hair. It used to be so bushy, she reminisced with a twinge of sadness. Outside, a car sped by, crushing the gravel. Someone whistled along.

"We could be mad–really. After all who can tell. We've nothing. We are mad, really."

"It isn't easy to be mad," the man said. "The likes of you and I can never be mad. We are too damn conscious of ourselves. Too self-absorbed. You are your own prisoner, and I my own. The mad are a free people. That's why the world fears them and puts them behind bars. Wants to forget them. But you may shackle a mad man however you will, he'll always be free. How strange: we who are captives walk around in the world unrestrained, and the truly free are put away!"

"Then what shall we do to become mad?"

"Keep dogs!" the man said. They laughed.

A long silence ensued.

"Can't sleep," she said.

"Yes."

"Power's out; can't even watch a movie on the VCR."

"Yes. If we could just fall asleep, we may be able to have a dream."

After a brief silence he said, "Let's play."

"In the dark?" she giggled like a teenage girl.

"I mean with words. I'll tell you a story, a short one, then you tell it back to me, changing it along."

"Changing it along–how? When did I ever know any stories?"

"Just the day before yesterday after watching a TV play, you said it should rather have been written in such and such way–remember? Well, think of my story as that TV play."

She lowered herself upon him, supporting herself on her elbows. "Here we go," she said.

"Where?"

"Tell your story. That's all."

"All right. Listen. Once upon a time there lived a man in a rundown neighbourhood of Baghdad. He was a nice and pleasant man. He inherited a little money. Which soon ran out and he was reduced to dire straits. One night he had a dream in which he heard someone say: Get up and betake yourself to Cairo. There by the baker's on the western side of such and such bridge there lies buried a great treasure. Dig it up and make use of it. When the man woke up, he thought that a dream was, after all, a dream; it would be foolish to put one's trust in it."

"Treasure reminds me to ask you to take out my jewelry from the bank locker day after tomorrow. I'm planning to attend the Friday wedding. So don't forget."

"Don't interrupt! When the same message was repeated in a dream three nights in a row and the tone of the invisible interlocutor grew increasingly insistent and threatening, the man decided he could no longer ignore the matter. Then again, no compelling reason required him to stay on. So he left Baghdad and, after enduring great hardship, arrived in Cairo. There he found the bridge and, sure enough, the baker's shop on its western edge. However, there was a problem. The site was by a very busy thoroughfare. Traffic never let up on it, day or night. At night, with the rush over and only a few passersby around, there was always an armed squad patrolling the place. How in the world was he to dig out the treasure? The man was annoyed and regretted having been talked into such a profitless venture merely by a voice in dream. One day he sat by a corner on the edge of the bridge, his head hung low in disappointment. It had grown night. A few pedestrians still trekked along. Here and there a shop was still open. All of a sudden, one of the guardsmen, who sported a handlebar mustache, and who often joked around with his fellow guardsmen, approached the man. For some time now this guard had been watching the man loiter in the vicinity of the bridge. The man's garb and demeanor further gave him away as a stranger. Naturally the guard was intrigued. He asked the man why he wandered in the area and why he looked so glum. The man told him the whole story. Whereupon the guard broke into a loud laughter and said, 'You are an absolute idiot! You saw a dream and right away, without bothering to think twice, went dashing out. Now you sit moaning. Oh dear, I too had a dream last year and heard a similar voice urging me to set out for Baghdad. There, under the jujube tree in the courtyard of the house of so and so in such and such neighbourhood, I was told, lay buried the accumulated treasure of seven kings. Night after night the same voice frightened and threatened me, but I let the words drop in one ear and go out the other. So, man, listen to me and go back home. For nothing'll come of dreams.' Saying this the guard moved along but the man was absolutely stunned. It was his own name which the guard had mentioned. The name of the neighbourhood was also correct. And to top it all off, he had a jujube tree in the courtyard of his house. Right away he knew the meaning of his dream. He immediately returned to Baghdad and lost no time in digging out the treasure. All his problems were solved in one fell swoop."

"That's all?"

" 'That's all'–whatever do you mean? This is mysticism, my dear. Quite beyond you!"

"Maybe."

The stillness around them deepened further. They could clearly hear the clock ticking away in the adjoining room: as if a pair of tiny hands were pounding away, softly but incessantly, in an effort to dig out and pry open something from somewhere.

"You give up?" the man asked.

"No. Let me think," she said. And the man tried to conjure up a face–a familiar face, especially when it was absorbed by deep thought: forehead creased with a couple of lines, dark, thick eyebrows, jet-black eyes, with a faraway look, mouth a little contorted, as if from the exertion of thinking. Would there still be lines on her forehead?–the man thought. He groped for the woman's hand and held it. Then locked his fingers into hers.

"No. The story didn't end that way," the woman said, all of a sudden.

"Oh!"

"By the time the man returned to his home in the environs of Baghdad it was already night. He was wiped out from fatigue. He had bought some fried fish on his way home. He thought he'd warm it up, eat, and then rest. The treasure wasn't running away, after all. He'd worry about it tomorrow. He had warmed up the fish and barely taken the first morsel when there was a knock at the door."

"Wow!"

"He got up and opened the door. And who did he see? The same moustachioed Cairene. They both were struck with amazement. Then the guard said, 'Oh I see, so you're the one who lives in this house. Well then, my dream was a true one.' When the man's amazement wore off he said, 'I've got this fish, not a whole lot, but you're welcome.' The moustachioed guard didn't waste a minute. Promptly he sat down and began eating. When they'd finished eating, the guard said, 'After I spoke to you I was struck by the thought that my dream might be a true one. Without further ado I set out for Baghdad. I already knew where I was headed for. I just asked for the address as I went along. The sight of the jujube tree in the courtyard reassured me and as soon as you appeared at the door I knew the days of want and indigence were over.' The two shot the breeze for quite awhile. The guard recounted with great gusto all he'd endured. Evidently, some of the episodes were pure fabrications. All the same, he knew the art of making a story sound interesting. When sleep overwhelmed them, they retired for the night.

"When they got up in the morning, the guard said, 'The treasure's as good as ours. No rush. Let's go out and see a bit of the city. I've heard a lot about Baghdad. And don't you worry about the expenses. I've got ten gold pieces on me.' Happily, they went out sight-seeing. Had it been a small place they might've tired of it in a couple of days. Not Baghdad. It was improbably large and full of attractions: carnivals, fairs, a hundred different amusements and entertainments, numerous promenades and recreation parks. Out before the crack of dawn, they never set foot in the house before dark: strolling in a park once, luxuriating in a meadow next. Or they went boat-riding on the river, or just wandered through the sprawling suburbs. They went through every neighbourhood. Old, dilapidated palaces seemed to attract them the most. They felt a particular fondness for them. The new ones, full of splendour and magnificence, these they only looked at from outside with a transient joy. The fellow, he knew Baghdad like the back of his hand. Who lived where, what happened where, he knew every last thing about the city by heart. The guard, on the other hand, had a thousand stories at the tip of his tongue. Their tongues knew not how to tire, nor did their feet. Every night they went to bed firmly resolved to dig out a little treasure the next day. But the next day they consoled themselves saying that the treasure was, after all, theirs, so why the rush. 'We still haven't seen such and such part of the city,' they would say. 'So let's go there today.' And that's how the days passed. Their clothes soon turned into rags. They'd make do by patching them up. When hunger overwhelmed them they headed for a soup kitchen. Hand in hand they combed the streets of Baghdad all day long, or wandered amidst its gardens and ruins."

"And the treasure?"

"Well, if they didn't dig it up, what can I do?"

"You've screwed up the story beyond all recognition."

"You asked me to alter it as I went along. And so I did. I don't know what's good or bad."

Neither spoke for a while. At last, the man said, "Go to sleep!"

"How?" the woman shot back irritably. "I would if I could. Seems I can't."

"Well then, let's go out. We'll watch the stars. That'll help us fall asleep–at least that's what they say."

"Nonsense!"

"Come on. We'll watch the stars. No harm in watching."

They put their slippers on and stepped out into the small backyard. They stood on the grass and looked at the sky strewn randomly with innumerable stars, some shining brightly, others twinkling faintly. Their arms strung across each other's waist, they stared at the sky. The universe looked chopped up into unbelievable distances. God knows across what distances the light had to travel before it reached them.

"Grandpa knew all their names by heart," the man said.

"How far the stars are!" she observed.

"How far? You mean how close?" the man said.

"Close?"

"That's why they're visible."

"How perfectly cool is their light!"

"That's because the night is cool. It makes their light feel cool too. Merely an illusion."

"What if we found an abandoned child here–wouldn't that be fun?"

"What's the use? We'll bring him up, worry our heads over him, he'll grow up and one day leave us."

"That's never stopped parents from bringing up kids."

"A dog never leaves its master."

"I'm feeling chilly."

Slowly, they walked back in. The man felt as though some of the stillness of the sky, a deep, dark, far-reaching sky, had somehow become entangled with their bodies and crept in right along. Still the space outside looked brighter compared to the pitch darkness of the room.

They lay down, next to each other, and it was as if they had just climbed down from a high place and, exhausted, had stretched out on a slope to catch their breath. Sleep, too, is a star, the woman thought. A dog barked in the distance.

"This story. . ." she began.

"Which story?"

"Ours. What if we tried to change it?"

"How?"

"Like get up and leave. Chuck everything. The house. The things in it. Everything. Just keep moving. On and on. Sleep where night overtook us. Eat with contentment whatever we could find. No particular place to go. Only a road to walk on. Walk on and on. Nothing to own. Absolutely nothing. And no regrets either."

"We don't have the guts for that."

"We don't?"

"Yes. It's all very well to ramble on like this. But when you get up in the morning, you'll be able to see this house clearly. . . the things in it–then? Yes, then? Tell me! What do we have to show for a lifetime of toil except this great pile of material things. We can't leave. We're much too sensible for that. We couldn't make such a terrible mistake. Neither you nor I."

The woman drew a long breath and then placed both her palms on the man's cheeks, as though trying to hold a great big bowl.

"What a pity," she said, "that we can't even go . . . I mean, can't even become free."

Translated by Muhammad Umar Memon

JEELANI BANO

Some Other Man's Home

All the houses look terribly alike–I'm afraid I might end up in some other man's home. That fear kept haunting me as they took me away from the hospital.

The doctors at the hospital had said I had been badly hurt in an accident–they must have lied–otherwise I should hurt somewhere–they seemed to look at me with suspicion–they kept watching me as if any moment I'd jump out of my bed and run away.

And then it happened–what I was afraid of.

God knows what strange house they have brought me to!

No sooner had they forced me down on a bed than some woman began shrieking, "Ooooh! How terrible! He can't be *my* Hamid. Nothing could've happened to *him*."

Then some child asked, "Who's that, mummy? Who's that all coiled up in daddy's bed?"

Now there couldn't be any doubt: I had been brought to the wrong house–that's what I was afraid of all the time.

What's going to happen next?–what if the man of the house comes back and finds me here?–run . . . run. . .

But there were people around me, holding me down–"Calm down, *bhabi,* calm down," I heard someone say in the next room. "He'll get crazier if you won't. Try to make him happy. Get him to like it here."

Make me happy?–like it here?–what imbecile won't take care of his family himself but force another person to sleep in his bed?–I must've fallen among robbers–they want to rob me–where are my keys?

What fool's house is it, anyway?–there's hardly any light in this room. . .

Why hasn't the sun come out today?–I hope they didn't lock it up too–perhaps it's night now–how did that happen?–but if it's night there should be stars and the moon–"Uncle Moon, so far away; Uncle Moon so far away"–who's there?–come in, come in–is it Mr. Sun?– yes, the sun ought to be up now–but suppose one morning it doesn't come up, what would I do then?

I won't be able to shave–nor would I be able to drink my tea–how can anyone shave in a dark room?–I might cut my neck–that fool doctor at the hospital had said, "Don't ever try to shave yourself!"–why did he say that?–did he think I had lost my hands in that accident?

How would I get my shaving things now?–I seem to have lost my keys–all my things are gone–I've been robbed–there must be robbers living in this house–how they stare at me!–their eyes bulge–they whisper to each other all the time–then there's that boy Fazlu, who brings me my meals–every time he sees me he grins like an idiot–the fool.

Perhaps they've all gone mad due to some accident–perhaps they were going somewhere in their car and suddenly. . .

God, how my head hurts!–did someone hit me with a rock?–I must retaliate–I must hit back with a bigger rock–I should give someone a good thrashing. . .

But I just don't feel like getting out of this warm, soft bed right now–also, I'm scared of the man who keeps peeking at me through the transom–he gives me such mean looks–he seems to gloat over my troubles. . .

"Go away! Get away from me! Leave me alone!"

My shouts brought Nimmo waddling to my bedside–she's a plump woman. . .

I'm not sure how I happen to know her name–she pretends I'm her husband–that's a good one, isn't it?–I'm sure I've never seen an uglier face, or a more hateful woman–I flatly told her I won't touch her, not even with my slippers–but she keeps coming back, again and again– she tells me to shut up and lie quietly–it makes me wonder: was she the wife of some poor beggar like me in her previous birth. . .

Nimmo came into the room and asked, "Who are you shouting at?"

"That fellow up there, why does he keep staring at me?" I pointed at the man in the transom.

"God have mercy!" Nimmo shouted, striking her forehead with her open hand. "That's no man–that's you. Don't you even remember yourself?"

Now how can that be true?–how can that man be me?–and if he is indeed me then who am I?–which of us is the real me?–this is just terrible–it could get pretty sticky for me if these strange people found out that the real me was someone else–I had better find some hiding place for myself–where's my blanket?–now I won't respond, no matter how hard someone calls. . .

"He isn't insane," someone speaks angrily in the next room. "Why don't you folks get him some medical treatment? Doesn't anyone want him to get well–to give all of you a hard time again?"

". . . so much property . . . big savings account . . . seven hundred rupees per month in pension. . ."

That must be Nimmo's husband–probably he's gone mad–or are they conspiring against me?–they want me to go mad?–did they cut me into two . . . put one part in the transom?–they must have kidnapped me from the hospital. . .

Who's here now?–who's pulling at my blanket?–I'm not here–I'm over there, in the transom. . .

It's Nimmo again–with a plate of grapes in her hand–who are these other people with her?–perhaps she's brought them to watch the show. . .

With great affection she puts a grape in my mouth–she says, "Come on, Hamid, be nice. See, your aunt's here, also Nishat and Akhtar. Or have you forgotten them too?"

"How're you feeling now?" a man asks, sitting down on the bed.

"Aha! I begin to see now," I say to the man–I've recognized who he is–"You're that man in the hospital–you must've come to give me a shot"–I quickly grab a vase to defend myself–"Get out of here–or I'll let you have it in the mouth."

Nimmo starts to cry, but I give her a kick–I say to her, "Stop acting! You think I'm some pet monkey to show to your friends. If you aren't careful in future I might make you dance for them."

It looks like I'll have to get away from this place–now that would be something–one day they'll come into the room and find I'm gone–then they will have something to cry over. . .

But this other me, he's really spoiled everything–he has his eyes fixed on me all the time–now why did that happen?

Why did I break into two?–what can one-half of me do? . . .

One day Nimmo sent two children into my room–a boy, Pappu, ten or eleven–very suspicious–very much on his guard–he seemed to think I had a rock in my hand–and a very pretty little girl–like the doll that goes chun-chun when you turn the key in its back.

"Come here, Chun-Chun," but she ran up to the bed before I could finish–Pappu tried to stop her, but she threw her arms around my neck–her lovely hair spread on my chest. . .

"Daddy, daddy," she said, "how did you hurt your head? Pappu's scared of you, daddy. You're not going to spank us, are you?" Then she cupped my face in her hands and whispered, "Get me a little airplane, daddy, then both of us will fly away."

"Yes, we'll fly away, very far away. Grrr, grrr, zoom, zoom."

Suddenly the two of us were flying around in a small airplane.

"Ta-ta," Chun-Chun waved to those contemptible people below us. "Ta-ta, ta-ta," I shouted too.

"Stop, stop! What do you think you're doing?"–those curs have got hold of me again–"Don't be so wild. You're not well"–Nimmo grabs from the back–"Get down, Munni. You can't ride on daddy's shoulders anymore. He's not feeling well, you know."

"Let go of us"–I try to free myself–"We're flying to Delhi. We're going way far away. Ta-ta, ta-ta. . ."

But Chun-Chun had to get down–I too was forced back on the bed–then Nimmo came and sat down near me.

"Thank God," she said, her voice all cream and honey–"Thank God, you still remember your children"–then she touched my face and snuggled closer–"I swear to you I was so scared you might have forgotten your children too. I don't know what we'd have done then."

"Why? What's the problem?"–I push her away from me.

"Why! You think I'd go out and get a job at my age. Thanks to your pension we still somehow manage, but only barely. What else do we have now? Just a little bit of property. I tell you, I envy Imtiaz's mother. She lived in luxury till the day she died. Why did you then marry me? Where would I go now with these small children?"

Nimmo must be crazy–one moment she's crying, the next she begins to giggle–so unpredictable.

Suddenly she puts a piece of paper before me–"Here, sign it"–she coyly says.

What's this now?–something to make me her slave for life? What if it made my split permanent?–one part peeking through the transom–the other lying here snared by these thugs. . .

"What are you looking around for? Hurry up and sign the paper."

Nimmo must be standing on hot coals–she is so agitated–I closely look at the paper–1000–1000–numbers come into focus, then disappear. . .

"Aha! So that's what it's all about–money!"–I quickly sign the paper.

"Mummy, what would you've done if daddy had forgotten how to sign his name?" That's Pappu–next to Pappu, Fazlu–behind Fazlu, Shimmi–then some other Ummi-Pummi–they form a circle around me. . .

"Just think, all the money would've been lost if the sahib had forgotten how to write!" That's Fazlu–he has teeth like the seeds of a rotten melon. . .

"Shut up!" I pounce upon him. "Who the hell are you to talk of money? And why the devil must you flash your teeth every time you see me? Am I a clown? Are there horns sprouting from my head?"

They burst into laughter. . .

A suspicion crosses my mind: has my appearance changed in some way?–do they know I'm split in half?–that one half of me sits in the transom?–perhaps that's why they keep staring at me–what's more amazing, the I in the transom also stares at me like them. . .

Perhaps I shouldn't act so wild–the other day I chased a fly all over the house–so many light bulbs got smashed–the glass cabinet was knocked over–Nimmo said everyone was watching my show–you might have thought all the movie houses had closed–that all the people looking for entertainment had come into this house–there were so many of them.

Some of them even put on their own shows–a matinée was going on in the dining room–that cute girl, Shimmi, was the heroine–a tall, dark man was the hero–quite a romantic show it was–plagiarists!–I've seen such cooing couples in every Hindi movie–they seemed ready to burst into a song–"You're my moon, I'm your moonlight"–God! I'd have gone crazy if they had–"Cut, cut!" I shouted–they were so frightened they actually stopped–the hero leaped out the door and ran away–the heroine threw herself at my feet–"Daddy, please forgive me"–now she was shedding false tears. . .

I pulled her away–the way the father does in that movie–"And you forgive me too, for I can't play in your trashy movie."

Just then Chun-Chun came into the room–the lap of her frock

was filled with paper cuttings–"Quick, daddy, I've brought you lots of money"–she dropped the strips of paper in my lap–they turned into currency notes–then she started picking them one by one–"With this note we'll buy a big cake, with this, an airplane–with this, some cigarettes for daddy and with this we'll buy a daddy. . ."

"You're silly!"–that was Pappu again–"You don't buy daddies with money."

"You can too. Didn't you buy us all with money, daddy?"

"Of course, I did. I bought all of you with money. You're all my slaves. Here now–line up all of you!"

I gave the order, but no one listened.

"Pappu's stupid," said Chun-Chun. "Mummy says if one has money one can buy anything."

That gives me an idea–perhaps I should try to buy back that other I. I grab all the money and push her away–"Get Out! This is my money."

"No, it's mine," Chun-Chun begins to whimper. "Daddy's taken all my money. I want my money back."

Nimmo comes into the room.

"What'll you do with those scraps? Let Munni have them."

"I'll buy my other I with it. You want me to remain split in half for ever?"

"God have mercy!" Nimmo's frightened by my scolding. "Go on, children, go and play outside. Your daddy's about to have another of his fits."

She locks me inside the room and goes away. . .

I'd also like to kill all my enemies, but I don't have my gun–it was borrowed by the man who killed Kennedy–he hasn't brought it back– would I otherwise let so many wild and useless people run around freely?–particularly Nimmo and Fazlu, and that Imtiaz?–the three ought to be shot–you'd see how brightly the sun shines that day–how people laugh . . .

"Bang . . . bang . . . bang!" I make my fingers into a gun and begin to shoot–those who come within my range fall–right and left–Nimmo– Fazlu–that pig-faced doctor who sent me by force to another man's house–the clerk in the pension office who smirks every month when he sees me–they're all dead–now we can have some fun–eat and . . .

How hungry I am today!–I haven't eaten anything for the last twelve months–I'll have some kababs today–hot and spicy–and if I don't get my kababs I'll roast that Imtiaz and gobble him up. . .

"Bring me some kababs! Quick! Kababs wanted!"

Instead of kababs, Imtiaz comes into the room.

He too is a member of this strange household–his darling mummy insists that the worthless creature is also my son–curse the thought!– I think we were mortal enemies even in our previous lives–there's nothing in his eyes but contempt and hatred for me–whenever I see him I say to myself, "Just wait, one day I'll get you. . ."

I wish I knew who pays for this boy's fancy airs–every time he passes by he blows cigarette smoke into my face–he and Nimmo constantly fight over money–at night he comes home very late–past midnight and dead drunk–he thinks I don't know the smell of alcohol–who really amazes me is that brazen Nimmo–his darling mummy–how dare she tell me this scum is my son!

I may be old, but I know the world–sometimes I so wish to slap his face–that should quickly make him recall his real father–but then I get scared by his muscles–I begin to pity the man who had him for a son.

As usual Imtiaz starts giving orders: "Hurry up! Get dressed. Today is the 7th. We must go and get the pension."

I enjoy these monthly excursions–I have so much fun wandering in the streets–we get the money but when I try to put it in my pocket, Imtiaz takes it away from me–he buys me some ice cream–then he leaves me at the house and goes away–his mummy shrieks and shouts. . .

On the 7th of every month so many people try to drag me away with them–Nimmo says I belong to her–she wants to take me with her to get the pension–Imtiaz says I belong to him alone, that only he should take me out. . .

But today I pay him no attention–just to spite him–"Where are my kababs? Bring me my kababs. I'm hungry."

"Please change your clothes first," he says with a great show of affection–"Today I'll buy you kababs with all the pension money."

How kind he is to me today!–he doesn't scold me–nor gives me a push to make me change my clothes–to hell with kababs!–I don't want any–I won't even go out with him–why should I go to get the pension?– why shouldn't I just crawl back under the blanket?

I won't get up–that's right–that's what I'll do today–it's such a nuisance: change clothes to go anywhere–the whole house gathers around–one person gives me a shave–another scrubs my arms and legs–Imtiaz himself irons my clothes–then he helps me put them on too–that day he's so concerned about "what people might say" . . .

People–people!–who are the people the residents of this house are so afraid of?–if I ever find out I'll give them all the dirt–that the other day when Nimmo had gone out, Imtiaz opened the safe with a key of his own and took out some jewelry–that any day now Shimmi will run away with that swarthy fellow–she too has plans to open the safe–every day I hide behind this curtain and watch what goes on–one day Pappu was picking pieces of meat out of the dish on the table and gobbling them down when I surprised him–later they were all muttering: "How did he get in there?" "How long was he hiding there?" . . .

And that Fazlu–what a rascal he is!–he brings me my meals, then sits down and gobbles them himself–one day, after he leaves the room, I put my ear to the door and listen–he tells Nimmo that he had fed the sahib. . .

"No, no. I haven't eaten anything. I'm starving. Give me some food." I run into the room and shout at them.

"God almighty! What does he want now?" Nimmo says to Shimmi. "Just now Fazlu fed him and now again he's hungry!"

"You might get sick from eating too much," Shimmi tells me, pushing me towards my room.

"No. I'm starving. I haven't eaten anything. You can ask Fazlu."

Instead of an answer, Fazlu looks at Nimmo and starts laughing.

"But why did you have to come here? You'll only make a mess on the table. Go to your room. I'll send you something to eat." Nimmo pushes me into the room and bolts the door from outside.

"Don't push my daddy–don't hit him," Chun-Chun shrieks outside the door–she is crying.

"Shut up! Be quiet! Daddy's darling!" Nimmo starts spanking her.

"Open the door." I beat my head against it. "Open the door."

It is opened.

Have they killed her?–wiping the blood from my face I look for Chun-Chun–she's standing in a corner scared to death–we run into each other's arms. . .

Nimmo has thought up another trick to keep me confined to this room–she brings all sorts of people to talk to me–to keep me happy, she says.

Two days back she brought a crazy man to see me–he had a false beard which flapped in the air–he kept grabbing at it as if he were scared of being exposed–the moment he saw me he clasped me to his breast–as if we were old buddies.

"Well pal, how are you?" he asked heartily. "Feeling better now?"

"You tell me, how're things with you? Care to sell this beard of yours?"

He jumped back, but I grabbed his hand and pulled him down beside me–no harm in having some fun with a loony.

He pulled himself free and moved away to sit on a stool.

"I thought of coming to see you several times, but I was afraid you might not even recognize me," he said, smoothing his beard.

"That's true," I reply, "You have changed a bit since you went crazy."

I don't know why he started to laugh–they say mad people always consider others to be mad–perhaps the old rascal thinks I've gone crazy?

"You know, pal," he says after a few moments, "you know, I do feel bad about you being sick. But what can we do? It's as God sees fit."

"And I just adore this beard of yours. Won't you let me have it for just one day? Chun-Chun and I want to play cops-and-robbers."

At that he jumps up and starts for the door–then stops and remarks somewhat pompously: "Talk some sense. I understand your wife didn't even bother to get you treated. Anyway, did you hand over all your pension to these people or did you save a little for yourself?"

Again that damn word!–it seems I'm only the name of a pension– no one sees me as a human being–they see only an amount of cash– none of them talks of anything else–I wish I could peel this pension off my face and throw it away–but in that case, would I even be visible to anyone in this house?

I don't remember how or when I got rid of that nut–I heard Fazlu say that when I tried to pull at that guy's beard he was scared out of his wits and ran away–what else could I've done–how else do you treat a loony?

Another such character came into the room the other day–he too acted as if we were old buddies–started telling me of all our good times together–all lies–then on the sly slipped into his pocket my expensive Parker–he smoked all my cigarettes too–then, as he was leaving, he made a great show of telling me how he had been looking after Nimmo–trying to cheer her up so she won't be heartbroken from my illness–finally he proudly declared that it was he who had brought me here from the hospital–when I heard that I couldn't restrain myself any longer.

"So it's you who threw me into this hellhole! But why? What did you gain from torturing me so?"

"Nothing yet," he replied with a smirk, "but I will, soon enough."

"I'm calling the police. I'll expose you." I twirled the dial of the telephone."Hello, hello."

"Give me my telephone." Chun-Chun came and pulled it out of my grasp–it is her telephone– "Here, let me do it," she said, "Whom were you calling?"

"The police. Get them to come quickly or else the criminals will get away."

"Hello." Chun-Chun put the receiver to her ear and sat down on the floor–she had a serious look on her face–"Come quickly. They're bothering my daddy. They're not giving him food."

After a while both of us got tired of that game.

"That's it. Now let's go and catch the thief." And we earnestly set out in pursuit.

"Sssh! Don't make any noise," Chun-Chun said, putting a finger to her lips.

We crawled on our knees from room to room–suddenly my head struck the foot of a bed–someone jumped down–"Thief, thief," I started shouting, and grabbed his leg–"Hurry, bring my pistol. I've got him."

"We caught the thief! We caught the thief!" Chun-Chun began to clap and shout.

"Let him go, please let him go. The children might come. Please don't shout so." That was Nimmo.

I looked more carefully–how amazing–the thief was the man who a moment ago had been talking to me!–by now the whole house had gathered there–Shimmi–Pappu–Imtiaz–Fazlu–they looked flabbergasted–first they looked at me, then at the man–then they walked out of the room without saying a word–what cowards! They don't even have the guts to tell off the thief.

That night I could hear Nimmo muttering in her room: "No, he isn't mad. He's just shamming. He pretends to be careless about himself, but he never stops watching me. . ."

One day an amazing thing happens.

What do I see but that the night has ended–the people are up and around–there is light in the room–but I don't see any sun–did the thief steal the sun?–my anxiety grows–then Chun-Chun comes in with her telephone–I immediately tell her the terrible news: "Someone stole the sun last night."

"What! Where did it go?" Chun-Chun is horrified–in this house none is smarter.

"Who knows! Didn't you notice how dark it was? Now I'm lost. Without a sun how can there be a day? When can I now get out of the bed?" I start crying.

When she sees my tears Chun-Chun throws down her toys and rushes to cling to me–she spreads her golden hair on my chest.

"I'll buy you a sun this big," she says, spreading wide her arms–then she opens her hand, "See, I've two paisas."

"Silly! No one can buy the sun." I laugh at her foolishness.

"Then how did it come to you?" she asks, with wide open eyes.

Well!–now we had another problem on our hands–how did the sun come to me in the first place?–and why did it come?–did the sun also know about my pension?–did it hear about that other I too?

"Who's he?" I ask Chun-Chun, pointing with my finger.

"That?" For a long time she stands there looking at the other I–her neck stretched upward–then she says, "That's daddy."

"Whose daddy?" I'm glad–he turns out to be someone else.

"My daddy," she says, putting her palms on her chest for emphasis–then she adds, "That's you."

Me?–a shiver goes up my spine–even these children know that I've been cut into two! "Do you know who hung me up there, Chun-Chun?" I ask her furtively–first making sure no one was listening.

"Mummy did," she likewise whispers into my ear. "One day she put you behind the glass, tied a cord and hung you up there."

She put me behind the glass?–tied a cord?–in other words, I've been executed!–hanged till dead–I'm no longer alive–I have nothing to do with this world now–why am I then lying in this bed?

I get up and quietly stand against the wall, but just then Nimmo barges into the room–she's been cross with me ever since I caught the thief–however, now her voice is soft as butter–first she tries to pull me away from the wall–then, when she fails in her efforts, she flops down on the floor near me.

Even so she starts acting very important–she refers to my pension as her pension–to her children as "my children"–she says she needs thirty thousand rupees–she wants to sell the house and also take out all the money in the bank–so that Shimmi can be married off–so that Imtiaz can be given his share and then kicked out for good.

I listen–like some real-life, hapless husband–these talks of pensions and bank accounts bore me to tears–but after a while I couldn't take it anymore–I start scolding her–"Be quiet! I won't listen to you anymore. You've killed me. You put a cord round my neck and strangled me. I'm dead."

She falls at my feet. "Please forgive me, Hamid. Please forget what happened that night. I'll never deceive you again."

"Ha! Why should I forgive you?" I kick her away. "You stole my sun. It was never so dark before." I kick her again. "And you took away my pistol. Now I can't shoot the thieves. Do you know how many thieves are lurking in this house? What kind of a place is this anyway? Some film studio where people constantly act out romantic scenes? No, I refuse to take part in your stupid plays."

Just then I happen to look up. "Who put that noose around my neck? You cut me up and hanged me. Now I can't even show my face anywhere."

Nimmo begins to shriek–I keep hitting her with anything I can get hold of–some people rush into the room–they try to stop me–I hit them too and they run away–I chase them–today I'll kill the whole lot–I'll shoot them all.

"Come! Come everyone! See what this man is doing!" Nimmo is shouting to the neighbours. "Today I'll have all the property transferred to my name!"

"Go ahead and try." Imtiaz enters the room. "I'll take daddy with me."

"You think so? You'd better not even come near him." Nimmo shrieks at him, waving her hands. "Some lover of his daddy! I know why you want to take him with you. So you can swallow all by yourself the seven hundred of his pension. You'd better not even try it. He's all the support left for my little ones."

The two are fighting so loudly it's impossible to understand them–I drop the rock in my hand and start to think–will Imtiaz really take me away from this crazy place?

That other I shouldn't get a whiff of it, I tell myself–I want to give him the slip–now it should be his turn to tackle this bloodthirsty bunch.

"Come Chun-Chun, let's get out of here." I pick her up in my arms–she seems scared by the fight raging around her.

"Where are we going?" She drops her doll and its tiny bathtub–she makes herself comfortable against my shoulder.

"We're going far away . . . very far away . . . where the sun is."

I open the gate of the house and step out on the street–the people inside keep fighting–they don't even try to stop us–perhaps they weren't fighting–perhaps they were mourning someone's death–the sun's death, perhaps, or my pension's. . .

"Daddy, daddy," Chun-Chun is saying, "Imtiaz Bhai was hitting mummy. He wants your pension."

So my pension is not done with yet?–what should I do now?–I'm scared–Imtiaz might start hitting me too.

"Daddy, you must throw away your pension." Chun-Chun advises me. "Throw it into the river. Then no one will fight." Then she starts clapping her hands. "Look daddy, we found the sun! There it is, trying to hide in the river. Let's hurry and catch it."

It's indeed the sun–so it wasn't stolen after all!–it only tried to hide away from us in the river.

"Run faster, daddy. Mummy is coming behind us. She's coming to catch you." From her perch on my shoulders, Chun-Chun keeps me informed.

What should I do now?–I begin to run faster–but I see no place to hide–there is nothing but water in front of us–where can we hide from Nimmo?–"Come Chun-Chun, let's hide in the water. Let's see how they catch us then. . ."

Translated by C. M. Naim

RAM LALL

The Grave

I hadn't been able to sleep at all. The journey had been long, and very tiring. I felt as if I had travelled for years on end, not just two days and nights. The pain in my joints seemed to have settled in for good, and my aching eyes were determined never to let me sleep again. It looked like I was destined to wander–lost, bedraggled–from one city to another, for ever and ever. . . .

I was coming from Jabalpur. My wife, Bilquees, and our three children, Hamid, Najma, and Nasreen, were with me. We had changed trains at Allahabad; our present train was taking us to Lucknow; at Lucknow we were to get another train for Iqbalpur, our final destination.

I have never liked to visit Iqbalpur. Since our marriage I have been there only twice, and that too because Bilquees insisted. It's her home; she tries to spend there a few days every year.

I should also tell you something about our life in Jabalpur before we had to leave the place. I lived there for eighteen years, holding a well-paying job with the Transport Department. I was also the proud owner of a house which was both beautiful and comfortable. It embodied years of hard-earned savings. Any wife would rightly have been proud of her husband for it. But not Bilquees. She never expressed any appreciation for either its comforts or its beauty.

As a matter of fact, she never looks with approval at anything that strikes my fancy. I love to invite my friends for big meals, she hates the very thought of it. I am addicted to bridge; she never even tried to learn the game. And yet, I have always loved her immensely. She entered my house twelve years ago to become its crowning glory, and the passing years have not lessened my love for her. Why she doesn't like my house, why she feels like a stranger in it–these questions have never bothered me. On the contrary, I have always found delight in her, for she has given me three lovely children. When I see them I forget every sorrow–I feel I lack in nothing, that I am at peace with the whole world. Every time Bilquees looks at me with a smile I feel an increased urge to live. But I have also often seen a terrible grief in her eyes. In such moments my entire universe appears to come tumbling down around me, and I am seized by a feeling of utter loneliness. Then Hamid and Najma and Nasreen rush up to me with their smiling faces, or Bilquees herself will shake me by the shoulder, asking, "What's the matter, Khalid?" and I come back to this world, my heart and mind again rid of any shred of melancholy.

It was bitterly cold that night. I am not a poet so I don't have the words to describe the cold. All I can tell you is that it was the first week of January, and a cold wave had gripped us for two days. In our panic to flee from Jabalpur, we had left the bedrolls at home and carried just two blankets with us. One of them now lay over Hamid and Najma, the other covered Bilquees and Nasreen. I myself huddled inside my overcoat as I sat leaning against the shuttered window, reading the prison letters of Maulana Azad. Books are the only friends of those who are forced to be alone or who prefer solitude. As are also cigarettes. Usually I don't smoke much but that night I found a new pleasure in lighting one cigarette after another.

As I read and smoked, I kept thinking of Iqbalpur. It was our destination, but I wasn't going there of my own desire. In fact, the opposite was the case. It was Bilquees, as I told you, who used to go there every year. I had always refused to accompany her. But this time I couldn't say no. I immediately agreed when Bilquees suggested that we leave Jabalpur and take shelter in Iqbalpur. I would have agreed even if she had suggested some other place. I was prepared to go anywhere, so long as I could hope to see the happiness return to the eyes of my frightened children.

We didn't have any close relatives in Iqbalpur. I never had any relative there, but Bilquees's whole family used to be there at one time– her father, mother, grandfather, and so many more. Now they were all gone. Her parents were dead and buried there, as was her grandfather who, before his death, had been so eager to move to Pakistan. Most of the others had in fact emigrated. Yet Bilquees kept going back to where there were many graves, but no one to look after them. Every monsoon caused one or two of them to cave in, creating a vacuum unbearable even to think of. The two trips I had had to make had been enough for me. That place had none of the peace that I felt in Jabalpur or in several other cities where I knew hundreds of people. Walking around in Iqbalpur had been like walking over tracks laid across hidden pits–at every step I felt I was liable to go crashing down some dark hole.

Bilquees had now only one, quite distant relative living in Iqbalpur, an "aunt" named Rahmat Bua. I doubt if she was really her aunt, but Bilquees always stayed with her on her visits. Rahmat Bua was the oldest woman alive in Iqbalpur. Now in her eighties, she was of the generation of Bilquees's grandfather; she knew the entire family, those who rested in the graves as well as those who had emigrated to Pakistan.

Bilquees would have emigrated too, just as her grandfather had wanted her to. He had, in fact, chosen for her a young man–some relative of his–who had gone and settled in Lahore. It was the grandfather's right to choose her mate, for she had spent more time with him than with her parents. And it was the grandfather who had personally tutored her in Arabic, Persian and Urdu. But when the time came for Bilquees to take that all-crucial step, her father blocked her way. He wanted to keep his daughter in the country where he lived. His resolve caused a split within the family. It even caused the death of the grandfather, who couldn't bear the disappointment. He died the day I took Bilquees to Jabalpur as my bride.

When Bilquees visited Rahmat Bua, she heard many stories of her grandfather. Stories that had made him such a well-known figure in that town. Bilquees herself remembered a lot of things about him–his peculiar laugh, his curious cough, his rages, his recitation of the Qur'an, his abundant joy while explaining the couplets of Sa'di, so many things.

Some of those who had emigrated to Pakistan would also come every once in a while to visit with Rahmat Bua. The old lady kept track of everyone. On her return from one of those stays with Rahmat Bua, Bilquees would act as if she had been visiting with her own mother. She would tell me about each and every relative of hers. She would tell me even if I didn't ask her. She would even give me the news of that "depot supervisor" in Lahore Cantonment who was himself now a father of several children.

For some time I hadn't been paying much attention to the book in my hands. As I thought about Iqbalpur I had kept staring at Bilquees's face. Once when she changed sides her *burqa,* which she had been using for a pillow, fell to the floor. I picked it up and tucked it back under her head. She was startled and opened her eyes, but seeing me smile she went back to sleep. I lit a fresh cigarette and searched for the line where I had stopped.

Again I couldn't concentrate on the book for long. I kept seeing a vision of Bilquees as she had been twelve years ago, a simple girl of seventeen whose major attraction was not the extraordinary length of her glossy, black hair but those enchanting features which she had inherited from her Pathan ancestors, who had come and settled in India so many generations ago. Her body was firm and lofty–like the mountains of Khyber. But that wasn't all. She also had eyes that were limpid like the pale blue sky of the northern plains, eyes that, in an Eastern girl, always betray a quiet intelligence and a passionate love. If ever those eyes displayed the littlest hurt I felt severely anguished. I had chosen my path and laid down my course, and Bilquees had always come along behind me, though with uncertain steps, as if carrying some monstrous burden. But today, when I was travelling with her to Iqbalpur, I was myself uncertain. Perhaps it was this sense of defeat which now lay upon my heart like a rock.

Suddenly, in the pale, sickly light within the carriage, I became aware of a ray of dawn's glow which had come peeking through the fog-covered glass of a window. At the same time, quite unexpectedly, the train ground to a halt at some station. It wasn't supposed to stop anywhere before Lucknow, but it had. I disengaged myself from my thoughts and tried to listen to the sounds outside. Someone walked by, his heavy steps crunching the gravel. The engine, having been forced to a sudden stop, made loud panting noises.

When several minutes passed and the train didn't start, I opened the door and looked out. It was some small station, enveloped in fog. A high length of the platform, one small single-storey building, and scattered lights, close and far, yellow, red and green. The wind was still. A bit away I could see the station master in his office–he was busy writing in a fat register in the light of a hurricane lamp. I watched him for several minutes, then turned to look at the porter who was limping towards the rear of the train, carrying a mug of hot tea to the guard. I recognized the sound of his steps: it was he who had passed by my closed window earlier. When he came close I could see nothing of him except his heavy overcoat and the large, dark turban which muffled his face. "What station is this?" I asked him. He didn't even bother to look at me. As he went limping by, he muttered, "Nigohan."

Nigohan! I was startled. I had completely forgotten that there was such a station just before Lucknow. Perhaps because it had been night every time I passed that way before. Also the train had never before stopped there as it did today.

I got down to question the porter some more, but he was already too far away. I walked around a bit on the platform to see if there was a sign that said Nigohan, then went over to the station master and asked him the same question. He confirmed what the porter had told me. I could feel a curious wave of joy rising within me. I strode out of the office, turned, and leaned my head back to look at the very top of the building. There, in the increasing glow of dawn, I could see where it was written: NIGOHAN.

How the place had changed! Before, there had been only one room for the station, and the platform had not been so high either, just level with the ground. By now I was bursting with joy. I wanted to rush back to Bilquees and tell her the good news that our train was in fact standing at Nigohan station. But before I could do so, another, most marvelous thought almost overwhelmed me. I felt I'd go mad with ecstacy. I ran back to the station master, pulled out our tickets, and laid them down on the table in front of him.

"Sir, the train will be here a bit longer, won't it? We can get down here if we want to, can't we? Do you think it would cause us any trouble if we left this train and took another later in the day?"

The station master only nodded his head in assent to all my questions, but the look he gave me betrayed some surprise. I could no longer suppress my excitement and blurted out everything.

"You see, sir, I'm originally from this village. But it's been twenty-five years since I was here last. Don't you think it's a strange coincidence that our train made this unexpected stop? I think it stopped here just for me?"

Chuckling to myself, I stepped outside, then rushed back in and asked, "Are you sure the train won't leave right away? I also have my children with me, you see."

"No sir, it won't. You can take your time. There's another train coming from the opposite direction and it has priority."

"Oh!" I exclaimed, and went loping to my compartment.

Bilquees had just woken up, and finding me gone and the door open, was looking around in some confusion. In my exuberance I grasped her face with both hands, but she immediately slapped them away–after all, there were other passengers, asleep in the compartment. I ignored my impropriety and went on, "Quick, Bilquees, get the children up. We must get down here–at this station. And hurry up. This train is just waiting for the tracks to be cleared, then it will leave."

I started waking the children myself. I called their names and shook them. Bilquees, obviously, had no idea of my excitement; in fact, she looked rather apprehensive. She grabbed the sleeping Nasreen to her breast and exclaimed, "Oh God! What's happening?"

The look of terror on her face wiped out the smile bursting over mine. Just a few minutes earlier, I had gaily loped across the platform, but now my feet felt heavy and shackled. I stood still, gazing into Bilquees's eyes. When we were leaving Jabalpur, even in the midst of extreme dangers those eyes had frequently glimmered with triumph; now, however, there was only stark terror in them.

After a few moment's silence I began to recover. I could feel my elation slowly coming back, my body once again became alive. Forcing a smile on my face, I said, "There's nothing to fear. We're getting off here only because we want to, and we'll go on later as we please. There is no danger. The danger was only where we had started from."

Eventually all of us got off the train. Hamid and Najma, their hands stuffed into their coat pockets, squatted down on the gravel platform to watch the rush of the second train as it went hurtling by on the other side. Nasreen clung to her mother's breast; Bilquees had wrapped her in her burqa to protect her from the cold. I grabbed the two blankets and our solitary suitcase, and moved towards the waiting room. Bilquees followed me, scolding the children for lingering behind.

Soon enough the full light of morning spread everywhere. Bilquees still looked rather peeved at having to get down there, but she had lain down on a cane settee and covered herself with a blanket. Hamid and Najma were running around outside on the platform, while little Nasreen stood with a dazed look on her face, peering through the screen doors.

Suddenly Hamid called me to come out. When I joined him, he pointed in amazement at the porter who was limping towards us, a garland of extinguished signal lamps around his neck and half-empty bottles of kerosene oil in his hands. It was the same porter whom I had encountered earlier. Then his face had been covered against the cold, but now I could see it clearly. He too was looking at me as he limped closer. We couldn't remove our eyes from each other's face. When he was quite close, he asked, "Khalid Bhai?" then stopped a few paces away just to make sure if I was indeed Khalid.

"So, it's you, Ramdas!" I exclaimed, both amazed and delighted, and rushing forward embraced him, the garland of lamps and all. Tears glistened in his eyes, and his dark face under the several day's growth of beard seemed to shine. I asked, "Why are you limping?"

"It's my wretched joints, Khalid Bhai," he replied. "But you tell me about yourself. What brings you here? Did you lose your way? Looks to me, you must be some big "officer" now. I'm right, aren't I?" And he laughed.

I grabbed his shoulders and hugged him a second time. Then, with a lump in my throat, I said to my children, "You know who he is? He's my childhood friend. We used to play together in this village. See those houses over there?–that's our village. The stories of our past are written all over it–isn't that so, Ramdas?"

When he vigorously nodded his head in agreement, the garland of lamps around his neck jangled, and the children's faces lit up with smiles.

Ramdas made some tea and served us himself. There was a tiny market near the stationhe went there and brought us some hot *jalebees* dripping with syrup. Then all of us set out to see the village. I was feeling some pride in showing them around–it was my village. The children were also excited to learn that their father was once a child like them and used to run around there. It always amazes children– and also delights them–to learn something of their parents' childhood. I was enjoying my children's amazement and delight. I love to play with my children, to tease them, to do things that would make them burst into laughter. I know all the ways to keep them happy. And when I see their laughing faces I feel as if heaps of flowers have been suddenly burst into bloom around me.

Bilquees was with us. She walked along in her burqa, the veil lifted from her face. She wouldn't laugh or smile, nor would she ask me about anything. The children kept bursting into peals of laughter as I reeled off the names of my childhood companions–Shabbu, Navabu, Gursharni, Ram Bhajva–but Bilquees's face showed only a faint disdain.

The village had changed altogether. Now there were several houses in that wide open space between the village and the station where we used to chase each other. And I couldn't find the pond into which, one Eid day, a boy had pushed me. When I had returned home, my festive clothes soaking wet, my father had given me a good spanking.

When Hamid heard about my getting spanked, he began to giggle. "All right, daddy," he said, "now tell us just how your daddy spanked you."

"The way it's usually done."

"No. I mean, did he use a cane or did he. . . ?"

"He slapped me," I said, laughing. "Like this," and patted his cheeks.

Now Najma spoke up, "But, daddy, you never spank us!"

I looked at Bilquees with a mischievous smile and said, "Because your mother spanks you enough, that's why."

Najma ran over to cling to Bilquees's leg and said, "No, she doesn't. She's always nice to us."

I wanted to show them my old home. Twenty-five years ago my father had sold that house to pay for my education in the city. When we reached that spot, an entirely different house stood there. Its occupants didn't even know me. As a matter of fact, except for Ramdas, no one else in the village had so far recognized me. And none seemed likely to. Most of the villagers, when they couldn't find any land to farm or money to start a little shop, tended to migrate to the nearby city to work in its factories or pull cycle-rickshaws. I walked through the lanes of my past like a stranger. In front of the mosque I paused to recall the imam who had taught me how to say my prayers. When we reached the old primary school, I searched for that corner where I used to sit and study, and where the teacher would sometimes force me to contort my body in punishment for not completing my homework–but I couldn't find the place. The children ran along with me. They were having great fun. Even I felt as if my childhood had come back in the form of a boy and was walking beside me.

We made a wide circle and finally wandered back to the railway tracks, but now at the other end of the station, the northern end, towards Lucknow. Suddenly I began to feel strangely restless. I started looking around for a long-forgotten spot. There used to be a mango tree near the tracks, and the tracks themselves curved by that tree. But now there was neither the tree nor that curve in the tracks.

"What are you looking for, daddy?" the children began to clamour.

"When we used to live in the village," I told them, "I had a lovely puppy for a pet. He was so tiny–he seemed to hug the ground when he walked. And he had long, shiny brown hair all over him. The hair covered his eyes too. He had such adoring eyes–sometimes we would just sit gazing into each other's eyes."

"What was his name, daddy?"

"We called him Puppy."

"Puppy! It's such a sweet name."

"Where is he now, daddy?"

"How did you get him, daddy?"

"An English officer gave him to my father. My father had long worked under that Englishman. In fact, my father got Puppy from him for me. And Puppy became my dearest friend. When he first came, he used to bark at me; later he just adored me. He would come and lick my shoes. If I whistled, he would come running up immediately. He always followed me when I went out to play. I had put a collar round his neck which had tiny bells sewn to it. When Puppy ran the bells went: tinkle-tinkle-tinkle!"

The smiles on the children's faces broadened and their eyes began to shine. Bilquees had squatted down on the tracks, tired after all the walking. I stood facing the kids, and continued.

"I trained Puppy to fetch the ball. When I played *gilli-danda* with other boys, Puppy would run and fetch the gilli on his own. Then I trained him to carry my satchel. I had to commute to Lucknow every day to go to a school, and every morning Puppy would carry my satchel for me to the station. There I would take it from him and board my train. When the train started moving, Puppy would run alongside the tracks. But he could run only a little distance, for soon the train would gain speed. Then Puppy would stop, usually near that curve, and go back home.

"One morning, there we were, all the boys, sitting in the train and calling out to Puppy, who was bouncing along, barking with excitement. The louder we called his name, the faster he tried to run. Then the train entered that curve. That day Puppy also tried to turn and follow along. But the curve was too sharp–even if a man were running he could stumble and fall under the train. And so that day when Puppy tried to turn with the curve, he couldn't and fell under the wheels."

The children's mouths fell open in horror.

"Puppy was killed instantly," I went on. "We pulled the alarm-chain and the train stopped. All of us clambered down and rushed back to where Puppy lay. He was already dead, cut to pieces. The gravel and cinders around him were splattered with warm blood. When I saw the blood I broke into loud cries. . . ."

"Then? Then what happened, daddy?" Hamid could barely ask. Najma's throat was dry too–she tried to but couldn't say a word. Nasreen's terrified eyes were fixed on my face. And, for the first time, Bilquees was also listening to me intently.

"Then we gathered the pieces of his body," I started slowly, "and carried them over to where the mango tree was. There we dug a hole in the ground and put Puppy inside it. We then filled the hole with dirt and covered the spot with many stones–to mark the grave of our dearest friend. After that day, every time we went to Lucknow we never failed to look out for Puppy's grave."

"Where is that grave, daddy?" one of the children asked.

The grave was not there anymore to be seen. Its every trace was gone. Only the memory had survived. As my eyes circled around looking for Puppy's grave, they suddenly met Bilquees's eyes. Who knows how long she had been staring at me! Her eyes were full of feeling for my search. As I looked back at her, a rueful smile flickered over her face. She stood up and walked over to me, then taking hold of my arm she softly asked, "Would you like us to stay here for a few days?"

Translated by C. M. Naim

PARVEEN SARWAR

Hearth and Home

She saw Shamsul Islam for the first time in the gala event at Uncle Abbas's silk farm. A lean, short man, with a rich brown complexion, his half-closed eyes sparkled with the desire of a bright future. And he spoke Urdu with a Bengali accent. He had an M.A. in History but was more inclined towards the arts and music. The thing about him which most impressed Shakira was his apparent determination.

There were government as well as nongovernment officials among the guests, local people as well as foreigners. Everyone toured the farm first: saw the silkworms busy at work, the cocoon stage, and, finally, silk threads being made and spooled by machine. Tea was next, followed by a variety show put on by the local art circle in which Shamsul Islam took the lead.

A stage had been set up in a large hall. Here young men and women wearing colourful costumes were gathered in small bands. Each in turn came forward and did their presentation. First the *bhawaiya,* then the *bhatyali,* then a song after which the dances started. In addition to the regional dances of Bengal, dances from all the provinces of Pakistan–the Baluchi *tapka,* the Sindhi *jhumar,* the Pushtu *kathak,* as well as the *luddi* and *bhangra* from the Punjab–were presented with persuasive authenticity to preserve the spirit of unity. Tunes were struck up in the *chatka* and *gambhir* mode. When Shamsul sang some patriotic songs with great fervor, Shakira could not hold herself back any more. An unseen force drew her backstage, where she said, "I'll sing the *aiman.*"

Shamsul, who had by this time come down from the stage and was about to direct the next dance sequence, heard her and looked at her greatly amazed.

"You don't believe me."

"No, no! It's fine. Please come." He then called, "Vinod!"

A brightly dressed, cheerful youth bobbed over. Shamsul said something to him in Bengali and the youth nodded and went over to the other side.

"Miss . . . ?" Shamsul gave her a questioning look.

"Shakira."

"Miss Shakira, which instrument would you like to accompany you?"

"Any would do, but the *tabla* is a must, hmm?"

"It'll be there. I've instructed Vinod."

"Fine."

"First Vizay will do a solo. Then you. What do you say?"

"Perfect."

And when Vijay came up to the mike and introduced her, her face flushed with anticipation. She stepped confidently forward through the applause.

Shamsul's melodious flute joined her beautiful voice, backed by a *sarangi* and violin. Both lost themselves in the ebb and flow of a beautiful *raga*. When the spell broke, Shamsul was awakened from a colourful dream.

This was followed by some short skits. Barman recited a *ghazal,* Bengali style. Zuhra and Anuradha presented a Bengali duet. Last of all, Shakira sang a *mahiya.* Before the curtain fell, the national anthem was sung. Shamsul and Shakira's voices seemed to merge. Both their hearts beat as one, with understanding, sincerity and, above all, patriotism.

The curtain fell. The guests began to leave, amid smiles, laughter and warm goodbyes. Shamsul was involuntarily drawn towards her. "Thank you, Miss Shakira," he said. "Your voice is sheer *mazic!*"

Shakira didn't feel like replying. She just smiled.

"It was a cuckoo bird from the Punzab, I'd say."

"Oh no, Mr. Shamsul Islam. Nothing like that."

"This isn't just the *mazic* of Punzab or Bengal but of all Pakistan." Shakira burst out laughing.

"Have you had some training . . . ?"

"Yes."

"Miss Shakira," he rotated his hands around each other, "I used to think that only a Bengali woman could really understand the spirit of music–but now I've changed my mind."

"No single region can have a monopoly on art."

"No, no. Certainly not!" Shamsul nodded his head emphatically.

"Anyone who works hard . . ."

"Absolutely. Absolutely."

Shakira had thought that he would excuse himself after a short chat, but Shamsul was not about to be gotten away from that easily. He leaned over and asked her secretively, "Miss Shakira, would you join me in my mission?"

"Mission? Is this some *missionary* work?"

"Oh, no," he countered quickly. "Nothing of the sort."

"Then what is it?"

"Well, it is . . ." he put his hand on his chest. "Well, I and my associates have formed an Art Circle. You've just seen one of its programs."

"Oh I see–so this is the Art Circle."

"Yes. It needs a lot of work on the music side, though."

"For example?"

"For example, a Music Academy devoted exclusively to Urdu and Bengali singing–as a completely separate branch of our Art Circle."

Shakira was looking at him uncomprehendingly. Totally absorbed in his plans and mission, he suddenly grabbed Shakira's hand, brought her into the hall cluttered with empty chairs, sat down in one spot and said, "We're the same. You know it."

"Hmmmm."

"And you also know that between East and West Pakistan there's a gap of a thousand miles."

"I know all that."

"Miss Shakira, we're now *one*. Our souls are *one*. Our God is *one* and our Prophet is *one*."

"So?" Shakira was visibly impatient.

"So? We still don't know each other, do we? I don't know who you are and you don't know who I am."

"Well–what can I do about it?"

"I'll tell you." He put his hand on the back of the chair in front of him. "What we'll do is sing together. We'll translate lots of Urdu, Bengali, Punzabi, Pushto and Sindhi songs. Then we'll set them to music."

"It'd take a lifetime. Besides, I am afraid I don't have your determination," she said, getting up. "I'm only here for a few days and then

I have to go back."

"Miss Shakira," he said, without bothering to get up, "when I spot someone suitable for my National Mission, I don't let them slip away. No, sir, I don't. I draft them!"

Shakira burst into laughter seeing him so utterly serious. Then straightening the hem of her floral sari, she tried to humour him.

"I'll get someone back in Lahore to translate those songs for you and . . ."

"Certainly not. Lahore won't do at all. You'll have to stay here in Dhaka and give us your help."

"There are others here who can help you. Besides, it will be a lot easier for me in Lahore to . . ."

"I don't want to hear another word, Miss Shakira."

"Then it's useless to continue," she said, decisively, showing her immense irritation, and continued, "I can't leave my parents, my brothers and sisters to come here and live for your amusement."

She did not even bother to say goodbye and stamped out on to the farm's main lawn. She looked up at the overcast sky above. Lightning was flashing through the dense clouds in the distance.

In addition to being a successful businessman, Uncle Abbas was a travel buff. When Pakistan was created, he had settled down permanently in Bengal. His silk business was thriving splendidly. Thousands of Bengali and non-Bengali labourers were employed in the daily business of breeding silkworms, tending their cages, packing the skeins of thread they helped manufacture for export.

He was a generous man whose ambition was as high as his farm was wide. He had never married, living alone at his sprawling German-style farm in a red brick bungalow nestled comfortably in a grove of banana trees beyond which there were open fields with shady mulberry trees and an interminable green expanse.

Coming to her room Shakira found her dinner neatly laid out for her on the table. She wasn't hungry so she quickly changed and slipped into bed. She started to read a book but her mind was elsewhere, preoccupied with Shamsul. He surely was an odd fellow, who'd just ramble on, caring little to listen to others.

"Some people are just pests," she concluded, "and he's one of them."

She put the book down on the table, turned off the lamp and went to sleep.

The rain pelted down all night, producing a metallic music on the peaked corrugated iron roof. The trees whistled in the strong wind. When she woke in the morning she found everything sopping wet. She was immediately reminded of home. It rained as fiercely in Lahore, too. During the monsoons the cuckoo's song dripped down like juice to sweeten the mango. East or West–the sky's the same everywhere. So are the clouds. And thunder.

She opened a shutter of the window at her bedside. Outside, people were moving about cautiously through the puddles of water. A large gang of labourers, wearing burlap sacks on the head for rain coats, had already arrived at work, which must go on, no matter what the weather.

She was still busy taking in the greenery outside when she was jolted by the sound of a motor scooter. Somebody stomped in and stopped outside her door. It was Shamsul, who was asking her if he could come in.

"Oh no!" Startled, she hurriedly covered her head with the hem of her *dupatta* and froze.

"May I come in, Miss Shakira?" he repeated.

She pulled herself together. "Come in, come in Shamsul Sahib."

"Salam alaikum. I came early today."

"Is everything alright?"

"Fine."

"Then why have you come?"

He sat down in the chair and joyfully said, "Haven't you seen how pleasant it is?"

"Yes . . . very . . ."

"I thought I'd take you to Narain *Ganz*–for an outing, that is."

"What's there?"

"Thought I'd show you the *pat kol*–I mean show you round Badrul Dada's mill."

"You mean the jute mill?"

"Of course."

"But Shamsul Sahib, today . . ."

"I've got big plans for today. There's a lot to be done."

"But I have other plans that don't match yours."

"No if's and but's–please."

Shakira was put off guard by his authoritative manner. She said evasively, "Please have some breakfast first."

"I've already had breakfast."

"At least a cup of tea."

"All right."

She quickly slipped through the door to get away from him but he darted right after.

Uncle Abbas was reading the newspaper at the breakfast table. As soon as he noticed them, he put aside the newspaper and started chatting. The subject was mostly business. He had plans for establishing a poultry farm on a large scale.

"The land's been purchased. Thousands of labourers can be put to work. Along with that they can also do some agriculture."

"Nice idea," Shamsul observed.

"If only you could be persuaded to join us . . ."

"I?" Shamsul started, then proceeded cautiously, "Well, I have started an Art Circle, with a full-fledged Music Academy attached to it."

"Oh forget that," Uncle Abbas said peering through his glasses. "Why waste your time on song and dance? Do something worth your while, young man."

Noticing Shamsul's face contort with displeasure, Shakira quickly moved to hand him a cup of tea and said, "You put your own sugar."

Shamsul set the cup down on the table as though he were spoiling for a fight.

Uncle Abbas babbled on about how important poultry and vegetable farms were for the country's prosperity and progress.

"And cultural institutes–what do you have to say about them?"

"Young man, where are you going to get culture when you can't get pure and affordable food? Who ever heard of a starving man dancing?"

"You're right." Shamsul, who didn't want to get too involved in the argument, just laughed and lowered his head.

Uncle Abbas started explaining that local varieties of chickens had been already procured but the order for the white and red English variety would have to wait until proper arrangements to house them had been made.

Shakira had no interest in the topic, so she ignored it and asked Shamsul instead, "What plans do you have for *your* academy?"

"I," Shamsul picked up some confidence, "well, I will sing to the whole world and glorify the name of my country."

Uncle Abbas tipped his glasses up on his forehead, gawked at Shamsul, and said shaking his head, "Some plans you've got, young man."

"All we need now is some cooperation from the older generation–like yourself."

"You don't expect me to start singing and dancing at my age, do you?"

"Oh I don't mean that. I meant funds."

"Ah . . . that's the crux of the matter!" Uncle Abbas banged his fist down on the table. "It all boils down to money–always. Without it everything comes to a screeching halt."

"Never mind," Shamsul quickly turned his face away. "If Miss Shakira could be persuaded to join us, we will overcome all difficulties."

"Sure you will. Take her along. She'll help you out a lot."

And that slight hint was enough. Shamsul grabbed Shakira's hand and dragged her all the way to where his scooter was parked.

Uncle Abbas gave a prodigious laugh. "That's just fine. Doing something is better than doing nothing at all. What's the use of sitting around the house vegetating."

Everything looked fresh, washed clean in the bright sunlight. Once outside, Shamsul said with a touch of sarcasm, "Miss Shakira, you'll have to stop this 'no' business."

"What 'no' business?"

"Just that you always say 'no' to everything. Well . . . we should quickly get married."

"Who?" she screamed in disbelief.

"You and me . . . that is, East and West."

"But . . ."

"I don't believe in courtship. It's a waste of time. We shouldn't stoop so low. Marriage is a business. Fifty-fifty."

"But I am already engaged."

"So what, I am too!"

"Zaheer's a big journalist, Mr. Shamsul Islam."

"Hashmat Ara isn't exactly a bad looking girl either. She is very pretty, altogether like a doll. But she doesn't have a good voice."

"Back where I come from girls don't marry outside the family."

"Same here. Very, very conservative people."

"Please don't talk like that." She was beginning to feel offended.

"Miss Shakira," his voice dropped, "I suggest we think about the matter with a cool head."

"I don't have to think about it."

"I want to have a link with the West wing," Shamsul explained solicitously. "We are *one*. We must have an understanding before we get together and sing Urdu and Bengali songs."

Shakira stood in silence. She looked peeved.

"This geographical gap between us—we must close it once and for all."

Shakira suddenly felt it was an erudite philosopher, a thinker, a politician, a great national leader who was talking to her in the person of Shamsul. What he was saying began to appeal to her. But she felt diffident, almost vexed, about the thought of breaking the chains of tradition that bound her inexorably to her family, her milieu and her history.

"I'm not the sort of person you might think." He leaned closer. "I can give up Hashmat Ara for my mission."

"It's not a question of West, you know . . ." Shakira pulled back, her thoughts terribly confused. Zaheer was her ideal . . .

"Perhaps you think I'm a pauper."

Shakira was unable to reply.

"Sure I'm penniless. Sure my family is rustic. But they're all well off. Have no fears, Miss Shakira."

"When did I say that?"

"All right. I'll spell it out for you." He turned again to face her. "Look, we've got a jute mill in Narain *Ganz*. Whenever I want I can get a share and join. After all, my brothers, Badrul and Qamrul, are already working there."

Shakira's mind was soaring above the expanse of East and West.

"Our house is very small but it has everything. My mother does all the work by herself. My sister Tara helps her out. Father has set up his own textile mill. We are all Muslims, devout and true Muslims."

Shakira just stood there, lost and uncertain. Finally she asked, with more than just a trace of bitterness, "What are you driving at?"

"Revolution!" he said, putting his hand on hers that was resting on the scooter. "Everyone likes change."

What insanity!—she thought.

"What's this, marry in your own family and stay glued to one place for the rest of your life!"

"So what?"

"So what? So, I must marry Hashmat Ara and rot here in Dhaka, and you with your Zaheer in Lahore–is that it?"

"Certainly!"

"Certainly not! We've got to break this *caze* we've built around ourselves. You won't, I know. But I *will*."

"I can't even begin to think about it."

"You'd better. There's still time. Why do you think I've been beating my brains out since this morning–no, since last night?"

"Heaven forbid!" said Shakira, pulling her ears.

"Look, Miss Shakira, we'll travel from village to village, from town to town, telling people about unity. You know, about love and affection and sincerity?"

"I know," she grimaced.

"Our country sorely needs these things, now more than ever."

There was such unassailable charm in these words that Shakira felt she was ready for a complete change in her life. When she had a talk about the matter with Uncle Abbas, he hastily scribbled a letter off to Lahore and said as he closed the envelope, "He's a crazy, emotional Bengali. Says one thing but will do just the opposite."

It wasn't the time to stand there abashed, like some eastern girl, so she quickly retorted, "What he said was right, uncle. We do need *unity* badly at this time."

"You can achieve this unity without necessarily getting married."

"But one must prove by actual practice what one believes in merely as a theory."

"Shakira, child," Uncle Abbas began as he swivelled in his chair, "it's practically impossible for a plant from one region to take root in the soil of another. Surely you know that."

"This theory has already been proven wrong, uncle. If the soil of the other region is suitable, it will then not only take firm root but also grow sturdy in no time."

"No!" Uncle Abbas snapped crisply. "There's always a tidal wave poised to uproot it. I say this for your own good."

"A strong, healthy plant always stands up against the worst storms . . . and prospers."

No amount of argument was going to persuade Shakira; but Uncle Abbas tried one last time, tenderly, "I know these Bengalis inside out, a lot better than you think you do."

And then he fell silent. What he was saying could not have impressed Shakira at all. His life and all his affairs had become inextricably bound to Bengal; he had settled in this land and said his farewell to the Punjab–how could his words now have carried any weight with anyone, let alone Shakira?

Shakira had now started to accompany Shamsul on his trips to all parts of Dhaka: Tej Gaon, Gulshan, Tongi, Ramna, Lal Bagh, the University, the Stadium–what place was there they hadn't wandered through aimlessly! Together they set up an office for their Music Academy, where they translated songs and set them to music, and gave cultural programs in different parts of the city before crowds of people who looked up to them, sang songs of unity with them, and showered them with flowers.

Daddy's letter from Lahore was curt. Her sister, brother, mother, just about every relative was peeved at the thought of her marrying a Bengali, as though she was about to renounce her religion. Everyone was unanimous that marriage never has brought two nations together, nor it ever will. The dismal end of some such historic marriages was before everyone. All cross-cultural marriage has ever succeeded in doing is to ruin the lives of the very people whom it was supposed to have brought together.

Seeing her waver once again, Shamsul quickly proceeded to allay her fears in a gentle, reassuring voice, "My grandfather was a prominent worker in the Muslim League. He lives in a continuous state of ritual purity. We all offer prayers regularly. Everyone is very religious, devout and conservative. And you won't go outside your family to marry. What a pity!"

Shakira gave him a look of faint, joyous optimism tinged with amazement.

"Take these old *mosjids*. My elders contributed liberally towards building them. They all had faith in Shah Zolal and Saiyid Shahid . . . and Tito Mir was their ideal. Everyone can manage a conversation in Urdu."

Shamsul had to work on both sides. And it wasn't easy. When Hashmat Ara heard about it, she cried herself hoarse. And Boro Ma, who had never ever in her wildest dreams imagined the tender green shoots of the Punjabi grass growing in her own backyard, flew into a rage.

"But she'll massage your legs, mother . . . and she'll take care of the housework also," Shamsul repeatedly explained to Boro Ma in Bengali.

But Boro Ma could scarcely be convinced that a girl reared in a radically different environment would bring her happiness. She would just sit crying by herself when Shamsul wasn't around, or would be overcome by a surge of grief while embroidering a bedspread, or break into uncontrollable sobs while boiling rice. Seeing her slowly consumed away by gloom, Bharati would come over and sit down beside Boro Ma to console her. After all they had been such close neighbours for so long. Holi, Divali, Durga Puja–Boro Ma always wholeheartedly participated with Bharati's family in their Hindu festivals. And it was Bharati who had taught Boro Ma how to put a *tilak* on her forehead in the manner of the Hindu women. On the festivals of Eid and Baqar Eid Bharati would come over with her children and the two families spent the whole day in lighthearted joke and banter. Together Boro Ma and Bharati would go to the shrine of Shah Jalal and offer flowers at his grave. Their sons Shamsul and Vinod had grown up together, and together had nurtured their passion for song and dance.

So Bharati would explain to Boro Ma that there was no difference between a young man and a head-strong horse. "Suppose Shamsul were to run off headlong one day, you'd be left to cry for the rest of your life!"

Bharati's reasoning made sense. Boro Ma could scarcely agree with her more. She would quiet down. But the next instant the thought how it would disgrace her among her kith and kin–as though she were bringing an untouchable in her home–would make her choke. After all, relatives were a strange breed: forever poised against you, on the lookout for the flimsiest pretext to run you down.

Finally, after many a day's thought, maternal affection won out over her misgivings. Her son's heart was like a bubble which she could not mend if it broke.

Even if they were all miffed, Uncle Abbas, Badrul Bhaiya, Dada, Qamrul, Boro Ma, everybody participated in the wedding preparations with the pretense of genuine happiness. Bharati handled everything from decorating the house to greeting and receiving the guests herself, keeping Robin Chacha constantly on the run. Vinod and Tara wrote out the guest list. Badrul Bhaiya got together with Vijay and made arrangements for the preparation of Punjabi and Bengali foods.

Dada gave a helping hand to one and all in their respective chores, but mostly occupied himself with keeping Boro Ma's sagging spirits up.

On the wedding day the sky had cleared after a light rain. The air had an earthy fragrance. The smell of rice paddies came wafting across the distant fields. Everything appeared fresh and colourful. When Shakira–her head covered with a golden dupatta and the red *bindiya* blazing in the centre of her forehead–stepped into her new home, she felt as though she would revel in these colours for the rest of her life. All around her would be green and gold, and not even the slightest shadow of anxiety to cloud her happiness. Life was so pleasant!

When Bharati took Shakira's hand and helped her down the carriage, Qamrul remarked rudely, "There, that's Boro Ma's job."

Bharati quickly put her hand over his still gaping mouth and glared him down from head to foot. Then she pushed everyone aside and said, "For the past four months I've been doing all the dirty work around here just for this day. Just what are you trying to say?"

Qamrul was struck dumb. He shoved his hands into his waistcoat pockets and whirled on his heels. He knew very well the influence Bharati enjoyed over Boro Ma. Better not meddle with her or else she would have Boro Ma throw him out of the house in a minute.

And then he saw Bharati embrace Shakira, kiss her, and escort her in the house through the doorway decorated with fluttering red and green flags.

Bharati seated Shakira on the rush mat in the decorated room. And then she put her hands on her waist and exulted triumphantly, "There now, take a look."

Everyone crowded around, straining to see the bride. Badrul Bhaiya, walking by the room, preoccupied with a number of chores, reacted as though he had suddenly remembered something important. Standing in the door frame, his head bent, Qamrul fumbled through his pockets, patted awkwardly the inside pocket of his *khaddar* shirt, then stuck his hand inside. Everyone burst out laughing.

"The money comes out hard, doesn't it, Badrul Bhaiya?" Vijay chortled nearby.

To hide his embarrassment, Badrul quickly went over to Shakira, thrust his hand forward and dropped the money in Shakira's hand. He then bent slightly to look at her face half-covered with the bridal veil and said, "The bride . . . she's just like a lotus bud." And continued, jokingly, "The bud of Ravi has come to dwell along the banks of the Padma!"

Tara glared at Qamrul: certainly, this wasn't the sort of thing to joke about now. Qamrul quietly sneaked away.

But the cat was out. Everyone gathered around began to whisper. Realizing the situation, Boro Ma rushed to the scene, as if driven by an urgent desire to see the bride. She lifted Shakira's veil in a way as though she were throwing an open challenge to her kith and kin to shut up once and for all: here, take a good look at this enchanting face. If she doesn't look Bengali then what else does she look like? The same sharp eyes, fine-honed features, and rich brown complexion. Even the hair is the same: long and thick and smelling of coconut oil. And the same melodious voice. . . .

Boro Ma stood in silence. The onlookers were breathless, as though a piece of the moon had fallen before them. Tears were poised on Shakira's lashes. Yes, indeed, she was Beauty incarnate!

"Bhabi . . . is so beautiful." Priti drew a deep breath.

"Who says bhabi's not Bengali?" Kiran said after looking at Shakira's hands and feet dyed orange-red in henna.

"What's the matter? If she isn't a Bengali now, she will become one soon." Bharati dropped the veil over Shakira's face. Everyone was jolted, as though out of a dream, and began to laugh.

"Yes, she'll change a lot."

Everything calmed down. The sparks of unease and suspicion, afloat in the air until a little while ago, began to die out. Brimming with maternal affection Boro Ma spontaneously left for her room, returning a minute later with a lot of jewelry. "I secretly saved the money to have this jewelry made for my daughter-in-law," she said to Shakira in a way to draw everyone's attention and to make them have a good look. "Now all of this is yours: these bracelets, these earrings, this forehead pendant–everything." Then taking an embroidered bedspread she had been working on and a patchwork quilt out of a bag, she said, "Here, daughter. I've put lots of love into each stitch. Just for you."

Although Shakira didn't understand everything Boro Ma was saying, she could feel her sincerity. She involuntarily threw her arms around Boro Ma and wept. At that precise moment she remembered her own mother who hadn't even had the decency to answer her letter, let alone offer her a few words of blessing.

She couldn't miss her mother more.

The girls scurried off and soon dragged Shamsul along. Laughing, he stuffed Shakira's mouth with some *sondesh.* This was a comforting moment which bolstered her courage and made her forget her mother. After all, Boro Ma was her mother, too. Sweetness trickled down her throat as though it would permeate her whole life.

Shamsul spontaneously broke into a love song; its every word sinking deep into her soul. If it wasn't for her, then who was it for?

The song ended, and Priti asked through the ensuing applause, "Isn't the bride going to sing?"

"She isn't done blushing yet," Bharati concluded emphatically.

"But she will sing. She will sing tomorrow." Tara seemed to know everything.

The girls raised hell with their laughter. They joined hands to form a circle and in an atmosphere heavy with the scent of roses, marigolds, aloe woodsticks, and perfumed rubbing pastes began to dance.

Priti, Hameeda, Tara, Anuradha, Zahida–it was as if a constellation of stars had fallen to earth. Their long hair, flower-braided, fluttered across their swaying hips, and their fine, diaphanous Banarsi dupattas kept slipping down their shoulders, and the red bindiyas sparkled and blazed ever more brilliantly on their foreheads.

Every now and then Shakira felt someone whispering into her ear– "We are one. . . . From East to West. . . . From the sands of Arabia to the yellow and red mountain regions of China. . . . From the waters of the Nile to the dust of Kashghar. . . . There is no difference between us, not in thoughts, not in customs, not in traditions, not in beliefs. . . ."

The girls were getting worn out from dancing. Shamsul grabbed Shakira's hand and said as he helped her up, "Now this is your home. You'll get tired if you keep on blushing so much."

They left hand in hand. Shamsul brought her into a brightly-lit room where Bikram and Vinod were chatting. Bikram hurriedly got up from an upholstered chair and presenting a sitar to Shakira said, "An artist's gift to a fellow artist. Can there be a worthier gift?"

"Oh," she smiled and unconsciously plucked the strings. A sweet tingling spread through her body.

"But I won't talk about music," said Vinod. "I consider literature to be equally important." He had Nazrul Islam's *Ugni Bina* in his hand. He toyed with the book and continued, "One must read *Gitan-jali* and Nazrul's poetry to understand the Bengali soul."

"But does bhabi know Bengali?" asked Bikram as he looked at Vinod.

"I hope so."

"Well, if she doesn't today, she certainly will tomorrow," said Shamsul as he gave the two a look of deep appreciation. Then he turned to Shakira. "Come on, now," he said with good cheer. "It's your own home. Don't be so shy. Say something. Laugh."

A childlike smile danced on Shakira's lips.

And then Shakira really took root and started to grow like a tiny plant in her own courtyard. For a few days after their wedding Shamsul mostly stayed home. They went out for walks together. This other world of her rebirth was enchanting: the winding rivers; the murmuring brooks; line upon bright line of brooding egrets on the wet sandy beaches at sunset; the rush of sailboats on the twinkling starlit water; grove after grove of swaying coconut and betel-nut trees, with their waving fronds; the wind rustling mischievously through bamboo and banana leaves; the flashes of lightning in the gathering dark clouds; and the claps of thunder. . . .

Whenever the rain prevented her from accompanying Shamsul to the Music Academy, she would spread her mat on the veranda near the *lajwanti* vine. She really enjoyed doing her lessons to the pitter-patter of the raindrops. When the rain came down hard, she would really perk up. She would look joyfully at Tara and say: *"Dhakate bor-sha-kale khub honghota hoy* (In Dhaka it is very cloudy in the rainy season),"* and then turn the page of her book and continue, *"mushaldhare brishti hoy ar rasta-ghat bhije jai* (it rains heavily and the streets are flooded.)"

Tara would laugh at her simplicity and single-mindedness and say, *"Bhabi, apnar desh kon* (Bhabi, what is your country)?"

"Amar desh Pakistan, poshchim Pakistan ar purbo Pakistan—dwiti bhag (My country is Pakistan. West Pakistan and East Pakistan—both parts)."

Tara would drop her work and come and sit next to her. *"Poshchim Pakistaner kon bhag* (What part of West Pakistan)?"

"Ponzab (Punjab)," she beamed.

"Ki Ponzab-te brishti hoy na (Does it rain in Punjab)?"

"Kokhan (When)?"

"Barsha-kale (During the rains)."

Sitting there she would be invaded by memories of home: the Ravi flowing melodiously in its course, the dusty town of Shahdarah whose groves of ancient date palms still reverberated with the sounds of grandiose caravans long since gone by. She would hand over her book to Tara and mull over many things. It would repeatedly occur to her that if she had married Zaheer, they would have certainly gone to Swat or Kaghan for their honeymoon. Her mother would have been overjoyed and her father would have felt fulfilled in her. Since the wedding, only Bajiya had come from Lahore. In a closed room at Uncle Abbas's, Bajiya embraced her tightly and kept crying her heart out as though Shakira had strangled herself. Between sobs she said, "You have caused father and mother tremendous pain. They look miserable! Sick! They're being eaten up inside. You're a murderer, Shakira!"

She felt like a criminal, scarcely able to reply. When Bajiya finally went back to Lahore, she didn't even care to say goodbye to Shakira.

But why was she thinking about all that? She didn't feel sorry. She hadn't done anything wrong. She would shake this train of thought off and get up, then go over and sit down next to Boro Ma and help her make rice crispies.

Despite her age, Boro Ma worked as hard as a busy ant, all day long. She had a little house which she had planted ivy on. She swept and mopped all by herself. She even raised chickens. Outside the house was a pond filled with pink and white lotus blossoms. She would sit right there on the bank and scour the brass utensils to a glittering shine. She would wash the clothes and spread them on the trees to dry, then dive right into the pond. Then after her muslin *dhoti* dried, she would come right back to the kitchen and make such mouth-watering rice and coconut sweets that Shakira would forget everything.

Over a period of time Shakira gained Boro Ma's confidence and, with it, the control of the pantry. She slowly took over her work and gave her a rest. Shakira would massage her legs and scalp. She took over the responsibility of everything from husking the rice to cooking the food. She began to feel a sense of belonging when occupied with the cleaning and kitchen work as though she'd been doing it for years. And whenever she got a break from work, she'd sit down with a Bengali book.

As time wore on, the world of song was buried within the confines of those four walls. She'd feel tired every time there was a cultural show, which made Shamsul wonder. What plans they'd made together! The sorts of things they had wanted to do and show to the world! Whatever happened to those grand plans? How things had changed, and so imperceptibly!

"I'd like you to translate a song, Shakira Begum," he would say to her.

"I'll do it," she would reply, nonchalantly.

"When? It really is important."

"It may be important, but Boro Ma hasn't been feeling well."

"She'll never feel well."

"But now I have to do all her work."

"Leave it. It's her work."

She would give him an anguished look, but a preoccupied Shamsul would continue, "Vinod wrote the song. It's a great one."

"I'm sure it is." She'd quickly begin making Boro Ma's bed. "Yesterday I brought her some medicine but it didn't do any good, and now she has a bad cough."

"Huh. Medicine won't work its magic in a day," he would say, irritated.

"She has a headache and perhaps even a fever."

"She'll get better on her own."

"How will she just on her own? We'll have to take her to a doctor."

"Tell her to go herself."

Shakira would stop her work and glare at him. "You don't care about your mother at all?" she would ask.

"Whoever does?"

Shamsul's caustic attitude would burn into her soul. She would sit down next to him with head bowed. He had been prone to making such heartless remarks for the past few days.

"The song is really first class. It's about unity." He'd sing it for her in Bengali. "We've got the tune, now all it needs is to be put into Urdu."

"Get a secretary," would come Shakira's exasperated reply.

"What about you, Shakira Begum?"

"What will Boro Ma say?" she'd say, looking around.

Shamsul would get up without saying a word, frightening Shakira, and she knew she'd have to do something to keep peace around the house.

When she'd hurry through the housework, Boro Ma, sitting on the straw mat, would try to cheer her up. "All of your Boro Ba's ancestors came from West Pakistan and settled here."

Shakira would lapse into thought: What was the difference between all of them and her? Granted there was a space of a thousand years between them and herself, but every person's relationship to life was the same. How many generations have to be buried before one can be called an inhabitant of the land his dead are under?

For the previous few days Boro Ma had been getting weaker. She wanted someone to be near her all the time, and she'd talk on so that Shakira didn't have a break to think about her own ancestors. Who were they? What were they? and where did they come from?

Boro Ma would sit there and show her how to weave mats and sometimes how to make wicker baskets. She was good at her work and had made lots of handbags and furniture.

Shakira was intelligent and quickly learned much from their talks. When there was no more work, she'd help make Tara's trousseau. She'd make such dazzling embroidery that Boro Ma would feel overjoyed. Both would put their heads together and talk of close, sweet things for hours on end.

Boro Ma yearned to see her courtyard filled with children. After four years of prayers and waiting, Munna was born and she was ecstatic. For Shakira, the sky was bluer and the trees greener.

"This is a new shoot, nourished by the blood of East and West." The sight of Munna filled her with unbounded joy. "His roots run deep, stretching from the Padma all the way to the Ravi. All his ancestors were from the West."

"My Munna will be a great singer," said Shamsul one day after silently walking up behind her. She was sitting in the courtyard rocking Munna's cradle. In the sparkling golden sunlight Munna seemed like a little sleeping angel.

"He'll conquer the world with his songs!" Then Shamsul lifted him up and swung him around so hard that Munna began to bawl.

"He'll fall! Hey! Hey!" screamed Shakira, alarmed. She shot up and took him back into her arms.

"You don't know how to hold babies."

"You think I've been holding them all my life?"

"And I have?"

"Speak Bengali, Baba."

"No, Urdu."

"My Munna will speak Bengali and he'll be a great Bengali poet. A real Nazrul!"

"My Munna will speak Urdu," Shakira said, putting Munna's cheek to hers, "and he'll be a superb Urdu poet. A real Iqbal."

"No way. Munna will be a Nazrul. A *Bengali* poet."

"Munna will be an *Iqbal.* Not just for Pakistan but a poet of the whole Islamic world."

"Nazrul's a better poet than Iqbal," Shamsul jabbed at her for his own amusement.

"Ha! Who believes that?" She wanted to parry his mean thrust.

"Iqbal's message is universal, while Nazrul just sings about *his* land."

"Nazrul's book *Ugni Bina* is beyond compare."

"Yeah, sure. I've read it." Shakira bristled. "If God gave you the sense to read *Bal-e Jibril,* then your eyes would pop open."

"My eyes are open as far as they go, Shakira Begum," said Shamsul, stamping his feet.

Shakira, who in her imagination had dug her heels into this land, suddenly found herself faltering. She didn't have the slightest idea why such trivial things had suddenly become annoying. The distance between them began to grow.

"I said, Munna will speak Urdu!" she screamed.

"Why Urdu?" snapped Shamsul. "I'll make sure he's educated."

"Because Urdu is the national language."

"Who goes along with that?"

"Shamsul," she sobbed. The building storm suddenly blew itself out. Was it some weakness in her or a change in the political climate? She felt as though she had been dipped in icewater right up to her neck. She looked into Shamsul's fiery eyes and said gently, "He can speak both. Both will be his languages. Now what's wrong?"

Shamsul couldn't bear to stay there any longer. He left in a huff. After that he never picked up Munna with any joy. Now he'd try to keep his distance. He would come home late and Shakira would stay awake waiting for him.

Time wore on. The unrest grew. Munna was growing up. He was barely a year old when the atmosphere grew ominous. The sweet songs of unity between East and West went sour and didn't rhyme anymore. The cacophony of shouts and slogans was deafening. The tide of placards and banners surged up. Ghirao, strikes and arson were commonplace. Brother Badrul and Qamrul spent most of their time at the jute mill. Dada was already standing guard over his textile mill. Shamsul was in cahoots with Vinod and Vijay. Shakira had no idea what they were up to. All day long Boro Ma would stay huddled with Bharati. Everyone was secretive. How did everything change so fast? Shakira felt cut off from everybody.

From morning that day the walls of the house shook with the sound of bullets and shellfire. Rattled, Uncle Abbas announced, "Our lives are in danger!"

"I don't have anything to fear. I'm in my own home."

Her unshakable confidence sent Uncle Abbas back with much of what he wanted to say left unsaid.

Shakira would think that she was a symbol of sacrifice and love. What could anyone do to her? But the way Boro Ma had about-faced –she had never expected that. Boro Ma would cry hysterically, tear her hair, beat her breast. Her feet would feel like they were being jabbed with needles. And as quick as she would hear a gunshot, she'd leap over to confer with Bharati. How she had changed! She'd glower at Shakira with such burning hostility as if she would suck the blood from her veins and leave her writhing in the slaughterhouse.

"You will get us into trouble," Boro Ma exploded with all her might. "You'll bring us untold suffering."

Shakira, her chin on her knees, vacantly staring off into space, was thinking: am I not a Bengali now? Let someone talk to me in Bengali. I'd reply in pure, polished language. Haven't I pored over Bengali literature? Let someone have a discussion with me. Can't I sing *bhatiya?* Can't I enchant others with a Bengali folksong? Can anyone cook fish and rice better than I? I can even make coconut sweets and rice crispies. I can embroider, weave wicker baskets and . . . and . . .

Boro Ma's screech jolted her out of her feeling of love and belonging. She felt as though even the storm's slightest gust was enough to uproot love's tender sapling.

"The song of unity will turn into a dirge, Shakira," Shamsul said worriedly. "They'll douse Munna with petrol and set him on fire! They'll drag you through the streets of Calcutta . . ."

Shakira gave him an unbelieving look. Shamsul was out of his mind. He was yelling, "For God's sake go back to the Punzab!"

She was shaken to her soul. She grabbed Munna and clutched him to her breast as she cried uncontrollably. Her tears fell and soaked into the very ground that up to now she had thought her own.

The factory smokestacks stopped belching smoke. The sky was covered with an ominous cloud of smoke from the tanks spewing shells. Crows and vultures descended on the rotting bodies in unending hoards. The blood of East and West flowed together, staining the hands of Abel as well as of Cain.

Boro Ma would now constantly stick with Bharati. Shakira's presence was a threat to her life. Anuradha had taken Tara to her village. And Shamsul–no one could say what he was up to.

Markets of human bones and flesh had opened in the streets and towns. The Hindu merchant happily danced on piles of skulls.

Uncle Abbas's silk farm had already been looted and he'd decided to go back to the Punjab empty-handed.

"You should go with your uncle, Shakira," said Shamsul unemotionally.

". . . And you?"

"I'll stay here. This is my country."

". . . And Munna?"

"He'll stay with me, of course," he said.

Shakira couldn't comprehend any of this. Shamsul continued, "He's Bengali. He's my son."

"I can't give up my Munna," she said wistfully.

"Tara'll look after him."

Shakira let the tears roll down her face. That was all she could do; she would like to die beside all of them but who would know.

When Shamsul saw how desolate she was, he softened a bit and said gently, "There's only hatred out there. I don't even know what will happen to me."

Her tears continued to flow. Now they were her constant companions.

"When I'm out there, I belong to my friends. I forget that I have ties with both East and West. When I come in here, then . . ."

Shakira continued to silently pat Munna. After so many days Shamsul had finally sat down with her. She didn't have the courage to complain about anything.

Who knows how the house caught fire that night. Boro Ma put all the blame on Shakira for not putting out the fire in the hearth. There was always a fire in the hearth but it had never gone out of control and that night she had carefully extinguished it. She had even carefully put away all the dishes in the cupboard. Only when she had finished all the kitchen work and come out had she seen Vinod's fleeting silhouette in the moonlight.

The fire was quickly extinguished but she spent the night on burning coals.

Shamsul was in a quandary: he couldn't stay in the house, nor could he go out. He'd endlessly try to prove his loyalty and patriotism to his friends but to no avail. In their eyes he was a Punjabi agent who had married a non-Bengali woman.

Finally, with her heart sinking, she picked up Munna and walked barefooted into the starry night. Shamsul walked along, drained, an empty shell of a man.

Barely saving their lives, enduring adversity and starvation, when they finally reached Lahore via Bangkok, Shamsul had left his soul somewhere behind.

Uncle Abbas took them in and put them up in a two-room flat. Shakira now started rebuilding her nest twig by twig. In her spare time she would tutor the neighbourhood kids or embroider bedspreads. Shamsul had found work as a musician and worked by contract.

Out of consideration for Shamsul, she didn't allow her house to have a Punjabi air. She grew creepers on a bamboo trellis off the veranda. She laid rush mats in the rooms. She hung pictures of fishermen in sailboats floating on the waves of the Ganges and Padma and scenes of lush rice fields basking in the golden sunlight. Now she cooked only Bengali dishes. Deep inside she didn't want to see Shamsul grow apart from her in mind and heart. She would weave beautiful baskets and ceaselessly arrange flowers in them. She would make colourful quilts. She got rid of all her old clothes and adopted the sari as her dress. She'd smile when she'd put a flower in her hair and in every way try to greet Shamsul in a distinct Bengali manner.

She was busy sewing when he came in one evening. He silently prowled through the whole house, then went over to her and said, "Will Lahore ever come to be a Dhaka?"

"What do you think?" A beautiful smile played across her lips.

"Me?" Contempt spread over his face. "Shall I *really* tell you?"

This alarmed Shakira. She looked over his face vacuously trying to catch even a glimmer of past love.

He sat down on the stool and began pulling off his shoes. He radiated hatred. Acrid superiority boiled up in his face. Wrinkling his nose, he said, "Gardens–no good. No real rain, just dried up clouds. I've taken a look at your Punzab. A real good look. The rice is rotten and the fish stinks."

"Shamsul!" she yelled, anguished. "It's the same rice here that used to be sent over there to you people. How can you say all this?" Shamsul broke into a crazed cackle.

"We'll get even with you Punzabi people for this army action."

"Tell me, Shamsul, for God's sake tell me. What does any government in the world do to suppress a rebellion?"

"I've heard it all." Shamsul was not about to give in.

"I've never seen rebels walking away with garlands around their necks in any country. Little do you know the Hindu mentality."

"I don't need to."

He was now completely fed up with her. He had often thought that if his wife had been Bengali, he would have stayed in Bengal and wouldn't have had to be tossed around like this.

Now he had started hanging out with his Bengali friends. Together they formed a Bengal Club where they would vent their rage. All day and all night they'd talk about the separation of East Pakistan and sing songs of Bengali patriotism. They'd play cards and occasionally also chess. They'd smoke endlessly and vow to sacrifice their lives for their rights and their hopes.

Shakira would look despairingly from one imprisoning wall to the other like a caged bird with Uncle Abbas's words ringing in her ears, "He's a crazy sentimental Bengali; he'll say one thing but do just the opposite."

Little had she suspected Shamsul would change so much.

She passed the period of the December War in unmitigated suffering. Now even Munna's antics and infectious laughter couldn't cheer her up. She stumbled around aimlessly as though she had knowingly taken the wrong path. She was in a constant state of mourning. Whenever she opened her mouth to say something, tears would precede her words.

On the day the news of the Pakistani army's surrender in Dhaka came, the Bengal House was done up like a bride. It was an unexpected shower of happiness. Sweets were passed around and consumed joyfully. The celebration went on late into the night. Everyone danced drunkenly, congratulating one another on their freedom.

Shamsul staggered into the house with glazed eyes. Shakira was standing at the window, sorrow personified. Her hair was in disarray and her face unwashed, not to mention her clothes unchanged. Life no longer held any attraction for her.

"*Zoe* Bangladesh!" Shamsul plopped down on the stool and slammed down his coat. She gave him a forlorn look.

"You didn't say *zoe.*"

She didn't answer but her eyes welled up with tears.

"An independent and great country! Bangladesh! How I'm happy today!"

Shakira turned away.

"Well? Why does my happiness bug you so much. *Why?*"

She looked out the window and stammered, "Sh-Sh-Shamsul?"

"Yeah?"

"I wonder why we got married."

"Me, too. Hashmat Ara was all right."

"That's what I regret."

"What's that?"

"That if today I'd been married to Zaheer, then . . ."

"That's fine," sneered Shamsul. "You're still stuck on Zaheer!" he screamed with burning jealousy. "I'm not staying here any longer. I'm going to Canada, and my son Munna with me." He leapt over to Munna who was playing on the floor.

"Lay a hand on Munna and . . ." Shakira shrilled and struck forward like a bruised serpent.

"And what?"

"I'll jump to my death in a well," she said without thinking. Darkness swirled around her.

"Oh, a well. If you had the urge to commit suicide, then you should have offered yourself in Dhaka, and at least I could have said you died for unity."

That threw her for a loop.

"You of all people say something like that? You?"

"Yes, me. Shamsul. I said it."

"You weren't like this before."

"Circumstances have made me like this!" he bellowed. "You Punzabi people have looted our homes. You started an army action. Your army has razed Bengal. You've exploited our rights, you vagabonds!"

"Come to your senses," Shakira said gently as she sat down next to him and patted his shoulder. "Don't be misled by the enemies' lies.

Look at your home."

"I have no home. You've done a great injustice to us Bengalis."

"Injustice? What kind of injustice? Think with a cool head."

Shamsul's eyes burned into her.

"Look at me. Just look at me. Haven't I been a victim of injustice?"

"Not a bit."

"I abandoned my home and my country for you, Shamsul."

"I'm going to Canada. Our worlds are completely different."

"What about Dhaka?"

"I'll see how things go. I can't live there with a Punzabi wife."

"But you're Bengali."

"I'm not Bengali anymore. I go there and they'll kill me. They'll say, 'His wife is Punzabi.' I stay here and I'm a dead man. They'll say, 'He is Bengali! Kill him!' "

"No, Shamsul. It's not like that."

"This isn't my country."

"Our country is Pakistan. East and West Pakistan."

Shamsul leapt up and, putting his hand over her mouth, yelled, "My country is Bangladesh. That's it!"

She pushed his hand away, "East Pakistan," she screamed from the depths of her soul. "East Pakistan, not once, not twice, but a hundred times, East Pakistan!"

"Bangladesh!"

"East . . ." She made it that far when Shamsul pushed her aside violently. She fell face down on the floor. Tears flooded her eyes and sobs squeezed from between her lips.

Shamsul stamped out, never to return. His entire world shrank to the confines of the Bengal Club. Shakira's world was ripped apart. Even playing with Munna gave her no happiness. Every so often Uncle Abbas would put his hand on her head and gently say, "I told you. A plant from one region can't be transplanted to another."

Now she would sit quietly by him. Whenever there was work, she would quietly get up and do it–her only respite from feeling suffocated and terribly lonely.

Then one day Uncle Abbas told her that Qamrul alone had been able to make it to Karachi.

"Why did he . . . ?"

"Shamsul phoned today and said that Qamrul came via Nepal."

"Did he say anything else?" Shakira couldn't hide her eagerness.

"He had a lot to say. But he kept coming back to, 'I'm ashamed of the way I've treated Shakira.' "

Try as she would, she was unable to contain her tears.

"He's coming here today. Qamrul's coming, too."

"What's here for him, uncle?"

He didn't care to reply, expressing, as it were, through his silence, "You know best."

Shakira was restless throughout the entire day and even though she tried to overcome her anxiety and concern by acting nonchalant, her true feelings were apparent in her every action.

It was evening when Shamsul entered downcast and with bloodshot eyes. Shakira turned away and went into her room. He followed like a whipped child.

"Shakira," he said in a voice that she had yearned so long to hear. "I came to apologize."

"For what?"

"Because I made you miserable."

"You were going to Canada."

"No! No!" Shamsul quickly put his hand over her mouth.

"What brings Qamrul here?"

Shamsul heaved a sigh, then put his head in his hands and said, "Brother Badrul, Dada . . . everyone. The Hindus murdered them all. The Marwaris plundered their jute mill."

"But they were Bengali. They had lived on the land for generations."

"They were Bengali . . . but Muslim."

". . . and Boro Ma?"

Shamsul's face blanched. His throat tightened. In a choked voice he said, "Vinod sold Tara off in Calcutta and hacked Boro Ma to pieces."

". . . and Dada?" asked Shakira, numbed.

"They tied him up with rope, doused him with petrol and . . ." He couldn't go on. He was drained.

After a pause, Shakira spoke up. "You've got your Bangladesh after all. Its soil is dyed with your blood. Shout, 'Long live Bangladesh!' Now you're a free citizen of an independent country."

"Shakira! Shakira Begum!" Shamsul pleaded. "We didn't want this sort of freedom."

"Now there will be a Hindu Raj and all you Bengalis will be slaves of the Hindus. Say it! Long live Bangladesh! Say it! Say it! Long live Bangladesh!"

For five months Shakira had ached to spit the boiling poison in her heart into Shamsul's face, but Shamsul pleadingly stretched out his hand to her. Shakira curtly brushed it aside. Shamsul grabbed her hand with a feeling of utter helplessness. It was an entreaty. There was the soft, light warmth which was there the very first day. Amazed, Shakira looked hard at him. There were tears in his eyes.

Then, still clutching her hand, he sat down on the floor and bitterly cried, "We are one, Shakira Begum."

Shakira wiped his tears with the corner of her sari and looked at him as though she didn't believe a thing he said.

Translated by Muhammad Umar Memon and Wayne R. Husted

IKRAMULLAH

The Needy

Late in the morning every day, following Nooran and holding firmly
on to the same bamboo staff, Fattoo and Bakhshu could be seen going
through the city streets and roads, feeling their way with their feet and
singing loudly until they reached the steps of the Jamia Mosque. Then
fat Bakhshu plunked down noisily, his legs crossed, leaning against
the pillar which stood at the foot of the steps to the right. Next to his
left knee sat Fattoo. Nooran would lay the staff under their knees,
place the aluminum bowl in front of them and go to get hot tea from
the vendor who sat on a cotton rug a little distance from them with his
samovar. Horse-drawn tongas passed by, tapping along the road. Cars
went honking and raising dust in the street. The sound of firm, young
feet, the dragging spash of old feet inserted in slippers; the twitter of
children going to school–every sound filtered through their cocked
ears as they sat there waiting for the tinkle of a coin in their bowl.

A whole crowd of beggars used to gather there, in front of the steps
of the Mosque, waiting for some good fortune to befall them. One of
them humbly pleaded for charity. A few stared at the passersby,
eagerly racing a few paces after them, before returning to sit down
near the steps. Another simply stood there silently, extending his begging bowl–the image of sorrow incarnate. Yet another repeated the
same line over and over again from a eulogy for the Prophet, sounding like a record with the needle stuck. And yet another recited
devoutly and in all humility some nonsense as though it were a verse
from the Qur'an. Some, apparently unconcerned with begging, sat on
the steps, one leg on top of the other, mending their rags. And some
sat and nodded, having hung their tattered quilts and ugly blankets on
the stair wall to dry. In all this rumpus, Fattoo and Bakhshu raised

their cry of "Give, O generous ones, in the name of the Lord" in so high-pitched a voice that they could be heard above the din in the street.

After finishing the tea, Nooran would sit close to Bakhshu's right knee and, perhaps, to give them heart, sometimes join her voice to theirs. Bakhshu, sitting between the two of them, evinced great aplomb and confidence. His shirt stayed open at the chest casually revealing a bushy growth of black and grey hair. This growth seemed to join his disorderly beard going all the way up to the deep sockets of his eyes where slices of red flesh could always be seen quivering. On his head was a veritable forest of salt-and-pepper hair. He always kept his bison-like neck turned so that his ear could stay in line with the bowl. Fattoo was thin, middle aged and, in his own way, very meticulous about his clothes. On his head he wore a fez, red at one time, now black with grime. He wore a long coat buttoned up at the collar, its original colour untraceable because of its numerous patches of different colours; however, its buttons, of different sizes and colours, were always properly done. In his bluish cadaverous face his marble-white swollen eyeballs revolved slowly and aimlessly. The only growth of hair was on his chin, and it had turned inward like a goatee.

The three of them–Fattoo, Bakhshu and Nooran–had just about appropriated this particular spot near the Mosque. If anyone else attempted to occupy it, the blind men's repeated hits with the staff and Nooran's endless obscene swearings made sure that the attempt came to nothing. When the tinkle of a coin came from the bowl, Bakhshu would extend his hand and take the coin out. Then slipping his hand along Nooran's thigh he would bury the coin in her fist, at the same time giving her a gentle pinch. Fattoo, impatient to find out what the coin was, would stop his call, bend down towards Bakhshu and ask him, "What was it?" Finding no answer from him, he would extend his arm across Bakhshu's back and pull at the hem of Nooran's headcloth and ask her, "What was it? You tell me."

"A ten-paisa coin. What else do you think?"

Part believing her and part not, he would say, "Maybe you are right, but to me it sounded distinctly like a quarter-rupee."

Then Bakhshu, in a decisive tone of voice, would settle the matter: "Gone are the days when people parted with quarters. Nowadays even a ten-paisa coin is a great blessing."

Bakhshu and Fattoo had been living together for many years. On the bank of the city's open sewer, they had built a sort of hut for themselves with crooked pieces of wood and a piece of rusted tin used as a roof. From the same tin they had made the four walls and even fashioned a door. Their hut was the safest place possible in the city. The Municipal Committee did not bother them, nor did any landlord ask them for rent; they didn't even fear being evicted by someone else desiring to occupy that spot.

The only problem was that of the bad smell of the sewer, but gradually their noses had become used to it. From their hut the glaring city lights seemed distant like the twinkling stars. In this hut, buried in silence and darkness, the noise of the city reached them as if it were coming from another world. Sometimes when a car took a turn the hut was suddenly bathed as though by lightning, only to plunge back into darkness just as quickly.

Almost a year ago, having gone through two or three husbands and tried her luck on the city streets, and despairing in her middle years both of husbands and clients, Nooran had been forced to become a beggar and had turned to the steps of the Jamia Mosque. She sorely regretted being childless. At her age now, when her blandishments had lost their appeal and her coquetry and playfulness seemed distinctly ludicrous, the children would have been so useful. There was nothing she had not tried; she had made vows at shrines, bought amulets from spiritual guides, tried spells and necromancy, but all proved utterly useless–she couldn't conceive. She who as a streetwalker could clean her clients out playfully now found it difficult to ask for charity. A few times she did muster enough courage to extend her hand and beg for money, but no hearts warmed to her plea. She was neither a cripple, nor sick, nor even young. Being crippled or sick, a disadvantage in her previous profession, would have helped greatly now. Her youth had brought her to the streets earlier; now her good health was driving her to her ruin.

What strange paradoxes does nature bring out! Nothing ever seems to work in the same way twice. What was a blessing yesterday becomes a curse today. Young girls were collecting alms with both hands. Coins were constantly falling into Bakhshu and Fattoo's begging bowl. In her small dirty eyes a new idea sparkled suddenly. She came and sat down on her haunches near Bakhshu. He become conscious, as he slipped a coin inside his deep shirt pocket, that someone was near him. He assumed it was a beggar trying to establish a perch.

Fearing the loss of his monopoly Bakhshu spoke in some heat, "Get lost, you, or I'm going to use this staff on year head. This is our place. Go beg somewhere else." Fattoo also ordered, "Be off, man. No one else besides us can beg here!"

Making her voice full of entreaty, Nooran answered, "O brothers, I am not a beggar. I just sat down to have a little rest." Then slinking away a little she added, "All right, if it bothers you, I'll move away."

Contented by her replies, the two of them once again began voicing their pleas. In the meanwhile a passerby tossed a coin towards them and moved away. The coin struck the rim of the bowl and bounced off to the ground. Bakhshu finding the bowl empty started scouring the ground with his hands looking for the coin, as a dog looks for a thrown bone with his snout. Nooran picked up the coin, cleaned it by blowing air on it from her mouth and put it on Bakhshu's open palm, saying, "Here, take it. It's a half-rupee."

"Oh, really! A full half-rupee!" Then he addressed Fattoo, "Hey, we nearly lost a fortune. It's so nice of this good woman to have picked it up and given it to us."

When they were tired of screaming their requests, Bakhshu got up and started walking towards the tea-seller, feeling his way with his feet. Nooran jumped up to help him and held his hand saying, "Oh, dear, how could you do that, walking without any support? What if you had stumbled? Why did you not tell me what you wanted? What am I here for?"

Never in his life, ever since he had been weaned from his mother's breast, had Bakhshu met with such an overflow of human sympathy. What mankind owed to him, he was used to receiving it in the form of a few tossed coins, and both he and mankind were content with this arrangement. The touch of the unknown female hand and the tone of voice full of concern swept him away in a torrent of pleasure as a piece of straw is swept away in a flood. The slices of pink flesh in the sockets of his eyes quivered vigorously. For the first time in his life that day, in his empty eyes he felt a violent emotion which wanted to erupt and wash everything around in its effulgence. Confused and perturbed he stood, as if in the square of a magical city, panting like a bull. "I . . . I . . . for tea . . ." he tried to speak, but Nooran led him by the arm to his usual perch. "You sit here quietly. I'll get tea for you," she assured him.

That night Nooran tagged along with them to their hut. Now, every morning, before leaving for the Mosque, Nooran diligently locked the hut and tied the key to the drawstring of her trousers. On the way back in the evening she bought flour and lentils, etc., and cooked the meal inside the hut. That kept the hut both warm and lit and saved money on both counts. When the food was ready, she brought both the men near the fire and made them sit down. Then she placed the bowls of lentils in front of them and made them hold the flat bread in their hands. Feeling with their hands, they first determined the location of the bowls and then, fixing them firmly on the ground, began eating noisily. After the meal Nooran talked to them about the day's income and expenditure. Whatever was left, she divided it up in three parts, giving Fattoo his and keeping Bakhshu's and her own share with her. Fattoo used to check each coin by feeling it, count his share and often protest. "Today was Friday," he would grumble. "We should have got eight annas each. There are only six." Feigning helplessness Nooran would say, "See, such is my luck: I slave for him, I cook for him, and I feed him; all the same, he accuses me of cheating." Seeing such injustice being done to "his" Nooran, Bakhshu would flare up: "You bastard; you call us dishonest. You wretched son of a bitch, pick up your things and get the hell out of here. Right now!" Both hands spread in front of him, a subdued and crouching Fattoo would slowly walk back towards his cot. Behind, a smile of triumph would spread on Nooran's face. Tucking a small pouch full of bank notes in the belt-loop of her trousers, she would place a loving hand on Bakhshu's shoulder and implore him, "Oh, forgive him. His bad habits can't be helped." If Nooran hadn't already estimated that two blind men can attract the public's attention and sympathy more easily than one, she would have driven Fattoo out of the hut a long time ago. Her business-woman's mind had become convinced long ago that Fattoo's departure would reduce their income by more than a half.

Nooran and Bakhshu would then lie down on the cot and wrap themselves inside the same quilt. Alone, Fattoo would nurse his loneliness in his bed and hear the sweet slow whisperings of love coming from the other bed. Sometimes Nooran's suppressed laugh would jump out of the quilt and fall on his ears like molten lead. He would squirm and wrap the quilt around his ears more firmly.

Never before in his life had he felt so alone. His cot felt to him like his grave. He thought of going to Bakhshu and telling him how lonely and wretched he had been feeling of late. He and Bakhshu had been sharing everything in their lives for the past thirty years, but Bakhshu had had Nooran to himself for a whole year. He wanted him to share her with him, lend him her sweet whisperings for one night. What harm could there be if her laughter boiled over from his quilt for one night? But the fear of receiving incessant blows from Bakhshu held him back. Burning in the cauldron of desires, whenever Fattoo found Nooran alone in the hut, his mind became filled with loudly hissing, poisonous vipers of passion. Perturbed by the dreadful hissing of the thousands of snakes, Fattoo, in sheer desperation and without the least constraint, would try to hold on to that feeling of coolness called Nooran and pull her towards his chest, but the pelting down of abuse from her lips, as she herself squirmed in his arms to get away from him, would quickly drive away the madness which had earlier transported him to the very gates of heaven. He would once again return to his usual inferno of consciousness where he smouldered away like a wet log moistened by care and caution. If only he could catch fire and incinerate! The whole of him and in one fell swoop! That, at least, might put an end to this constant smouldering! One evening when Bakhshu had gone out of the hut for a while, Fattoo unloosened the pouch stacked with bank notes from his belt, placed it in front of Nooran's feet and stood there, his hands folded together. Nooran was sitting before the fire baking the flat bread. He told her that he was willing to offer all that money to her, and whatever else he earned from that day onward if she would once, only once, come to his bed. For a moment Nooran was tempted. Her hand moved towards the money, but then it occurred to her that she could take that money away from him whenever she wanted. Where could he take it? But if she allowed him even a little liberty, he would come totally undone. His demands would increase everyday and if Bakhshu found out about the two of them, her whole game will be ruined. She was lucky to have found this roof over her head; where else would she go looking for another one? Showing deference to the intensity of his feeling, she spoke to him patiently: "Fattoo, come on, keep your money. You know it well I'm Bakhshu's woman. Why do you talk like that?"

"But you were never married to him—were you?" Fattoo said. "And, besides, I'm not asking you to do it every day. Just once—that's all."

"Listen," Nooran said, "I've told you many times before, if you don't stop this nonsense, I'll have to tell Bakhshu. He will blow up. A fight won't be good for you. Use your brains sometimes."

Fattoo flared up suddenly. His white, round marble eyes quivered fast, and despite his effort to subdue his voice, a sharp cry emitted from his clenched teeth and frothing lips. "Use brains! Brains! You bitch, you bastard!"

As his anger subsided, he fell into an abyss of despair. He was no longer conscious of his loneliness or helplessness, nor did he feel any jealousy; he was no longer sad at someone else's victory, or at his own defeat. Each and everyone of his desires had been crushed. Nooran, in rejecting him, had shredded his personality and thrown the bits to the wind. Many times he tried to locate himself within his being but failed. The bubbling laughter from the bed nearby now fell on him as water on stones, making no impact at all.

After that incident he became totally unconcerned with Nooran. Neither her closeness nor his own loneliness perturbed him. He suggested to Bakhshu, "Look, Bakhshu, Nooran has perforce become our partner. She's of no use to us. I think we should ask her to move out. We can easily get our food from the inn-keeper as before." But Bakhshu answered him curtly: "If you don't want to live with us, you are free to pick up your things and leave." With a pert response like that Fattoo could do nothing but give up and wait patiently.

One day after going through the city, when their group reached the steps of the Jamia Mosque, they found a blind young boy of eighteen or nineteen sitting in their place and in his melodious voice singing "Call me to the city of lights, Prophet." Earlier on whenever someone by chance or mistake happened to occupy their place, they would drive him away. Likewise, today, Bakhshu told the boy, "Go somewhere else, young man. This is our place." The boy moved his neck sideways like a parrot and, smiling, said, "The land belongs to God. You can sit here just as I can."

This enraged Bakhshu. The veins of his neck and forehead swelled up. Giving the boy a hard push, he said, "Get away from here you pig's off-spring. I told you once, politely, to do that. I don't want to hear any more nonsense from you." Nooran and Fattoo also started screaming their heads off and swearing. The boy staggered a bit but then steadied himself, and with the help of his bamboo staff, walked over to the other side of the steps. There he stood next to the pillar and began singing his "Call me to the city of lights" again. After settling down, these three also started bellowing their "Give, O generous ones," sounding like torn dreams. The boy's voice, like something sweet and magical, was attracting the passersby. He sang continually, one eulogy of the Prophet after another. Coins were raining down in his begging bowl. The tinkling of the coins in his bowl was like bullets hitting the breasts of these three. It was almost noon and they hadn't even collected enough money for their lunch. They were squirming to see their livelihood being thus stolen from them. What to do? Bakhshu threatened to hit him with his shoes and shove him down the steps. But Nooran said disdainfully, "What difference would that make? He would pull people with his sensuous voice wherever he is." Bakhshu said, "In that case, get him off this street altogether." Fattoo peevishly resisted the idea, "You are not the boss of a gang of thugs to be able to do that. If we make too much noise, people will more likely beat up on us . . . with their shoes." Bakhshu suggested, "Maybe then we should give up this place and go sit outside the gate of the District Courts." Nooran said, "But what sense is there in giving up a place we have had for years. There are many beggars outside the courts. We don't know if we'd get any proper place there." Then suddenly Nooran thought of something. Moving the two closer to her by their shoulders, she whispered, "Why not ask him to join us?" Fattoo and Bakhshu vehemently disagreed, but Nooran explained, "Listen. Don't be stupid. We can double our income by making him our partner. He looks like a simpleton come straight from the village. It doesn't look like he has a place to eat or sleep. He is surely a stranger in town. He is blind. In a new place how is he going to live? He would need help at every step. Let me talk to him. I'm sure he'll agree. We have nothing to lose." The two finally relented, "Alright, as you wish."

That evening Nooran was leading a troop of three men to the hut. Their income had really doubled because of that blind boy, Ahmad. Day and night, the three of them would fawn on him, treating his every wish as a command. Ahmad–who back in the village, had been a mere unclaimed orphan, loudly singing eulogies of the Prophet every Friday at the village mullah's behest and begging for scraps of food– had suddenly become well-to-do and important. He was happy with and proud of this change in his life. With Ahmad's entry into the group, Bakhshu started losing the importance he had had in Nooran's eyes. Ahmad's sonorous voice seemed to her a more dependable support than Bakhshu's strong arms. She still slept in Bakhshu's bed but the warmth of affection was disappearing now. Many a time Bakhshu complained, but each time she would excuse herself on account of not being well. Now Ahmad was the focus of all her attention. She engaged in pleasantries with him, pinched him and excited him by touching and nudging him. When he became eager to embrace her, she would coax him, "Wait. . . Not yet. . . Not yet." One night when Bakhshu was fast asleep, she quietly woke the owner of the sensuous voice and took him outside the hut. There she held his face in her hands, kissed him and said, "The time for our union has come. We are leaving this city to go somewhere else, where there'll be just the two of us. Why should these other two share our income?" Then she came back inside the hut and removed the money-belt from Fattoo's hip. He was awake and knew that she had already left Ahmad outside the hut and was now stealing his money. He also knew that she was running away with Ahmad and would never return. All the same, he kept quiet. When she had loosened and taken away his money belt and walked out of the hut, Fattoo breathed a sigh of relief, turned over in his bed and went to sleep.

Translated by Faruq Hassan

SURENDAR PARKASH

The Scarecrow

Hori, Premchand's fictional hero, had become very old–so old, indeed, that even his eyelashes and eyebrows had turned white, his back had become bent, and big, blue veins had started to jut out underneath the coarse dark skin on the back of his hands.

During this time he had fathered two sons, neither of them alive any more: one died while bathing in the Ganges, the other resisting the police. Why did he have to resist the police? There isn't much to tell. Whenever a man becomes aware of himself and begins to feel the agitation around him, he runs afoul of the police; naturally. Well, some such thing . . .

Old Hori's hands relaxed briefly on the handle of the plough, quivered a little, and then tightened again. He yelled at his animals, urging them to move on, and the ploughshare went ripping through the earth.

The sons had wives and a total of five children: three belonged to the one who drowned in the Ganges, two to the other who died resisting the police. The responsibility of providing for all of them had fallen on Hori's shoulders; blood had begun to course through his decrepit old body.

The sky was unusually red that morning. Five grandchildren, bare naked, were bathing at the well in Hori's courtyard. His older daughter-in-law would draw water from the well and throw it over their bodies one by one, as the children frisked about, rubbing their bodies and splashing water. His younger daughter-in-law was baking big, flat, round breads and stacking them up in a basket. Inside, Hori had changed his clothes and was now fixing his turban. That done, he looked at himself in the mirror standing in the niche in the wall: his entire face was a web of wrinkles. Hori closed his eyes, and standing before a small image of Hanuman Ji hanging on the wall near him, he joined his hands and bowed reverentially. He then walked through the door out into the courtyard.

"Ready?" he asked in a loud voice.

"Yes, Bapu," the children, all of them, cried in unison. The two daughters-in-law quickly fixed the edges of their saris on their heads and began to work faster. Not one was ready, Hori could see that; all of them were lying. And he thought: how indispensable lying was for human existence! A true blessing from God! For without lying, wouldn't people just drop dead–one after the other, there being no excuse to live any longer? First we tell a lie, then, trying our damndest to prove it true, we inevitably prolong our lives.

Hori's grandchildren and daughters-in-law all threw themselves with a zest into proving true the lie they had just uttered. Meanwhile, Hori gathered his harvesting tools from a corner. And now they were truly ready.

Their grainfield was flourishing. The corn was ripe and today was harvest day. It looked like a holiday. Everyone seemed eager, indeed impatient, to get to the field right away. Just then they saw that a radiant sun had enveloped the whole house in its magic.

Hori threw his towel-cloth over his shoulder and thought: What a fortunate time has finally arrived! No more threats hurled by the revenue agent, no more fear of the *banya*–the skinflint village creditor–the tyranny of the *Angrez,* or the landowner's ever-present share in the crop! Lush, green stalks, filled with grain, swayed before his eyes.

"Come, grandpa, let's go," the oldest grandson grabbed his hand, while the rest of the children wrapped themselves around his legs. The older daughter-in-law closed shut the door of the hut and the younger one balanced the bundle of bread on her head.

Invoking the name of Lord Hanuman, they came out the door into the alley, where they took a sharp right towards their field.

The village alleys and by-lanes had begun to hum with activity. People were going to or returning from the fields. Every face was lit up with happiness and every eye glowed from the exhilarating sight of crops ready to be harvested. Hori felt that life certainly looked different today. He turned his head involuntarily to look back at the children trailing behind him. But they looked as the children of farmers always do: dark-skinned and emaciated, who could be so easily frightened by the mere sound of a jeep, or the soft stir of the change of seasons. And the daughters-in-law . . . oh well, they looked like widows of poor farmers, their faces buried deep inside the mantles drawn over their faces, poverty hiding like lice in every single fold of their meager clothing.

Hori let his head droop and moved along. Past the last village house stood the open fields, with a Persian wheel nearby. A dog slept under a *neem* tree, without a care. In the cattle shed some distance away, a mix of cows, oxen, and water buffaloes belched away uproariously after gorging themselves on fodder. Up ahead, as far as one could see, were grainfields–swaying, golden. Beyond them, past the small ravine to one side, was Hori's lonely little tillage, full of ripe stalks that swayed languorously in the breeze. Walking down the dirt trail Hori and his little clan looked, from a distance, like pieces of cloth, each a different colour, crawling on the grass. They were headed for their field, beyond which was a *thal,* a spread of barren land without any vegetation at all. There was just a little lifeless dirt, into which one's feet sank as soon as one stepped into the sprawling dry stretch. The dirt had become as powdery as the bones of his two sons after cremation: how they first popped like corn and then crumbled in the hand like grains of sand. The thal was slowly encroaching on the neighbouring land; it had already spread out a good two arms' length in the last fifty years, Hori remembered. He had desperately wished that it wouldn't spread to his field, not at least until his children had grown up. Afterwards, it didn't matter. By then he would have himself become part of some such barren stretch.

Endless trails . . . Hori and his little clan trekking along . . . barefooted . . .

The sun was looking down from the eastern window of the sky.

They had walked quite some distance and their feet had become coated with dust. Everywhere around them people were busy harvesting the crops. They greeted the passersby with "Ram! Ram!" and then with a surge of quite uncommon energy cut down the culms with their scythes and put them aside.

Hori and his clan crossed the ravine one by one. The ravine was bone dry. The clay at the bottom, mixed with sand, was without a drop of moisture, its surface etched with strange patterns and tracings–

marks left by water's meandering feet.

Up ahead they could see their field, lush and swaying in the breeze. Their hearts bubbled with excitement: the crop, after harvesting, would fill their granary with corn and their courtyard with fodder. Then, sitting on the bed–their one and only piece of furniture–they would feel the rare, absolute joy of eating *bhat,* those gargantuan belches coming after the belly is filled. . . . They all thought this at the same time.

Suddenly Hori stopped in his tracks. He was looking at the field in absolute astonishment. The rest of them looked back and forth from Hori to the field. Hori's body was animated by a sudden burst of energy, as though from a flash of lightning. He took a few steps forward and shouted at the top of his lungs:

"Who the hell are you?"

There was a stir in the stalks. They all saw it and followed Hori with big, hurried strides. Hori shouted again:

"Who is there? Speak up! Who is stealing my crop?"

But the cornfield returned no answer. They had come quite close to the field now; they could hear the sound of the scythe clearly as it went rasping across the stalks. They were frightened a little. Then Hori, picking up courage, challenged in a loud voice:

"Who are you, you bastard? Why don't you answer?" He drew his scythe, ready to attack.

Suddenly something like a skeleton arose from the far side of the field and, it appeared, began to look at them cheerfully.

"I'm . . . I'm Hori's scarecrow!" he introduced himself, waving the scythe.

They were frightened; a few muffled screams managed to escape from their throats. Their faces went pale, and white crust formed on Hori's lips. They froze. They stood stock still for a while. How long was that while? An instant? A century? Or, perhaps, even a whole age? None of them could tell. They weren't even sure they were alive, until they heard Hori's voice, trembling with rage.

"It's you . . . Scarecrow. But I made you to look after the field–I built you with pieces of bamboo, didn't I? And gave you that Angrez hunter's outfit–remember, the one who hired my father as a game flusher? The hunter was so pleased with him he gave him his torn khaki outfit when he left India. And yes, your head, which I made from an old clay cooking-pot. I put that hunter's pith helmet over that pot–

remember? And you lifeless dummy, you're stealing my crop?"

Hori rattled on, walking over to the scarecrow, who was still looking at the lot of them, softly smiling, as though supremely unaffected
by any of Hori's tongue-lashing. As soon as they drew nearer, they saw
that about one-fourth of the crop had already been harvested and the
scarecrow stood near the heap with scythe in hand smiling sweetly.
They wondered where in the world the scarecrow got the scythe. They
had been looking at him for months now. Lifeless scarecrow, who always stood with both his hands empty. But today–today he looked
very much like a real man, of flesh and blood, just like them. That did
it. Hori flew into a rage. He took a step forward and gave the
scarecrow a nasty push. But the scarecrow didn't so much as budge
from his place, though Hori, by the force of his own shove, was flung
several feet away. Everyone shouted and ran towards Hori. He was
holding his waist and trying to get up. They helped him. He looked at
the scarecrow, full of apprehension, and said, "Scarecrow, you . . .
you've grown stronger than even me! Even me . . . who made you with
his own hands, so that you would guard my crop."

The scarecrow was smiling, as usual. He said, "You're getting upset
over nothing, Hori Kaka! Look, I've harvested only my share of the
corn. Exactly one-fourth–"

"But, but who gave you the right to steal what belongs to my
children? Who are you to begin with?"

"I do have a right, Hori Kaka, I really *do*. Because I *am;* and besides, I have been guarding this field."

"But I put you here thinking that you were lifeless. Never heard of
inanimate objects claiming a share. And this scythe–where did you get
it from?"

The scarecrow burst into a resounding laughter. "You really are
naive, Hori Kaka. You talk to me, yet think of me as lifeless?"

"But who gave you this scythe and life? I surely didn't."

"I got them on my own. The day you split the bamboo to make me,
brought the tattered clothes of the Angrez hunter, painted my eyes,
nose, ears and mouth on the cooking-pot long since in disuse–well,
that very day life had started to stir in those things. Together they
formed me, and as I stood here waiting for the crop to ripen, a scythe
slowly began to grow out of me. And today when the crop has ripened,
I find a scythe in my hand. All the same, I haven't stolen your property. I waited for today, when you would come to harvest your crop, and

have taken out only the portion that is rightfully mine. Why must you get so upset about it?"

The scarecrow said it all, slowly and deliberately, so that everyone would understand him clearly.

"No, it can't be. This is a conspiracy. I DO NOT CONSIDER YOU A LIVING PERSON! Period! It is all an illusion. I shall take the matter to the *panchayat.* You throw this scythe right away. I shall not allow you to take even a single stalk!" Hori shouted. And promptly the scarecrow dropped the scythe, smiling.

The village council was set up in the *chaupal.* The village headman and his deputy were present. Hori sat with his grandchildren in the middle. A feeling of tremendous sadness made his face look lifeless and withered. His two daughters-in-law stood with other women to one side. They were waiting for the scarecrow to show up. Today the panchayat was going to give its verdict. Both disputants had already given their statements some time ago.

At long last the scarecrow came along, walking in his graceful un-hurried manner, full of verve and brio. All eyes rose towards him. He was his usual self–relaxed and smiling. The moment he stepped into the chaupal, everyone involuntarily stood up, bowing their heads out of reverence. The scene stabbed poor Hori right in the heart. He felt that the scarecrow had come to own the conscience of everyone in the village–why, he even had the verdict of the panchayat in his pocket. Hori felt like a drowning man, desperately flailing his feet and arms against a particularly strong current.

Finally, the *sarpanch* gave the verdict. Hori's whole being trembled. He accepted the panchayat's verdict, and he agreed to give the scarecrow a quarter of the crop. Then he got up and held forth before his grandsons:

"Listen, this perhaps is the last crop of our life. The thal is still a little ways from the field. I advise you never again to set a scarecrow as guard over your crops. Next year, when the fields are ploughed and sowed again, and the elixir of rain has made them sprout, tie me to a bamboo and stand me in the field . . . in place of the scarecrow. I shall keep watch over your crops, until such time as the thal has crept forward and devoured your field, and made its dirt into powder. Don't ever remove me from the field. Let me stay there, so that when people look at me they will be reminded that they mustn't place scarecrows in their fields, that scarecrows are not lifeless, that they become animated on their own, and that scythes grow out of their bodies. And so they come to claim a quarter of the crop as their share."

Hori then proceeded slowly towards his field, followed by his grandchildren and, behind them, his daughters-in-law. And behind them all came the other people of the village, their heads bent low.

Coming close to his field Hori fell down and died. Promptly, his grandchildren began to tie him to a bamboo pole, as the other people watched.

The scarecrow removed his hunter's hat from his head, placed it on his chest and bowed his head.

Translated by Muhammad Umar Memon

ENVER SAJJAD

The Cow

One day they got together and finally decided that they really ought to take the cow to the butcher.

"We won't get a penny for her now," one of them said. "Who'll buy that bag of bones?"

"But dad, I still think if we treat her . . ."

"You keep your trap shut, smart aleck!"

Nakka shut up and moved off to one side. His father, pulling at his beard as though he would pull some ideas out of it, sat down and put his head together with the other grown-ups.

If I even so much as open my mouth, they all behave like butchers. Since I came to know myself, I've known "Spotty"; and from the day these people have been thinking about giving her to the butcher, moment by moment I feel more orphaned. What can I do? They all laugh at me for taking care of her so much. For loving those bones.

Unable to hold off any longer, Nakka blurted out: "Why don't you send her to the vet instead of the butcher?"

"You don't understand that she can't be well again. Why waste money treating her?"

Don't I really? Just yesterday mum recorded my fifteenth birthday!

"Just let her be treated . . . who knows?"

"Don't meddle with your elders!"

I really wish that I, that I . . . could take all of you to the butcher.

Then together they proceeded to chain up the cow. But it was as if the cow knew exactly what was going on. She wouldn't budge an inch from her spot, not even when they beat her. They just couldn't get her to move. Nakka was standing off to the side glassy eyed, trying to understand.

Bravo, my Spotty, my Cow, my Gaumata! Don't move! You don't know how these people are planning to deal with you. Don't move, otherwise, otherwise, if you do . . .

The cow was rooted to her spot. Every now and then she would just turn her head to the side to look at the boy. A little way away the cow's calf was sitting unconcerned tied to a stake by a rope. The clubs rained on her bones but her calf seemed supremely indifferent to it. Nakka's ears too were slowly, ever so slowly becoming numb.

Tired out, the grown-ups sat down and put their heads together again. They decided that even if they got her going, it was possible that she could drop dead on the way; therefore, it was better to haul her in a truck. At least she could be picked up and loaded into a truck.

The next day the truck came.

Hearing the sound of the truck, the cow turned and looked. Then she blinked her eyes and stuck her nose into the manger where Nakka had just thrown some fodder before going to look at the truck.

"You're not really going to . . ." He couldn't believe it.

"So what do you think–we're joking?" asked one.

"Dad, please give me the cow. I'll . . ."

"Oh, Big Mister Veterinarian" said another.

"Dad, without her I'll . . ."

"Oh, Romeo!" said the third.

The fourth, fifth, all these big people–the pigs–they're all alike, and dad, who thinks he knows it all, what's got into his head, anyway?

"Son, even by giving the truck driver ten rupees to take her, we'll come out ahead."

Oh you miserable merchant, take the money from me, take it from me! . . . but . . . I don't have it in hand, but when I grow up, I'll . . .

"Ha-ha-ha!"

When, when I start earning some . . .

"Ha-ha-ha!"

But by then Spotty's bones will have been ground to dust . . . What, what, just what can I do?

One of them went over to the manger to lead the cow away. Nakka went along behind him to see what was going on. The grown-up unfastened her chain. The cow looked over at Nakka with some unchewed fodder clenched in her teeth, then picked up her hoof to go.

"Don't! Don't! Don't!" screamed Nakka.

"Shut up!"

The cow stood up.

The grown-up gave the chain a jerk.

"No, Spotty, don't!"

"Are you going to shut up or would you rather I pulled your tongue out?"

Nakka shut up. The grown-up pulled the chain again forcefully, "Move it lady. The truck driver isn't going to stand around all day for you."

The cow's eyes were bulging out of their sockets and her tongue was fluttering in its captivity, but the bagful of bones stood its ground. Nakka smiled, but just as suddenly became sad.

She has . . . she has been sold. She'll have to go . . . but . . . I'm certain if we spent a little money and treated her . . . then . . . then . . . but what can I do with those grown-ups? If I were only a vet myself . . . and there, that calf doesn't seem to care if his mother is being beaten black and blue and he's standing out there looking around like an idiot . . .

He stopped, searching for more words.

Then one of them had a brainstorm. He grabbed the cow's tail and gave it three or four nasty twists. She started running from this pain in her rump. He looked over at Nakka and laughed.

The pain in her rump drove the cow right to the truck. Nakka's heart throbbed madly.

Pig! God damn you!

The truck driver dropped a plank on the ground for the cow to climb on. The cow put a hoof on it.

"Don't get on!"

"Cut out his tongue! He's scaring her!"

Nakka again shut up and moved back. The cow looked first at the plank, then at Nakka.

Pig! God damn you! Nakka's head was bent in shame. *What else can I do? What else can I do?*

Right up to that moment the cow wasn't frightened, but then, suspicious, she looked this way and that before giving out a big hiss.

My Spotty knows! My Spotty knows climbing the board will put her in the truck! But she doesn't know why she shouldn't get on the truck!

They all got together and rained clubs down on her back; her legs quivered but she did not budge. When they got together for a second assault, she was ready to take off to get away from this pain but suddenly dad had a bright idea. He whacked her right on the mouth. She turned back around to face the board.

Puffing away, dad said, "Come on, sons!"

They all got together again and rained clubs down on her.

Nakka was standing at a distance–immobile, unfeeling.

"It won't work out this way," one of them said, catching his breath.

"What then?"

They were still leaning against the truck and thinking, when God knows what got into the cow that she abruptly turned and took off, raising a cloud of dust as she went past Nakka like a perfect stranger.

Nakka was stricken.

"Look out, look out! She's over on the left," warned one.

"Naturally," dad said as he combed his beard with his fingers.

The cow was licking her calf. Dad's eyes sparkled deviously. "Bring that calf over here! We should have used this trick yesterday. We'd have even saved ourselves the money for the truck."

Nakka was paralysed.

One of them grabbed the calf's rope. Nakka's tongue quivered. The cow paused briefly, picked up her hooves and hesitantly followed the calf and passed near Nakka. A curse slowly rolled off his tongue. The calf clopped up the board and into the truck. The cow came to the board and stopped. Perplexed, she looked at her calf and then very slowly turned her head to look at Nakka. One of them quickly pulled out some fodder and put it in front of the cow. She took some stalks with her teeth, then after a pause, let them drop to the ground. She put one hoof on the board, then another.

God knows what happened to Nakka. Suddenly, a torrent of fresh, hot blood coursed through his entire body. His ears sizzled red and his head rattled. He ran to the house, got his father's double-barreled shotgun and fed two shells into it. Completely out of his mind, he ran outside, put the gun to his shoulder and took aim.

He looked with open eyes. The calf was outside the truck chewing away at the fodder the cow had dropped. The cow, tied in the truck, had her head stuck outside looking at her calf. One of them was sitting in the truck preparing to take the cow away. Dad was standing outside running one hand through his beard and shaking the hand of the driver.

Then I don't know what happened. Who did Nakka take aim at? The cow, the calf, the driver, his father, himself? Or else he's standing there, still aiming?

Somebody go there and take a look and tell me what happened next. I just know that one day they got together and decided to . . .

Translated by Muhammad Umar Memon

BALRAJ MANRA

Composition One

WHAT AM I TO THE SUN?
I–ignorant, helpless, sick–unable to say a thing.
In those days the question WHAT AM I TO THE SUN? was locked in the prison of my mind.
I had no keys with which to fling open the gates to this mind-prison and let out the question and, with it, free myself.
Who has the keys?
I–ignorant, helpless, sick–who could I ask?
In those days living under a spell:
Here the sun would rise; there I would awake. The sun would start its journey, I would start mine. We would move forward, onward, leaving milestone after milestone behind along the way. Here the sun would set; there I would fall asleep.
How did it happen?
I don't know. I have never looked full face into the sun.
When first I fell asleep in the sunset, I was facing it. A cool breeze flowed softly, very softly, while the sun smiled through the rustling foliage of the *neem*. I was sunk deep in my armchair, soaking up the balmy weather. Every now and then I felt a gentle, mysterious ebb and flow, sweet sensations–sweet, mysterious sensations–the sun smiling through the rustling neem foliage. The shadows of the neem waltzed on the cool, emerald velvet of the smooth mowed lawn. The mellow, absolutely charming drunkenness of three successive glasses of Diplomat whiskey.
The smiling sun began its gradual descent.
I pulled the chair behind the neem trunk and fell drowsily into it.
The sunshine lay as a pale sheet over the emerald turf.
Suddenly it began to shrink.

Lifelessly, my hands dropped, my legs dangled lazily, my eyelids began to droop. The last bit of sunshine flickered for a moment and shrank completely as I felt drowned in a compulsive, heavy sleep.

When I opened my eyes, it was a pale sun smiling sadly on the eastern horizon.

Never before had I slept so long.

From that time it became a routine. Here the sun would rise, there I would awake. The sun would start its journey, I would start mine. We would move forward, onward; milestone after milestone was left behind along the way. Here the sun would set, there I would fall asleep.

In the mind-prison something uneasy began to stir

Something I had never experienced.

I failed in trying to give some meaning to the stir, but my efforts continued. The sun would rise, I would awake; the sun would go down, I would sleep. It went on and on. Only after the passing of an age was I able to give some meaning to that strange stir.

WHAT AM I TO THE SUN?

I–ignorant, helpless, sick–unable to answer.

Strange to say, that stir came to resemble a question locked in the mind's prison.

WHAT AM I TO THE SUN?

I–ignorant, helpless, sick–unable to say a thing.

Ignorant because I was unable to answer.

Helpless because I could neither overwhelm the sun nor overcome myself–for here the sun rose, there I awoke; here it sank, there I slept.

Sick because–desperately and continuously–all my veins needed the sun's rays.

To rise with the sun, to sleep when it set became a torment–a torment because my relation to the sun was beyond comprehension. I knew I could not rest until I had determined the precise nature of this relation, for WHAT AM I TO THE SUN? echoed and re-echoed in the prison house of my mind.

The pity of it, I had no keys to this prison so that I could fling open the gates and let out the question and, with it, free myself.

Who has the keys?

I–ignorant, helpless, sick–who could I ask?

And so it went: Here the sun appeared on the eastern horizon, there wakefulness touched my lashes. The sun, pale and sad; I, withered and gloomy. The sun far, far away while my taller shadow spread obliquely westward. The sun would begin its course and my slanting shadow would keep it company. When the sun began to rise slowly from the eastern horizon, my shadow began to dance slowly round and round me. As the sun came towards me, my shadow would shrink. The sun atop my head; my shadow under my feet. The sun moved slowly westward; my shadow lengthened towards the east. The sun sank here and there I was overcome by sleep.

Is my shadow my bond to the sun?

I would try to grasp the basis of this all.

Is my shadow my own?

Filled with misgivings, I would falter, feeling unable to go on.

Is my shadow the shadow of the sun?

Are the sun and I twins?

After thinking so hard and so often, all I knew was that I was ignorant, helpless, sick. But the realization of my ignorance, helplessness, sickness was no answer to my misery–the mystery remained inscrutable.

One day, as the sun moved forward on its course, a stranger, a complete stranger, the wind, whispered past my ear:

"Innocent friend! you are the centre of sun and shadow–shadow and sun revolve around you."

Thenceforth it was so: Here my eyes opened, there the sun rose; here I set out on my journey, there the sun set out on its journey; moving forward, onward, leaving milestone after milestone behind; here I fall asleep, there the sun goes down.

Translated by Muhammad Umar Memon

MUHAMMAD UMAR MEMON

Lucky Vikki

"Why are you making all this fuss? Don't you see that the photograph itself is out of focus? Even a blind man can tell that!" Saeed, the most balanced and centred and calm person among us all, tried to explain as rationally as he possibly could to the ugly photographer who, undisturbed by it all, went busily on retouching some negative. Saeed's words couldn't have fallen on deafer ears. For us this calamity, the ruin of the picture, was far more earthshaking than, say, the Agadir earthquake, or the fear of the Super Power confrontation in Laos and Cuba, or even the possible outbreak of the Third World War. That monstrous, misshapen photographer, on the other hand, went on calmly retouching the negative–as though God Almighty, the Lord of the heavens and earth, had created nothing besides his pencil with the two-inch-long pointed tip and that damned negative. Not even once did he bother to raise his head and look at us.

His prodigious indifference, his mammoth equanimity truly burnt me up. I picked up our group photograph and slammed it down on the glass-top counter and roared: "You think the money we gave you was ill-gotten? Don't you see the picture is so bloody out of focus that no one is even recognizable? Who let you become a photographer, eh?"

When I slammed the picture down, my hand hit the glass-top of the counter. The slap disrupted the photographer's composure, but only for the briefest moment. Shaken a bit, he paused for a second. Inadvertently, his pencil registered a little more pressure than usual on the negative, but that was all. It was as if he had physically absorbed the shock of my little display. But he still didn't bother to look up. He pushed back the thick glasses that had slid down to the tip of his nose. Then he picked up his cigarette from the ash tray, took a couple of puffs, coughed a little, shifted a bit and resumed his work.

This threw me into a fit of rage. It was a rare opportunity by all counts, one that we could be rightly proud of: The chairman of our Society had commissioned to have a group photograph taken after the farewell party which the junior grad students had thrown for our graduating M.A. class. He had also agreed to pay for the photograph out of the Society's funds. For my own part, I had managed to persuade Shah Ji, the vice president of the Society, to have the words "B.A. (Honours), Departmental Representative" printed after my name on the photograph, so that after I was finished with the University I would at least have a memento of my life there–well, you know, something to brag about.

It was not exactly that I was dying to serve the promising sons and daughters of the nation that I had run for D.R. two years in a row. The purpose of this whole exercise simply was to get an insignia for my blazer pocket and a pin for my tie. I was looking forward to wearing the blazer and the tie during the winters. Then I would have proudly walked down the interminable hallways of the University, shrugging my shoulders every now and then, looking busy and important. But what could I do now? That whole purpose had gone down the drain. Success had eluded me at the very last moment. The first time I decided to run for the position of the D.R., the elections were delayed for so long that when I finally got around to asking for the insignia, I found out that all such tokens of self-glorification had already been doled out. The second time, the president of the Students' Union had ended up in jail for his alleged involvement in some political affair. As a result, all the activities of the Union were suspended indefinitely. The prospect of receiving the insignia and the pin had again evaporated. And now that I was about to earn the small honour of having my photograph taken, the wheel of fortune had decisively turned against me. To Saeed the loss was not a serious one. He had many times been captain of soccer teams, both in college and the University; he already had a whole pile of blazer insignias and group photographs. And as for Shah Ji, well he was a typical Pathan from the Frontier for whom the only things that truly mattered were commitment to studies and the display of the typically northern hospitality.

In other words, this honour was important only for me. That was why after promising Shah Ji and Saeed to meet them at seven o'clock at the photographer's, I had rushed there. I was the first to arrive and had asked this dolt of a photographer to show me the picture. One look at the print and I knew I had been exposed to the full fury of a powerful earthquake; it had levelled everything and dashed to the ground all that was valuable and meaningful in my life. All those rosy dreams of a future were shattered: bottles of soda pop began to explode in my brain. This stupid, ugly photographer had snatched away whatever little glory I had hoped to gain. The photograph was so fuzzy that I felt like smashing his head with the heavy paperweight lying on the pile of memos on his showcase. I could only grind my teeth in anger and wait, restlessly, for the arrival of Saeed and Shah Ji. Three heads, I thought, would be better than one.

They had hardly entered the studio when I threw the photograph at them and spoke with bitterness and sarcasm: "See if you can recognize your blessed faces in this! Some photographer huh! Wouldn't settle for less than fifty rupees! And what have we got here? Have a look!"

They too were just as shocked to see the photograph. Shah Ji was, perhaps, also worried that the chairman might doubt his integrity. He could think that Shah Ji had made a shady deal with some third-rate photographer in order to siphon off the Society's funds.

"Mister, what kind of a picture is this? It's so dim . . ."

"This print not for you. This only a tesht copy. Still to do re-touching on it. Then you see. It will be thousand times besht–what?"

"What are you talking about, man? Are you trying to rip us off or what? This picture . . . and becoming best? Not a chance!" Shah Ji said, astonished. "There's no way in the world this picture will become any better. Come on, you must be joking!"

"Then is it my fault? Ice-factory wall was casting shadow in the cafe. I told you make the photo here in studio. You disagreed. Didn't listen. Now if there was shadow in cafe lawn, then, my friend, is not my fault."

"What kind of a photographer are you?" I roared. "Why didn't you tell us clearly that the photograph would come out this bad?"

"No photographer can doing that. You have to take this picture– what! What will I do with it?"

"Why will we have to take it!?" I shouted "I can't figure this fellow out. I don't know what he means by saying we have to take it. Listen, you! Our money wasn't ill-gotten that we can waste it on a picture like this. You claim to be a photographer and you don't even know whether the picture will turn out all right. How long did you say you've been doing photography? Thirty years? Twenty?"

Seeing my dreams shattered this way, I lost patience. I cannot recall how much abuse I must have heaped on the fellow. He however was not perturbed by any of that. Inching forward his pumpkin-like distended belly, he continued retouching the negative. On the other hand, I, like one who suffers a loss in indigence, had been transformed because of my grief into the living image of Schopenhauer's philosophy.

"Listen," I said to him, "you will have to take another picture. You know damn well we are students. Even normally we are hard up. And look at you–you own such a big studio. If one of your photographs turns out bad, surely you can afford to take another one. But we cannot afford to pay you an extra penny."

"How you can blame me for bad picture?"

"I don't know how we can or cannot, but I do know that if you cause us any more trouble, I am going to bring all the students from the University down here. One charge by them and your whole studio will be in shambles. What do you say to that, brother?"

But my threat had no effect on him whatsoever. It was like trying to make an etching on water. Without raising his head he said with perfect serenity: "Mister, why you making these empty threat? I told you, not my fault. Not take another picture."

"Why the hell not?" I thundered.

Suddenly it struck me that from his accent he seemed to be a Gujarati. Why not try to reason with him in his native tongue? It might work. So I asked him in Gujarati, "Where are you from, mister?"

At that he was startled. He readjusted his glasses. The corners of his fat drooping lips, coated with layers of sealing-waxlike paste from his incessant *pan*-chewing, suddenly fluttered like the flesh of a newly slaughtered goat. He understood my attempt to trick him. Realizing that this community-relationship would cost him dearly, he neatly lied his way out of my trap, and banking on his favourite expletive ("What!") answered:

"I from Karachi–what!"

"Are you ever going to come straight, man?"

"What can I say, mister? You people using force on me. I told you. Come day after tomorrow. Try other print. Will be thousands times better."

"But this print is so hazy that nothing except the tie is visible. The next might become a little bit better, but it will never be perfect," Saeed said, disappointed. "There is hardly any hope!"

"Mister, give it try. I make it really good–what!"

"Well, it's the same old story. No shopkeeper ever finds fault with his own wares, and the whole world is yellow to a jaundiced person. Come on, man, be reasonable." Saeed was still intent on bringing the photographer round with politeness, but I was enraged by the continuous cawing of the man.

"Stop this nonsense and return our money. We didn't give you an advance for this kind of rip-off."

He didn't bother to answer me but kept busy with his retouching.

"Alright. Well then, what will it be?" I tried to get a final word from him but Saeed pulled me back by the shoulders. He moved forward and said sternly, "Mister, you'll have to take the picture again!"

The photographer's petty-mindedness came to the surface. He threw his brush-holding hand in the air, describing a curve with it, and said, "Oh, yes? Why I take the picture again?"

"Because you have spoiled the earlier one."

"Who says I spoil it? Are you a photographer–what?" he hissed loudly.

"And are you? You who don't even know whether a picture will turn out well or fuzzy?"

"In Firdaus Cafeteria no photographer can be taking clearer picture than this."

"Why not?"

"Because ice-factory wall was casting shadow and because on back wall was a creeper."

"But was your brain asleep at that time? Why didn't you warn us?"

"Oh, stop my brain-hammering. Come day after tomorrow and try second print."

"And who will be responsible if the second one turns out just as awful?"

"I am not. You might think that also bad!"

"Are you out of your mind? We haven't been bitten by a mad dog to go bothering a photographer if he takes a good picture." I couldn't take any more of this arguing. I pushed Saeed away and moved near the photographer and said, "You finish your job honestly or you'll have to deal with the whole University crowd in your studio." Then I announced my decision as categorically as I could: "You will have to take the picture again and we shall not pay you an extra penny. That's it."

Shah Ji, who had been quietly watching all these goings-on, said, "This dolt doesn't give a damn, does he."

The photographer also gave us his final decision. "I not taking another photograph. Now you leave. Come back day after tomorrow— what! On Sunday."

Incensed by his refusal I said, "How dare you say no?"

"Well, no second picture. This my decision."

"The hell with your decision."

"Watch it, mister. Watch language. I not your father's shervant!"

"What?" I stepped forward, bringing my hand in a semicircle to give him a hard one across the jaw when my eyes caught sight of a girl standing in front of a man who sat behind the glass counter near its edge. My body suddenly went numb, as if buried under tons of ice. All the tension and fury flew out of me as air does from a punctured balloon. Helpless, I looked around in embarrassment. Seeing this sudden change in me, Saeed and Shah Ji, like perfect fools, looked around to find the reason. When they saw at the edge of the counter what I had seen, they understood everything. And, like me, they too began looking around, slightly ashamed, pretending that nothing unusual had happened.

She must have been the daughter of one of the well-to-do families who shop at Elphi. Wow! What a shapely figure! Breasts like wine goblets placed upside down! Like two restless doves! So full, so perfect! Eyes that could kill with one look! A thin line of collyrium coming out of the corners of the eyes and arching like a taut bow! And the spell of the eyes themselves–Lord! A sleeveless shirt of Chinese silk sticking to her body, as though it was itself the skin! Every contour, all arches, curves–everything fully visible! She was leaning on the counter, her elbows resting on the glass, holding her doll-like face in her cupped hands, and saying something to the man sitting behind the counter. The man moved the phone forward towards her. When she reached out to dial we could see a thin layer of fine powder covering the shadow of her clean-shaven underarm. We stared at her, dazed.

Our eyes were glued to her body, watching her every move. When she picked up the hand-set from the cradle, our hearts throbbed fitfully. Lord knows who that lucky fellow was, lucky to be the object of her smiles and good cheer!

She dialed the number. A few minutes later, while staring at us she spoke into the phone, "Hello, Vikki." We all stood motionless, everyone feeling extremely embarrassed, each one only concerned about what impression he had made on her. Perhaps she thought we were some uncouth, illiterate, uncultured cads, coming to blows with the photographer.

Avoiding each other's eyes, each one of us was staring at her, each wishing he were that lucky Vikki.

"Yes, misters," the photographer spoke, "come two day after tomorrow. Try second print. Will be thousand times besht!"

I turned back and, helpless, looked at him. A vague yet very clever smile, the smile of a seasoned man, played on his slightly parted lips. His eyes showed his age, the experience of a whole lifetime, the illumination of a veteran's business acumen.

"Yes, yes. Try making it good," we said, almost in unison. And after casting a final, dissatisfied look at the girl, we stepped out of the studio.

On our way back we had an intense talk about her. Our keen imagination had already stripped the last stitch of clothing from her body. We visualized her body with all its sharp lines, in all its glory peering through the fine, transparent silk. Feasting on that image, we gratified all the gargantuan desires of our dissolute minds.

About an hour later, when the lights on the Elphi had begun to twinkle and when that lusty agitation in our minds had subsided some, we began squabbling. We were blaming each other and asking why, on what basis, really, had we agreed to accept that worthless picture from the photographer.

Then, suddenly, in the shadows of the flashing neon signs, I began thinking: that shrewd photographer–he really knew his business.

Translated by Faruq Hassan and the author

ANWER KHAN

The Pose

God knows what got into her head. She abruptly broke her stride and slipped into Shandar Cloth Store. Then she opened the door of the show window and, deftly, removing the lovely mannequin, stood herself in the plastic dummy's place and assumed its pose.

It was evening. The street was packed with people, but they were so preoccupied as they went their way that none of them noticed what she had just done.

Why did she do it? She probably didn't know that herself. True, she was something of a daredevil in her childhood. But now she was a grown young woman, a college student smart, sophisticated, urbane. Even the most daring boys at the college got cold feet walking with her. What she'd just done, well, it just happened. It was entirely unpremeditated.

Standing in the show window she felt a strange sense of comfort wash upon her. She was now, after all, a part of this bustling marketplace. She could also look closely at the place, the whole of it, standing in just one spot, without having to move. Walking as one of the crowd or while shopping, she never felt herself a part of the life around her–the bouyant, strident life, full of vigour and excitement.

Her tense body gradually became unstrung, and an unprovoked smile came to her lips. She quite liked it–standing with one foot slightly forward, the hem of her sari going over her head and then dropping down to wrap itself around the joint of her right elbow. She looked positively ravishing. She could stand in her new posture forever, she thought, overcome by a sudden impulse, although her knees had already begun to ache from the pressure.

She was just considering easing up on her heels a little when her eyes caught sight of a peasant who suddenly cut through the crowd on the sidewalk and came over to the show window and began gawking at her with eyes at once full of lust and wonder. His eyes seemed to say: Incredible! These craftsmen can be so skilful! How they make stutues that look like real people!

It was good the glass panel stood between them, otherwise the country bumpkin would certainly have ventured to touch her.

The peasant perhaps wanted to linger on for a while, but the scouring glances of the passersby forced him to move on. As soon as he had moved away, she relaxed her feet a little. Even shook them a bit. But now her lips began to feel dry. "Just a little while longer," she told her lips under her breath, "and then I'll take you to a restaurant and treat you to a glass of ice water, followed by a steaming cup of some finely brewed tea." Her thirst let up a bit and she slipped back into her former pose.

She certainly had no wish to exhibit herself like this to the pedestrians. Perhaps the thought had never even entered her mind. Rather, it pleased her to think that she was now a full participant in the teeming life around her. It was a strange feeling. She had never experienced it before.

"Oh God!"–the expression came from the lips of two college girls– "how lifelike!"

Their voices, travelling along the glass panels and filtering through the holes in the steel stripes holding the frame, came upon her softly, as if from a great distance.

The two girls gawked at her with admiration as they exchanged a few words among themselves, while she looked at them with tenderness. She was happy. Incredibly happy. No one had looked at her so appreciatively before. At least not in her presence. Like a kind and caring queen receiving the adulation of her subjects, she sustained her regal pose until the girls had once again melted into the crowd and disappeared from view.

"Let's see who comes next?" she thought to herself.

Her feet had again started to protest. This time around, though, she sent them a warning, a rather stern one: Scoundrels, stay put! Can't you wait even a little? She wouldn't care a hoot about their protest, she decided.

She was still congratulating herself on her firmness when she caught sight of a cop who had just separated from the crowd and after taking a pinch of chewing tobacco from a box he held was rubbing it with his thumb. The moment he saw her, his hand stopped dead, his mouth fell open, and his eyes widened. She stared at the cop sweetly. The cop's eyelashes began to flap frantically; he rubbed the tobacco hastily and stuffing it between his lower lip and tooth practically stuck his eyes against the glass of the show window.

She was overcome by a powerful urge to laugh, but managed to stop herself with the greatest difficulty. Suddenly her feet began to itch uncontrollably. There was even a slight, involuntary tremble. But the cop thought it was a mere illusion, or the effect of the tobacco.

The cop stared at her for a long time. He would withdraw a little, then come back and inspect her closely. This went on for so long that she began to tire. Is the idiot going to leave the place at all?–she wondered. She was feeling uncomfortable. She knew she couldn't go on standing in that pose. All the same, she also knew that she was safe inside the show window. Where would she find such protection outside?

Thank God the cop finally decided to leave, and she drew a breath of relief, loosened her hands and feet, straightened up her tense back, indeed even massaged it a bit. Night was approaching and the crowd had thinned down to a few swift-footed pedestrians.

Soon it will grow dark, she thought. She'd better get out of here while there was still some light. The cloth store must be emptying out. Somebody might see her getting out of the show window. She'd have to be very careful . . . and fast. And yet there was such comfort inside the show window! How she wallowed in that pleasure! Another ten minutes? Why not . . .

She was still mulling over this when she spotted her girlfriend Sheyama on the sidewalk. Right away she sprang into her former pose and held her breath. Sheyama threw an inattentive look in her direction and because her thoughts were elsewhere, the danger, luckily, was averted. The thought that some of her acquaintances might spot her here had not occurred to her until Sheyama came along. This was precisely the time when her older brother returned from work, she recalled with horror. He's already suffering from a heart ailment. What if he saw the family's honour exposed so shamelessly out on the street? Wouldn't he drop dead?

Two boys appeared in her field of vision. They were returning from school, their satchels glued to their backs. They looked with zesty curiousity and pasted their faces–eyes and all–flat against the glass.

"Hey, she's real," the voice of one of the boys entered her ear faintly. Once again she wanted to laugh.

"Punk–it's plastic," the other boy said. "Whoever uses a live model?"

"But she looks so real. Seems she'd open her mouth and start speaking any moment."

"That's because of the evening. In proper light, you'd see."

"Hi!" the boy said as he winked at her mischievously.

The other one broke into a gale of laughter. Then he too waved at her and said "Bye!" and the two walked out of her field of vision.

As soon as they were gone, she suddenly began to laugh, but just as suddenly, became very nervous.

A young man was looking at her with perplexed eyes from across the glass. When their eyes met, he smiled. She smiled back, if only to hide her trepidation. She quickly grabbed the plastic dummy, and tried to install it, pretending to be one of the store attendants.

The youth's eyes were still riveted on her.

Arranging the sari around the mannequin she looked at the youth from the corner of her eye to see who he was looking at. His eyes lingered briefly at the plastic figure, then bounced off it and became glued to her.

She backed up, supremely confident, opened the door to the show window and walked out.

None of the store attendants saw her go out, or if they did, she was so agile and so fast that they couldn't figure out what had happened. The doorman didn't notice as he was busy talking to one of the sales clerks.

Confidently she strode away, briskly but lightly, happy and satisfied. As though she'd just unloaded the entire pestering weight of her body and soul. After she had walked away some distance, she turned around and looked back. The youth was still staring at her, perhaps with wonder.

She quickly turned down another street.

Translated by Muhammad Umar Memon

ASIF FARRUKHI

Fertility

This was a cat's life–her own life, as it was lived by her, a cat. What objection could I have to her doing with that life whatever her little cat-like heart desired? She was, after all, a cat. If I had any concern at all, it was with the difficulty that would come later, with the kittens. In the end, it was them I would have to do something about.

And my cat did have kittens–regularly. At first I simply used to give them away to different households. But this just made room for more, and so even though I would find new homes for them, their numbers did not diminish. The time came when all the houses of all our friends and relatives had cat's in them–cats we had given away; but we still had more than we wanted. People began to avoid coming to our house, fearing that we might furtively get them to take yet another kitten off our hands. At first these people accepted them as pets, but later took them only because we were so insistent. Later, the time came when our friends, after *we* had gone to see *them,* would begin checking under tables and beds, making sure we hadn't left behind another one when we departed. They had no desire for any more. But neither was it possible for us to find space enough in our own home for the cats' ever-increasing numbers. What else could we do but look for new homes for them? At the same time, I didn't want to trouble anyone–people or cats. I took every precaution to see that our kittens didn't end up where they might remain unloved or unwanted, where they might not belong, where they couldn't settle comfortably with the people or furnishings of a specific house. After all, raising cats isn't some kind of negotiable affair, where you can haggle and barter about

227

this or that. You have to establish an attachment.

So now I had a problem. All the kittens we had managed to get rid of were a short time later replaced in newer numbers. I had more cats than I needed, and I just didn't know what I was going to do with them.

Initially we had been all smiles over the arrival of the new litter of kittens. I felt a strong attachment to the mother cat, and I loved her no matter what she did. When the time came to deliver the kittens and I saw her labour pains, tears began to flow down my cheeks. And after the kittens had been born–well, as I said, I was all smiles, and my chest swelled with pride. Picking up those tiny newborn pink-white darlings–they were like toys, really–I danced around the house. Agitated, the mother cat would call out behind me. "Silly," I chuckled, "I'm not trying to steal your babies away." Very carefully, I put them back. The mother cat looked at me and meowed as though she were saying thank you, and then began to lick them. For their part, the blind and oh-so-weak kittens purred and began to feed at their mother's teats. The mother gave them their milk, and I stood enraptured watching the whole affair. I was happy because she was happy. Now, though, if she wants to forget about all this, then that's her business. It was I, after all, who took it upon myself to see that she had a proper diet, and it was I who supervised the kittens, concerned that their father might pick up their scent and come around to prey on them. (I really didn't care which of the wild, wandering neighbourhood cats was in fact their father. But whichever one it was, I did feel that he was our common enemy.)

The mother cat and I–together we continued to watch the kittens grow. I remember the day when their eyes opened for the first time. Led by the mischievous innocence of those brand new eyes as well as by the explorer's desire hidden in their needle-sharp claws, the kittens began to explore every nook and cranny of our house, the house which for them was the entire universe. They would make leaps onto the soft quilting of the beds, roll about on the rug, get underfoot, get caught up in the shrubs, and simply play among themselves. The mother cat would grab each one in turn by the neck, carrying them in her mouth from one corner of the house to another, and, like soft cotton balls tumbling across the house, they would end up with their faces nuzzled in their mother's stomach, nursing.

In the days that followed, their eyes began to sparkle, a crispness of muscular strength became evident in their soft purring, and their skin began to fill in with fur. They no longer followed the mother cat wherever she went; rather, they scooted about on their own in the nooks and crannies of the house searching for God knows what. The mother just lolled in the sunshine, watching them as though slightly fed-up, as though she couldn't be bothered. Occasionally she would let out a soft, admonishing meow. Later she gave up doing even this. Annoyance took the place of disinterest. In the evenings I would put out a saucer of milk for her, and if the kittens so much as came in her direction she would let out a threatening growl. The mother had of her own accord managed to distance herself from the kittens. But for me, removing them from the household had become a problem. And this was just the *first* litter of kittens.

People then started telling me to get somebody to drop them off somewhere. ("The Empress Market is a good spot. There are always lots of cats hanging around the butcher shops there, . . ." I was told.) My feelings were hurt even to think such a thing. After all, hadn't I even sewed a silken quilt for them?–how incredibly adorable they looked lying on it. ("You're spoiling those kittens as though they were the firstborn children of your dearest friend!" my friends chided me. These very same people would *now* call it "cold hearted" wouldn't they.) I could just see what would happen if I simply turned them loose: they'd wander around lost in vacant lots and bushes, attacked by blood-thirsty dogs and harassed by passersby. They'd have to forage for their food in narrow backstreets. They'd learn the ways of ferocity–for survival's sake–and turn out like those seasoned cats who lie on rooftops keeping an eye out for pigeons perched alone, who unnoticed snatch edible morsels lying about in alleys and backstreets. This isn't the kind of life I had in mind for them, but neither could I keep them at home.

The next time my cat had kittens, instead of being a pleasurable event, it turned out to be sheer misery for me.

Then somebody told me what the English do with kittens they don't want to keep–they take them for a dip. I put them in a basin of warm water. ("They feel less pain if the water is warm," I was told.) The kittens were very small and vulnerable. They had yet to complete even their very first day in this world–a world in which no one was willing to accept them. I picked them up from their mother's side and put them one by one into the water, which caused the surface to tremble a bit. Was it a whirlpool I was seeing, or was it their final struggle? I couldn't tell. Were there bubbles rising to the surface of the water, or had tears fogged my eyes? By the time I had wiped my eyes and looked, the surface of the water was calm, and at the bottom they looked like stones lying on the bed of a pond. I picked them up out of the water and for a moment I thought they looked just as they had only a minute before. Before I broke down completely, I threw the kittens onto the trash heap. They lay right there until the garbage truck came along to take them away, like some child's abandoned, lifeless toys upon which the flies had begun to settle.

The cat had become anxious. When she passed in front of me I would get flustered and avert my eyes, and I would look at my hands which seemed to be turning blue from all the water. I blew on them gently, and felt the blood return to them. The cat was looking for her kittens. She was walking all around the house like some restless, lost soul. She would come wandering in from the lane outside, look about in the rooms, and calling to her kittens she would leap out the window and begin to search in the flower beds. She didn't touch the milk that had been left out for her. At night her howls sounded like some old woman's periodic wails for the dead. ("That's the fire of maternal instinct . . ."–those people could even find a name for this.)

I too felt like crying for all the sorrow the cat was going through. Seeing me in the corner of the room wiping my eyes with the edge of my *dupatta,* someone had laughed. "Don't worry. She'll get over this in a couple of days. She'll be fine, you'll see. Your cat's just a little slut anyway." Hearing this, I gulped. I felt my hackles rise, and there was reproach in my eyes–sorrow-filled reproach for my cat.

I saw for myself that she didn't grieve very much for the kittens–or rather, that those profligate alley-tomcats didn't *let* her grieve. Those people who want to can go ahead and laugh, but I was shocked to find out that this was my cat's true character. From the very beginning I had wanted to keep her away from those tomcats. At the time she was given to me as a gift, I was told that this cat was extraordinary because of the rare and unusual pedigree she bore. Kittens of this sort are sold for lots of money, and those who know about cats are always on the lookout for them. You can only get such kittens by formal breeding within this pedigree, and maintaining the pedigree requires constant attention. (So is all this the reason she was given to me? To keep my mind off things?) "Don't let her roam around. . . Those alley cats will ruin her. . . . And even if they don't ruin her, the mongrel kittens will be worthless. . . "

I kept my cat under heavy restrictions. I thought I had brought her up in line with my own disposition. She never poked her nose into the pots and pans in the kitchen, nor did she ever ruin the rugs or bedding. But she did begin disappearing at night. After licking her saucer of milk clean, she was nowhere to be seen in the house. Late at night, you could hear her and the other cats calling to each other from the bushes, followed by the shrieks and growls they made fighting. I thought that the constant companionship of only one human wasn't good for a cat, that she needed to play with her own kind, so I didn't prevent her from going outside. Several times I saw her standing in front of another cat, staring at it with impudence, raising her tail, offering a challenge to battle. Growling in turns, they would attack each other and disappear tumbling into the bushes. One day, she brought one of her playmates home with her. This other cat was somewhat larger than mine, and its colouring was somewhat like that of the membrane which forms on top of a cup of tea after it's been left out too long. Its eyes were devoid of any friendship–rather they were hard looks, looks of disdain. I was determined to shoo it out of the house, to chase it away, but despite my threats, it stood its ground. It was waving its tail like a whip. It opened its mouth to snarl at me, exposing its glistening, needle-sharp teeth. I stepped back, and seeing this, it too retreated a bit. But to my surprise, when it turned back to leave, I saw that there was a pair of testicles hanging like ripe walnuts underneath its upright tail.

I couldn't allow my cat to play *that* kind of game, but she had seen the way out, and all my coaxing and sweet-talking wasn't about to stop her. I must have convinced myself that I should just go ahead and let her do what every other cat does. And yet, each night before going to bed I would shut every door and window, cutting off any access she had to her life outside the house. Even so, she managed to escape–I have no idea how. In the morning when I'd get up, I'd find her waiting on the doorstep along with the newspapers: her delicate skin cut here and there, all scraped up, her paws full of mud–filthy from head to toe. As soon as I'd open the door she'd jump up into my arms. She'd begin to rub her head against me and treat me to a chorus of gentle meows, as though she were expressing her limitless joy and satisfaction. She looked like some satiated, happy woman.

This all must have been about the time she had her first litter of kittens. I gladly put up with them, too–and I let my cat know that I did–even though they took after their father. So she can't claim that I loved them any less because of this. Before this time I didn't acknowledge, even to myself, that I was disappointed at all. Disappointed . . . and embarrassed. And before I even had a chance to put any of this out of my mind, she managed to present me with yet another litter.

Now she had made this into a habit. Not once did the kittens of one litter ever resemble the kittens of another. Sometimes they were spotted, sometimes they were striped. And with each litter it got more and more difficult for me to find them a good home. Just how difficult, only I can know. Still, I never reprimanded her. And even if I had, she wouldn't have cared less. I was watching the part I played in her life become progressively smaller and smaller, while the part played by those wild, profligate tomcats (who so evidently were her lovers) grew and grew. Very infrequent were the days when she stayed home with me. When I coaxed her, she'd make her way over to me and sit down at my feet. She ate her food whenever she felt like it, and would then lie down for a bit of repose on a soft pillow in front of the fireplace, as though nothing had happened at all. On some days, a strange madness would overcome her. She would leave and stay away from the house for days on end, and when she returned, it was only because she sought solace after suffering the scrapes and scratches from one of her fights somewhere. I'd clean her abrasions in warm water, and when I sat down to apply the ointment, I'd end up having to smear it over her entire body. Soft purring would emanate from her throat and she'd begin taking playful swipes with her paws at my hands. She'd pull away from me hoping that I'd follow, and then–just like that–she'd come over to play with me. She had put on the coy, coquettish airs of much-pampered women. There was no way I could have known, but news of her upcoming "special days" spread fast among all the toms in the neighbourhood. They would cry all night long under my window, and the balefulness of their night-hidden wails and howls would keep me awake. How many times did I see them?–climbing up onto the window sill in the impatience of their desire, finding the screen blocking their entrance into the house, clawing at it with frustrated paws, hovering like evil spirits. I was determined to stop her, but my cat would quietly slip out. Her restlessness would get her up and she'd begin to pace around the room looking for some way out to the source of those cries. She too, in just the same manner, would begin to cry in response. It's a mystery to me how and when she managed to get out. But all night I'd have to listen to the thuds of their jumping about, to the shrieks and cries of their fighting and chasing. A few times I decided to get up and go catch both her and her boyfriend, and so I followed the noise they were making. But she never gave me the opportunity–she was a very clever cat, and she carried out her business well removed from prying eyes. And as for the neighbours, they were aware only of when those shameless, stray tomcats quit loitering around our house, which was also the time that our cat's stomach would begin to swell.

"Your cat has become a whore," I was informed, as though I had no idea. But more than the accusation itself, I dreaded its thunderous, courtroom-like tone.

After some time, the neighbours came and gave me a graft from a rose bush. I didn't ask them, but I did ask myself why it was that whenever they brought me something I was supposed to amuse myself with, it was always offered as though it were Mira's cup of poison. I disposed of that question as I would the poison, and gave myself completely over to taking care of that graft. It was ordered from Punjab especially for me. I had to take care that it flourished, because it was expected of me. I had a bed made for it, I prepared the soil and watered it, I put the graft into the soil, and I proceeded to wait for the dry sprig to sprout some green leaves. One stem remained exactly as it was–dry and leafless. The other one sprouted very tender shoots. I watched these shoots grow and bud, too. But I knew then that there was something wrong with the graft, that it was not flourishing the way it should. This time though, I didn't unilaterally decide on the cure, but rather I asked everyone for suggestions and remedies. I tried out whatever anyone told me. Someone said that roses just don't do well in Karachi soil, so I had the soil of the flower bed replaced. Someone said to mix tea leaves into the soil around the roots, so I did that too. But still the plant didn't grow. It remained withered, like a sick child. When it did manage to put out a blossom, it was small and a pale dull red.

Then someone told me what the English do to make their plants grow–they talk to them. My face must have shown my incredulity, because I was then told that plants have sense perception, that they are living beings, and that they respond to the emotions of the one talking to them. I swallowed hard and thought to myself, "Oh, I wish I looked like a clinging vine . . . I wish I really *were* a clinging vine! If someone were to want to communicate with *me,* I'd grow full and green, living my life piggy-back on some broad, strong tree limb."

But, regrettably, I wasn't even a plant. Subsequently I thought, "Why should the rose's growth be stunted because of my disappointment? Let it blossom." I talked to it. I told it about myself. I told it how promiscuous my cat had turned out.

When the rose's chilled leaves shook in the wind, I took them to be agreeing with me–they were commiserating with me. I didn't suspect that I had made yet another mistake. I should not have told the graft about myself. I had become so used to living my life only one moment at a time that I completely neglected to consider how detrimental such tales of woe would be for the rose. *Anyone* listening to such tales couldn't help but wither and die. And sure enough, the rose responded accordingly–no blossoms, no leaves.

My mistake in communicating with the rose was to make it my confidante, because when it did finally respond to me, it did so by producing a bud which turned into the puniest of blossoms. This was an ailing rose which had somehow failed to grow strong.

I was pleased, however, with the fact that the rose even bloomed at all. But when I went outside to check on it, yet another shock awaited me–it had been infested by aphids.

The aphid-ridden blossom's colour was faded, the petals were withered, and they were marked with the inevitable signs of death.

Now I had only one choice left. I went inside and got a scissors, and without flinching I closed the shiny metal blades and snipped the blossom from the plant. And not just this blossom, but also the one withered bud which was just beginning to show its head on another branch.

And as I was snipping that bud, it became clear what I should do with the cat.

Depressed, I logically and methodically laid out all my options before me and considered them on my own. I couldn't just turn the cat out. So this was not a viable solution. On the other hand, I also couldn't allow her to continue doing whatever she wanted without some means of restricting her. Otherwise, her nocturnal escapades with the stray tomcats would never end, nor would the series of kittens, the disposal of which was my unpleasant duty.

The onslaught of kittens had to come to an end–kittens which were proceeding from her womb as though they were a deluge emerging from the old woman's oven in Noah's time, threatening to overrun the entire planet with cats.

And besides, the speed and numbers with which she could produce kittens seemed like an insult, a distinct mockery of me by means of her own fertility. She was pointing out her superiority. She was taunting me in her brazen, arrogant manner, as though her disobedience were my defeat. And she must pay for it.

This time when I called her, the cat had no idea of the danger at hand. She came strutting over to me and began to rub her body up against my leg. "Slut," I cursed her under my breath, and purring she leaped up into my arms. Even then she had no idea that my grip on her that minute found its strength in the fire of my rivalry. She made no attempt to escape from my arms, even when I immersed her head in the basin of warm water. And by the time she did try, it was already too late. She writhed in agony, and then rolled over onto her back. I turned her over and, spreading out her four paws, tied them to the sides of the basin (just like that film of the surgical operation they were showing on TV in those days, as some kind of entertainment). I took the pruning shears I had used on the rose plant, and plunged its shining blade into her hide. And since I was a regular, dedicated viewer of that TV show, I had no trouble determining, in the midst of her entrails and bleeding veins, the part of her anatomy which was guilty of her exceptional fertility. I cut it out with the scissors, just as I had the rosebud. I was examining it, holding it between the blades of the scissors. Blood was surging forth. There was no way to stop it. The entire basin was becoming red–thick, stout blood in the turbid water; fresh blood. The bursting freshness of this red jet of blood struck me like a spear directly in my chest, and my heart began to sink with a feeling of irreparable loss. This blood has to stop. How would I bring her back now?–I suddenly thought. I had never seen how the doctors on that program got the patient back up on his feet. My heart began to sink, and I put my hands into the basin as well. I touched the cat's lifeless body with those numb hands, wondering whether or not she would respond if I tried to communicate with her. But blood kept spilling from where I had cut out the source of her fertility. It dawned on me that I had the ability to take life, not to give it: the very reason I was deprived of fertility. Just like a stretch of land forever remaining arid, devastated and disfigured by salinity.

Now no cat will come soft-footed up to the doorstep of my life, asking "Shall I come in?" No, those times are over. On balance, my punishment is my life alone, without my cat.

Translated by Griffith A. Chaussée

MUHAMMAD MANSHA YAD

The Show

They cover a long distance in the dark and arrive at the river bank at day break.

Here and there the bank is littered with dead and half-eaten fish.

"Father, this is the work of otters."

"Yes, son," says the older man, "this is precisely what they do. They keep killing the fish and piling them up. But when time comes to eat them, they fight among themselves and ruin the game and bloody themselves."

"All these fish!" says the boy. "Wouldn't the river run dry of fish if they kill so many in just one night?"

"This could happen, if the otters keep multiplying."

The two put their bags down on the bank and look across the river at the village they are headed for. The minarets of the village mosque are clearly visible, but there is neither a boat nor a bridge to cross over to the other side. Troubled, they look at the river. It appears uniformly deep and wide at every point. The older man broods a while and then says, "Son, let's place our trust in God and plunge into the river."

"Whatever you say, father."

"What if we drown?"

"We won't repeat the mistake."

"You've turned out to be quite smart, Jamura!" the older man laughs and says.

"But, of course. I'm your son–am I not?"

"We certainly would have plunged, . . ." the older man stops, thinks some, and then says, "but for this dream I had last night."

"What dream, father?"

"It was a very frightening dream, son."

"What did you see?"

"Oh Jamura, I saw that there was a big crowd. I'm standing in the middle of that crowd with the spotted snake curled around my neck. The children are clapping and older people are throwing coins onto the sheet spread on the ground. Just then the snake, whom I've nurtured with the same loving care as I have you, suddenly bites into my neck and empties its poison."

"And then?"

"And then darkness begins to fall before my eyes. Peoples' faces begin to dim and their voices fade out. I feel I'm falling deeper and deeper into the well of a deathly sleep. As I'm drowning, I muster all my ebbing strength and call after you in the darkness."

"Then?"

"Then I wake up with a start hearing my own cry and, lo, I see it's midnight, the moon has gone, the dogs are howling ominously and the breeze, heavy with dew, is moving about balefully."

"What happens next?"

"My eyes fall on you. You are lying all curled up from the cold. I throw the sheet over you, just as I always do in the arena, when I slash your throat and then make you leap back to life. But at that melancholy hour of the night I felt that the manner in which I threw the sheet over you was distinctly ominous. And my sleep left me."

"Just from that," the boy says, "you concluded that we should not enter the river?"

"Yes, son. It doesn't look like a good day for us."

The older man sits down and stretches out his legs to rest. The boy, still full of energy, starts clambering up and down the hills at a run. Suddenly he shouts: "The bridge, father, I can see the bridge! It really isn't all that far!"

The word "bridge" sends a current of fresh energy through the man's decrepit old body. He stands up and sprints off to the hill and gazes at the water flowing downstream. Then, overwhelmed by a sudden rush of happiness, he says, "Yes, the bridge isn't all that far. But . . . the path is riddled with difficulties."

"That hardly matters, father."

They pick up their gear and start walking along the river on the path which takes them through formidable cliffs and steep slopes, hills, ravines, dangerous fjords, thick jungles, prickly brambles and dry grasses that injure their feet. But they keep moving along. And the tall minarets of the village mosque across the river move right along with them. They are exhausted from walking on what looks like an endless trek. Morning turns into noon, noon into afternoon, but the bridge still looks just as far as when they had started. Which prompts the older man to say, "It is very strange, Jamura–the bridge keeps moving ahead."

"And the village too," the boy says. "The minarets are walking right along with us."

"Strange, isn't it, Jamura?"

"Very strange, father."

"I'd say, son, it's some kind of spell."

"Want to know what I think, father? We make fun of people all the time. Today, well, today we are being laughed at."

They keep trudging along. The afternoon dwindles. They are exhausted from walking. Their lips are crusted from drinking the river's muddy water over and over again. Their clothes are torn to shreds and their feet are bleeding from walking through the thorny brush. Still the bridge and the minarets of the village mosque beyond remain as distant as ever.

"Stop, son," the older man says. "Perhaps we are not fated to reach the village across the river. We'll keep walking on and on but will perhaps never reach the bridge."

"What shall we do then?"

"Let's go back."

"No, father. What good will it do to go back? We've aimed for the village across the river–haven't we? Besides, men don't give up easily."

"You've a point there, son. Even our women folk don't easily scare from the fury of the waves. They plunge right into the river with nothing but pitchers of unbaked clay to keep them afloat."

"Good, father, so then let's jump into the river."

"No, son, you'll tire. Besides, we've all this gear to carry."

"Don't worry about me, father. As for our things, we'll have new ones made once we get there."

The older man says nothing. He puts the stuff back down and gazes off into the river waters. Then breaks into a song:

Deep is the river
the boat rickety and old
And fearful tigers stand watch on the river bank . . .

The boy chimes in, completing the lines:

I too must visit my lover's abode
Would that someone came along.

Suddenly they hear the sounds of dogs barking and cattle lowing.
"These sounds–right in the middle of the jungle?" the boy says.
"Looks like there's a village nearby–I mean a different village."
"Looks like that."
"Let's spend the night in this village. We'll have a good night's rest and then we can start off again early in the morning. What do you say, son?"
"As you like."
The older man thinks for a bit and then starts off after the sounds. The boy trails behind him, casting furtive glances every now and then back at the village across the river. Gradually they pull farther and farther away from the river bank and come upon a small village.
Abruptly the older man stops short. He looks overhead at the jujube tree and asks dumbly, "Jamura, it couldn't be. . . ."
Jamura too looks into the tree, then picks up a rock and hurls it at the foliage. Berries come tumbling down. He picks one up, tastes it and quickly spits it out. "Yes, father," he says, "it's only *neem*. Horribly bitter."
"God take care," the older man says. "Neem right along with the jujube. It doesn't bode well. Son, it's some spell."
The boy just gawks at the sky without speaking a word.
"Those are swallows, son."
"Yes, a whole flock of them."
"Must be looking for food."
"Or something else–who knows?"
"What else, son?"
"Elephants."
"No, son, no. They are not those swallows. These are the kind who just sit on the backs of elephants, have a good time and chirp."
"Let's get out of here, father. This place doesn't look right."
"God will take care, son," the older man says. "Let's do a little business here in this village. We'll spend the night here and be on our way early in the morning."

"Whatever you say, father."

They step into the village, dump their gear in an open space, and scan the area. The boy spreads out a sheet and sits down on one of the corners. The older man yanks out his small kettle drum and flute from the gear and begins to play them both.

In no time a crowd of children materializes and begins to gather around them. The faces of father and son light up with hope and satisfaction. The older man looks at the boy meaningfully and shakes his head, as if saying, "Fine, now we'll earn enough to spend the night splendidly."

The older man continues playing the flute and drum, becomes tired and says, "Son, it's a strange village. My arms are frozen stiff from playing the drum and my chest has gone dry from blowing into the flute, and we have yet to see an adult man or woman with a coin to spare."

"They might be deaf, or they might have plugged their ears with cotton. Who knows?"

"Why so, son?"

"Because if one never gets to hear good news, then a time comes when he's so fed up he doesn't want to hear anything at all."

"Bravo Jamura, you've learnt your lesson well. Now tell me this: what makes you think they have never heard good news?"

"I see it written on the faces of these children, father."

"Jamura, you're a smart boy."

"Look who is my teacher."

"You are right, son. They do look like orphans."

"It even occurs to me that they have themselves driven their parents out of the village."

"I wonder if we haven't tumbled into the wrong place."

"Yes, it looks like that."

"Not a single adult man or woman in the whole village! Looks as though all the adult population has gone away to other villages to perform shows as we do."

"Then they will surely come back. We must wait for them."

"Why?"

"Just to find out who is the better showman: you or they."

"No, Jamura, no. These children scare me. They look so strange."

"Well then, let's get out of here."

"Yes, son, that makes better sense. But let's just ask these children where all their elders have disappeared to."

"We are elders ourselves," a brat blurts out from the crowd. "Do we look like youngsters to you?"

Father and son are taken aback and exchange uncomprehending glances. They still haven't quite recovered from the shock when another tiny child addresses them in a perfectly adult voice: "The Scribe has spoken the truth. Now you two get on with your show and be on your way. We don't permit those who think they are bigger and older than us to stay in our town a minute longer than is necessary."

"You mean to say that not a single person of adult height lives in this village?"

"We don't let them," a boy chuckles and says. "We get rid of them–right away."

"So this village. . ." the older man stammers.

"Yes, this is *our* village and I *am* its chief. But don't waste our time. If you can perform some very good tricks, why, we will surely reward you. Enough. Now get on with your show."

"We are not quite done watching the show before us." The boy remarks.

"You! Mind your manners, boy!" the chief shouts angrily. "Or else . . ."

"My, my," the boy breaks into a laugh, "you do behave like a chief's son."

"Chief's son? Damn it, I *am* the chief!"

"Yes, yes–he is our chief!" a whole bunch of small-ones affirm vociferously. But the boy keeps laughing. Then, edging close to the older man, he says, "I wonder whether we haven't wandered into the land of dwarfs."

"Showman–what's this nonsense?" the chief screams. "He is calling us dwarfs? Tell the impudent brat to shut up, or get the hell out of our village."

The older man looks about in numbed silence, then says to the boy, "Jamura, be quiet. This is some spell."

"What spell, father? These kids . . ."

"They're not children, my son," the older man cuts him short.

"Then what are they?"

"Take a close look at them, Jamura. They have grey hair and they have wrinkles on their faces. They are advanced in years but their brains are still unripe. I'm afraid they could be quite dangerous."

"Strange."

"Very strange, son. God help us."

Presently a few dwarfs walk in carrying cots and wicker stools. The chief, along with crowds of his midget population, sit down on these. The chief says in a commanding voice: "Let the show begin!"

The older man throws a perplexed look at the spectators, then begins to take things out of the bags.

First, he produces three balls and sets them on the ground. Then he covers them with three bowls, mumbles "abracadabra" and blows over them. One by one he lifts the bowls. Presto, the balls have disappeared.

He looks at the audience, expecting applause. But they are unmoved. They just stand or sit in motionless silence.

Next the old man puts the bowls back on the ground face down. When he picks them up one by one, each reveals a ball underneath. Again he looks at the chief and others among the audience, again expecting applause. But they seem totally unimpressed by the trick. They neither move nor applaud.

Then he removes a rupee coin from his pocket. He turns it into two rupees, then the two into four, and exclaims, "Gracious gentlemen! True lovers and connoisseurs of art! I'm no magician. This is merely sleight of hand. Were I a magician, I wouldn't have come here; I would've just stayed home minting money."

"We know that," the chief interrupts him. "Just get on with the show."

"Well, then, get into the act yourself," Jamura says. "What are you waiting for?"

"Showman—this impudent brat . . ." the chief snaps, bristling with rage.

"Chief, I beg your pardon," the older man implores and, with a gesture of his hand, tells Jamura to be quiet. He then pulls out trick after ingenious trick to amuse them: He makes a perfectly empty glass become filled all by itself; turns the filled glass over without spilling a drop; closes his hand over a handkerchief and when he opens it, lo, the handkerchief has changed colour; swallows a lighted cigarette and makes the smoke come out of his ears; wraps a spotted snake round his neck and makes it bite him; swallows a knife clean and then makes it come back out . . .

But none, including the chief, is amused. No one claps or applauds.

Which leaves him terribly upset. In desperation he makes an announcement:

"And now for my grand finale I shall slit Jamura's throat and, after I've killed him, bring him back to life."

Suddenly the chief and his subjects break into wild applause. The man is simply shocked. Earlier, whenever he made the announcement for this trick, which he usually saved till the end, the greater part of his audience reacted with horror and tried to persuade him not to do it. But these folks–what kind of brutes were they that they went into such ecstatic applause at the mere mention of slashing a throat?

He makes Jamura lie down on the ground and as usual pulls a sheet over him. Then he jerks out a butcher knife from his bag and, running his hand along the blade, says:

"Gracious gentlemen! True lovers and connoisseurs of art! What father can slash the throat of his own son? Only prophets have the guile and the courage to do so. This is but a game, a trick, an optical illusion. All for the sake of this wretched stomach which must somehow be filled . . ."

"Don't waste time with your prattle!" the chief thunders.

"Plunge the blade," shouts someone in the audience.

"Yes, plunge the blade, plunge the blade," the audience chime in, shouting at the tops of their voices.

The man tries to overcome his nervousness, then comes up to Jamura wielding his butcher knife and slashes the boy's throat.

The audience breaks into ecstatic screams, applauds widely, whistles and boos, throws coins on the sheet, and without bothering to observe his being brought back to life begins to slink away.

Slowly the place empties out.

The older man calls, "Get up, son, and collect the money."

But Jamura doesn't respond.

The man nervously uncovers the sheet and is horrified to see Jamura lying in a pool of blood, his neck actually severed.

The showman's cries begin to echo throughout the village.

Translated by Muhammad Umar Memon

SALAM BIN RAZZAQ

Ekalavya–The Bheel Boy

Hiranyadhanus, the Bheel, with his only son Ekalavya in tow, traversed jungles and deserts, crossed rivers and ravines, mountains and valleys, and, after enduring great hardship over weeks and months, finally reached the outskirts of Indra-Prasth.

The day was far along by the time they entered the city, and the shadows had begun to shorten. The streets were sparkling clean and shops opened for business, vibrant with jostling crowds of shoppers. Priests–their colourful ceremonial marks pasted across their broad foreheads, hair neatly braided, and their sacred threads hung diagonally across their bodies from the left shoulder to the right hip– came clip-clopping out of temples on their wooden clogs. People would see them and immediately prostrate before them reverentially, while the priests accepted this obeisance by raising their heads. Every now and then a mounted soldier, his sword hanging from his waist, a fringed diadem on his head, passed by. A few beggar boys, heads completely shaven except for a short, thin braid resting on the neck, and bare-bodied, except for a saffron-coloured *dhoti* draped around their waists, their foreheads smeared with ashes, went about collecting alms in their begging bowls.

Just then Hiranya, the Bheel, appeared on the street holding his son's hand. As soon as the priests saw him, their foreheads creased with displeasure. People busy shopping momentarily turned around to look at the Bheel and his boy. By chance, the eyes of a mounted soldier also fell upon him. He spurred his animal on and promptly overtook Hiranya. He cracked his whip in the air and asked in a thundering voice:

"O Chandala! What brings you to the city this early? It isn't even a Thursday."

"I haven't come to buy or sell anything. I have merely come to see the illustrious and the mighty Gururaj Dronacharya."

"Gururaj Dronacharya?" repeated the incredulous people who had promptly crowded on the scene.

"Yes, him."

Hiranya's throat was fast drying up; he was finding it hard to bear the lance-sharp eyes of the people.

"You are a wretched Sudra," the mounted soldier rumbled, "yet you talk about meeting Gururaj. Don't you know that's a sin?"

"Yes, Scion of a Kshatriya, I know that it is a sin. But a child's fancy has driven me to commit it."

"Whose child?"

"My own, O Guardian of the Kingdom!" Hiranya replied, looking at Ekalavya who stood holding his finger.

"And what is his fancy?" the soldier asked, looking closely at the skinny, dark-coloured little thing who stood holding a small bow in his other hand, with a quiver full of arrows hanging from his shoulder.

"Son of a Kshatriya, this fortunate one insists on learning archery from none other than Dronacharya himself, the Most High."

Hearing this the soldier looked at the people gathered around them. They all appeared positively shocked by the diminutive Bheel's insolence. Then he cleared his throat and said, "O Wretched Man, Guruvirya Dronacharya teaches archery only to sons of Brahmins or Kshatriyas. You are neither. What makes you think you can get him to teach you archery?"

But this time it was Ekalavya who raised his head and answered. "I'll persuade him with my skill."

"Well then, show us your skill," the soldier said, smiling with ridicule, as he looked at the people who also nodded derisively.

Quickly Ekalavya straightened his bow, took out an arrow from the quiver and scanned the area with his restless eyes. He spotted a water fowl in the sky. The Bheel boy strung his bow, slightly stretched out his left foot, rested his right knee on the ground, took aim and released the bow. The arrow whizzed out. The next instant the water-fowl fell right at the boy's feet, its body skewered by the arrow.

Everyone–the soldier included–peeled their eyes and gawked now at the bird, now at the boy. Some even cheered, "Bravo! Well done!" in spite of themselves. The bird fluttered briefly and then the life ran out of it. People, overcome by both surprise and adulation, began to whisper:

"What perfect aim!"

"Who is this son of a Bheel?"

"Where are the two coming from?"

"Who have they come to see?'

"Rajguru Dronacharya."

"Rajguru? Really?"

"Yes. This son of a Bheel has come to learn archery from Rajguru. Or so it's said."

"Son of a Bheel and wanting to learn archery from Rajguru–that's an outrage!"

"Rajguru won't teach him. No, never!"

"Of course he won't. This man's just a Bheel. And Rajguru Dronacharya is of such elevated status!"

"Well, let's just see."

The soldier, as immobile as a statue, stared at Ekalavya for a while, and then after clearing his throat once again said, "Well, all right, you can go and see Rajguru if you must. But I'm telling you, he's not going to teach you anything. How will he teach *you* the art which princes no less than Bheema and Arjuna are learning from him?"

"But if I could just see him once," Hiranyadhanus pleaded, "my visit to the city, all the hardship I've had to endure, will have paid off."

"Gururaj must be instructing the princes in the woods of the royal palace. If you can betake yourself there somehow, you'll be graced with a sight of him."

Thereupon the soldier spurred his horse on. The horse lurched forward. The crowd moved to let the horse pass, and the soldier trotted off.

Hiranya seized Ekalavya's hand and the two began to walk towards the royal palace.

At the gate of the enclosure behind which lay the woods they were stopped by the gatekeeper, who said, "O Chandalas! Watch where you're going. Don't you know evil spirits are not permitted here?"

"Lord, have mercy! Permit us to see Rajguru Dronacharya Ji. Just once! Please! For the sake of God, do us this favour!"

"Shut up, Vile Man! You're but an infernal being, yet you want to have a vision of Mahaguru Dronacharya? Don't you know, by merely uttering Mahaguru's name with your vile tongue, you've already defiled it, which is an unpardonable sin. That's crime enough to stick a red hot rod into your mouth."

"Mercy, Son of a Kshatriya, mercy!" Hiranya joined both hands begging for the gatekeeper's forgiveness, and then promptly touched the ground with his forehead.

Seeing Hiranya humble himself thus, the gatekeeper's anger subsided some. He raised his eyebrows and offered the question, "Why do you want to see Acharya Deva?"

"For the sake of this obstinate brat. He has gotten it into his head to learn archery from Acharya Deva."

The keeper of the royal gate burst into laughter, and went on laughing for a while. Then he said, "You look a little crazy too. Oh dear! What makes you think that Acharya Deva will consent to teach archery to a Bheel's son?" He raised another resounding guffaw, "Ha-ha-ha!"

"Lord, I know I'm being very impudent. But I felt helpless before a child's insistence. I had to come here. If only I could see Acharya Deva once, I will fall on his feet and implore him. I'd do exactly as he says. But I must see him."

"And you there, wretched son of a Chandala," the gatekeeper suddenly accosted Ekalavya. "Do you know how to shoot arrows?"

"Lord, he knows but a little," Hiranya Bheel said quickly.

"That tree over there," Ekalavya pointed. "Pick out any of its fruit, any at all, and I'll pluck it down by your feet."

"Lord," Hiranya quickly intervened, "please don't mind; he doesn't mean it."

The gatekeeper ignored Hiranya. He stared at the boy and said, "Look, if you are unable to fell that bunch of three mangos over there in one shot, I'll seize your bow and arrow and have you and your father beaten about the head with a shoe ten times over. Agreed?"

"Agreed!"

Hiranyadhanus froze. "Lord, please let it go. Forgive him. He's just an ignorant little boy." Then he grabbed the bow and chided the boy, "Ekalavya! you argue with the Lord, where is your shame?"

"No, no! Don't stop him! Let him shoot. And if he misses, be prepared to receive ten blows over the head with a shoe."

"Lord, you are the master. You can strike me now. You don't need an excuse."

"No, the deal's struck. He must shoot." Then looking at the boy, the gatekeeper said, "Go on, shoot!"

Ekalavya strung the bow, took aim, and pulled the bowstring all the way to his earlobe. The arrow shot out with a whiz and the next moment the bunch of mangos plunked down near them. The gatekeeper's mouth fell open at such superb deftness, his eyes riveted incredulously on the bunch.

Ekalavya bowed and saluted him reverentially.

Just then some commotion was heard inside the enclosure. The gatekeeper started and turned round to look. "Well, well, what do you know?" he said. "Acharya Deva's palanquin is coming along."

He beckoned Hiranyadhanus and Ekalavya to step aside and unsheathed his sword with a flourish and stood at attention with the sword held before his face.

Shortly four palanquin-bearers briskly strode out of the gate carrying a golden palanquin in which sat Rajguru in all his pomp and glory.

Clad in a silken dhoti, his sacred thread in place, caste mark on his forehead, crown on his head, ears strung with jeweled ornaments–Rajguru's face emitted such radiance it was impossible to behold him. Two bodyguards holding tall lances came trailing behind the palanquin. Suddenly Hiranya threw himself in front of the carriage and, joining his hands in a gesture of reverence, touched the ground with his forehead. The armed guards made a dash for the Bheel and tore him from the ground.

"Guru Deva," Hiranya implored. "Please listen to my petition, I beg you."

The guards began to drag him away to one side, but the Bheel kept on his humble litany, "Guru Deva, hear me out. Please. Just once. Then punish me however you will."

The Rajguru kept looking at Hiranya with his shinning eyes for some time and then raised his hands, making a gesture for the guardsmen to let go of the man. And the guards released him accordingly.

Once again Hiranya prostrated himself on the ground and joining his hands in a gesture of extreme humility entreated, "Devaraj, I am Hiranyadhanus, the Bheel. And this is Ekalavya, my only son. He's dying to learn the art of archery. If Your Highness would just so much as give him a place by Your feet, he'd be able to satisfy his heart's desire. Lord, don't be angry. I know this is an outrage, but what could I do? I'm powerless before this childish insistence."

Rajguru Acharya lifted his eyes and looked at Ekalavya. The boy immediately made his obeisance. The Rajguru beckoned him to come close.

"Why do you want to learn archery?" he asked.

"So that I may protect myself against beasts in the jungle and against enemies in the village."

"You do know, don't you, that archery is taught only to sons of Kshatriyas? You are a Bheel, and yet you talk about learning archery. Such insolence is punishable with your life."

"Guru Deva, just give me the permission and I will sacrifice myself at your feet."

Rajguru Dronacharya smiled artlessly. "Son of a Bheel," he said, "you are very clever. But we really cannot take you as our pupil. This is forbidden by our laws. All the same, we give you our blessing."

Guru Deva Dronacharya made a sign. The guards promptly withdrew from the Bheel, and the bearers moved on with the palanquin. Ekalavya and his father kept looking at the palanquin carrying Guru Deva Dronacharya away. When it had disappeared from view, father and son withdrew to their forest.

Subsequently–the story goes–Ekalavya made himself a clay image of Guru Deva Dronacharya and made it into a living mentor before whom he persevered in perfecting his skill at archery. The day came when none could equal him in that art.

Then thirty-five hundred years later, it so happened that Ekalavya was reborn in the household of a poor labourer, who also went by the name of Hiranyadhanus. When Ekalavya became five years old, Hiranyadhanus put him in a municipal school. The boy turned out to be an exceptionally bright student. Day and night he worked hard at his study, always securing the highest marks in his exams. He very much wanted to become a doctor. After he graduated from high school with top honours, Hiranya took him to a medical college.

As luck would have it, the self-same Guru Deva Dronacharya turned out to be the principal of that college.

Ekalavya filled out the admission form. His scores were so good that Guru Deva Dronacharya called him into his office cubicle. He recognized the father and son right away. He smiled and said, "Come in, Ekalavya, do come in." Then, looking at the father, "Well Hiranya, how are you?"

"I am fine, by God's grace, Maharaj."

"So what do you do these days?"

"Lord, I work as a day-labourer in a mill."

"I see. A menial worker, huh, yet you want to make your son a doctor–why?"

"He certainly will become a doctor, Maharaj, that is if you're kind and willing to do us a favour."

"Don't say that, Hiranya, please don't. You don't know that we are still quite as helpless today."

"How can you possibly be helpless?"

"Dear God, thirty-five hundred years haven't taught you a thing! Poor Hiranya, still the same old idiot!"

"My Master, I certainly don't wish to sound impudent, but back then we were considered Sudras. Today we are no longer considered quite as servile a caste. So what possible obstacle could there now be in accepting Ekalavya as your pupil?"

"That's precisely the problem, Hiranya. Times have changed. If you were still a Sudra, or a Harijan, I'd have had no difficulty admitting Ekalavya against the B.C. quota. Today your not being a Sudra is the biggest stumbling block. Ekalavya couldn't be more unfortunate: when he should've been born to a Brahmin or a Kshatriya, he chose a Sudra; and when he should have been born into the family of a Harijan, he chose a non-Harijan household. *You* tell me now, what should I do?"

"Do what you will, Master, but don't send us back in disappointment. I've come to you full of hope."

"We are truly helpless, Hiranya."

"Lord . . . Master . . ."

"Peon!" Principal Dronacharya called his servant, who promptly appeared. "Show in the next candidate!"

Dronacharya turned his face away from Hiranya and Ekalavya. The peon made a gesture for them to exit the room, as he called out the name of the next candidate.

Translated by Muhammad Umar Memon

Notes and Glossary

ZAMIRUDDIN AHMAD ("First Death")
bandigi: a term of salutation indicating respect and deference, usually employed in addressing Hindu traders; *sala:* literally, wife's brother; colloquially, the most common word of abuse; *pandan:* an ornate metal box in which betel leaves (*pan*) and other chewing materials that usually go with it (such as cured lime, catechu, grated betel nuts, tobacco, and cardamom pods) are kept; also used by housewives for keeping petty cash; *abba:* father, daddy; *amma:* mother, mummy; *murgha:* a common punishment for boys; the boy is required to assume the posture of a rooster (murgha) by bending over, passing his hands under his knees to hold his ears, and to remain in that posture for the duration of punishment.

QUDRATULLAH SHAHAB ("The Plague in Jammu")
qawwali: Muslim devotional hymns sung in assemblies of the devout, usually at a saint's shrine; *sattu:* parched-grain flour; *burqa:* a two-piece wrap-around used as a veil and cover for the body, used by Muslim women in public; *dupatta:* a long, wide scarf worn by women over the shoulders, bosom, and head; *fatiha:* the opening chapter of the Qur'an; generally the term includes this chapter and some other verses of the Qur'an which together make up the prayer for the dead; *durud:* a formulaic prayer praising and blessing the Prophet Muhammad; *bismillah arrahman arrahim:* "In the name of Allah, most benevolent, ever-merciful" the general Islamic invocation of God; it prefaces every chapter in the Qur'an except the ninth; it is used by

Muslims extensively before embarking on an activity; *pir:* a Muslim saint; *pan:* see Ahmad, above.

QURRATULAIN HYDER ("Hyena's Laughter")
bindi: a dot, a mark; here, ornament for the forehead usually worn by Hindu women; *tabla:* a pair of Indian drums.

ABDULLAH HUSSEIN ("The Refugees")
'idgah: a large space (may or may not be enclosed) where the prayer on the two major Muslim festivals of *'id* takes place; *qasba:* a small town, a large village; *du'a:* a personal prayer usually following the ritual prayer; a supplication; *burqas:* see Shahab, above.

HASAN MANZAR ("The Beggar Boy")
'idgah: see Hussein, above; *pan:* see Ahmad, above; *milad:* celebration of the nativity of the Prophet Muhammad; however, milad here stands for the ceremony in which poems praising Muhammad are chanted as a gesture of thanksgiving following the successful culmination of a project or deed; *kalima*: the Muslim profession of the Unity of God and of Muhammad as God's Prophet; required for conversion to Islam.

KHALIDA HUSAIN ("Recognition")
The title of the story, "Pahchan," means both "recognition" and "identity"; *burqa:* see Shahab, above; *kalima*: see Manzar, above; it is also recited during ritual prayers and when hearing of a death or spotting a funeral procession.

JEELANI BANO ("Some Other Man's Home")
bhabi: brother's wife, sister-in-law; but never wife's sister.

RAM LALL ("The Grave")
burqa: see Shahab, above.

PARVEEN SARWAR ("Hearth and Home")
tabla: see Hyder, above; *sarangi:* a violin-like musical instrument; *raga:* a musical mode; *ghazal:* a lyrical poem in Urdu; *dupatta:* see Shahab, above; *mosjid:* Bengali way of pronouncing the more familiar

masjid (mosque*); tilak:* a ceremonial Hindu caste mark painted low on the forehead between the brows; *bindiya:* same as bindi (Hyder, above); *khaddar:* the coarsest cotton fabric; *bhabi:* see Bano, above; *sondesh:* a Bengali sweetmeat; *dhoti:* a cloth worn round the waist, passing between the legs and tucked in behind; *zoe:* Bengali pronunciation for the Hindi and Urdu *jai*–victory! or *jiye*–long live!

SURENDAR PARKASH ("The Scarecrow")
Hori is the protagonist of the novel *Ga'odan* (The Gift of a Cow) by the famous Urdu and Hindi novelist Munshi Premchand (1880-1936); *panchayat:* village council; *chaupal:* community place; *Angrez:* the British, singly or collectively; *thal:* a stretch of arid, barren land; *bhat:* a simple, watery rice dish with lentils; *sarpanch:* head of the village council.

MUHAMMAD UMAR MEMON ("Lucky Vikki")
pan: see Shahab, above.

MUHAMMAD MANSHA YAD ("The Show")
"They are not those swallows" is an allusion to the Qur'an 105:3; it is said that in the year 570 C.E. Abraha, the Christian Abyssinian viceroy of South Arabia, marched northward to destroy Mecca. He was leading a large army, which also included a number of elephants. Abraha's attempt, however, was foiled by an act of God. A large flock of *ababil*-birds (swallows) swooped down on the invading army and pelted it with stones, thus forcing it to withdraw.

SALAM BIN RAZZAQ ("Ekalavya–The Bheel Boy")
Bheel: a non-urban mountain race that resides in the forests and hilly tracks of central India; their caste status is very low; *Indra Prasth:* ancient name of Delhi; *Chandala:* a member of the most degraded of mixed castes; an outcast; a wretch; *Harijan:* "God's child," euphemism for an untouchable.

Contributors

ZAMIRUDDIN AHMAD was born in Fatehgarh (India) in 1925 and emigrated to Pakistan in 1947. He was educated at Aligarh Muslim University and later at St. Andrews College, Gorakhpur, and Allahabad University. He has worked as a journalist in India, Pakistan, the Middle East and U.K. and also as a broadcaster for the BBC, the Voice of America, Radio Pakistan and Pakistan Television. He started writing fiction in the early 1950s. His writings include about forty short stories, numerous critical essays, radio plays, and TV serials. In his critical monograph *Khatir-e Masum* (1990), he explores the dimensions of female sexuality across the entire range of Urdu poetic genres. A Hindi translation of some of his stories appeared under the title *Pahli Maut* (Delhi, 1985). *Sukhe Sawan,* his first Urdu collection, was published in Karachi in 1991. The story included here first appeared in the literary journal *Saughat* (Karachi, 1962). In 1971, Mr. Ahmad moved to London and lived there until his death in December 1990.

JEELANI BANO has been writing fiction since 1954 and has so far published two novels, two collections of novellas, and four volumes of short stories. Practically all her short fiction has been translated into all the major languages of India, and many pieces have also been translated into English and Russian. Her novel *Aiwan-e Ghazal* (Delhi, 1976) was so well received that it was translated into fourteen

255

Indian languages and will also be shown on Indian TV. She has been the recipient of numerous literary honours, among them the Soviet Land-Nehru Award for 1984. She traveled to the U.S.S.R. in 1985 to receive it, returning twice to that country in 1986 and 1988. She also enjoys writing children's stories and radio, TV, and stage plays. She holds a Master's in Urdu literature and is a literary consultant to the Ministry of Education, Government of India, as well as an advisor to many official and semi-official agencies for the appreciation and promotion of Urdu. She lives in Hyderabad (India) with her husband Anwar Moazzam, an eminent Urdu poet and academician. "Some Other Man's Home" ("Paraya Ghar") is the opening story of her collection by the same name (Hyderabad: Urdu Markaz, 1979).

CAROLINE J. BEESON studied Urdu at Cornell University and the University of Minnesota, Minneapolis, and at Hyderabad (India).

GRIFFITH A. CHAUSSEE was born in Racine, Wisconsin, in 1963. After a B.A. from the University of Chicago, he moved to the University of Wisconsin (Madison) where he took a Master's degree in South Asian Studies, with concentration in Hindi literature. He spent the 1989-90 academic year in Lahore (Pakistan) studying Urdu. Currently, he is enrolled in the Department of Comparative Literature.

ASIF FARRUKHI, whose real name is Asif Aslam, was born in Karachi in 1959. He took an M.B.B.S. degree from Daw Medical College (Karachi) in 1984 and a Master's degree in Public Health from Harvard University in 1989. He is now Senior Instructor in the Dept. of Community Health Sciences, The Aga Khan University, Karachi. He's been writing fiction and criticism regularly since 1979 and has so far published three collections of short stories and a book of interviews, besides contributing a rather large number of book reviews to a number of Karachi-based English newspapers and magazines. He has also translated widely from Hermann Hesse, Ayn Rand, Ernesto Sabata, G. Karnad, and Satyajit Ray. *Shahr-e 'Alamat* (an account of his trip to Berlin where he spent two months at the Goethe Institute as a fellow) is in press. "Fertility" ("Zarkhez") is taken from the third collection *Chizen Aur Log* (Karachi: Ahsan Matbu'at, 1991).

(RAJA) FARUQ HASSAN was born in 1939 at Lyallpur (now, Faisalabad, Pakistan). He holds degrees in English studies from the Universities of Punjab, Leeds, and New Brunswick and has also taught in Pakistan and Canada, where he permanently settled in 1968. Since 1972 he has been teaching at Dawson College, Montreal. He has published two volumes of poetry and numerous translations of Urdu poets and prose writers and has also co-edited *Versions of Truth, Urdu Short Stories from Pakistan*. A selection of his poems in English translation will appear shortly from Canada.

INTIZAR HUSAIN was born in Dibai (India) in 1925 and was educated at Meerut and, later, at Lahore (Pakistan). Creative writer, critic, and translator, he has published five volumes of short stories, three novels, a novella, and a volume of critical essays. The *Journal of South Asian Literature* devoted an entire issue to him in 1983, and a selected translation of his short fiction appeared under the title *An Unwritten Epic and Other Stories* in 1987. An English translation of his novel *Basti* will be published by the University of Minnesota Press. He makes his home in Lahore. After working for nearly three decades as a columnist for the daily Urdu newspaper *Mashriq*, he has recently moved over to the English newspaper *The Frontier Post*. "The Back Room" ("Dehliz") is taken from his collection *Shahr-e Afsos* (Lahore: Maktaba-e Karwan, 1973).

KHALIDA HUSAIN was born in Lahore in 1938. She started writing fiction in 1963 under her maiden name Khalida Asghar. After half a dozen brilliant stories, including the memorable "Sawari" ("The Wagon"), she disappeared from the scene after her marriage in 1965, reappearing after a silence of some twelve years. The fiction she has produced since her second appearance deals almost exclusively with the problems of female identity in the male-oriented and largely tradition-bound society of contemporary Pakistan. She has so far published three collections of short stories, some of which have been translated into Hindi and English. She is now settled in Rawalpindi, where she teaches English at Military College of Engineering and Technology. "Recognition" ("Pahchan") is from her first collection of the same name (Karachi: Khalid Publications, 1981).

ABDULLAH HUSSEIN is the pen name of Muhammad Khan who was born in 1931 in Rawalpindi (Pakistan) and now makes his home in London. Trained as a chemical engineer, he practised that profession for more than a dozen years in Pakistan and the U.K. before deciding to devote full time to writing. His short stories and novels have received wide critical acclaim in India and Pakistan; his first novel *Udas Naslen* (1963) received the Adamjee Award, Pakistan's highest literary prize, and has been translated into Bengali, Chinese, Hindi and Punjabi. A Chinese translation of his second novel *Bagh* (1982) is underway. All except one of his short stories, of which he has published two volumes, are available in English translation under the titles *Night* and *Downfall by Degrees*. "The Refugees" ("Muhajirin") appears in his collection *Nasheb* (Lahore: Qausain, 1981).

WAYNE R. HUSTED holds a Master's degree in South Asian Studies from the University of Wisconsin, Madison, where he is now finishing a doctorate on Shi'ite Islam in India. He spent an undergraduate year at Agra (India) to study Hindi and Urdu, and a graduate year at Lahore (Pakistan) to study advanced Urdu. He has co-translated numerous contemporary Urdu writers.

QURRATULAIN HYDER received her M.A. in English literature from the University of Lucknow. She has published extensively: seven novels, several collections of short stories, and translations into Urdu of such writers as Henry James, T.S. Eliot, and Truman Capote. In 1968 the Sahitya Akademi (Indian Academy of Letters) awarded her a prize for her collection of short stories *Patjhar Ki Avaz* and her celebrated novel *Ag Ka Darya* has been translated into fifteen Indian languages. She was one of the editors of *Imprint* magazine (Bombay);

Contributors

after which she worked for many years as a member of the editorial staff of the *Illustrated Weekly of India*. She is widely traveled and in 1979-80 was a writer-in-residence in the International Writers Program of the University of Iowa. In 1990, she was the recipient of India's highest literary prize, the *Bharatiya Jnan Pith Award*. She now lives in Delhi. "Hyena's Laughter" ("Lakarbagge Ki Hansi") is taken from her collection *Roshni Ki Raftar* (Karachi: Friends Publishers, n.d.).

IKRAMULLAH (CHAUDHRY) was born in 1930 in Jandiala, a small village in the Nawan Shehr District of Jullundur (India). He finished high school in Amritsar. After Partition his family moved to Multan, where he received a B.A. in 1953. Two years later he took a law degree from University Law College at Lahore. After practising law in Multan for a few years, he joined the insurance trade in 1965, retiring in 1990. He has been writing fiction since 1962. He has published a collection of short stories, *Jangal* (1972), and a novel, *Gurg-e Shab* (1977), banned within six months of its publication by the Punjab Government. "The Needy" ("Muhtaj") is taken from his collection *Jangal* (Lahore: Sang-e-Meel Publications).

ANWER KHAN was born in Bombay. He holds M.A. degrees in Urdu and Persian and is currently employed at the Bombay Port Trust. His first short story appeared in 1970, and he has since published three collections of short stories and a novel. "The Pose" ("Poz") is taken from his latest collection *Yad Basere* (Delhi: Takhliqkar Publishers, 1990).

RAM LALL (CHHABRA), who was born in 1923 in Mianwali (now in Pakistan), is by far the most prolific writer in Urdu: fifteen volumes of short stories, four novels, two travel accounts, and a book of literary criticism. Among his other writings are four books for children, a screen play for the film *Dil Akhir Dil Hai*, a television film, and many radio plays. He was an honourary president of the Progressive Writers' Association, U.P. Chapter (1978-86), and a vice-chairman of the Uttar Pradesh Urdu Akademi (1981-85). He retired, in 1981, after working for forty-three years with the railway department, and now lives in Lucknow. "The Grave" ("Qabr") is taken from *Ram La'l Ke Muntakhab Afsane* (New Delhi: Seemant Prakashan, 1984).

BALRAJ MANRA was born in 1935 in Jhingarkalan (now in Pakistan). After Partition his family moved to India. Manra joined the Health Department of the Municipal Corporation of Delhi as a laboratory technician in 1956 and has recently retired. He has written about three dozen short stories, some of which have been translated into many regional languages of India. *The Altar,* which includes translations of eight of his stories, was published by Writers' Forum, Delhi, in 1966. A story of his was anthologized by *Short Story International* (New York) and another appeared in *New Writing in India* (Penguin, 1974). He has tastefully edited the avant-garde literary journals *Mi'yar* and *Shuur.* "Composition One" ("Kampozishan Ek") is taken from the Lahore-based literary journal *Savera,* no. 38 (1966).

HASAN MANZAR is the pen name of Syed Manzar Hasan who was born in 1934 at Hapur and raised at Gorakhpur (India) before emigrating to Pakistan in 1947. After finishing his medical studies at Lahore, he worked for a time with the Dutch Merchant Navy, in Saudi Arabia and Nigeria. Later he studied psychology at Edinburgh University and took up a teaching position at Malaya University, Kuala Lumpur. He is now settled in Hyderabad (Pakistan), where he runs a private psychiatric clinic. He has so far published three collections of short stories. Currently he is working on a fourth collection and a novel. "The Beggar Boy" ("Ramsarna") is taken from his collection *Nadidi* (Hyderabad: Agahi Publications, 1982).

NAIYER MASUD was born in 1936 in Lucknow. He holds an M.A. in Persian and two separate Ph.D.'s in Urdu and Persian, and is a professor of Persian at Lucknow University. He is not a prolific writer, but what little he has written has been well received. He has so far published two collections of short fiction. His other published works are translations of Kafka and several contemporary Iranian fiction writers, a book on the now nearly extinct art of *marsiya*-recitation and a selection from Faqir Muhammad Goya's *Bustan-e Hikmat,* commissioned by the Urdu Academy, U.P. In 1977 he visited Tehran at the invitation of the Ministry of Culture, Government of Iran. "Obscure Domains of Fear and Desire" ("Ojhal") appears in his collection *Simiya* (Lucknow: Nusrat Publishers, 1984).

MUHAMMAD UMAR MEMON was born in 1939 at Aligarh (India) and emigrated to Pakistan in 1954. He was educated at Karachi University and, later, in the United States, where he took a Master's in Near Eastern Languages and Literatures from Harvard and a Ph.D. in Islamic Studies from UCLA. He is now Professor of Urdu, Persian, and Islam at the University of Wisconsin, Madison. He writes fiction and criticism in Urdu and English and has also translated widely from modern Urdu fiction, of which he has published four volumes. He has edited *Studies in the Urdu Ghazal and Prose Fiction,* and a book of his on religious polemics, *Ibn Taimiya's Struggle against Popular Religion,* appeared in 1976. "Lucky Vikki" ("Tab-e Nazzara Nahin") is taken from his collection *Tarik Gali* (Lahore: Sang-e-Meel Publications, 1989).

C. M. NAIM hails from Barabanki (India), where he was born in 1936. He was educated in India and the United States and has been teaching Urdu humanities at the University of Chicago for a quarter of a century now. He has written several major articles on Urdu poetry and prose fiction and has also translated numerous modern Urdu poets and short-story writers. A co-founder and a former editor of the *Journal of South Asian Literature,* he also edited until recently the *Annual of Urdu Studies,* and is editor of the collection *Iqbal, Jinnah, and Pakistan: The Vision and the Reality.* He is currently working on an annotated translation of *Zikr-e Mir,* the Persian autobiography of Mir, one of Urdu's foremost poets.

SURENDAR PARKASH is the pen name of Surendra Kumar Oberoi, who was born in 1930 in Lyallpur (now in Pakistan). He studied Urdu informally from his father, a shopkeeper. After the country was divided in 1947, his family emigrated to Delhi, India; the changed circumstances never permitted Parkash to finish high school and he was obliged to work at a number of menial jobs before being hired as a scriptwriter at All India Radio, Delhi. In 1971, he moved to Bombay to seek employment in the film industry. He has since written scripts for TV serials and films, among them *Vijay, Apna Jahan,* and *Anamika.* He has published three collections of short stories, of which the third, *Baz Go'i,* was the recipient of a Sahitya Akademi award in 1989. He is currently working on a fourth collection and a novel. "The Scarecrow" ("Bajuka") is taken from *Baz Go'i* (Delhi: Educational Publishing House, 1988).

JAVAID QAZI was born in Pakistan in 1947. He came to the United States in 1968 to study and finished a doctorate in English literature at Arizona State University in 1978. He writes fiction and his work has appeared in *Kansas Quarterly, Sequoia, Chelsea,* the *Toronto South Asian Review, Massachusetts Review* and the *Anais Nin: International Journal.* He lives and works in California.

SALAM BIN RAZZAQ is the pen name of Shaikh Abdussalam Abdurrazzaq who was born in 1941 in Panwil in the Maharashtra province of India. He finished high school in 1960 and published his first short story two years later in the literary magazine *Sha'ir.* He is the author of three collections of short stories, two in Urdu and one in Hindi; he has also translated Marathi fiction into Urdu. Currently he is putting together for Maharashtra State Urdu Academy a two-volume selection of Marathi writing in the last twenty-five years, which he is also translating. He lives in Bombay where he teaches in a school run by the Municipal Corporation. "Ekalavya–The Bheel Boy" ("Yklavyah") is taken from his collection *Mu'abbir* (Bombay: Kahani Publications, 1987).

MUHAMMAD SALIM-UR-RAHMAN, who was born in India in 1934, is an eminent Urdu poet and critic, who started his literary career with the translation in Urdu of Homer's *Odyssey*. He worked at one time as editor of the best modern Urdu literary journal *Savera* and as associate editor of *Nusrat*, a weekly. Since 1963 he has been contributing book reviews and literary columns to the Lahore-based English daily, *The Pakistan Times*. He has published a great deal of poetry, half a dozen short stories, and numerous translations from English into Urdu and from Urdu into English; three of his English poems once appeared in *Poetry North West*. The first volume of his critical work on ancient Greek literature is in Press. "Voices" ("Awazen") was published in *Mihrab* (Lahore: Maktaba-e Mihrab, 1989).

JOHN ROOSA was born in Cincinnati, Ohio, in 1962. He holds a B.A. in liberal arts from Tufts University and is now a graduate student in South Asian history at University of Wisconsin, Madison. He has studied Hindi and Urdu in both India and Pakistan.

ENVER SAJJAD was born in 1936 in Lahore. He first wrote in the traditional vein but later adopted a more innovative approach to writing fiction. He is also a painter, writer of radio and TV plays and actor. He studied medicine at Lahore and Liverpool (U.K.) and is a physician by profession. His active involvement in politics during the Bhutto years got him into trouble with the Zia regime. As a result he was imprisoned both in 1977 and 1978 and banned from the state-owned radio and TV. He founded Pakistan Artists Equity in 1970 and was chairman of Pakistan Arts Council, Lahore, from 1973 to 1975. He is the author of three volumes of short stories, two novels, and a book of critical essays. "The Cow" ("Ga'e") is taken from his collection *Iste'are* (Lahore: Izhar Sons, 1970).

PARVEEN SARWAR was born in Aligarh (India) in 1928 and received her early education there. After Partition her family relocated in Lahore, where she took a bachelor's degree in arts from Kinnaird College and another in education from Lady Maclagan Training College. Although no collection of her fiction has so far appeared, she has published well over a hundred short stories in the most prestigious Urdu journals and is considered a major writer. She is also well known as a writer of children's stories. She lives in Lahore. "Hearth and Home" ("Ghar Angan") is taken from the journal *Naya Daur* (Karachi), nos. 63-64 (n.d.).

QUDRATULLAH SHAHAB was born in Gilgit in 1917 and spent his childhood in Jammu. He worked for some time in the civil service of India and later, after Partition, joined the civil service of Pakistan, where he held numerous offices, including that of Ambassador to the Netherlands. He is, however, best known to Urdu readers as a master short-story writer and the main architect of the Pakistan Writers' Guild, a government-sponsored agency for the organization and aid of Pakistani writers. His published works include two collections of short stories and *Ya Khuda!* a novella about the problem of rehabilitating the refugees made homeless in the wake of India's partition. "The Plague in Jammu" ("Jammun Men Pleg") is the opening chapter of his voluminous autobiography *Shahabnama*, which was completed just before he died in 1986 and was published posthumously (Lahore: Sang-e-Meel Publications, 1987).

MUHAMMAD MANSHA YAD was born in 1937 in Shaikhupura District, Punjab. He holds an M.A. in Urdu Literature and another in Punjabi and a diploma in civil engineering. His published works include a volume of Punjabi short stories, six collections of Urdu stories, and several anthologies, which he edited. He lives in Islamabad, where he is Deputy Director, Capital Development Authority, Government of Pakistan. "The Show" ("Tamasha") is taken from his collection *Khala Andar Khala* (Rawalpindi: Matbu'at-e Hurmat, 1983).